Brian P.

W9-BNV-450

Sir Henry Merrivale Takes Charge

"Y'see, son, this business is not all bath-salts and lilies on the pond. It's messy. It's got claws. Pretty certainly in the past, and maybe in the future, we're dealin' with murder."

We will send you a free catalog on request. Any titles not in your local book store can be purchased by mail. Send the price of the book plus 35c shipping charge to Belmont/Tower Books, P.O. Box 270, Norwalk, Connecticut 06852.

Titles currently in print are available for industrial and sales promotion at reduced rates. Address inquiries to Tower Publications, Inc., Two Park Avenue, New York, New York 10016, Attention: Premium Sales Department.

SKELETON IN THE CLOCK

A SIR HENRY MERRIVALE MYSTERY

Carter Dickson

BELMONT TOWER BOOKS ● NEW YORK CITY

A BELMONT TOWER BOOK

Published by
Tower Publications, Inc.
Two Park Avenue
New York, N.Y. 10016

Copyright © 1948 by William Morrow and Co., Inc.

All rights reserved

PRINTED IN THE UNITED STATES OF AMERICA

Published by special arrangement
with William Heinemann Ltd.

The policeman, passing through Moreston Square at three o'clock in the morning, saw lights still burning in the windows of the top-floor flat at 16. And he smiled to himself.

That would be Miss Ruth Callice's flat. The chimes from St. Jude's Church rang the hour, rippling through the little eighteenth-century square and lapping it in security. Police-Constable Davis glanced up at a quarter-moon over the rooftops. No more, he thought, of *one* thing. These narrow red-brick houses, these white-painted window-frames and pane-joinings, wouldn't burst or burn amid a nightmare of noise. At least, P. C. Davis amended with the skepticism of all his tribe, not just yet.

In front of the door of number 16 stood a heavy shiny car, a new one to rouse envy. Again he looked up at the lighted windows, lulling against rooftop and sky.

Miss Callice was—nice. And he didn't mean it in any smug or smarmy way, either. Young, good-looking, but (still his mind would find no better word) nice. There were people up there, the men in black ties or white, the women in high-cut or low-cut dresses, sometimes as late as three in the morning, like this. But never any disturbance; seldom any drunks. They went in talking; they came out talking. What did they find to talk about?

At that moment, in the living-room on the top floor, John Stannard, K. C., was employing his most measured tones.

"Let's suppose, Ruth, your theory is correct. In that case, what would be the most dangerously haunted place in the world?"

Miss Callice, on the sofa under silver-shaded wall-lamps, made a protest.

"I didn't say it was my theory," she pointed out, and looked at her two companions. "It doesn't necessarily mean I believe in—"

"Say it," Stannard urged dryly. "Don't be afraid of a word; or you'll never get near the truth. Say it. 'The supernatural.' "

It would have been difficult to tell Ruth Callice's age, though she could not have been more than twenty-eight. And P. C. Davis's definition of niceness would be hard to analyze even by closer observers.

Frankness? Honesty? True; but these qualities, when too strongly observable, are suspect because they may be assumed. It may have been that she completely lacked coquetry; never thought of it, never noticed herself; though she was undeniably pretty and her rounded body, in the oyster-coloured evening-gown, was far from unnoticeable as she sat coiled on the sofa.

The light, smoke-misted, glistened on her light-brown hair. She rested one elbow on the arm of the sofa, her arm straight up, fingers turning over a cigarette that had gone out. When she changed her position, the light altered the complexion of her face and shoulders from pale to pink-pale. Her straight-forward eyes, dark-brown, regarded Stannard deprecatingly.

"I only said—" she began again.

"Let me put the case to you."

"Oh, my lord of the law!"

"My dear Ruth, it's not necessary to mock at me."

Ruth Callice was genuinely astonished. She sat up. "Stan! I never thought any such thing!"

"Never mind," chuckled John Stannard, K. C.

He had one of those heavy voices, roughened into what for him was unjustly called a whisky-voice, which can make any statement sound abrupt. Thick-bodied, not overly tall, he picked up his cigar and settled back in the easy-chair. Out of a roundish face, roughened like his voice, the brilliant black eyes peered sardonically. Though he had reddened during those remarks with Ruth, this may have been a matter of the drinks.

"A man dies," Stannard went on, after a gust of cigar-smoke. "His soul is heavy with evil; with spiritual poison; call it what you like. He may die a natural death; more probably, he commits suicide or is killed. In any case—"

Here Stannard made a chopping motion with his hand.

During this time neither Ruth Callice nor John Stannard had glanced at the third person in the gilt-and-silver room: a young man who sat some distance away from them, his head down and his hands on his knees, near the empty fireplace and the grand piano. At the barrister's last words he did look up.

"Your dead man," continued Stannard, "in a spiritual sense is chained there, He's what the books call earthbound. Is that correct?"

Ruth gave a quick little nod of absorbed attention.

"Yes. That, you see," she threw out her hands, "*is* what would make some of these houses so horribly dangerous, if it

6

were true. It wouldn't be like an ordinary haunting. It would be like . . . like a man-eating tiger."

"Then why don't your psychical researchers do the obvious thing?"

"The obvious thing? I don't follow you."

With the cigar Stannard gestured round at the bookshelves.

"You tell me," he retorted, "that at Something-Old-Hall there's a psychic strangler, and at Somewhere-Low-Grange there's an earthbound force that can crush you to death. It may be so; *I* can't say. But I can tell you a far better place to look for evidence. If what you say is true, what *would* be the most dangerously haunted place on earth?"

"Well?"

"The execution shed of any prison," replied Stannard.

He paused, letting the image sink in. Then he got up and went to the coffee-table beside the sofa. His black hair, showing no grey and brushed to a nicety round his head, gleamed in contrast to the reddish, roughened face. The white shirtfront bulged and crackled. Picking up the decanter, he poured a very little whisky into his glass.

"But that's—horrible!" Ruth cried.

"No doubt," Stannard agreed dryly. "All the same, think of it for a moment."

The sofa-syphon hissed.

"Your human tiger, at the very high point of his rage and desperation, is dragged to the execution shed and has his neck cracked on a rope." The strong, faintly husky voice pointed it vividly. "If anybody would leave an earth-bound soul in that place, he would.

"Believe me," Stannard added abruptly, "I've defended too many murderers not to know that many of them are decent honest fellows. There-but-for-the-grace-of-God, and all the rest of it. When you hear the foreman of the jury say 'not guilty,' you feel half sick with relief. You pat yourself on the back for the rest of the week."

Ruth's eyes were fixed on his face.

"I've heard," she said, "that only two persons you defended on a murder charge were ever . . . well, executed."

"Much exaggerated, my dear. Much!" Stannard chuckled; then his expression changed. "But I've seen the other kind of murderer too. That's why I don't scoff at spiritual evil."

He lifted his glass, drained its contents, and put it down.

"By God, it *is* true to say they don't know the difference between right and wrong. Not at that time. Mostly they go to the rope with indifference; outwardly, that is. But not inside. They're boiling crazy. Society hasn't understood them. Society has persecuted them. They want to tear . . ." Stannard spread out his hands. "That's why I say, Ruth, that a place like Pentonville or Wandsworth must be deadly. Hasn't any psychical researcher ever thought of spending a night in the execution shed?"

Ruth lifted her shoulders.

"I don't know," she confessed. "I never thought of it." And she turned towards the young man who was sitting near the fireplace and the grand piano. "What's *your* opinion, Martin?"

Martin Drake looked up. Like Stannard, he was dark. Unlike Stannard, he was tall. But his cat-green eyes, now absent minded, had a sardonic quality which sometimes matched Stannard's. He looked thin and he looked ill.

"Oh, I suppose they've thought of it," Martin Drake answered. "But they wouldn't be allowed to. The Prison Commission would have a fit."

"Right," chuckled Stannard.

(He missed no glance Ruth Callice turned towards Drake. There were currents in this room, not quite like a usual social evening.)

"But I wish we could do it," the young man said unexpectedly, and struck his clenched fist on his knee. "Lord, how I wish we could do it!"

Ruth's voice went up. "Spend a night in a . . . ?"

"Oh, not you!" Drake smiled at her; it lightened the illness of his look to kindliness and affection. "I suppose, actually, I meant myself."

"But whatever for?"

Stannard, who had returned to the chair with his cigar, spoke gravely.

"You mean, Mr. Drake, that since the war you have found life in England dull and intolerably frustrating?"

"If—you want to put it like that, yes."

"Will you forgive me, Mr. Drake, for saying you are very young?"

"Will you forgive me, Mr. Stannard, for saying that you are a little pompous?"

Again Stannard chuckled. Perhaps he was doing this too much. His lips were drawn back from the teeth in a fixed, pleasant smile; his small black eyes glittered.

"Of course I forgive you," Stannard said heartily. "I have achieved—" he glanced at Ruth, evidently himself feeling young and callow at forty-five, and hating it—"I have achieved

8

some small success in this world. That breeds pomposity sometimes. God knows I try to avoid it." His tone changed. "Are you serious about wanting to meet earthbound spirits?"

"Quite serious."

"Ah? Suppose I arranged it?"

Ruth Callice was now sitting bolt upright on the sofa. Her lips opened as though in expostulation, but she did not speak.

"It couldn't be done!" Martin Drake said.

"Not at the prisons I mentioned, no. But what about Pentecost?"

"Pentecost?"

"You've never heard of Pentecost Prison, Mr. Drake?"

"Never."

Stannard crossed his knees comfortably and addressed Ruth.

"Fifty years ago Pentecost was one of our model local prisons." He paused. "I use the word 'local' prison to distinguish it from 'convict' prison. At local prisons, offenders serve sentences only up to two years; executions are always performed there.

"In '38," Stannard pursued, "Pentecost was closed. It was to be enlarged and modernized. Then came the war. The Government took it over with the usual rubber-stamp excuse of 'storage purposes'. Ever since then it's remained the same. It's not under the control of the Prison Commission; it's controlled by the Ministry of Works. I—ah—have some slight influence at the Ministry. I might get the keys for a night or two. Now do you begin to understand?"

"By George!" the young man said softly. His long, lean figure grew tense; his upper lip was partly lifted as though at the scent of danger. "I'd be eternally grateful, Mr Stannard, if you could."

Stannard, too, seemed to have been struck by a startling new thought. Seeing that his cigar had gone out, he dropped it into a standing ashtray beside the chair.

"Extraordinary!" he said, and his face grew more red. "I've just remembered something else."

"Remembered what?" Ruth asked quickly.

"Pentecost is in Berkshire. It's under a mile or so from a place called Fleet House, a big Georgian house with a flat roof." His little black eyes stared at the past. "Eighteen years ago—or was it twenty? yes, twenty!—a man named Fleet, Sir George Fleet, pitched off that roof within sight of a lot of witnesses. It was accident, of course. Or else . . ."

"Or else?"

9

"It was a supernatural murder." He spoke without smiling.

Martin Drake brushed aside this reference to Fleet House.

"Do you honestly think you can get the keys to the prison?"

"Oh, I think so. At least I can try. Where can I reach you tomorrow?"

"I'm afraid I've got to be at Willaby's Auction Rooms all morning. With a friend of mine named Merrivale." Unexpectedly, a reminiscent grin lit up Drake's dulled eyes. Then he became sober again. "But I can make a point of being at my rooms in the afternoon, if that's convenient? I'm in the 'phone-book."

"You'll hear from me," Stannard assured him.

Loud in night-stillness, the clock at St. Jude's rang the quarter-hour after three. Stannard got up, brushing a trace of cigar-ash from his waist-coat. He drew a deep breath.

"And now, my dear," he said to Ruth, "you must excuse me. Middle-aged barristers can't keep late hours like you young people. I'll ring *you* tomorrow, if I may."

Throughout this conversation Ruth had kept her eyes fixed on Martin Drake. Doubt, uncertainly, showed in them and troubled her breathing under the oyster-coloured gown. Stannard noticed that Drake, though he got up politely, made no move to leave. It was a dead hour, dull on the wits and opium to the emotions. Yet something wrenched in Stannard's heart as his hostess followed him to the door.

In the little hall of the flat, every inch of wall-space was occupied by shelves of bright-jacketed books. Ruth Callice was the owner of a fashionable bookshop in Piccadilly, which she managed herself; that was how she and Stannard had met. A dim little ceiling-lantern burned in the hall. Stannard picked up hat and rolled umbrella from an oak chest.

"It was awfully nice of you to come," Ruth said.

"Not at all. The pleasure was mine. May I see you again?"

"Of course. As often as you can."

She extended her hands. Stannard, the suave, had considerable difficulty in managing his hat and umbrella.

"Thanks." He spoke gruffly. "I'll remember that. No; I can manage the front door. Thanks again. Good-night."

The door, closing heavily after him, made a hollow vibration. For a moment Ruth stood staring at the door. Then she returned to the sitting-room. Though both windows were wide open to the warm July night, she made a feint of attempting to push them higher to let the smoke out. Martin Drake, his back partly turned, was standing by the fireplace lighting a cigarette. Ruth went softly over to the grand piano and sat down.

She hesitated. Common-sense, practicality, shone in the dark-brown eyes as she lifted her head; a perplexity verging on impatience. But this expression faded, with a wry twist of the mouth, as she began to play.

The tune was *Someday I'll Find You.* Its saccharine notes riffled and rippled, softly, through the room and faintly out into the square.

"Ruth!"

"Yes, Martin?"

"You're one of the finest persons I ever met," said the young man, and threw his cigarette into the fireplace. "But would you mind not playing that?"

Ruth closed her eyes, the lids shiny and dark-fringed, and opened them again. "I'm sorry, Martin." Her fingers rested motionless. Without looking round Ruth added, "Still searching for her?"

"Yes."

"Martin, dear. Isn't that rather foolish?"

"Of course it's foolish. I know that. But I can't help it. There it is."

"You met her," Ruth pointed out dispassionately, "for just one evening."

"Long enough, thanks."

"And you haven't seen her for . . . how long?"

The other's reply was immediate, almost mechanical. "Three years. One month. And four—no, five days. I'll tick off the calendar this morning."

"Oh, *Martin!*" The piano-keys jangled.

"I've admitted it's foolish. But how many things, the closest things, are governed by reason? Answer me that!"

"You were both in uniform," Ruth persisted gently. "It was in that scramble and hectic whirl just after D-Day. You don't know anything about her, except that she wore a Wren's uniform. You don't even know her name, except the first, and she admitted that was a nickname."

It was as though, in remonstrance, Ruth attempted to press and prod with every detail.

"A station buffet at Edinburgh!" she said. "A station platform! A train tearing through the blackout, with you two," her voice strengthened, "kissing and swearing you loved each other. Martin! Lots and lots of people have had adventures like that."

Martin Drake's face was white. Ruth, with her consummate tact, should have noticed this.

"It wasn't an adventure," he said quietly.

11

"No. Of course not. I didn't mean that. Only—suppose you do find her, and she's married?"

"Curiously enough," retorted the other, with a brief return to his mocking air, "that possibility had occurred to me in the course of three years, one month, and five days." He lifted his shoulders. "What could I do? Murder the husband?"

"Well, but . . . suppose she's engaged. What would you do then?"

"Try to cut him out," Drake answered instantly. "Not that I could, probably. But—" he lifted a clenched fist, dropped it, and then cleared his throat—"use every trick, fair or unfair, to cut the swine out and get her back again. That needn't lead as far as murder, of course."

There was a silence. Still Ruth did not look round. The doubt, the indecision in her eyes, had grown stronger.

"Ruth!" her guest began apologetically.

"Yes?"

He went across to her, stood beside her at the piano, and put his hand on her bare shoulder. "Thanks," he added, "for not asking the obvious question."

"What obvious question?"

"How many Wrens," he went on, with a kind of fierce and shaky cheerfulness, "how many Wrens, at a time like that, must have said, 'Oh, just call me Jenny.' Jenny! Jenny! *I* know it. So do several of my friends, who think it's funny. But it's not funny. That's the trouble."

Ruth reached up and disengaged his hand from her shoulder; rather quickly, he thought. She did not admit or deny that she had thought of asking any such question. She looked straight ahead, unseeingly, at the music on the piano-rack.

"What did you think," she asked, "of our friend tonight?"

"Stannard?" Martin Drake's face clouded. "Stannard's a damn good fellow. I'm sorry I called him pompous. Nerves. If he can really get permission to spend the night in the execution shed at that prison . . ."

"If you two go there," Ruth interrupted quickly, "I'm going too. Did you notice that Mr. Stannard seemed rather—embarrassed?"

Drake was startled.

"The Great Defender? Embarrassed? Why?"

"Oh, no reason," said Ruth, with a lift of her head that made the soft brown hair gleam. "No reason! No reason at all!"

And again her fingers moved over the piano-keys.

Downstairs, under the moon, the sleek black car still waited before the door of number 16. Inside the car, his thick arms

12

round the steering-wheel, John Stannard sat where he had been sitting for some minutes. Once more he heard the strains of *Someday I'll Find You* drifting down from the lighted windows on the top floor.

This time Stannard trod on the starter. As the motor throbbed into life, he revved it to a hum which deepened into a roar. Then, very gently, he put the car in gear and drove off towards Kensington High Street.

Chapter 2

On the following morning, Friday July 11th, the blue-and-white flag was up at Willaby's in Bond Street to show that there would be an auction that day.

Martin Drake saw it as he turned out of Brook Street at a quarter to eleven. London in 1947, dazzling under its first really warm summer since the beginning of the war, winked with show-windows against dingy brick or stone. It heated the body and strengthened the spirits. Martin, freshly shaven and as well-dressed as clothes-coupons permitted, felt his own spirits lift.

But that always happened on a sunny morning. It was the night he dreaded.

He hadn't, Martin reflected, been drunk at Ruth Callice's flat last night. Merely a trifle muzzy, and blackly depressed. He had an impression that some remark, some reference made by Stannard (he could not remember it now) ought to have had significance. But his mind was closed to so many things. He had almost become maudlin in the presence of Ruth Callice's obvious sympathy. He was so fond of Ruth that under any other circumstances . . . but there were no other circumstances.

Jenny!

The silent oration he addressed to himself ran something like this:

You are London's prize fool. You admit that. At the age of thirty-four you have had, to put it very conservatively, some slight experience. Your conduct is not made more supportable by those people, two or three friends at the Savage Club, who know about it.

13

"My dear old boy," one of them had said, "all you need is thus-and-so. With so many willing dames about . . ."

Or old Hook, with his touch of grey side-whisker and his twinkling eyeglass, who always quoted Leigh Hunt:

> *Jenny kissed me when we met,*
> *Jumping from the chair she sat in—*

And this, though you had to smile, touched a raw spot. It was, in so many ways, expressive of Jenny. Jenny, blonde and slender, in the blue uniform and hat which at first glance made her seem unapproachable. Jenny's eagerness, her sincerity, almost her naïveté.

"*A station-buffet at Edinburgh!*" Ruth had said. "*A station platform. A train tearing through the blackout, with you two kissing and swearing you loved each other.*"

Hell!

When such things happened to other people, Martin reflected, or even happened in stories, they had at least a trace of dignity. This hadn't.

In the hush just before dawn on a summer morning, the express from Edinburgh stops at Rugby. Heavy boots clump and bumble along the wooden platform. Misshapen shadows, interweaving, loom up against the dim blue station lights and the faint glow from the services' tea-canteen. Captain Drake of the Gloucesters, and (rank and unit unknown) Jenny, hand in hand, stumble out to get a cup of vile tea. In the confusion and milling on that dark platform—every private's kit seems to swing and bang for a yard in each direction—you lose Jenny's hand.

That was all.

Eight minutes later, when the whistle blew and the doors slammed, Martin jumped into the train. He staggered along the corridors, over kit and luggage and bodies, calling Jenny's name. Two or three times he was answered, not seriously. There were cheers. The drugged dawn-wind blew drowsily. When they reached King's Cross, he swore to himself, it would be all right. But, when that mob charged through the barriers, he couldn't find her either.

That was all too, except for the long waiting.

Ahead of him now, on this brilliant morning of July 11th, loomed the dun-coloured premises of Willaby's. Sedate and solid, hushed and holy, Willaby's yet wore an air of expectancy. How many treasures from the houses of the great and the near-great, of furniture and china and silver, of

14

tapestries and pictures and armour: how many of these have passed under the hammer at Willaby's, perhaps, no man can compute. The porter—who recognized Mr. Martin Drake as a black-and-white artist of something more than national reputation—respectfully held open one door.

"Morning, sir!"

"Good morning." The image of Jenny, held in abeyance, started up again like a toothache we think vanished overnight. "Er—have they started yet?"

The porter eyed him reproachfully.

"Not till eleven, sir. *As* usual. Got your catalogue?"

"No. I'm just looking on today. What's up this morning?"

"Furniture and carpets, sir. Mainly seventeenth and eighteenth century."

To judge by the subdued murmur of voices from upstairs, there must be a fair-sized crowd. A number of persons were mounting the broad, dingy staircase. At the top it opened into a large, square room, walls panelled in some material which resembled faded brown burlap, where they displayed specimens of future auctions. Beyond it lay another large room, with towering bookshelves. Both of these rooms opened, at right-angles, into the main auction-room.

"Hel-*lo*, Drake!"

A face, half-remembered, drifted past and was lost. Martin returned the greeting vaguely. He heard a fashionably dressed woman talking, with greed and not for antiquarian reasons, about the display of carpets. An old man with a white moustache, obviously a dealer, stood hunched over his catalogue.

The main auction-room was long and high. Sunlight sparkled against its grimy glass roof. At the rear, blue-smocked attendants lounged or stood with arms folded in front of a line of ticketed exhibits. The auctioneer's desk, like a high-set rostrum, faced out over a very long horseshoe-shaped table, covered with green felt, round which would gather the chairs of the eagerest bidders. Martin had loathed crowds—no matter how soft-voiced or shuffling—ever since that night on the train. The whole room seemed to hiss at him.

"Get it dirt-cheap if the dealers don't . . ."

"Jump in at the beginning! That's when people are cautious, and . . ."

No!

Just off the main hall, at the right, opened another showroom smaller and narrower than the others. Here were displayed the items for the next sale, which would be on

15

Monday. Arms and armour, of course! That was why he was here!

On two tables along the narrow sides of the room, and a long one down the centre, they had thrown rapiers, daggers, hand-and-a-half swords, even two-handed swords. Many were tied in bundles, most of them unpolished. Round the walls there hung, very highly polished, the more obvious of the choice items. The only other person in the room was a girl, at the other end of the centre table, her back towards him, searching through a handbag.

Martin looked round.

The walls glittered with steel in low, dim-burning electric light. Halberds and guisarmes with long light shafts and undulled points. A wicked-looking main-gauche. What seemed to be—he took a step forward—a Thomas cup-hilt. This was Martin's hobby; he wished he had a Monday's catalogue.

Then the girl at the other end of the table turned round. And he saw that it was Jenny.

Silence.

Martin Drake was faintly conscious of a murmur of voices from the other room, and the ticking of his wrist-watch. But he felt alone, and amid the stuffiness of the arms-room, with Jenny. At first his chest seemed light, light and hollow; then he felt a sensation almost like physical sickness.

Jenny, blonde and slender. Jenny, with the wide-spaced blue eyes, the eagerness and the—no! not naïveté! some other expression! With intolerable vividness he remembered her, in the corner of the railway compartment, her arms round his neck, and moonlight draining colour from her face, the rattlety-clack of the train dimming speech. Even now she was wearing a dark-blue tailored suit with a white blouse. Martin tried to speak. All he could force out was the inanity of, "Hello."

"Hello," said Jenny in a voice hardly above a whisper.

He started to walk towards her. Though they were separated only by the length of the green-felt-covered table with its weapons, it seemed an enormous distance. Then he noticed something else.

You are not permitted to smoke at Willaby's. Fumbling in her handbag, Jenny found a tortoise-shell cigarette case, the kind that contained only very small cigarettes. Jenny took out a cigarette; and automatically he reached in his pocket for a lighter. But her hand was shaking so badly, as she lifted it, that she hastily put back the cigarette in the case.

Emotion caught these two like a net; it made them flounder;

16

it kept them half deaf and partially blind.

"Where were you on that train? I couldn't find you!"

The blue eyes flashed up.

"I—I stayed behind on the platform. I thought you would too, so we shouldn't miss each other. —But it's too late!" she added. "It's too late!"

"How do you mean, it's too late?"

Jenny turned away from him, but he swung her back again. The softness of her shoulder under the blue coat, the brushing of the yellow hair in a long bob against his hand: he had to remember where he was. Then he lifted her left hand. Though there was no wedding-ring on the third finger, it held an engagement ring both costly and in good taste.

(Well, you've been expecting this, haven't you? You've been prepared for it? Steady!)

"Do you love him?"

Jenny looked away.

"No. But I'm afraid he's very much in love with me. And then grandmother—and, of course, Aunt Cicely—"

"*Do* you love him?"

Still without looking round, Jenny shook her head violently.

"Who is he?"

"He's awfully nice. He was one of the original Battle-of-Britain pilots. And his record since then . . ." The soft, sweet voice, perhaps over-cultured in accent, trailed away. "Did you ever try to find me?" Jenny asked accusingly.

"Jenny, I've done nothing else ever since that night! But all I knew was your nickname!"

"Jenny is short for Jennifer. Surely you could have guessed that?"

"Yes, of course. Only I thought . . ."

"You thought—you thought I gave that name on some kind of casual adventure." She clenched her fists.

"No, so help me! But it was the only clue I had. Did you ever try to find *me?*"

"Yes, of course. And I did: easily."

"Oh?"

"You're Martin Drake. You're a famous artist. You live at the Albany, and you're not married. Only grandmother said— and, of course, Aunt Cicely—"

"Look here," said Drake with restraint. "Who the devil are these two powerful jujus, grandmother and Aunt Cicely? Can't they be tipped over like any other savage idols?" He glanced round. "And, by the way, can't we get out of here?"

"No! Please. Sh-h!"

"Why 'sh-h'?"

"Grandmother's here. She wants to get something at the auction. How on earth did you know *I* was here?"

"As a matter of fact, I didn't. I came here for a pre-view, to recommend one or two rapiers for Sir Henry Merrivale."

"Sir Henry Merrivale!" exclaimed the girl.

Jenny raised one hand as though to shade her eyes. On her flushed face, with the short nose and the rather broad mouth, was an expression he could not read. Martin noticed, absently, that beyond her was a stand of armour—a Cavalier half-suit, much blackened, with lobster-tail helmet—and behind it, on the wall, a picture depicting one of the loves of Aphrodite.

"Sir Henry Merrivale!" Jenny exclaimed. "You know him?"

"Slightly, yes. I went to him last week about tracing you. He said he'd help, but just for the moment he was too much engrossed in studying the subject of reincarnation."

"The subject of . . . *what?*"

"Reincarnation," explained Martin. "He thinks he may be the reincarnation of— Hold on! Wait! I've got it!"

For the rush of happiness at seeing Jenny, it seemed to him, had loosed a spell from his wits. He knew now why a certain cloudy reference should have been clear.

"Got what?" asked Jenny, with that eagerness he knew so well.

"Last night a barrister named Stannard mentioned a place in Berkshire: Fleet House, I think it was. He said there'd been some ugly business, twenty years ago, which was either an accident or a supernatural murder. And that's it, of course!"

"How do you mean?"

"A friend of Sir Henry's, Chief Inspector Masters, has been pestering him to take up the case. Masters wants to re-open it. It seems there's new evidence, anonymous letters or the like." Martin stopped short. "What is it? What's wrong?"

He interpreted Jenny's expression, now. It was fear. Again he became conscious of the room's stuffiness, and the weapons glittering round the walls. Jennifer said:

"Richard Fleet, my *fiancé*, is the son of the Sir George Fleet who died. Aunt Cicely, who's only an aunt by courtesy, is Lady Fleet. My grandmother is their closest friend."

"Listen, Jenny," said Martin, after a pause during which his throat felt dry. "There's only one question I'm going to ask you, but it's got to be answered."

"Yes?"

"Do you still feel as you did—in the train? *Do you?*"

"Yes," replied Jenny and lifted her eyes. "Yes!"

18

"Jennifer, dear!" interrupted a calm, authoritative female voice. It cracked their idyll to bits. Jenny started; Martin swung round guiltily.

And it is now time, in this chronicle, to introduce none other than Sophia, Dowager Countess of Brayle.

She had approached unheard. She was a large, commanding woman, her grey-white hair confined under a rakish fashionable hat, and her body so compressed into a dress of garish design that it almost, but not quite, failed to make her seem fat. Her voice, which forty-odd years ago had been called a 'pure contralto' as her nose had been called 'sweetly aquiline,' could often be heard speaking on public platforms.

The Dowager Countess, in fact, occasionally showed habits rakish and even skittish. At these same public meetings, for instance, she had a trick of taking two sweeping steps backwards, while raising her right arm and exclaiming, "Here's three chee-ah-s." Sometimes she even did this in private, to the mild-voiced protest of Aunt Cicely.

All her friends would testify to her good qualities: that she was fair, that she was generous, that she even had a sense of humour. She had perhaps every good quality except that of being likeable. But that did not matter. The Dowager Countess meant to get her own way, always got her own way, and accepted this as naturally as she expected a lamp to light at the click of a switch. Whether you liked her, or didn't like her, simply did not matter.

"When you see my composure ruffled," she would say comfortably, "then will be the time to criticize."

This imposing lady, a faint smile on her face and an auction catalogue in her hand, stood before the two culprits and waited with endless patience for someone to speak.

Jenny, pushing back her yellow hair, blurted it out.

"C-Captain Drake," she said, "may I present you to my grandmother? Captain Drake, Lady Brayle."

The latter's nod and glance flickered over Martin as though he had not been there at all.

"The auction," she said to Jenny, "has begun. Lot 72 should come up in a few minutes. I feel sure, Jennifer, that you will wish to be present? Follow me, please."

She swung round, her somewhat ample posterior conspicuous in the flowered dress, and moved majestically away. Jenny, on the other side of the long centre table, followed her almost parallel. Martin, with a raging heart, could only follow Jenny. At the far end of the table, however, Lady Brayle

19

wheeled round with her back to the open arch into the main auction-hall. She glanced at the weapons on the table.

"Ah—Jennifer dear," she continued with a sort of cold archness. "It occurs to me we must not forget our *fiancé*. Now must we?"

Jenny made an incoherent noise.

"Richard, or dear Ricky as we call him . . ." Lady Brayle paused. "Captain Drake. Let me see. You were in the Guards?"

"No. The Gloucesters."

"Oh. The Gloucesters." Her eyebrow indicated that she had momentarily scanned the army-list and found no such name. "How interesting. Richard, or dear Ricky as we call him, is one of our new breed of chivalry: our heroic and fearless knights of the air. Don't you think so, Jennifer?"

"Grandmother, he'd pass out if he heard you talk like that!"

But grandmother's contralto was now warming up with platform eloquence.

"You might give him, I think, some small present of arms. This fine old English blade," exclaimed Lady Brayle, picking up a Turkish scimitar of about 1885, and waving it in the air, "would surely be suitable. I am informed that the air-force seldom carry swords. But the spirit of it! You agree, Jennifer?"

"Yes, grandmother. But . . ."

"*You* agree, Captain Drake?"

Martin swallowed a heavy lump in his throat. This calm and indomitable old lady was trying to get his goat. He longed to take one dig at her, just one. But he feared its effect on Jenny. Just how much influence this doubtless-benevolent Gorgon exercised over Jenny, who three years ago had given her age as twenty-two, he could not yet estimate.

"Quite," he agreed.

"It is no use, Captain Drake," she smiled at him. "It really is no use."

"I beg your pardon?"

"But any criticism you might make of the weapons, of course!" said Lady Brayle, deliberately avoiding the issue and raising her eyebrows. The cold, shrewd grey eyes expressed astonishment. "This cute little dagger, now, with the sheath!" she broke off. "Perhaps *that* might appeal to dear Ricky, Jennifer. Or here, better still . . ."

Martin gritted his teeth. His glance wandered past her into the main auction-hall. For the most part the spectators, either in chairs or standing up, had pressed close to the long horseshoe table below the rostrum. In the cleared space outside and beyond them, approaching slowly and at a lordly pigeon-toed walk, moved a figure which sent Martin Drake's hopes soaring up.

"It's the Old Man," he breathed.

Chapter 3

The auctioneer's voice was small, thin, and at this distance all but inaudible.

"*Lot 55. A fine Queen Anne table, grained mahogany, drawers richly gilt, date circa 1721, originally . . .*"

The figure Martin had seen was a large, stout, barrel-shaped gentleman in a white linen suit. His spectacles, usually pulled down on his broad nose, were now in place because he held his head up. On his head was a Panama hat, its brim curiously bent, and in his mouth he clamped an unlighted cigar.

As he advanced, his corporation majestically preceding him, there was on his face such a lordly sneer as even the Dowager Countess could never have imitated. Indeed, a close friend of Sir Henry Merrivale would have noticed something a little odd in his behaviour. The brim of the Panama hat, to an imaginative observer, might have been arranged so as to carry sweeping plumes. As he rolled the cigar round in his mouth to get a better grip, his left hand rested negligently in the air as though on the pommel of an imaginary sword. Aloof, disdainful, he sauntered towards the armour-room.

"Or this, for instance!" cried Lady Brayle.

Martin drew his gaze back. Into the room, unobserved, had slipped another figure: the tiny old man, with the white moustache, whom he had seen hunched over a catalogue in the outer room.

From the table Lady Brayle had fished up a heavy iron shield—round, convex, its outer side scored with dull embossments—and balanced it on the edge of the table.

"Really, Jennifer, I might defy you to find a better present than this shield of our lives and homes! This monument of antiquity, this holy . . ."

21

The apologetic little man cleared his throat.

"I trust you will forgive the intrusion, madam," he whispered in a soft and creaky voice. "But the shield is not genuine."

"Not genuine!"

"No, madam. I could give you reasons at length. But if you will look in the catalogue you will find it described only as 'Scottish type,' which of course means . . ."

"Scotland," said Lady Brayle. "I believe the Fleets were originally Scottish. That will serve well enough. Look at it, Jennifer! Observe its beauty and strength of purpose!"

Lady Brayle was really thrilled. Also, she must have been a powerful woman. She caught up the shield with one hand on each side of the rim. Inspired, she took two sweeping steps backwards and swung up the shield with both arms—full and true into the face of Sir Henry Merrivale just as he entered the room.

The resulting *bong*, as H.M.'s visage encountered the concave side of the shield, was not so mellifluous as a temple-gong. But it was loud enough to make several persons in the auction-room look round. The Dowager Countess, for a moment really taken aback, held the shield motionless before H.M.'s face as though about to unveil some priceless head of statuary.

Then she lowered it.

"Why, Henry!" she said.

The great man's Panama hat had been knocked off, revealing a large bald head. Through his large shell-rimmed spectacles, undamaged because the concavity of the shield had caught him mainly forehead and chin, there peered out eyes of such horrible malignancy that Jenny shied back. His cigar, spreading and flattened, bloomed under his nose like a tobacco-plant.

He did not say anything.

"I suppose I must apologize," Lady Brayle acknowledged coolly. "Though it was really not my fault. You should look where you are going."

H.M.'s face slowly turned purple.

"And now," continued Lady Brayle, putting down the shield, "we must not be late. Come, Jennifer!" Firmly she took Jenny's arm. "I see Lord Ambleside and it would be *most* discourteous not to speak to Lord Ambleside. Good day, Captain Drake."

All might still have been well, perhaps, if she had not turned for a last look at Sir Henry Merrivale. Mention has been made of Lady Brayle's sense of humour. She looked at H.M., and her face began to twitch.

"I am sorry, Henry," she said, "but really—!" Suddenly she threw back her head. The once-pure contralto laughter, refined but hearty, rang and carrolled under the roof.

"Haw, haw, haw!" warbled the Dowager Countess. "Haw, haw, haw, HAW!"

"Easy, sir!" begged Martin Drake.

He seized H.M.'s quivering shoulders. Taking the squashed cigar out of H.M.'s mouth, in case the great man should swallow it, he threw the cigar away.

"Easy!" he insisted. "Are you all right?"

With a superhuman effort, no one knows how great, H.M. controlled himself or seemed to control himself. His voice, which at first appeared to issue in a hoarse rumble from deep in the cellar, steadied a little.

"Me?" he rumbled hoarsely. "Sure, son. I'm fine. Don't you worry about *my* feelin's."

"You—er—don't hold any malice?"

"Me?" exclaimed H.M., with such elaborate surprise that Chief Inspector Masters would instantly have been suspicious. "Oh, my son! I'm a forgivin' man. I'm so goddam chivalrous that if I was ever reincarnated in mediaeval times, which I probably was, some old witch must 'a' copped me in the mush with a shield practically every day. You lemme alone, son. I just want to stand here and cogitate."

Martin, so intent on Jenny that he could think of little else, for the moment forgot him. Jenny and her grandmother were standing on the outer fringe of the crowd, their backs to the arms-room: though Jenny, peering round over her shoulder, tried some lip-message which he could not read.

H.M., cogitating deeply with elbow on one thick arm and fingers massaging his reddened chin, let his gaze wander round. Presently it found the halberds and guisarmes, their long shafts propped upright against the wall. Slowly his gaze moved up to their points. Then, musingly, the gaze travelled out into auction-room and found the ample, flowered posterior of the Dowager Countess.

"Ahem!" said the great man.

Elaborately unconcerned, he adjusted his spectacles and took down one of the weapons. Holding it horizontally on both hands, he ran his eye along the shaft with the critical air of a connoisseur. But it was obvious, from his blinkings, that he needed more light. That was why he strolled out into the auction-room.

"One hundred and fifty . . . Sixty? . . . Seventy? . . . Eighty? . . ."

The auctioneer, a sallow dark man with a pince-nez and a cropped moustache, had an eye that could follow lightning. He never missed; he never misinterpreted. A nod, a mutter, a pencil or catalogue briefly raised: the bidding flickered round that horseshoe table, or out into the crowd, more quickly than the senses could determine. Nobody spoke; all bent forward in absorption.

"Two hundred? Two hundred? Do I hear . . ."

"Oh, my God!" breathed Martin Drake.

That was where he saw what was approaching, on stealthy and evilly large feet, the unconscious back of Lady Brayle.

The only other person who noticed was the timid little man with the white moustache, who had observed all these proceedings in silence. But the little man did not cover ground like Martin. Silently, in loping strides, he reached the side of the avenger; firmly he gripped the other side of the shaft, and looked at H.M. across it.

H.M.'s almost invisible eyebrows went up.

"I dunno what you're talkin' about," he said in a hollow voice—though Martin, in fact, had not uttered a word. He uttered one now.

"No," he said.

"Hey?"

"No."

H.M. altered his tactics.

"Looky here, son," he pleaded. "It's not as though I'm goin' to hurt her, is it? I'm not goin' to *hurt* the old sea-lion. Just one little nip and bob's-your-uncle."

"H.M., don't think I disapprove of this. I'd give a year's income to do it! But one little nip and I may lose the girl."

"What girl?"

"Two hundred pounds! Do I hear more than two hundred pounds?"

"The girl I told you about! There! She's Lady Brayle's granddaughter!"

"Oh, my son! You stick Sophie in the tail and this gal's goin' to adore you."

"No!"

Faintly the hammer tapped. *"Lord Ambleside, for two hundred pounds."*

"Sold!" cried Lady Brayle, in the midst of that shuffling and mist of murmurs which greet the tap of the hammer. "Did you hear that, Jennifer? And to our good friend Lord Ambleside too! Here's three che-ah-s!"

Playfully Lady Brayle threw up her arm like an opera star. She took two swinging steps backwards. And she landed full and true against the point of the shaft gripped by Martin and Sir Henry Merrivale.

The sound which issued from the lips of Lady Brayle at that moment would be difficult phonetically to describe. If we imagine the scream of bagpipes, rising on a long skirling note of shock to burst high in a squeal and squeak of outrage, this somewhat approximates it. For about ten seconds it petrified the whole room.

Jenny, after one horrified look, put her hands over her eyes.

The auctioneer, in the act of saying, "Lot 71," stopped with his mouth open. Two blue-smocked attendants, who carried each exhibit into the open space inside the table so that it could be exhibited during the bidding, dropped a Sheraton writing-desk bang on the floor.

"Mr. Auctioneer!"

Shaken but indomitable, Lady Brayle made her voice ring out.

"Mr. Auctioneer!"

Up from a hidden cubicle, to the auctioneer's right, popped that bald-headed gnome who at Willaby's takes your cheque or bobs up at intervals to see whether you are one whose cheque may be taken. He and the auctioneer seemed to hold a flashing pince-nez conference.

"Mr. Auctioneer," screamed Lady Brayle, and pointed dramatically, "I demand that these two men be ejected from the room!"

The auctioneer's voice was very soft and clear.

"Have the gentlemen been guilty of unbecoming conduct, my lady?"

"Yes, they have!"

"May I ask the nature of the conduct?"

Truth, stern truth, will not be denied.

"This old trout," bellowed Sir Henry Merrivale, snatching the weapon from Martin's hands, "thinks we stuck her in the behind with a halberd."

The meek little man with the white moustache, appearing at H.M.'s elbow, tapped him softly on the shoulder.

"No, no, no!" he protested. "No, no, no, no!"

H.M. turned round an empurpled visage.

"What d'ye mean, no?" he thundered. "Didn't you hear

25

Beowulf's Mother yellin' for the chuckers-out?"

"Not a halberd, my good sir! Not a halberd!"

"Ain't it?"

"No, I assure you! A fine seventeenth-century guisarme."

H.M., his feet wide apart, the shaft of the weapon planted on the floor like a noble Carolean soldier, now made the situation perfectly clear.

"This old trout," he bellowed, "thinks we stuck her in the behind with a seventeenth-century guisarme."

Through the audience ran a sort of suppressed shiver. Martin Drake noted, with amazement and pleasure, that it was not a shiver of horror. It was the spasmodic tension of those who try, by keeping face-muscles rigid, to avoid exploding with mirth. One elderly man, with an eyeglass and withered jowls, had stuffed a handkerchief into his mouth. Another lay face downwards across the table, his shoulders heaving. Even with the auctioneer it was a near thing.

"I feel sure, my lady, that there has been an unfortunate accident." He made a slight gesture to the blue-smocked attendants. His voice grew thinly colourless. *"Lot 71. Here we have . . ."* And H.M. and Lady Brayle were left alone in a sort of closed ring, surreptitiously watched.

"Henry," the old lady said calmly.

"Uh-huh?"

"I am compelled to tell you something. For nine generations," declared Lady Brayle in a shaky voice, "your family have held the baronetcy in a direct line. Yet speak I must. — Henry, you are not a gentleman."

"So I'm not a gentleman, hey?" inquired H.M., getting a firmer grip on the guisarme.

"No, you are not."

"Listen, Sophie," said H.M.., tapping her on the shoulder. "I'm going to show you just how goddam gentlemanly I really am. I've had a reincarnation. Got it?"

Lady Brayle, whose confused mind evidently connected this with some sort of surgical operation, stared at him. Swiftly, silently, the bidding rippled round the table, followed by the tap of the hammer. It was the words, *"Lot 72,"* followed by a sudden loud murmur to drown out the next part, which galvanized Lady Brayle. The spectators, though interested, seemed reluctant to bid.

"Shall we start it at five pounds? . . . Five? . . . Will anyone say five?"

"I really," cried Lady Brayle, "cannot continue this childish discussion any longer." In haste and anxiety, which often

26

happens at such moments, her contralto rang loudly. "Five pounds!"

"I was a Cavalier poet," said H.M. "TEN POUNDS!"

A horrible suspicion seemed to strike Lady Brayle as she whirled round.

"Henry, you are not bidding? —Twenty!"

"Lord love a duck, what d'ye think I'm here for? —Thirty!"

"Henry, this is *too much*. —Forty!"

"It's no good gettin' mad, Sophie. —Fifty!"

Lady Brayle, instead of directing her bids at the auctioneer, advanced her face towards H.M.

"Sixty!" she hissed.

H.M. also advanced his own unmentionable visage.

"Seventy!" he hissed back.

The buzz of voices, never before heard in such volume at Willaby's, rose like a locust-storm. Twisting and swaying, the crowd pressed forward to get a look at what was being exhibited. It is recorded that one lady, maddened, climbed up on a stranger's back so that she could see. Martin, his own sight obscured, tugged at the great man's coat-tail.

"Listen, sir! Take it easy! You don't even know what it is!"

"I don't care what it is," yelled H.M. "Whatever it is, *this* old trout's not goin' to get it."

"This is malice," said Lady Brayle. "This is insufferable. This is pure childishness. I will end it." Her voice rose in calm triumph. "One—hundred—pounds."

"Oh, Sophie!" grunted H.M. in a distressed tone. "You're playin' for monkey nuts. Let's make it really interesting. —Two hundred pounds!"

"Gentlemen," observed a voice in the crowd, "here we go again."

"Two hundred and ten? Two hundred and ten?"

But Lady Brayle, a very shrewd woman, clamped her jaws. Undoubtedly she knew that the old sinner in front of her, whose cussedness was without depth or measure, would cheerfully have gone to a thousand. Catching the auctioneer's eye, she shook her head. Then she adjusted the rakish fashionable hat on her grey-white hair.

"Jennifer!" she called.

But Jenny did not reply, nor was she in sight.

"You will meet me," her grandmother spoke carefully to the air, "at Claridge's for lunch. One o'clock." Then she turned for a final remark to H.M.

"I must tell you something else," she continued. Martin Drake saw, for the first time, the very real ruthlessness of her

27

mouth, and of the wrinkles round mouth and eyes. "You, and in particular your friend Captain Drake, are going to regret this for the rest of your lives."

And, drawing a pair of white gloves from her handbag, she marched slowly towards the outer room and the stairs.

There no longer appeared to be any comedy in this. Open war. All right!

Searching round for Jenny, Martin saw her signal. Along the long right-hand wall, where stood exhibits overflowing from those at the back, Jenny looked out from between a high lacquered wardrobe and a row of gilt-and-satin chairs. He went to her, and they regarded each other in silence.

"I ought to be furious with you," Jenny said. "I ought to say I'd never speak to you again. Only . . ."

Again he saw the contrast between the placidness of her appearance and the extraordinary violence of her emotions. Ancient Willaby's was treated to the spectacle of a girl throwing her arms round a young man's neck, and the young man kissing her with such return violence as to endanger the equilibrium of the wardrobe.

But the spectators had returned intently to their bidding. Nobody saw them except an attendant of thirty-five years' service, who shook his head despondently.

"I *do* love you," said Jenny, detaching herself reluctantly. "But—however did you have the nerve to take that halberd or what-do-you-call-it, and . . ."

"I didn't," he admitted. "When your grandmother let out that yelp—"

"Darling, you shouldn't have done it." (This was perfunctory.)

"—when she yelped, and everybody looked round, I felt about two inches high with embarrassment. Then I took one look at H.M., and I felt about nine feet high. There's something about the old ba . . . the old boy's personality. It's like an electric current."

The gentleman in question, having detached himself from the spectators, was now lumbering towards them in the aisle between bidders and wall. From the arms-room he had retrieved his Panama hat. He carried the guisarme like a mighty man of war, thumping down its shaft at every step. But, when an attendant took it from him, it was with such a deferential, "*If* you please, sir," that H.M. only scowled. Then he surveyed Martin and Jenny.

"Not for the world," he said querulously, "would I show any curiosity. Oh, no. But, burn me, I'd like to have *some* idea of what it is I paid two hundred quid for. They say it's back there somewhere," he nodded towards the rear of the room, "and I can't get it till the end of the sale."

"Please," urged Jenny. "Lower your voice. I can tell you what it is."

"So?"

"It's a clock. A grandfather clock."

"Well . . . now!" muttered the great man, and scratched his chin. A vast load seemed lifted from him. "That's not bad. That's not bad at all. I was sort of picturing myself goin' home with a fine big bit of needlework labelled, 'Jesus give you sleep.'"

"The clock," Jenny explained, "hasn't got any works inside it. There's only a skeleton, fastened upright to the back, with its skull looking out through the glass clock-dial."

The effect of this remark was curious.

Instead of showing surprise or even sarcasm, H.M.'s big face smoothed itself out to utter expressionlessness. His small, sharp eyes fastened on Jenny in a way that evidently disconcerted her. He did not even seem to breathe. The thin voice of the auctioneer sounded far away.

"A skeleton in a clock, hey? That's a bit rummy. Do you happen to know any more about it, my wench?"

"Only—only that they say it used to belong to a doctor in our neighborhood. Years ago he sold it, or gave it away, or something. Then he died."

"Uh-huh. Don't stop there. Go on."

"Well! Aunt Cicely, that's Lady Fleet, saw it in Willaby's catalogue. She thought it would be nice as a present for Dr. Laurier; he's the son of the old doctor, you see. Aunt Cicely *is* kind. But she's so vague, though she's still very pretty, that she asked grandmother to bid."

"Oh, my eye!" breathed H.M. "Oh, lord love a duck! I want a look at that clock. Excuse me."

"But—"

"Sure, sure. I can't take it away. But a little largess, I think, ought to get me just a *look* at it. You two stay where you are!"

Martin made no objection. His blood was beating with the nearness of Jenny, his wits whirling, his entire universe concentrated on Jenny; and, he knew, she felt in much the same way. •

"Now listen," he said. "Before the wires can get crossed again: what's your full name, and where do you live?"

"My name is Jennifer West. Grandmother—grandmother's made me hate titles so much we won't bother with the rest of

29

it. My mother is dead. My father's lived abroad since the beginning of the war: in Sweden. I live at a place called Brayle Manor."

"Is that anywhere near Fleet House?"

"About half a mile south of it. Why?"

"Look here." Martin hesitated. "This engagement was— arranged. Wasn't it?"

Jenny hesitated too, and would not meet his eyes.

"Yes, I suppose you could call it that. We're practically broke; haven't a bean. The Fleets are very wealthy. Aunt Cicely . . ."

"Go on!"

"Well, Aunt Cicely's only weakness is that she *is* a bit of a snob about titles. Her husband gave I don't know how much to party-funds so he could get his knighthood. But that's not all! Richard is really . . . fond of me. Richard—"

"Or 'dear Ricky, as we call him.' "

"Darling, you *mustn't* talk like that!"

"Sorry. Do you know what black bile is? It's jealousy. Sorry."

"He really is nice. He's a great athlete, and very intelligent too: a double-first at Cambridge."

Fierce, tense, lowered whispers! Their voices were so soft, as they stood against the brown wall between the gilt chairs and the lacquered wardrobe, that no bidder could have complained of disturbance. Over a grimy skylight the sun alternately strengthened and darkened.

"If you don't mind," said Martin, "we'll omit the list of Richard's accomplishments. Jenny, I'm going to smash this marriage to blazes. Is that all right with you?"

"I think I should hate you if you didn't. But grandmother . . ."

"There is a technique with grandmother. You saw it used today by a master hand. How long are you staying in town?"

"We've got to leave this evening. I'm—I'm to spend Saturday and Sunday at Fleet House."

"Richard?"

"No! Not particularly!" The blue eyes grew puzzled. "It's something rather mysterious."

"How so?"

"Well, there's a friend of Aunt Cicely's, and mine too, named Ruth Callice. This morning, very early it seems, Ruth rang up Aunt Cicely. She asked if she could come down for the week-end, and bring two guests. I don't know who the two men are; but Ruth said Aunt Cicely would like them. Ruth said she

30

had some tremendous project, about the old prison. She said it *might* not work, but she'd know for certain today whether some Ministry would say yes."

Then, very quietly, Jenny added: "Why did you jump when I said 'Ruth Callice.'"

Martin had not jumped. But, as they stood together negligently against the wall, their hands were locked together. Each tremor, each blood-beat, almost each thought, seemed to flow from one into the other. And women, at times like these, have an emotional power which is almost like mind-reading.

"Yes?" murmured Jenny.

"Because I'm one of the two men. I was in Ruth's flat last night."

"Oh," murmured Jenny, and her gaze moved away. He felt, in the literal sense of touch, something wrong. "Do you know Ruth well?"

"I've known her for years! She's one of the finest persons I ever met!"

"Oh. Did you ever tell her anything about—us?"

"Yes, several times. I'm afraid I got rather emotional about it last night. She cheered me up."

"How nice," said Jenny, and suddenly tried to wrench her hands away. He held tightly. "Then didn't she ever tell you who I was? Who 'Jenny' was? Why didn't she?"

"Probably because she had no more clue than I had."

"Oh, yes, she had. She knew who I was. She knew all *I* knew about you, because I told her. Three years! And in the meantime, I suppose . . ."

It occurred to Martin Drake, quite accurately, that Jenny must feel about Ruth Callice much as he felt about Richard Fleet. He must stop this nonsense. But such talk is contagious.

"If it comes to that, why didn't you get in touch with me and tell me yourself?"

Jenny's pale complexion was flushed, and she was trembling.

"Because you thought it was just a casual adventure. Oh, yes, you did! Or else you'd have found me—somehow. *You* had to come to *me,* don't you see? Won't anybody leave me a little pride? Please let me go."

"Jenny, listen to reason! You know how I feel, don't you?"

"Yes. I think so."

Jenny's resistance fell away. It was trivial, a brushing of the wing in those fierce whispers. The hands of the clock on the far wall stood at a quarter past twelve; the morning's auction would soon be over. And yet, in the state of mind of these two, all unintentionally they were precipitating tragedy and disaster

31

which moved closer as steadily as the ticking of the clock.

"And now," she said, "you've been invited to Fleet House."

"Ruth and Stannard can go there. *I* can't.'

"Why not?"

"Damn it, you can't accept a man's hospitality and then tell him you're going to break up his marriage. Isn't there a hotel or a pub somewhere near?"

"Yes. There's one almost opposite Fleet House. That's where—" Jenny paused. Into her eyes came the same fear he had seen once before. She threw the thought away. "What are you going to do?"

"I'm going to put up at the pub. Tomorrow I'll see Mr. Richard Fleet, and Aunt Cicely, and as for grandmother: this afternoon, I think."

"No! You mustn't! Not this afternoon!"

He gripped her shoulders. "If I could only tell you, Jenny, how much—"

"Oi!" said the voice of Sir Henry Merrivale.

H.M. was standing very close to them. How long he had been there Martin could not tell, but it might have been a long time. H.M.'s hat was in his hand, and his expression was malevolent. Martin bumped back to reality.

"Well? Did you see the clock?"

"Uh-huh. I saw it. And it seems my first wild and wool-gatherin' notion," here H.M. massaged his big bald head, "is no more use than a busted kite on a calm day. But there's got to be *some* explanation! Or else—" With no change he added: "So you're putting up at the pub, son?"

"You listened?"

"I'm the old man," said H.M., austerely tapping himself on the chest as though this constituted all necessary explanation. "And I'm a bit glad you *are* stayin' there, if there's room for you. Masters and I will be there too."

Somewhere, noiselessly, an alarm-bell rang.

"Chief Inspector Masters?"

"Yes. Y'see, son, this business is not all bath-salts and lilies on the pond. It's messy. It's got claws. Pretty certainly in the past, and maybe in the future, we're dealin' with murder."

Chapter 4

Martin Drake did not see the skeleton in the clock until late on the following afternoon, when he saw it in the bar-parlour of the Dragon's Rest near Rimdown.

The Dragon's Rest, to be exact, boasted two bar-parlours in its long frontage. The inn, in that remote corner of Berkshire, faced westwards over a road running north and south. From the windows of either bar-parlour you could see, almost opposite—set well back from the road behind trees and clipped lawns—the white Georgian facade of Fleet House. By craning to the left, you could just make out in the distance the two square towers of Brayle Manor. By craning to the right, you could more distantly discern the round greyness of Pentecost Prison: six stone wings like spokes inside a stone wheel.

Both Pentecost and Fleet House, Martin felt, would hold bitter dreariness at night. Also, he was on a wire of nerves.

For he could not forget yesterday's events. Jenny had permitted him to go with her only as far as the foyer at Claridge's, where she was to meet grandmother. She had made him promise, solemnly crossing his heart, that he would see Richard Fleet first, Aunt Cicely second, and grandmother third.

Martin returned to his rooms at the Albany. After putting through a complicated and exasperating series of 'phone-calls, he managed to book a room at the Dragon's Rest. Then, under the huge arched window which had served a Regency artist, he tried to make new sketches of Jenny from memory. They displeased him. Presently the telephone rang.

"Stannard here," announced the hoarse, hearty, half-chuckling voice.

He could picture Stannard leaning back in a swivel-chair, the black hair plastered with nicety on his round head, the black eyes twinkling. Martin could almost hear the pleased creak of the swivel-chair as Stannard shifted his stocky bulk.

"I hope, Mr. Drake, you haven't forgotten our little talk last night?"

No, he hadn't forgotten it. But he could think only of Jenny.

33

Why, and in what crazy moment, had he insisted on this vigil in the execution shed?

"Because I'm glad to say," Stannard pursued, "that I have been successful. For a night or two at least we are masters of Pentecost Prison."

"Good! Good! Good!"

"Our good friend Ruth has helped us. A friend of hers has been kind enough to invite us all to spend the week-end—"

"Yes. I know."

"You know?"

This time an edge did get into Martin's voice.

"Mr. Stannard, it's a vitally personal matter; I'll explain when I see you. I can't stay at Fleet House. But you'll find me at the pub just across the way."

There was a slight pause.

"You'll travel down with us, of course?" inquired Stannard. "Noon train from Paddington to Reading, change for Newbury, then bus for the rest. Devilish awkward, being without petrol."

"Sorry. I'm afraid I've got to take an earlier train."

Now there was a definite pause. He knew Stannard had detected something odd in his tone, and that Stannard was examining the 'phone curiously.

"Shall I—ah—make excuses to our hostess and young host?"

"No. They'll have learned about it when you arrive."

"Shall I make excuses to Ruth?" This was said very casually.

"No." Martin clipped off the monosyllable.

"Ah. It should be very interesting to visit Fleet House," mused Stannard, "especially as I once had some slight acquaintance with its late owner. Just as you like, my dear fellow. Good-bye."

Martin replaced the telephone. He looked round his sittingroom, on whose walls much of his own work hung framed amid his collection of rapiers. It *had* occurred to him that afternoon to ring Ruth Callice and ask her what the devil Ruth had meant by her secrecy about Jenny. But Ruth was a good fellow; Ruth must have had some real reason; he put the thought aside.

That was how, next morning, a grey bus with dropsical wheels rattled him up in Rimdown crossroads at half-past eleven. Not far ahead he could see the Dragon's Rest, with its three tall and broad gables in a straight line, set up on a little rise on the east side of the road.

The Dragon's Rest was a beamed house of great age. Behind

it lay rolling fields, the glitter of a stream, and the largish oak-wood he later identified as Black Hanger. Not a blade of grass stirred, nothing stirred, in that hollow of silence and heat.

Mr. Puckston, the landlord, took him up to a first-floor bedroom facing west. Then Martin's first move was to clatter downstairs again to the telephone at the back of the saloon bar, and get in touch with Fleet House. He was answered by an informal and chatty maid.

"Mr. Richard? Oh, he's driven over to the races at Newbury."

Martin's heart sank. He put obvious questions.

"No, not back to lunch. But he'll be back in the afternoon, because there's people coming. Would you like to speak to his mother? She's in the garden."

"No, thanks. You say he drove over. Can you describe the car?"

"Oh, it's just an ole black car. Makes a lot of noise."

"Do you happen to know the number?"

"Are you kidding?" asked the maid, who had evidently been out with American troops.

"As soon as he comes back, will you ask him to ring Martin Drake at the Dragon's Rest? It's very important. Will you give him that message?"

"You have a nice voice," said the maid. "I sure will!"

Martin went back to his room fuming. To follow Richard Fleet in the crowds at Newbury races would be certainly to miss him, even if there were a photograph for identification. The minutes ticked on. He had lunch in the scrubbed oak dining-room, the food being incredibly good. But always he prowled back to the bedroom, also clean and surprisingly comfortable despite the humps of age in the floor.

Pulling back the thin white curtains at one window, he kept glancing across the road to where—some three hundred feet away—Fleet House raised its square, uncompromising face of white-painted stone. Being on higher ground, he could look across almost to the topmost row of windows. Over trees and clipped lawns, he could see a flagstone terrace before the front door.

Flagstones. That was probably where Sir George Fleet had
. . .

Martin saw no sign of an ole black car. But someone was moving on the terrace, woman in a long filmy dress with a red sash and a broad straw sun-hat.

And Martin yielded to temptation.

On a table beside his bed, with its spotlessly mended white

counterpane, lay an old-fashioned brass telescope of the short and folding sort. He pulled out its few bands and focussed the end one. The image sprang up close and clear, just as the woman turned her head round and up.

Aunt Cicely.

He remembered Jenny's soft voice: "Aunt Cicely *is* kind. But she's so vague, though still very pretty." The westering sun was in Martin's eyes, though the telescope shielded it. Aunt Cicely must be into her fifties. Yet she had an Edwardian air, Martin thought: the sort Sargent had painted so well. With her pale blonde hair under the broad sun-hat, face turned up, she seemed (through the telescope, at least) almost young and rather fragile.

Furthermore, she had recently been crying.

Martin shut up the telescope. What *was* the air of sheer coldness which seemed to breathe out of Fleet House? Probably his professional imagination. But . . .

This situation was getting to be damned awkward. He had not seen Ruth or John Stannard. But then he had not seen H.M. or Masters either, though the landlord told him they had booked rooms. Half-past two and a quarter to three.

It was past four, the cigarette-tray full of stubs, before he made a guess which he should have made before. He hurried down, fumbled with the small 'phone-directory, and rang Brayle Manor.

If grandma came to the 'phone? All right! But it was a male voice which answered, evidently a butler.

"Is Mr. Richard Fleet there?"

"Yes, sir. Whom shall I say is calling?"

Martin spoke deliberately. "This," he said, "is an enemy. Tell Mr. Fleet that an enemy is waiting for him at the Dragon's Rest to give him a message of great importance."

If young Fleet had an ounce of sporting blood in his body, Martin thought, that ought to fetch him. He expected further questions. But the unruffled voice merely said, "One moment, please." And then, after a long minute, "Mr. Fleet will be with you immediately."

Got it!

At this hour of the day, the whole inn was so quiet that you could hear the wainscot creak. Mr. and Mrs. Puckston must be enjoying their afternoon nap. The Dragon's Rest had three front doors, one in each gable. As Martin unlocked the first one, which was in the saloon bar, the snap of the key sounded like an act of guilt.

Moving on to the first bar-parlour, on his right, Martin

unlocked the front door there. This was a cosy room, its walls thickly hung with sporting prints and with quite genuine antique hunting horns of the early nineteenth century. Somewhat decaying leather chairs stood at the tables, and at either side of the black marble mantelpiece.

Then Martin turned round, and saw the skeleton in the clock.

The clock stood in the angle of the wall, south-east, beyond the mantelpiece. It was about six feet high, including its platform-base, and of dark polished wood elaborately wrought at the top. Through a round glass dial, with gilt numerals and hands, the skull-face looked out.

And the clock was ticking.

No! Wait a minute! It couldn't be ticking. The clock-case had another glass panel, oblong, so that you could see the skeleton behind a brass pendulum: which was motionless.

The illusion had been produced by a large square metal-cased clock, with a small pendulum, on the mantelpiece. Its slow *tick-tick* animated the hush of an atmosphere flavoured with the smell of beer and old stone. But the tall clock said nothing.

Yet it gave the watcher a slight start, the skull face a smug look in its dusky recess. Martin was conscious of golden shine lying through the windows behind him, of Fleet House across the road in its aloofness. He went over to examine the clock. As he had expected, the oblong lower panel opened on little hinges. He peered inside, he peered up.

With fine wires, and a heavier wire drilled into the head, the skeleton had been fastened to the back of the case; its feet and ankles partly concealed by a wooden fitting evidently designed to help the upright position. The clock-hands, like the pendulum, were dummies held by screw and spindle. You could adjust them to any position you liked. The hands now stood at ten minutes past twelve.

Tick-tick, tick-tick, tick-tick.

Richard Fleet would be here at any moment.

Martin drew back his head and closed the glass panel. How this reminder of mortality had got there he did not know. And it didn't matter.

He went through another door into the second bar-parlour. Dominated by a large iron stove rather than the usual fireplace, full of wicker chairs, this room was distinctly a comedown from the first. Nevertheless, Martin unlocked its front door. He had just turned the key when distantly, from the saloon-bar two rooms away, that particular door opened.

A voice called, "Martin!" He heard light, quick, running footsteps in tennis-shoes. And in the doorway of the second parlour, breathing hard, stood Jenny.

She wore a white tennis-blouse and white shorts, with a light pullover thrown over her shoulders. With her yellow hair somewhat tumbled, the colour of exertion tinted her face to more than mere prettiness. He stared at her.

"How did *you* get here?"

"On my bike." Choking a little to get her breath, she made a gesture towards the outside of the inn. "Darling, why did you send that message about being an enemy?"

"I had to get him here somehow."

"Grandmother was in the room when you rang up."

"Yes. I thought she might be."

"You hadn't said three words to Dawson before grandmother said: 'That is Captain Drake, I suppose.' Ricky said, 'Who's Captain Drake?' Grandmother said nothing at all. She just picked up her knitting and walked out of the room. Then I had to tell Ricky it was only a joke, but it *was* terribly serious. Afterwards I got old Riddle to insist the front tire of Ricky's car needed air—which it did—so I could get here before him."

"But you don't want to be present while we have it out, do you?"

Jenny's breathing was still quick. But the blue eyes regarded him steadily.

"If you want me to," she answered, "I'll stay here. I promise that. But I don't want to. I don't want . . . oh, God, no!" She shuddered. "The trouble is, you see, that I've got to know what happens. Just as *soon* as it happens." Jenny spread out her hands. "I'm sorry. That's how I feel."

"That's how a lot of us feel. Jenny! Do you still—?"

This was when they heard the loud cranking of a motor-car, emphasized by a loose mud-guard, approaching and drawing up outside the south wing. Once more the door of the saloon-bar, after a tentative rattle at its knob, was opened. Martin motioned Jenny (confound this sense of guilt!) to go out by the second-parlour door to the road.

"Hoy there!" called a male voice. "Hullo!"

Footsteps scuffled, hesitated, tramped through one room and then through two. In the doorway, inquiringly, appeared a tallish young man in sports coat, flannels, and with a blue tie skewered under one wing of his soft collar.

His mop of dark-blond hair was uncombed and unruly. He was on the lean and muscular side, carrying himself well. But first of all you noticed the quality of good-humour, which was

38

so genuine that it flowed from him and made friends immediately. His grey eyes, his bump of a chin, made it a strong face as well as a good-humoured face.

"Well," he said, "are you the enemy?"

"Yes." Martin could not help smiling back. "But not a personal enemy, if you follow me."

"Ah. That's good. Well, what's up?"

Selecting a wicker chair by the door into the first-parlour, the newcomer dropped into it and threw one leg over its arm. He began to fill a pipe from an oilskin pouch.

There was a long silence.

"Look here, old boy," expostulated Richard Fleet, who was fishing after a pocket-lighter.

"Yes?"

"Stop pacing up and down like a Norman baron. Get it off your chest. Spit it out. You're making me nervous."

"All right," agreed Martin. "It's about Jenny. I've been in love with Jenny for more than three years, though I've only seen her twice. I have reason to think she feels the same way about me. I haven't formally asked her to marry me, but we intend to get married. I hate to tell you this, but there it is."

Again silence. Richard sat partly sideways, motionless, his leg over the chair-arm, pipe and lighter also held motionless, looking up at his companion. His grey eyes were without any shade of expression. *Tick-tick, tick-tick* went the clock in the other room, noticeable now as well as audible.

"I'm sorry to tell you this!" Martin shouted. "But . . ."

Then he saw that there was a shade of expression, slowly moving in like a new blood in Richard's face, though for a second he could not interpret it. It was tinged with incredulity, but this did not predominate. Then Martin realized. The feeling was relief. Slowly young Fleet sat upright, and expelled his breath.

"Thank God!" he said.

Chapter 5

The words were so startling that Martin backed away until he bumped into the iron stove in the middle of the room. Richard Fleet hastened to correct any wrong impression he might have made.

39

"Mind!" he said, jumping to his feet and pointing with the pipe. "Jenny's the world's best. I'd do anything for her. I'm so fond of her that sometimes I've almost thought this plan would work. But—"

"But?"

"I grew up with her," the other retorted with extraordinary intensity. "Jenny was always *there,* from five to seventeen and onwards. Let's face it: I'm not physically attracted by Jenny. Whereas you, it's plain, have gone completely overboard physically; and that's the main thing. Yes, I know!"

He held up a hand, forestalling objection. He dropped pipe and lighter into his pockets. The grey intelligent eyes regarded Martin as though they knew, or thought they knew, the whole universe.

"They tell us a lot of things about companionship and community of interests and so on. Well, old boy," he grinned, "let's wait until we're old enough to have to bother with such things. The glorious part of all this is that I've gone overboard too. *I* want to get married."

Martin's sense of relief, he thought, completely overshadowed that of his companion.

"Congratulations! And very hearty congratulations! Who is she?"

Richard went over and carefully closed the second-parlour door.

"Susan Harwood. She lives on the other side of Brayle: the town, not the Manor." A shadow of worry crossed Richard's face, but his animation burst through it. "By God," he breathed, "this is the most magnificent . . . shake hands!"

They shook hands, fervently.

"Look here," said Richard, "what would you like?"

"Like?"

"Well," said the other, whose first impulse on feeling pleased was to give something to somebody, "what about my car with fifty gallons of best Black Market petrol? Or your choice from the gun-racks? Or I've got the finest book of telephone-num . . . no, you won't want telephone-numbers if you're going to get married. Neither will I." He pondered. "You know—by the way—what's your first name?"

"Martin."

"Right! Ricky here.' Again he pondered, "You know, if we plan this carefully, I'm damn sure we can wangle it."

"'Plan carefully?' What have we got to plan?"

"You don't know what you're up against," Ricky said

quietly. "No, wait! You think you do; but you don't."

"Family opposition?"

"You say that fairly contemptuously. Maybe Jenny hasn't told you everything." Ricky brushed the palms of his hands together; then gripped them in sinewy fingers. "I don't suppose you've ever played chess with Grandmother Brayle? *I* have. She ought to have been a man. She wants money, and she means to get it."

Though the sun was sinking, the many little panes of the second-parlour window were still tinged with gold. With both doors and windows closed, the room was hot and stuffy. Ricky went over to the window and stared out unseeingly.

"My mother," he continued, "is wonderful. But Grandmother Brayle has got mother"—he put his thumb in the palm of his left hand, and twisted it—"like that. And Dr. Laurier has more influence than anybody knows. As for Jenny . . ." He broke off. "Great Scott, there *is* Jenny!"

Martin hurried to his side.

In front of the Dragon's Rest, a slope of sun-glowing grass stretched down to the road. Across the road, beyond a short strip of grass, ran the low stone boundary-wall of Fleet House's park. Near the wall stood Jenny and Ruth Callice, apparently in casual conversation.

They made a contrast, against the trees and, somewhat towards the left, the white, square solidity of the house. Ruth wore a silk frock as though she were in London; her light-brown hair was done in some new upsweep style, with earrings. Jenny, in her white blouse and white shorts, lifted one shoulder as she spoke.

Ricky Fleet leaned his weight on the window-sill with both hands.

"You know," he said, "there's a row going on over there."

"A what?"

"A row. Don't ask me how I know; can't you feel it? Besides, I've been expecting one."

"Why?"

"I suppose," Ricky grunted, "I ought have been at home to greet the guests. But I start gassing, and time gets mixed up. Then Ruth rang up the Manor just before you rang me. Jenny talked to her." He hesitated. "Jenny wasn't any less gentle than she always is. But she sounded too—sugary. Like a woman waiting for a time and place to blow up. You know what I mean?"

Even as he spoke Jenny said a last few words, lifting her

41

shoulder, and moved away. She glanced towards the window where Ricky and Martin were standing. Her gait faltered and grew slow, but she continued; and automatically swung the thin blue pullover at her side. When Martin saw his companion's shoulders grow rigid, he realized something else.

"What the hell," Ricky blurted, "am I going to tell her?"

The door opened, framing Jenny against sunlight. Pouring embarrassment flooded into that room, holding all three motionless. Martin saw Ricky brace himself for an actor's role in some heroic speech of renunciation; he even saw Ricky glance at himself in a flyblown mirror to make sure the posture was right. But it was Jenny who spoke.

"It's all right," she said, looking at the floor. "I knew it was all right as soon as I saw you two shake hands."

The embarrassment remained, but the tension had gone.

"It wouldn't have worked, you know," growled Ricky.

"Ricky here," Martin said, "has been so decent about the whole thing that I don't know how to thank him."

"Nonsense, old boy! Nonsense!"

Jenny's eyes brimmed over as she regarded her (they hoped) ex-*fiancé*.

"You *are* a dear, Ricky."

"Not a bit of it, old girl! Not a bit of it!"

In another minute, Martin thought, he'll convince himself he really has made a heroic sacrifice.

"Martin," said Jenny, and hesitated. "Will you take me out somewhere tonight?"

At this change of subject, Ricky became natural again.

"That's not a bad idea! You can take my car. But where would you go for a beano in unexplored wilds like these?"

"That's not it." Jenny shook her head vehemently, still looking at Martin. "Will you just take me somewhere, and drive and drive and drive? I don't care where. Will you?"

"You know I will, my dear."

Jenny advanced into the room. Sinking into one of the wicker chairs beside a round table, she threw her pullover on the table. At this change of subject, abruptly introduced but well received, more emotion should have been drained away. And yet, in Jenny's case at least, it was not.

"Ruth Callice," she bit at her underlip, "says you and she and this barrister had some horrible idea of spending a night in the execution shed at Pentecost, to see whether there were any ghosts of hanged people. Ruth says you suggested it."

"Well . . . in a way I did, yes."

"She says you promised. But you won't go now, will you?" Martin laughed.

"Under the circumstances, Jenny, I think they'll make no difficulty about releasing me from the promise." He turned to Ricky. "Would you like to substitute for me?"

"Would I!" exploded Ricky. The words 'prison' and 'ghosts' had powerful effect. Again taking out pipe and lighter, his dark-blond hair falling over his forehead, he snapped on the lighter and kindled the tobacco with deep inhalations.

"Listen," he went on, with a waving gesture of pipe and smoke. "I've been trying to get a look inside that place for nearly ten years, ever since they hoicked the convicts out. But you can't *get* in, any more than the poor devils could get out. How are you going to do it?"

"Ricky!"

Jenny's small voice stopped him. He looked at her curiously. She was half lying back in the chair, the yellow hair thrown back, her face with a little more of its customary pallor.

"All the p-pleasant things," she stammered, gripping the arms of the chair, "have got mixed up with the dreadful ones. It was awfully kind of you to . . . to . . ."

"Rubbish. Let's get back to the subject of ghosts."

"All right," Jenny answered unexpectedly, "I will. Ricky, your mother's been very upset all afternoon."

Into Martin's head came an image of Aunt Cicely, with her tear-reddened eyelids, seen through a brass telescope from a bedroom window. But mention of Aunt Cicely seemed to act on Ricky as mention of Grandmother Brayle acted on Jenny, though in a different way.

"I know! I ought to have been at home in the afternoon!"

"No, Ricky. It wasn't that. Have you ever heard of a man named Stannard?"

"I don't think so. Why?"

"He's one of the guests. He and Ruth came down by an earlier train than they'd expected to. Ruth said she ought to keep an eye on Martin—"

(Here Ricky turned a surprised face, but Martin was looking at Jenny.)

"—and they got here about lunch-time. During lunch, Mr. Stannard started talking about the day your father . . . died."

Ricky took the pipe out of his mouth.

"Blast his impudence!" Ricky shouted.

"I honestly don't think it was impudence."

"No? It always upsets mother, though."

"You see," Jenny frowned, "Mr. Stannard said to Aunt

Cicely something like, 'I'm afraid we've met before, Lady Fleet.' Aunt Cicely laughed and said, 'That's not very complimentary.' Then Mr. Stannard said, 'Forgive me: I only meant I was at Fleet House on the day your unfortunate husband met his death.'"

"What did mother say?"

"Well, Ruth Callice tells me it wasn't a very merry lunch."

"Damn him!"

"Ricky, do you remember or did you ever hear of any 'Stannard' being there at the time?"

"No. Never."

"Nor I. In anything I've ever heard, or—read."

"But what *is* all this?" demanded Ricky. His pipe had gone out, and he put it down on the table. "You're as fretted as though you'd seen a whole crowd of ghosts. My governor's been dead for twenty years. It's a pity about mother; I'd like to wring Stannard's neck; but a little tact and we'll smooth it over."

"We can't smooth over the police," Jenny said.

She rose to her feet and appealed to Martin.

"I—I haven't said anything about what Sir Henry told us yesterday. I mean, at Willaby's. Partly because I was afraid of the rumpus, and partly because I never can tell whether he's serious or not."

Jenny turned to Ricky, and nodded towards the closed door of the other parlour.

"The police are *here*," she added. "They're in that room now. I saw them go in when I came here. There's a Chief Inspector from Scotland Yard, and the other man—well, they call him the Old Maestro. They're here to investigate. Sir Henry thinks your father was murdered."

The word, on Jenny's lips, sounded incongruous.

"Nonsense!" said Ricky. "He got vertigo and pitched over the parapet."

"Yes; but suppose someone did kill him?"

"Look here! Wait a minute!"

"I want to know who was at the house that day," Jenny went on, "and where everybody was when it happened. I was only five years old then. Ricky, how well do you remember?"

The other tousled up his hair, digging the fingers in.

"Some parts of it very plainly, and others not at all. Because they get mixed up with different years. I was barely twelve myself. Besides, I didn't see it happen. I was in the back garden with Miss Upton. She had a head-lock on me."

"Ricky, please do be serious!"

44

"I am serious! Can't you remember Miss Upton the governess, with a build like Sandow and yet that refined la-di-da accent coming out of her mouth?"

"Yes. I remember. She was with your family four years."

"Well, I mean quite literally she had a wrestling-hold on me. Because I wanted to watch the hunt go past." Ricky paused. "You know, Jenny-angel, this subject . . ."

"Yes! It's been taboo in our families for all these years. Let's tear it apart!"

"But why?"

"Have you thought," asked Jenny, and looked at Martin, "what the upset of a police-investigation would be in your house? And my house?"

Clearly Ricky hadn't. Up to this moment, it was clear, he had regarded the matter as nothing very important. 'The governor's been dead for twenty years; we've forgotten it; why bother?' Such might have been his philosophy. Now he sat down heavily in what had been Jenny's chair by the table, and picked up his dead pipe. The sun's glow was dimming to a pale, clear after-light through the open door to the road.

"Tell it," Jenny almost whispered. "Tell it!"

"It was October or November. I'm sure of that, because the trees were mostly bare and there were leaves on the ground. Also because they'd given me a new cricket-bat; and the governor asked what I wanted with a new one when the season was over; but cricket has no season for you at that age. There was some kind of special treat promised for tea, because a number of people were to be there.

"As I say, Miss Upton and I were in the back garden. Near the house, I think. There was a red sky to the west, with the bare branches of trees up against it. It wasn't very cold, and there was a clean autumny-tanging kind of wind. Then we heard the Ascombe Hunt.

"We'd heard faint noises before. But nothing to the uproar like this. We couldn't see anything, because the house was between us and the road. But the hounds were ding-dong and hell-for-leather on a breast-high scent. I knew they'd broken out of Black Hanger and across Guideman's Field just back of this pub here, and I guessed they were running to view.

"I started to make a bee-line for the front of the house. Miss Upton grabbed my arm. She was afraid I would run across and get among the field in front of somebody's horse, which had happened once or twice before. I kicked up a devil of a row until she got a head-lock on me. Then she said: "Richard, you may go to the front if I keep hold of your hand.""

"I said yes, and meant it. We started round the north side of the house, on the broad gravel drive. Then we heard a . . . well, a shout."

Ricky paused.

"I didn't think of anything being wrong, or even connect it with the house particularly. I knew my governor was up on the roof, trying to follow the hunt through a very powerful pair of field-glasses. As he always did when he had the rheumatics and it was agony to sit on a horse. But—

"Well, just as we were nearly to the front of the house, where there's a tap for the garden-hose, I distinctly heard Dr. Laurier's voice."

Jenny interposed. She had crept into a chair opposite Ricky, both of them with their elbows on the table.

"Was it old Dr. Laurier?" she asked. "Or the Dr. Laurier we have now?"

Ricky made a fussed gesture with the pipe. His eyes were hypnotized.

"Old Dr. Laurier, with the beard. The hounds were yelling, and there was the hallo-forrard. Only the hunt-servants had followed through the wood. Most of the field had ridden round; you could see a flash of pink coats coming round the edge of Black Hanger, and hear the horses. But I distinctly remember Dr. Laurier's voice saying, 'Get the table-cloth out of the hall.'

"In the front hall there used to be a piece of tapestry, worked with what I then considered very funny-looking knights; they had it on a table. That's the most distinct thing of the lot: *'Get the table-cloth out of the hall.'*

"Then we got round to the front terrace. There was my governor, lying face-down on the flagstones, looking just as usual: except that old Dr. Laurier, with the beard, was spreading the tapestry-piece over his head and I think his shoulders.

"I was so excited I looked across the road first: there were two men sitting on the roof-gables of this pub, and the hunt streaming beyond. Then there was something: I don't know what. Dr. Laurier straightened up. Your grandmother was standing beside him. When you're a kid, you never really know there's something wrong until you see the look on their faces. Dr. Laurier said, 'Miss Upton, take the boy away from here.' I could feel Miss Upton shaking through all her fifteen stone, and all of a sudden I felt as frightened as hell without knowing why. She turned me round and took me back. Then . . ."

Again Ricky paused. He put the pipe into his mouth and chewed at its stem.

"On my word of honour," he declared in that same hypnotized tone, and dropped the pipe again, "I haven't thought of this for years. Maybe you jogged it into my head. Maybe it's sheer imagination. But I have an impression that I looked *up*."

"Towards the roof?"

"No, no! I didn't connect the governor with anything like 'death' or all the terms you might imply. It was a vague kind of wonder what he was doing down here instead of up there. I looked at an upper window, I think to the right of the front door. And I saw . . ."

There was a sharp rapping on the inside of the open door to the road.

Martin Drake—shut out, almost forgotten, feeling a sharp twinge of jealousy at the absorption of these two in each other and their long familiarity—Martin jerked up his head at that rapping. The other two started as though they had been burnt.

In the doorway stood a wiry, middle-sized man whose pince-nez, except for its gold nose-clamp, seemed to fit into his eyes rather than advance outside them. His hair, cut *en brosse,* was iron-grey. In an ascetic face, with somewhat hollow cheeks, showed a narrow fastidious mouth. His whole air was one of fastidiousness and extreme precision; and he carried a medicine-case in his right hand.

Despite the bloodless mouth, his voice was vigorous if soft. He smiled at Jenny and Ricky, making the countenance pleasant and human, and then looked towards Martin.

"Captain Drake, I imagine?" he inquired. "I am Dr Laurier."

(So he's been talking to grandma, eh? Why did Lady Brayle persist with that 'captain' when they'd finished another war two years ago? Gossip, flying and twisting! How much was known?)

"Just Mr. Drake," Martin said, "if you don't mind."

Dr. Laurier bowed slightly. Next he turned to Ricky. You could imagine him, at a desk, pushing a group of small articles carefully into line.

"In my opinion, Richard, it would be very wise if you returned home at once. Your mother is not well."

Ricky twitched up his head. "You've been over there?"

"Yes." Dr. Laurier, not moving from the doorway, fired softly from a distance. He inclined his head. "I don't know

47

how many times I have told you that your mother has a definitely serious heart-condition. An unpleasant shock of any sort—" very slightly emphasizing the words 'of any sort,' Dr. Laurier's almost invisible pince-nez moved towards Jenny, and then Martin—"would be . . . most undesirable."

"Then if she heard—" Ricky checked himself. He also looked at Jenny and Martin. Wretchedness laid hold of him and shook him as though with hands.

"I'll go straightaway," he said, and got up.

"I hope," interposed Jenny politely, "my grandmother is well?"

And this was a different girl from the timorous one of yesterday. Martin saw that with a shock of hope. Though she seemed outwardly placid, her breast rose and fell under the white blouse.

"Your grandmother, Lady Jennifer," Dr. Laurier returned her smile, "is in excellent health. She was a bit disappointed, however . . ."

Jenny's tone expressed immense surprise. "Were you at the Manor too?"

"For a cup of tea; no more. As I say, she was a bit disappointed you were not there for tea. She wondered where you were."

"Oh, I've got to be out much later tonight. I shall have to go home and change, of course. But I've got to be out much later tonight."

Deliberately Jenny rose from her chair. Deliberately she slipped over to where Martin was standing, and took his arm. He put his hand over hers. Dr. Laurier made no comment and no sign: a grey-headed statue in the doorway, his pince-nez opaque, the medicine-case in his hand.

"And—Ricky!" the ex-*fiancée* called.

"Eh?"

"You will lend us your car for tonight, won't you?"

"Of course. And . . ." Despite his perturbation, the old smile kindled Ricky's face. "Look here, old boy. This man-of-honour business is all very well. But is there any real reason why you shouldn't stay with us instead of putting up at the pub? Can't you at least come over for dinner tonight?"

"I've been a fool," Martin blurted. "I'm always being a fool. But I had some wild sort of notion that everyone here was an enemy .. ."

"Who can tell?" murmured Dr. Laurier.

The words fell with soft, chilling weight. It was as though a dagger had thudded into a door; not too melodramatic a

48

comparison, because Dr. Laurier had a certain hobby. Martin felt Jenny's soft arm grew rigid against his coat-sleeve. And then: "I *beg* your pardon!" added the doctor, and stepped aside.

Ruth Callice, brushing past him with apology, stepped into the room.

In her unobtrusive way Ruth was urban charm, urban fashion, invading a country pub. Her grey dress, the dull-twinkling ear-rings, set off her dark-brown eyes and the full roundness of her neck. Ruth regarded everyone with smiling apology.

"Martin, dear," she said. "I've come to remind you about your promise for tonight."

Chapter 6

Some half an hour before Ruth's appearance, in the other bar-parlour with the clock containing its skeleton, Sir Henry Merrivale sat in a leather chair near the fireplace. Chief Inspector Masters stood opposite, behind a table on which lay a brief-case stuffed with documents.

And these two were carrying on in a way which would have sounded familiar to any friend of theirs.

"Now, now, Masters, keep your shirt on!"

Masters, large and burly, usually bland as a card-sharper, his grizzled hair brushed to hide an increasing bald-spot, was buttoned up in a blue serge and had assumed his witness-box manner. This indicated that his words would have weight and dignity.

"It might interest you to know, sir, that I've *got* my shirt on."

"That's right, Masters. Be like Me."

"These impossible situations," said Masters. "What do I care for 'em?" He reached out and snapped his fingers. "Not that! Oh, ah! And why? Because I'm resigned."

"*I* got a spiritual nature too."

Masters's blood-pressure soared, as was evident in his countenance. "But what I DO object to—"

"Easy, son!"

"But what I do object to," continued the Chief Inspector,

swallowing hard, "is the Assistant Commissioner wanting to dig up a twenty-year old case, because: first, he was an old friend of Sir George Fleet; and, second, he recently gets three anonymous postcards straight out of Colney Hatch. Now I ask you! Is that fair or reasonable?"

Delving into the neatly packed brief-case, Masters drew out three cards and pushed them across the table towards H.M., who did not even glance at them. H.M., with a malignant scowl, had folded his hands across his corporation and was twiddling his thumbs.

These cards, the ordinary twopenny-halfpenny sort you buy at any post office, had both address and message printed in small block capitals, with a pencil. They were postmarked in the town of Brayle, about two miles southwards, on July 5th, July 6th, and July 7th, and addressed, 'Chief of the C.I.D., Scotland Yard, London W.1.' The first card read:

Re Sir George Fleet: examine the skeleton in the clock.

The second card read:

Re Sir George Fleet: what was the pink flash on the roof?

The third card read:

Re Sir George Fleet: evidence of murder is still there.

"Lummy!" breathed Masters. "I've seen some scatty messages in my time, but this beats the lot." He squared himself. "Now I'll just take each point, sir. This clock, to begin with."

Both of them, in the old room hung with hunting prints, surveyed the tall clock. Standing cater-cornered in its southeast angle, its gilt hands and numerals faintly shining, the glass dial conveyed an impression that the skull had its chin tilted up so that the skull could see better. Like Martin Drake, Masters experienced the illusion that the *tick-tick* of the mantelpiece clock issued out of that dead case. It made Masters uncomfortable, which in his staid soul he resented.

"Sir," he demanded, "what's wrong with that clock?"

"Nothin'," H.M. answered simply.

"What's wrong with the skeleton?"

"Nothin'."

"Then why in lum's name do you want to bring it down here and stick it up in a bar-parlour?"

"Because, son, I can't do everything at once. I want to take that blighter out of his case—" H.M. pointed to the skeleton— "and put him on a table, and examine him thoroughly. I dunno who he is, son. But I can tell you who he's not. He's not Sir George Fleet."

50

"Oh, ah!" muttered Masters, with a sideways look. "So you thought of that?"

"Oh, my son! It was the very first wild and wool-gatherin' notion I did have, for no reason at all. But it won't work. Now the overall height of that clock, includin' platform and fancy top, is six feet. And the late lamented?"

"Six feet one inch tall," grunted Masters, with the heaviness of one who has studied much, "and with big bones."

"Right. Whereas the chap who's watchin' us," H.M. indicated the clock again, "was a little feller. Five feet five, about. Well-proportioned, small bones. Masters, I'll tell you what it is. That's an ordinary medical-school skeleton: varnished, articulated . . ."

"Meaning strung together with wire?"

"With fine cat-gut, usually. Besides, you couldn't possibly conceal the injuries to Fleet's head. Who'd want to?"

"Ah, and that's just it. What *about* the skeleton?" exploded Masters. "In all this record—" he brought his hand down slowly on the brief-case—"there's not a word to do with any skeleton in a clock. What's it supposed to mean?"

"I dunno. But an anonymous letter, postmarked Brayle, tells you to examine it. Five days later Our Sophie, on instructions from Cicely Fleet, waddles up to London to buy it for Dr. Laurier: son of clock's former owner. Don't you find that rather fetchin' and interesting?"

Masters took several paces up and down. The ticking of the clock seemed to trouble him.

"If we had one bit of evidence that this was murder—!"

"Oh, Masters. It was murder. Tell me something about George Fleet."

"Lummy, haven't you read this stuff in the brief-case?"

"Uh-huh. But I want to see what impressed *you.*"

H.M., his spectacles pulled down on his broad nose, closed his eyes. An expression almost of serenity crossed his unmentionable face. Masters, deeply suspicious of being done in the eye again, studied him warily. At length the Chief Inspector cleared his throat.

"Hurrum!" he said. "Sir George Fleet? Came of a well-to-do family in the Midlands, with a cotton-business. Family wanted him to be pukka Army; so did he. Boarding-school when he was a tiny 'un, then Harrow, then Sandhurst. Never finished Sandhurst; father died, and he had to take over the business.

"But he acted Army all the rest of his life, though he didn't join up in '14. Upright carriage, cropped moustache, dead-

51

keen on sport. Roared at everybody. Wanted a knighthood; got it; wanted a baronetcy so his title wouldn't die with him; didn't get it."

Still H.M. did not open his eyes, though his look was now evil. He grunted.

"Yes. That's why it's so rummy that . . . h'mf. What about his wife?"

"She lives just over the road, sir. You could go see her."

"I meant twenty years ago."

"Bit of a beauty, I'd say." Masters considered. "You've seen her photograph. Yes, bit of a beauty in the fair-haired, blue-eyed way. Completely gone on her husband. Idolized him. Do anything he said, and like it."

"Wait a minute, son. Does that mean she was all coos and clucks in public, and in private wept and twisted him round her little finger?"

Masters repressed a guffaw.

"No, it does not," he retorted dryly. "Old Chief Inspector Radford: if you've read his notes of that time—"

"I have. I've gone over other things too. Y'know, Masters, I may have been doin' you in the eye. Just a little bit."

Masters stiffened. Once more he became as wary as a heavy-game hunter near a somnolent water-buffalo.

"But it was only a telephone-call," pleaded H.M. in a bumbling way. "And it don't (burn me, it don't!) help with our real problem."

"If you hadn't sent that ruddy clock on ahead of us, and we'd got here—"

"You were tellin' me, Masters. About Fleet's wife."

"Now get this, sir! At that time there was only one person who ruled the roost in *that* house: it was her husband. Why, sir, he once tore up her favourite morning-room, or whatever they call it, and put in new panelling and a billiard-table. And she never said a word. I know what *my* old woman would have said.

"Changeable sort of gentleman, too. One time he had a collection of old swords and daggers. Got tired of 'em, and bang! overnight they went, and she had a room with nothing on the walls but hooks until he could put up antique guns instead. Now," Masters added grimly, "we'll come to the day of the accident. Because it was an accident, and I'll show you why. Come over and look at the house, Sir Henry. Just look out of the window!"

"I got a picture in my mind's eye, son. You just gush on."

Returning to the table, Masters sat down, took a blue-bound

52

folder of typewritten sheets out of the brief-case, and opened it.

"The date," he continued, "was November 4th, 1927. Just so. Let me emphasize a few points about that roof.

"It's a very big roof, flat and perfectly square. It's floored with cement; they used it for sun-bathing. On the edge of the south side there's a low chimney-stack, narrow and oblong, flat on top. In the middle of the roof there's another chimney-stack just like it, and a third on the edge of the north side. All in a straight line dead across the middle of the roof. Got it?"

"Got it. Sure."

"Just so. At the time this happened, there was nothing at all on the roof except two beach-chairs and a wicker settee, all of 'em pushed back dead against the little chimney-stack in the middle."

H.M., eyes closed, blew out his cheeks hideously.

"Stop a bit, son. What were beach-chairs doin' there in November?"

"It'd been a warm autumn, and still wasn't cold. They'd just been left there."

"Any smoke from the chimneys?"

"No. Not a fire lighted. Gas-range in the kitchen."

"What colour were the beach-chairs?"

Masters stared at him.

"How in lum's name should *I* know? This report deals with—"

"Now, now, Masters! Keep your shirt on!"

Again the Chief Inspector's forefinger, somewhat agitated by his blood-pressure, travelled down the typewritten lines.

"I don't have to explain this hunting stuff. You've read it. Sir George Fleet, even if he did act like a comic-paper colonel, really was a sport. First-class horseman and A-1 shot. He hunted except when he had (don't I know it?) the rheumatic pains in his side. On November 4th, about two o'clock in the afternoon, he was sitting in his study reading *The Field* when the gardener came to see him. This gardener said the Ascombe Hunt was 'drawing,' whatever that means, a big wood called Black Hanger."

H.M. sat up with ghoulish thoughtfulness.

"I say, Masters. Did you ever see me on a horse?"

"I daresay," the Chief Inspector said with heavy sarcasm, "you were one of the greatest horsemen in England too?"

"Well . . . now!" said H.M., with a deprecatory wave of his hand. "I wouldn't like to say that, no. But I had a steeplechaser, named Whoozler, who could take fences like the cow jumpin' over the moon. Besides, it'd âit in—burn me if it wouldn't!—with a former existence where . . ."

Masters stiffened.

"So help me," he swore, and pointed at H.M., "if I hear one more word about your reincarnation, just one more word, then back I go to tell the A.C. I'm through. I tell you straight: it gives me the creeps."

H.M. pondered. He peered round carefully, to make sure both doors were closed.

"Y'see, Masters, I'm not just sure I believe it myself, exactly."

"Ah!"

"But some of those books sound awful plausible, son." H.M. shook his head. "And it stirs you up, sort of (wouldn't it anybody?) to imagine . . . I say, Masters: couldn't you see me as a Cavalier poet?"

"In a pig's eye I could."

"But the feller was my own ancestor, curse it! His picture's the spittin' image of me. And I've just got a book on swordsmanship. And," added H.M., suddenly drawing himself up and glaring at his companion with awful dignity, "are we goin' to get on about Sir George Fleet, or aren't we?"

Masters shut his eyes, counted ten, and opened them again. There was a brief silence, under the ghost-clock and in the room of sporting prints. Then Masters went on.

"The gardener," he said, "told him the hunt was coming. So he picked up a pair of field-glasses, and started up for the roof. Now the only way to the roof is through a covered door at the very back, or west side, of the roof.

"Sir George walked straight to the front of the roof, a position just about over the front door below. He raised the field-glasses, and focussed them. It seems there was a lurid kind of red sky behind him, but it was clear light. Now get this, sir. The chimney-stacks were fifty feet behind him. He was alone on a concrete floor, *without anybody or any object within fifty feet of him.*"

Masters paused. He riffled over several pages, flattening them down with his fist.

"Stop the bus again," muttered H.M. "What about the field-glasses? I seem to remember readin' a story where there was hokey-pokey with field-glasses, and they stuck somebody in the eye."

Masters was now cat-like and bland.

"The fact is, sir, I thought you might bring that up. The

54

glasses were just plain field-glasses, as you'll hear in a moment. Accept that?"

"Uh-huh. Go on."

"Our *real* evidence," Masters continued, "comes from six witnesses on this side of the road. Two of these witnesses," he pointed upwards, "were sitting astride the gable-tops of this pub. And these two witnesses are clinchers.

"The Ascombe Hunt is disbanded now. But in those days, it seems, everybody hereabouts was keen about it. It beats me to know why. You'd think it'd make country people mad as hops to have a lot of horses and dogs tearing over private property and mucking it up. But they tell me it didn't. These six men, they were down in the bar. They heard about the kafuffle coming just about when Sir George did. And up *they* went.

"Our two chief witnesses are Arthur Puckston and Simon Frew. Mr. Puckston, who's still the landlord here, was astride one gable with an old brass telescope that belongs to the house. Simon Frew had a pair of big new binoculars he was very proud of.

"This pub's on high ground, sir. From the top you can see straight over and across Fleet House, covering the roof. During this time there was an unholy row in the wood. First one dog—"

"HOUND."

"—started to yell, then another, then a lot more, and before long: smack! out they came from Black Hanger, tearing across in the open. Now listen to what Simon Frew said, when he was astride the middle gable with his binoculars. All this question-and-answer stuff has to be polished up and made smooth into a statement. But here you are."

Again Masters smoothed out the turnover pages with his fist.

"'The field—'" he began, and stopped. "This 'field,' it'd seem, would mean the gents in the red coats."

"I got it, son. Well?"

Masters read slowly.

The field had just started to come round the far side of Black Hanger, almost facing us. It is a good distance away there and on higher ground than us. I put my glasses on them. The first few men were smiling and waving their hands. They seemed to be waving straight in my face. I knew it could not be me. So I turned my glasses round.

"Towards Fleet House," Masters interpolated grimly. "About three hundred feet, that's all."

Sir George was there. I could see all round him. He had his glasses to his eyes in one hand, and was waving with the other. Then it looked like somebody gave him a hard shove in the back. He stood there for a second. He shouted. He fell head-first. I did not follow him with the glasses because I was too surprised. I just kept looking round to see who could have pushed him.

It was a shorn statement. Yet Martin Drake, had he been there, would have seen the red sky with the silhouetted figure, and scented the autumn air, and sensed the rush and crash.

"I won't trouble you," Masters said drily, "with what you know. But just to hammer it home, sir! A bit of what Puckston said, the man with the telescope. His attention was caught by this yell Sir George gave."

And then spoke Mr. Puckston.

I looked round. I saw something pitch over the little ledge, but it was so quick I did not see what it was. I looked all over the roof, but did not see anybody or anything. I looked down. Sir George was lying there, and something was wrong with his head. Dr. Laurier ran out of the front door. Bert Hartshorn—

"Bert," Masters explained, "was the constable. He'd been at the pub, but naturally he (hurrum!) couldn't climb on the roof."

—Bert Hartshorn was coming up to the terrace. Dr. Laurier said something, and Bert picked up Sir George's binoculars and walked into the house. Dr. Laurier said something else, and Lady Brayle came out with some kind of cloth. I said aloud, 'The bastard is dead.'

To Masters it was one more case, with nothing more of drama than a blueprint. He closed the blue folder.

"There's more of Puckston," he explained. "And four others who were lower down in between the gables. But it needn't trouble us. Eh?"

H.M. groaned.

"Let's sew it up," suggested Masters. "The 'little ledge' Puckston talks about is a stone coping, just six inches high, which runs round the whole roof. You agree nobody could have hidden there? Or, if we accept the witnesses, attacked a big powerful man without some kind of struggle?"

56

"Uh-huh. I'm afraid I got to agree."

"You admit the fact that the roof was as bare as a biscuit-tin?"

"Well . . ."

"Sir George's injuries, for instance." Masters remained affable and bland, if anything more affable. "They were to the head, the arms, and one shoulder. That's not unusual, when somebody pitches from a comparatively low height. There wasn't another fracture or another mark on him. Not even," Masters lingered on the word, "a bruise."

H.M. made fussed motions.

"Don't leer, Masters. I hate leerin'. What's on your mind?"

"You were going to ask, weren't you, whether there was a bruise? Whether something might have been thrown or fired at him? Eh?"

H.M. only grunted.

"If it hit him hard enough to knock him over the edge," Masters pointed out, "it must have left a mark or a bruise. But it didn't. Finally, there's the evidence of the post-mortem."

Reaching with infinite effort into his hip pocket, H.M. fished out a case of his vile cigars and lighted one with relish. He seemed to have little relish for anything else.

"There was a possibility, just a bare possibility," Masters goaded him, "that somebody might have given him a drug—poison, even!—to make his head swim so he fell. But there was no drug, no poison, nothing."

"As I understand it, Masters, the post-mortem was performed by old Dr. Laurier. The family friend. So! Was there anybody assistin' him at the post-mortem? To sort of look on?"

Masters grinned.

"As a matter of fact, there was. A doctor from Newbury. I forget his name, but it's in the record. He confirmed the finding."

"O tempora," said H.M. "O mores. Oh, hell!"

Masters rubbed his hands together.

"Here's your victim," he explained, "on a concrete floor with no person or thing within fifty feet of him. He wasn't pushed. He had nothing thrown at him. He wasn't drugged in any way. What happened to him?"

"Son, I just don't know."

"You bet you don't. But I can tell you. Sir George was a man over forty, who'd just climbed some long flights of stairs. He got excited waving to the hunt; he came over dizzy, as anybody might; and he fell. Do you still want to know the colour of the beach-chairs?"

"Sure I do," retorted H.M. instantly, taking the cigar out of his mouth. "What's the pink flash?"

"Pink flash?"

"Certainly. See the second anonymous postcard on the table in front of you. Quote: *Re Sir George Fleet: what was the pink flash on the roof?* Go on, Masters: say it's a pink rat and I ought to be makin' faces at it."

"But there's not a word about a pink flash in any of this evidence!"

"No," returned H.M., "and there's not one word about a skeleton-clock either. But you'll find one standing just behind you."

Masters strode over to the middle of the room, where he jingled coins in his pocket.

"This chap Puckston," mused H.M. "I didn't realize he was still the licensee here. By that statement, he didn't seem to like Fleet much."

"There's nothing to that," Masters snorted. "It was only . . ."

Whether by coincidence, or at mention of the name, there was a discreet tap at the door to the bar. The door opened, to reveal the Puckston family: father, mother, and daughter.

To a befuddled Martin Drake, Arthur Puckston had been little more than a name and a voice. He was, in fact, a lean man with a freckled bald head, a harassed but conscientious smile; tall but stooped, with stringy powerful arms. Mrs. Norma Puckston, though stoutened and rosy, had fine black hair and was not unattractive. Miss Puckston, dark-haired and sixteen years old, was not unattractive either.

"I 'ate to disturb you, gentlemen," said Mr. Puckston, making an apologetic motion. "But it's five minutes to opening-time, and . . . well, do you really want this parlour for a private room?"

"We sure do, son," H.M. assured him. "If that's convenient?"

"Oh, it's *convenient*. But I shall 'ave to charge you a good bit extra. This being Saturday night, and other things. Even for the police . . ."

Three pairs of eyes surreptitiously watched Masters.

"Well, well!" said Masters, suddenly urbane and in his most cheerful manner. "How would you have learned I was a police-officer, now?"

"Things," said Mr. Puckston thoughtfully, "get about." He glanced up. "*You* ought to know that."

H.M. intervened.

"He's a copper, son. But he won't bother you. I'll see to that. Anything else?"

"Well, sir. If you wouldn't mind keeping the doors locked and the curtains drawn? It's that clock. You told me you were going to take the skeleton out . . ." Puckston's voice trailed away; his throat seemed to be constricted.

"Yes, I see your point," nodded H.M., taking several puffs of his (to others) venomous cigar. "You think it might put the customers off their beer if they saw me sittin' here with a skeleton on my lap like a ventriloquist's dummy?"

Miss Enid Puckston suddenly giggled, and was shushed by a look from her mother. The father, for some reason, took the girl's face between his hands.

"I'll be careful," H.M. promised. Behind smoke and spectacles, his eyes had taken on a faraway look. "I don't want to be chucked out of here. I'm always being chucked out of places, though burn me if I can think why. This is a fine old house, this is. Antiques, and real antiques."

"Oh, yes!" cried Mrs. Puckston in one gush. "Arthur always tries to—"

The doors of the Dragon's Rest, unlike those of most pubs, were solid and close-fitting. Little could be heard through them unless you bent close. But now, from beyond the closed door to the far bar-parlour, arose a sudden babble of angry voices, all clamouring together. One voice, a man's, clove through the tumult.

"I can't do it, I tell you! What's more, I won't!"

H.M. abruptly snatched the cigar out of his mouth.

"That sounded like young Drake." His own big voice boomed out. "Does anybody know who's there with him?"

It was the dark-haired and well spoken Enid who answered.

"Lady Jennifer, sir. And Mr. Richard Fleet. And a lady from Fleet House; I don't know her. And Dr. Laurier."

"So!" grunted H.M., and surged to his feet. "That's a combination I don't like." And, with his white linen suit rucked up and the gold watch-chain swinging across his corporation, he lumbered towards the door and opened it.

The heat of strained feelings was as palpable in the other room as its atmosphere of beer and old stone. But, except for Martin Drake, it was now empty. Martin stood by the stove, his dark eyebrows drawn together and the green eyes enraged. H.M., after giving him a dismal look, lumbered over to peer out of the open door into the road.

Some distance to the left along the Dragon's Rest, Jenny was

59

detaching a bicycle from the ivy and steadfastly refusing to look round. A light-haired young man in a sports-coat had just opened the central gate in the wall round Fleet House. Sauntering, her head high, a girl in a grey silk frock walked in the same direction. Though there was no visible sign of Dr. Laurier, you could hear a car-motor start up close at hand.

It had been a swift, decisive exodus. The emotional echoes still swung like bells inside your head. H.M., the corners of his mouth turned down, turned and surveyed Martin.

"You been havin' a good time?" he demanded.

"Listen, sir," Martin began. He paused for a few seconds, and tried again more calmly. "Yesterday, before Jenny and I left Willaby's, we told you pretty well everything."

"You did, son. Well?"

"But you didn't hear about the execution shed. You didn't hear——" Again Martin stopped. *"Women!"* he added, with one savage and sweeping gesture.

Then, shouting something, he also plunged out through the open door.

Chapter 7

Martin had slowed his run to a walk before he reached the central gate of Fleet House.

Well to the north and well to the south in the low stone wall, there was a wide iron gate through which a gravelled carriage-drive curved up to the front terrace and returned to the road again like the arc of a bow. In the middle of the wall there was a smaller central gate; from it a narrower path, between lines of trees, ran straight up to the terrace like an arrow to the bow.

Martin, his footsteps rasping on gravel, overtook Ruth Callice just as she reached the terrace. Ricky had already hurried inside to see his mother. This terrace was only a broad stretch of flagstones, with four shallow flagstoned steps leading up to it. Ruth hesitated at the top, and turned round at his call.

"Ruth!"

"Yes?"

He stood at the foot of the steps, looking up at her. Her softly rounded face had that clear-flesh tint he associated with youth and health. The dark-brown eyes were inquiring.

"Martin," she smiled, "you needn't apologize." Her expression grew whimsical. "I've been yelled at so often in my business career, especially by men, that I hardly notice it."

"I haven't come to apologize, Ruth. For the first time since I've known you, I think you ought to be put over a convenient knee and walloped."

Ruth's colour receded to pallor, and slowly returned.

"I won't quarrel with you, Martin."

"As a second point of fact, I didn't yell at you."

"You were fairly audible, dear. And please remember *only* what I said. I merely reminded you of your promise. Whereupon you and Jenny and Dr. Laurier began arguing as to whether or not it was a good thing to go ghost-hunting. All I said in the whole discussion was: would you come and see John Stannard before you decided. Then you yelled at me."

"That's why I'm here. To see Stannard."

He ran up the four steps and faced her. Round and above him stretched that white, and still cold, face of Fleet House. Four smallish Corinthian pillars were set flush into the facade, two on each side of the broad front door. Except for a small close-in balcony on each of the windows above, these were the only ornamentation. Eight windows on the ground floor, eight windows on the floor above, eight smaller windows on a smaller floor above.

Very high ceilings in the rooms, too. High, breathing cold like a prison! This Martin noted somewhere at the back of his mind as he ran up the steps.

"Jenny . . ." he began.

Ruth laughed. "Jenny thinks I've been your mistress for years and years. Isn't it exquisitely silly?"

"Not if she thinks so. Look here: if you knew who 'Jenny' was for all this time, why didn't you tell me?"

"Perhaps I had my reasons." A pause. "Perhaps I still have them." Another pause. "Perhaps I'll tell you tonight."

"Oh, no, you won't I—"

"Aren't you forgetting something?" Ruth asked sharply.

"Forgetting what?"

"That *I* was the one who arranged for us to stay here? That *I* was the one who deliberately arranged to throw you and Jenny together?"

This, it occurred to him, was true. It checked him in midflight, while Ruth smiled.

"Oh, Martin!" Her tone softened. "We've been such good —" the trailing of the voice implied 'friends.' She put out her hand, and he took it. "Now let's go in and see John Stannard!"

61

"Where is he?"

Ruth nodded towards the second two of the four windows to the left of the front door.

"In the library. Cicely, I'm sorry to say, hasn't been very well. You may not meet her yet."

"Tell me, Ruth. Do you know anything about what happened here nearly twenty years ago?"

"Yes. Almost everything."

With a common impulse they glanced over their shoulders. In the middle of the gravel path, down towards the gate, stood Sir Henry Merrivale. But he did not see them. H.M.'s fists were on his hips, his big bald head raised; and he was glaring with malignancy at something which appeared to be just over their heads.

Martin, looking up, could see nothing except the white-painted iron frame, crossing near the tops of the Corinthian columns, and folding flat a large old-fashioned awning, coloured orange. It could be let down to shade a long space before the front door. Then Ruth hurried him into the cool, not to say chilly, front hall. But her hand suddenly fell on his arm, warning him to say nothing as they saw what was ahead.

Fleet House had been built in the very early nineteenth century, in that pseudo-Greek classicism which began with the French Revolution and was continued by Bonaparte. The wide, dim hall had at its far end an arched window. A staircase had been built against that wall, sideways as Martin and Ruth faced it.

A little way up the stairs, outlined against the tall arched window, stood Aunt Cicely. Just below her was Ricky, asking questions. They were oblivious to any newcomers.

"Really, Ricky. It is nothing at all. I only wish to lie down."

The voice floated, with whispering-gallery effect, through the cool dim hall.

"But they said—"

" 'They said.' They always say." Seen closer at hand, in Aunt Cicely's faded prettiness there was some quality which was eerily familiar to Martin. Was it a faint resemblance to Jenny? Jenny thirty years older? "But there is something," she continued, "that you have got to learn. Very soon, I'm afraid. I have telephoned to Lady Brayle. Now don't detain me, please."

In her filmy Edwardian-looking dress, against the pallor of the arched window, she hurried upstairs. Ricky hesitated, irresolute, and then followed her. Ruth Callice almost impelled Martin to the left.

They went through a high, square, green-painted room, on

whose walls hung a collection of ancient fire-arms ranging from the match-lock to the Brown Bess. They emerged into a well-appointed library, of the same size and shape, with gilt cornice mouldings.

"Ah, my dear fellow!" said a familiar husky, powerful voice.

Stannard, in somewhat ungainly plus-fours, stood with his back to a white marble mantelpiece. On a round Regency table in front of him lay a large crackling document, once folded into many squares, now pressed open.

"Our hunt for man-eating tigers, in the psychical sense," he went on, "is almost ready. I have here—" he tapped the document with a pencil—"a plan of Pentecost Prison. I've investigated it this afternoon. Come here, my dear fellow! Let me show you the condemned cell and the execution shed."

Martin braced himself. "Mr. Stannard, I can't go with you."

"Can't go with me?"

"No."

For some seconds Stannard did not reply. Lowering his dark head, he put the pencil with great care in the middle of the plan. Martin sensed the hidden quirk at the corner of his mouth. Vividly he remembered Stannard at Ruth's flat on Thursday night: the chuckle, the too-fixed smile, the glitter of the black eyes, Stannard's too-frequent glances at Ruth. 'Will you forgive me, Mr. Stannard, for saying that you are a little pompous?' Martin remembered that too.

Then Stannard straightened up. "To tell you the truth, young man, I am not altogether surprised."

"Look here! Will you just let me explain?"

"Of course." Stannard inclined his head courteously.

"On Thursday night I didn't know something I know now. There was a certain girl—" here he saw Stannard's eyes narrow—"I'd lost for three years. On Friday I found her. There's what you might call family opposition, and everything is upset. I promised to take her driving tonight."

And now Martin recognized the other's posture. In imagination he saw Stannard, in wig and gown, standing behind a desk on counsel's bench: his head a little inclined to one side, listening in cross-examination with that air of polite incredulity and amusement which is all the more effective because it keeps a perfectly straight face.

"Indeed," Stannard observed. "You promised to take her driving." The inflection he put into the words was masterly.

"Yes!"

"When was this appointment made?"

"This afternoon."

63

"I see. You consider it sufficient excuse for breaking a previous engagement which has entailed some time and trouble, and which you suggested yourself?"

Fleet House, the chilly and wicked Grecian house which to Martin was beginning to seem like a prison, might have laughed.

"The circumstances are unusual," retorted Martin. He was conscious, under the black glitter of the eyes, how flat these words would have sounded in court. "I hoped you would release me."

Stannard slowly shook his head. He sent a surreptitious glance towards Ruth, who was sitting on a sofa turning over the pages of an illustrated paper as if she had heard nothing.

"I can't force you," smiled Stannard. "But 'release' you: no, I will not. The fact is, young man, you've lost your nerve."

"That doesn't happen to be true."

"Truth has many guises," said Stannard, dryly scoring a point while appearing to concede one. "It's unfortunate, too. I had devised a special test for your nerve."

"Nerve?"

"And for mine too, of course. Now it will apply only to me. Still," he chuckled, "I hope to survive."

"What's the test?"

"Does it matter? Since you are not interested . . ."

Martin took a step forward. *"What's the test?"*

Stannard's movements were deliberate. From a tapestry wing-chair beside the mantelpiece he took up a thick blue-bound book with faded gilt lettering on the back.

"I have been looking through Atcheson's *History of the Penal System*," he continued. The round face, roughened as though by a nutmeg-grater, looked pleased. "This was written in 1912, and there's a chapter on Pentecost. I hadn't realized what a fine lot of man-eating tigers were executed there. Old Mrs. Gill, for instance. And Bourke-Smith. And Hessler, who mutilated the bodies of women; Hessler actually tried to escape from the condemned cell.

"About ghosts," Stannard went on, "let me repeat my dictum. I don't say yes; I don't say no. What I can credit are the influences, released emotions. Haven't we all had the same experience, in a small way? We go into a house, usually an empty house. And for no reason at all someone says, 'I can't stand this place; let's get out.' "

Martin was about to say, "Like this." He also noticed Ruth looking furtively around, and wondered if it touched her too. Yet the library was a well-lighted room, two windows east and

64

two south, though green-shaded by the trees.

"The vibrations in that death-house," added Stannard, "must be like lying under a tolling bell."

"Never mind the vibrations. What's this test?"

"Ah!" murmured Stannard. He threw the book back into the chair and took up the pencil. "Observe this architect's plan of the prison!"

"Well? What about it?"

"You notice that the wings are like spokes in a wheel, with the outer wall as its rim. These shaded spaces between the spokes—" the yellow pencil moved briefly—"are exercise grounds, gardens, and so on: open to the sky. Our concern is Wing B—" again the pencil moved—"which is here. Wing B, on the ground floor, contained mainly offices for clerical work. But at the far end of it, *here,* is a self-contained unit. Behind an iron door it housed the condemned cell and the execution shed."

Ruth Callice had abandoned the paper and joined them by the table, where Stannard leaned on the crackling plan.

Ruth, Martin was thinking, couldn't have been brushed by any emanation from Fleet House. She had been here too many times before; she was a friend of Aunt Cicely; she would have remarked on it. Yes; but had Ruth ever said anything at all about Fleet House?

Stannard's yellow pencil was moving again.

"Pentecost, please remember, was not abandoned until 1938. It had the most up-to-date of neck-cracking methods."

"Stan," Ruth began in an uncertain voice, "do you think it's necessary to dwell so . . ."

But Stannard was looking at Martin.

"There was none of that hideous walk across a yard, into a shed, and up thirteen steps. The condemned cell at Pentecost is *here.* Opposite it, directly opposite across a passage eight feet wide, is the execution shed. The condemned man never knows it is there. He can be trussed up, marched across the passage, placed on a drop worked by a lever—"

Here Stannard made a chopping motion with his hand.

"—and plunge on a rope into a brick-lined pit. All in a merciful matter of seconds.

"My point," he added, after a slight pause, "is that these two rooms and the passage form a separate unit, a kind of self-contained flat, shut off by the iron door of the passage. Here is the key to that passage."

And he held it up. It was a large key, though it fitted easily into the pocket of his brown tweed plus-four suit.

"All the inside doors of the prison, of course, were unlocked at the time the government took it over for the infernal 'storage purposes.'" Stannard's face mocked them behind the big key. "However, I got this one. Shall I tell you how my test *would* have worked if you (most unfortunately!) had not decided to go driving?"

Martin, himself white as a ghost with wrath, merely nodded.

"The vigil," mused Stannard, *"would* have begun at midnight, outside the iron door to the self-contained flat."

Another nod.

"You and I," pursued Stannard, "would then have drawn lots. Whoever lost would have gone to the execution shed and closed the door behind him. The other would have locked the iron door, so that the loser would be shut into the flat.

"The winner," Stannard's mouth quirked, "would sit down outside the iron door, and wait. The locked-up man, of course, could move from the execution shed across to the condemned cell. But I cannot think that any swirling and pressing influences would hammer his brain less hard in the condemned cell than in the execution shed. He would be a rat in a spiritual trap. If he cried out for help, the man outside must unlock the iron door and let him out.

"The man outside, it is true, even the so-called winner, would have no easy time. If any spiritual evil raged there, he would be very close to it. You and I—one inside, one out—would remain there alone from twelve o'clock to four o'clock in the morning, when it begins to grow daylight. 'Spend the night' was I think the term you used?"

"Something like that, yes."

Stannard threw the key up and caught it.

"There it was," he concluded, with a husky sigh of regret. "What a pity you can't accept."

"Pardon me," Martin told him. "After you said you insisted on holding to it, I never said I wouldn't accept."

Stannard caught the key with a flat smack against his palm, and looked up.

"Meaning what?"

"That I do accept, with great pleasure."

There was a silence. If a short time before Fleet House might have laughed, now it seemed to be listening. Ruth, her white teeth fastened in her under-lip, hesitated.

"You mean that?" Stannard demanded.

"Naturally I mean it." Martin reflected. "We do all this, of course, in the dark?"

Stannard was slightly taken aback.

66

"No," he answered, after a slight hesitation. "Even in the best ghost-hunting tradition, that's not necessary. I have brought several portable electric lamps, with plenty of spare batteries. Each of us may have a lamp. If only," he added, "to read and pass the time."

"You know, Martin," Ruth said dreamily, "this means you won't see Jenny tonight."

Jenny! How to explain that he couldn't back out, literally and physically couldn't, if Stannard insisted? You touched a switch, you touched an emotion; you set forces moving, and you must go with them. Jenny would understand it. Surely Jenny would understand it! He could telephone her, and then go out to Brayle Manor.

"All the same," Ruth was saying in a troubled voice, "I almost wish I hadn't encouraged this. Or—arranged it."

"Arranged it?" said Stannard, and looked at her with genuine astonishment. "My dear girl, Mr. Drake suggested it. *I* arranged it." The blood came into his already reddish face. "I wanted to show you, my dear, that these young men, with their war-records and their infantile prancings, are not the only ones to be depended on."

Abruptly he pulled himself together, as though he had said too much.

"But—Stan." There was an affectionate note in Ruth's voice. "You didn't tell me these 'conditions.'"

"A little surprise."

"You see," Ruth braced herself, "*I'm* going to the prison. And other people are wild to go too. Ricky Fleet and even Dr. Laurier. When they were having that argument at the Dragon's Rest, Dr. Laurier said he'd consider himself insulted if he didn't get an invitation."

Stannard lifted his thick shoulders.

"I see no reason why a dozen shouldn't go," he said. "*If they all consent to leave the prison at midnight when the test begins.* You agree, my dear fellow?"

"I do."

"This affair is between the two of us?"

"By God, it is!" said Martin. "And, as Ruth says, you imposed the conditions. Now *I* impose one."

"Ah!" murmured Stannard, casting up his eyes in sardonic melancholy. "I fear, I very much fear, someone may be backing down again. However, what is the condition?"

"That both of you tell me," Martin replied unexpectedly. "what you know about the death of Sir George Fleet some twenty years ago."

Again there was a silence. Ruth, her dark-brown eyes wide with wonder, merely seemed puzzled. Stannard, his eyes quizzical, seemed to hold behind locked teeth some chuckle which shook his stocky body. It was at this point that Ricky Fleet, his hair troubled by ruffling fingers, came into the library.

"I second that motion," Ricky declared. He went to stand by Martin.

"Ricky, darling!" cried Ruth. He kissed her perfunctorily on the cheek, and pressed her shoulder. All this time his eyes were fixed in a puzzled, troubled way on Stannard.

"But you haven't met Mr. Stannard!" Ruth added, and performed introductions. "How is your mother?"

"Pretty well, thanks. She's taken a sedative. But it hasn't had much effect, and she'll probably be down to dinner. You know—" Ricky tugged his necktie still further in the direction of his ear—"a lot of talk about my governor's death always upsets her. But she never minds a reference or a comment, and we cured her long ago of any dislike about going up to the roof."

Still he was looking in that same puzzled way at Stannard.

"On my word of honour, Mr. Fleet," the other assured him gravely, "*I* made no more than a casual reference. Ruth will verify that."

"Then it must have been something else. She was all right at breakfast; though, come to think of it, she did look a bit disturbed and disappointed at breakfast. But nothing *wrong*. She keeps talking about . . ."

"Mr. Richard!" called a weary female voice from the doorway.

Martin recognized the voice, very quickly, as that of the maid who had answered him on the telephone, and who had evidently met more than one American G.I. She was a brown-haired girl in her twenties, combining an air of boredom with conscientiousness. Though she wore cap and apron, she lounged in the doorway with her weight on one hip.

"Yes, Phyllis?"

"Your mother," said Phyllis, "don't like trespassers. There's been a trespasser out on the lawn for one hell of a long time."

"Please don't bother me, Phyllis!"

"This trespasser," continued Phyllis, jerking her thumb over her shoulder in a way which may be seen on the films, "is a fat old guy with a big stomach and a bald head. I think he's nuts, because he gave the gardener some money. Now he's arguing

68

with the gardener about how high you can grow tomato plants and still get the best tomatoes."

"That's H.M.," said Martin. "Sir Henry Merrivale."

Stannard dropped the big key on the plan beside his discarded pencil. "Merrivale!" he exclaimed.

"Does that mean anything?" asked Ruth. "I think I heard the name from Jenny, but—"

"My dear Ruth." Stannard paused. "If I had that man against me in a criminal case, I'd think I had a walkover from the beginning and then suddenly discover I hadn't a leg to stand on. He's the craftiest old devil on earth. If he's here now, it means . . ."

Martin hurried to the nearer of the east windows and peered out sideways. He saw the crafty old devil almost at once. On the smooth lawn stood a tall stepladder, with a pair of pruning-shears near it. Beside it stood H.M. and a dour-faced man in overalls. H.M., glaring, was holding his hand in the air to indicate a tomato-plant of improbable height. The dour-faced man shook his head with a fishy smile. H.M. levelled a finger at him in question. The dour-faced man still smiled fishily. Whereupon H.M. climbed nearly to the top of the stepladder, turned round, and indicated a tomato-plant of such height that it could have been credited only by a believer in Jack and the beanstalk.

But Martin saw something else. Towards their left was the gravel path, tree-shaded, leading to the front door. Up this path marched the Dowager Countess of Brayle.

Martin swung round and addressed Ricky. "Do you by any chance want peace and quiet in the house?"

"God knows I do," answered the harassed Ricky, who was still glancing at Stannard to remember where he had seen the man before. "It's all I do want. Why?"

"Lady Brayle," Martin told him, "is coming up the path. Sir Henry is on the lawn."

"What about it?"

"Those two," said Martin, "act on each other like a lighted match in a box full of fireworks. Go out and grab 'em! Go out and bring 'em in here, where we can keep an eye on both! Quick! Hurry!"

Chapter 8

At one side of the broad leather-topped desk in the library stood H.M. At the other stood Lady Brayle.

Ricky's good-natured charm had worked, aided by the fact that he seized each by one arm. So they stood there, with their backs to the high glimmering-coloured books in the tall shelves, facing the group by the white marble mantelpiece across the room.

Grandmother Brayle had been at her haughtiest—"I *think* I have met Captain Drake—" during the few sketchy introductions. Today she wore heavy horsy tweeds, her grey-white hair without a hat. Without a flicker towards H.M., she looked steadily across and up at her own reflection in a mirror over the fireplace, and (incidentally) over the other group's heads as she faced them. It was H.M. who broke the thick silence.

" 'Lo, Sophie," he volunteered with surprising meekness.

"Good evening, Henry."

"Nice weather we're havin', ain't it?"

"That," murmured Lady Brayle, "is not altogether unexpected in July."

The length of the broad desk, with its inkpot and blue quill pen, separated them as though a leprous touch might be infected.

"Y'know, Sophie, we've been on speaking-terms for a good many years."

"Are you trying to appeal to my sentimentality, Henry? How amusing!"

"I say, though. Do you remember the night I took you to see Lewis Waller play *Beaucaire* at the old Imperial Theatre?"

"Please don't be ridiculous. Besides," Lady Brayle added suddenly, "your behaviour in that hansom was so utterly disgusting that . . ."

H.M. was stung. "Burn it, Sophie, I only put my hand—"

"It will not be necessary to go into details."

"But you didn't tell your old man so he'd come whistlin' after me with a horse-whip, which you said you were goin' to. What I mean: you were an A-1 sport in those days. Now you've turned into—" H.M. swung round. "Sophie, will you

70

believe me if I tell you that honest-to-God I'm trying to help you? And your family?"

Lady Brayle hiccoughed with mirth. "When, yesterday, you . . ."

"But I didn't know I was buying the clock, did I?"

"You must excuse me," the other said crisply. "I was summoned here by an urgent 'phone-call from Cicely Fleet. I do not know why. I—"

"Do you want the clock back?"

What effect this conversation was having on Ruth, Stannard, and Ricky, who were gathered with him beside the round table with the map, Martin could not tell. Ricky, he quite accurately guessed, had been told nothing about any attempt to buy a clock; and the water grew deeper. But Stannard, as a detached and sardonic observer of human life, sat down in the tapestry chair and, with pleasure, placed his fingertips together.

"Your behaviour yesterday," announced Lady Brayle, "was so despicable! So puerile! So childish—"

"Sure. Do you want the clock back?"

"Really, Henry." Lady Brayle seemed bewildered. "*I have no interest whatever in the clock,* except that I was asked to bid for it as a present for young Dr. Laurier." Her mouth tightened amid wrinkles. "And I should never allow Cicely to pay any such ridiculous price as . . ."

"Oh, Sophie! I'm not selling anything. It's yours if you answer me a few questions."

The other stared at him. "Questions? What questions?"

"Well," he said argumentatively, "when was the date you got that Willaby catalogue of the auction on Friday?"

"Really, Henry, I don't see—"

"I know you don't. That's because I'm the old man. Date?"

"Everybody knows," retorted Jenny's grandmother, "that Willaby's post their catalogues from London just a week before the sale. I must have received mine," she computed, "on July 5th."

"That's what I thought. But I had to be sure. Who else in this district subscribes to a Willaby catalogue?"

"Cicely, of course. And I think young Dr. Laurier. He is interested in arms and armour."

"What about Arthur Puckston, over at the Dragon's Rest?"

The wrinkles round Lady Brayle's mouth deepened, as though she were about to say she had no interest whatever in the Dragon's Rest. But human curiosity, it appeared, would not be stifled.

"Incongruous as it seems," she conceded, "Puckston does.

71

He is . . . one of our fine old yeomen. He is not well off, as few of us are; but he wants genuine antiques for his inn."

"Uh-huh. It was a possibility. Y'see . . ."

Aunt Cicely herself, in what seemed to Martin some informal pinkish robe with lace over it, interrupted them then. Her entrance was flurried and apologetic, but with such real charm that it seemed to lighten the chill of Fleet House. Though she had perhaps a trick of archness and rapid speech, not quite in keeping with her faded beauty, the personality triumphed.

Ricky sprang forward.

"Mother, I want to present—"

"Of course. How delightful of you all to come!" smiled Aunt Cicely, sweeping aside introductions, new ones or forgotten ones, by giving each of them a look of such pleasure that they all felt warmed.

"You must forgive me," she raced on, "for popping in here, like a cuckoo out of a clock, and not even dressed. But I *do* so want to have a word with Sophia, and she didn't come upstairs."

Lady Brayle seemed anxious to forget what she and H.M. had been talking about.

"We were merely discussing," said Jenny's grandmother, plucking a subject out of the air, "Dr. Laurier's interest in arms and armour. Come to think of it, yesterday in the arms-room I saw a shield and a fine old English blade which I thought of commissioning someone to buy as a present."

Sudden horror showed in Aunt Cicely's eyes, an expression which startled Martin Drake until he imagined it was one of her exaggerations.

"But you must never . . . !" she cried. And then: "Oh, dear, what am I saying? Dr. Laurier is *so* conservative that it really doesn't matter. Do come and talk to me."

They went. Yet not without a parting shot from the Dowager Countess as she turned at the door.

"Captain Drake," she said.

(Martin thought: shall I let them have it now, both of them? About Jenny and me? Ricky probably wouldn't mind. But the old dragon undoubtedly knows or guesses already; whereas Aunt Cicely would sob and call for sal volatile. Better hold your fire until you can blast the old dragon).

"Yes?" he said.

"Without doubt," said Jenny's grandmother, "you were thinking of telephoning to the Manor?"

"I was thinking of doing just that."

72

"When you ring," said Lady Brayle imperturbably, "you will be told that Jennifer is not at home. This, of course, you will disbelieve. Yet it happens to be true. I tell you so to save you trouble."

Fear, irrepressible however you tried, began to crawl through Martin.

"I pass no comment," said Lady Brayle, "on what does not concern me. Still! When Jennifer left the inn, I believe you were rushing in a somewhat frenzied manner across the road. You were calling the name of a young lady whom—ah—I think I have met in the past as well as today."

The old dragon's eyes seemed deliberately to seek Ruth without finding her. Martin, with a sick sensation, felt the props kicked out from under him.

"Jennifer, no doubt for some good reason, wished to visit some friends in London. Their address would not interest you. She left for the train in one taxi, while I came here in another."

Now, as Lady Brayle looked very hard at his own imperturbability, there was a grudging respect in her tone.

"Captain Drake, I have little respect for law. I would cheerfully steal and if necessary I would kill. But I am not a liar. Good-day."

Her flat-heeled footsteps, and Aunt Cicely's light ones, faded away. Stannard still sat motionless, watching the scene with less than amusement behind the pyramid of his finger-tips. Ruth kept one hand pressed to her breast, watching Martin. It was Ricky who spoke.

"You understand now what I meant, old boy?"

"Yes. I've understood that all along."

"What are you going to do?"

"Get that address in London, somehow."

"Phooey!" exploded Sir Henry Merrivale.

It was such a bellow that they all were touched by it except Stannard. Ever since that remark about Martin rushing across the road after Ruth, Stannard had been faintly smiling. Sir Henry Merrivale was standing behind the desk, surveying the quill pen with its blue feather. Ricky went over to him.

"Look, sir." He spoke with directness. "There's a lot more going on here than most of us can understand. Can you help?"

"Well, son, that's just what I was goin' to tell you." H.M. raised his head and spoke with the same directness. "Across the road," he indicated, "there's a snake named Masters. Chief Inspector Masters."

"Yes. I heard my gov—my father's death was being

73

investigated again. It's my mother I'm . . ."

H.M. shook his head.

"Masters won't bother your mother, son. He thinks it's all eyewash. I'm the one who believes there was hokey-pokey."

"It's a funny thing." Ricky had the same desperately undecided look. "Today I was giving Jenny and Martin here my personal reminiscences of what happened on the day of—well, the day it happened."

H.M.'s interests quickened. "So? You remember it?"

"Very plainly; but by fits and starts. Anyway, in telling them, I had just got to the point where Miss Upton and I came round the side of the house and saw him lying there with the tapestry-piece over his head. Then, as I told them, we started back. And I looked up at a window, the upstairs window on the first floor just to the right of the front door."

"You'd just got to there," interposed Martin. "What did you see?"

"The face," answered Ricky, "of somebody I'd never met. The face of a total stranger. Looking down like God. Even this afternoon I might have imagined I'd invented it, if I couldn't half-swear I've met the same man in this room."

Ricky swung round.

"Excuse me, Mr Stannard," he added, "but I think it was you."

Stannard's black eyes twinkled above the pyramided fingertips. He smiled, and Ruth smiled as one who shared the secret.

"Don't apologize, Mr. Fleet," the barrister urged him. "What you say is quite true. You *did* see me."

H.M. regarded him curiously. "So!" he muttered. "Then why is it there's nothin' about you in the record?"

"Because there is no reason why there should be."

"How d'ye mean?"

"I came down here, for one day, on a matter of business."

"Specifically?"

"Sir George wished to begin certain legal proceedings. He went to a solicitor in London, who hesitated and took counsel's opinion: meaning myself. I told the solicitor his client had no case. Would that do for Sir George? Oh, no. I must come down here and explain why. Being the rawest of young juniors then," Stannard spread out his hands whimsically, "I bowed."

"Uh-huh. What happened then?"

Stannard's eyes narrowed. His voice appeared to come from deep in his soft collar, where his chin was pressed. He glanced up at Ricky.

"If memory serves," he remarked, "that window you speak of is, or was, the window of your father's study."

"It's still a study, in a way," said Ricky. Ricky's eyes were fixed on Stannard with hard, cold, uncompromising, hostility. "The governor's trophies are still there, and one or two of mine. And the guns."

"Go on," H.M.'s very soft tone prodded Stannard, and the latter's shoulders lifted.

"Sir George raved," he went on, and now Ricky was pale with anger. "I talked. Some one came in to tell him about the hunt. He asked me if I were interested in hunting. I replied, I fear with truth, that nothing on earth interested me less. He took up a pair of field-glasses and excused himself to go up on the roof for a few minutes. Shortly afterwards I heard a shout and an unpleasant sound on flagstones. I went to the window."

The old, friendly, engaging expression kindled Stannard's face.

"Don't think me callous or unfeeling, I beg. I was shocked, of course. What struck me," his mouth twisted, "was the utter pointlessness of this tragedy. I stood there for perhaps five minutes. The dead man's pipe was still spilled on the desk-blotter. There were his guns behind folding glass cases. Then round the house came the large woman and the boy: that I remember as a symbol. The large woman and the grubby boy looking on horrified, looking on stupefied, as though they had seen the end of the world. Whereas they had seen the end only of (forgive me) an overbearing man who would be little missed."

Ricky started to speak, but H.M. shushed him fiercely.

"I gave my name and address to the local policeman," Stannard added. "But I was not needed. I took the train from Newbury: giving (I recall) a very callow statement to a newspaper reporter at the train. I have no connection with the Fleets, and never met any of them from that day to this."

"And that's all?"

"That's all," smiled Stannard, and Ruth joined the smile.

"Stung!" said H.M.

From the desk he picked up the pen with the long blue feather, and seemed to meditate aiming and firing it at one of the brass andirons opposite.

"Whole great big beautiful bloomin' possibility," he said, "and yet—" H.M. threw down the pen. He adjusted his spectacles, peering at Ricky over them. "I say, son. That roof. It's our last hope. Is there any possibility of seeing it?"

"Certainly. We use it more nowadays, for parties, than we

75

ever did. Like to come along, Martin?"

"Not for a minute," replied a bedevilled man whose thoughts churned round and round Jenny. "If you don't mind: in spite of what the old poisoner said—"

"*Poisoner?*"

"Lady Brayle. I was speaking figuratively. In spite of what she said, I'd like to use your telephone."

"At your service, old boy. Beside the stairs in the hall."

That was how, a few minutes later, Sir Henry Merrivale and Richard Fleet climbed several flights of dark steep stairs, and emerged under a metal hood with a door opening on the northwest corner of the roof.

Clear evening light, with a softness of air which could be felt like a touch, lay over the concrete surface. The roof, a hundred feet square and perhaps forty-five feet from the ground, had its floor painted light brown. At equal intervals, from north to south across the middle, stood the low white oblongs of the chimney stacks.

Just-before-the-war porch-furniture, of dulled chromium tubing and orange canvas seats, stood scattered about the roof. There were tables with orange tops, like the colour of the awning down over the front door. Two beach-umbrellas lay on the floor, ready to be put up. All these H.M. surveyed with displeasure.

A faint breeze moved here. Some distance over across the road you could see the three higher gables of the Dragon's Rest; and, on slightly rising ground behind them, the vast expanse of Guideman's Field and the wood called Black Hanger. To the north, much farther away, you could distantly study the round grey bulk of Pentecost Prison: its tiny windows unwinking, its air repellent even from here.

H.M., fists on hips, turned round.

"Oi! Son!"

"Yes, sir?" Ricky, the muscles tight down his lean jaws, kicked moodily at the floor.

"Don't let Jack Stannard get your goat." H.M. hesitated. His face seemed to swell and grow cross-eyed with embarrassment. "Looky here. Did you like your old man very much?"

"It wasn't that." Ricky shrugged it away. "The governor's very dim in my mind. He had his faults; he could wallop you like blazes. But—"

"But?"

"Well, he never minded how filthy dirty you got, or if you were in a fight. If you wanted something to do with games, he'd buy it for you before the words were out of your mouth."

76

Ricky dismissed this. "No; I was thinking about Mother. That swine of a lawyer must have said something . . . no, he couldn't have! Ruth swore he didn't upset her, and Ruth's as honest as the Bank of England. Never mind. What did you want to know?"

"I want to know," roared H.M., "the colour of the beach-chairs."

At this particular point the roof-door in the corner opened. Chief Inspector Masters, wearing a bowler hat and carrying the brief-case, overheard the last words as he stepped out on the roof.

"Goddelmighty," said Masters, very softly and wearily.

"By the way," H.M. told Ricky. "This weasel is the Chief Inspector I was telling you about. Don't pay any attention to him."

Ricky, though considerably more impressed by Scotland Yard than he could ever have been impressed by H.M., nevertheless turned back.

"You mean—the beach-chairs *then?*"

"Yes! Not this chromium stuff now. Do you remember?"

"Ho! Do I remember!" snorted Ricky. "The old lot stayed here from the early days practically to the time I was at Cambridge."

"Well? Colours?"

"The beach-chairs were striped green and black. There was a combination of settee and wicker chairs, also striped green and black."

"What about the floor?"

"It was painted dull grey, like the chimneys then."

"Nothing pink?"

"*Pink?* No; not unless it was carried up here like a coat or something."

H.M.'s expression grew murderous. "Looky here, son. I'm not doubtin' your word, but it was a long time ago. Can anybody verify what you say?"

Ricky considered.

"Miss Upton—no, she left two years later and they pensioned her off. MacAndrews, the gardener and handyman? No: Crawshay! Crawshay was the butler. Nobody has a butler nowadays except Grandmother Brayle. But he still lives at Reading; Mother can give you his address. And he'll tell you it's gospel truth!"

"Very interesting, sir," Masters observed satirically, to the surrounding air. "Are we getting on the track of that pink flash at last?"

77

H.M. stood for a moment, blinking. Then he turned round and lumbered towards the front of the roof, standing at the very edge. Masters, on the spot, could see the impossibility of anyone attacking Sir George Fleet in that fifty feet square beyond the chimneys of what had been bare concrete.

H.M. faced front, his feet apart and his bald head glistening. Then he turned round. His mouth was open.

"What a cuckoo I've been!" he breathed in a hollow voice. "Oh, my eye! What a thundering dunce!"

Now Masters had heard this tone before. And Masters, even with his mind made up, started a little. Both he and Ricky joined H.M. at the edge.

"Do you mean—?"

"No, no, dammit! I'm not *quite* on to something yet. But there were two pieces in the evidence I was forgetting. Was there anything *white* on the roof?"

Masters and Ricky exchanged glances. "No," the latter said, "unless—"

"Unless, as before," growled Masters, "somebody carried it up?"

"Y'see, I was forgetting that very bright-glowin' and lurid red sky everybody commented on. It might make something white seem pink, if only . . ."

Again H.M. paused.

"Also," he plodded on doggedly, "I had the whole conception and direction maybe a bit scrambled. I'll admit, fully and with a spit, that it's still an impossible crime. But look across at the pub there!"

"Ah, ah. Well?"

"Our witness named Simon Frew, the one with the powerful binoculars, was sittin' astride the centre gable. Just opposite us. Now Arthur Puckston, with the brass telescope: where was *he*?"

Masters pointed to their left.

"Astride the north gable. There!"

"That's right. Therefore he was lookin' sideways. Sideways." H.M. ruminated, like an ogre with a bone. "And there was nobody on the south gable. And . . . y'see, Masters, I didn't like Puckston's testimony one little bit. He didn't like George Fleet either."

Masters gestured impatiently with the brief-case.

"I told you there wasn't much in that! Sir George thought a pub across from his house was undignified and spoiled the view. But he couldn't even get Puckston's license revoked by the magistrates, let alone snaffle the land by some legal . . ."

"Legal, hey?"

"Maybe you've heard the word, sir?"

"Once or twice. That's what Stannard was doin' here on the day it happened, as sure as Moses had a beard." H.M. nodded vaguely. "Finally, you were goin' to tell me something more about George Fleet's field-glasses, only you didn't."

"For the last time," Masters said with powerful restraint, "there was NOTHING wrong with those field-glasses. They fell on the grass and weren't broken. Bert Hartshorn, the constable, took them into the house only a second or two after the gentleman fell. No murderous devices. No—"

"H.M. turned to Ricky. "What about you?"

"I didn't see them," retorted Ricky. "I . . ." He told his story briefly, much as he had told it to Martin and Jenny. "All these years the thing has seemed perfectly simple. Now you've got it so tangled up I don't understand it myself. Field-glasses, for instance."

"Pink flashes," amplified Masters. "Skeletons in clocks. God's truth!"

"I want to know what's wrong with Mother," persisted Ricky. There were lines of strain drawn from his nostrils to the corners of his mouth. The powerful hands and wrists dug into the pockets of his sports-coat. "I'm released from a marriage-obligation, or I'd hoped so; but am I released? Then this expedition to the prison tonight . . ."

"What expedition to the prison?" H.M. asked sharply.

They had all, by instinct, gone to the middle of the roof at its edge. Now, also by instinct, they moved back towards the furniture of darkened chromium and orange canvas.

At the rear of the roof, the staircase-door opened. Martin, somewhat drawn of face but with a gleam in his eyes, walked quickly towards them. Ricky signalled, "What did you find out?" and Martin signalled back, "Tell you later."

"You—" H.M. pointed his finger at Martin—"were shouting some gibberish about an execution shed, now I remember. What's this game tonight? All of it?"

Martin told him.

"I see," commented H.M., keeping an indecipherable poker-face. "Resistin' the powers of darkness and cryin', 'Ho!' All right. You two just nip downstairs, will you. Masters and I have got to have a little *causerie*. Don't argue, burn it! Hustle!"

Presently the staircase-door closed behind Martin and Ricky. It was very quiet on the roof, though a very faint murmur of voices floated from the Dragon's Rest. All about them the countryside, dark-green and somnolent, called a

79

visitor to lounge and drowse from worry. All, that is, except Pentecost Prison.

"Masters," said H.M., "we've got to stop this 'expedition.'"

The Chief Inspector, though uneasy and no longer satirical, remained practical.

"We can't stop it," he pointed out. "If they've got permission from the Ministry, there's nothing anybody can do."

H.M. lifted both fists. "Then we got to . . . stop a bit! What do you know about the inside of this jail?"

"Not much. We got the wire, a year or two ago it was, that Shag Fairlie was hiding out there. Remember when Shag broke Dartmoor? But it wasn't true."

"'Storage purposes.' What have they got stored in the place?"

"Paper," grunted Masters. "Bales and boxes and tied-up bundles! Stacked as high as your head and higher, through practically every corridor and cell and room! Only a little space so you can move between them and the wall. Oh, ah. I expect," his eye wandered round, "I expect anybody (hurrum!) anybody who was on the stout side wouldn't be able to get in at all."

Then every superior air dropped away from him.

"Fair's fair," snapped Masters, "and messing about is messing about. I ask you—straight, now— *is* there anything in all this 'pink flash' business?"

"There is. But that's not the main reason why we're here, Masters. We're here to prevent another murder."

Masters straightened up. The breath whistled through his nostrils.

"Another . . . ?"

"That's right."

"But whose murder?"

"Decide for yourself, son. In this whole case, where there are as many women as there are men, who would you say is practically certain to get murdered?"

Chapter 9

There was a bright quarter-moon, that night, in a soft blue-black sky without stars. The darkness caressed, it invited, anyone who sat under the hedgerows or followed the broad winding road. Its warmth would have stirred the blood of lovers, and doubtless did, somewhere under those trees.

The side road which led to Pentecost Prison had once been paved. Now, between the tall grass on each side, it lay cracked and broken and ridged because it had not been repaired for decades. The motor-car, with one wing banging, jolted badly on its surface. But, since the road was straight, the car's headlamps picked up far ahead the high iron double-gates against a rounded face of bricks once painted grey.

A few seconds more the car jolted off the asphalt to a gravel circle now thick-grown with weeds. The handbrake ticked back with a decisive wrench and the clanking engine was shut off, letting in stillness.

First John Stannard jumped out of the car, from the front seat. Then Ricky Fleet from behind the wheel. Then, from the back, Martin Drake, Ruth Callice, and—still to the surprise and very faint discomfort of the others—'young' Dr. Hugh Laurier.

"I am extremely grateful . . ." Dr. Laurier began. But his voice rang out loudly, and he stopped. The clock on the car's dashboard indicated the time as twenty-five minutes to midnight.

Footsteps swished among weeds. Someone laughed nervously.

"Got the lamps?" called Ricky's voice.

"Here," came the husky assurance of Stannard; and he chuckled.

"Shall I leave these car-lights on?" Martin demanded.

"Yes," assented Stannard's voice. "After all, three of you will be leaving in twenty-five minutes."

Seen only by car-lamps, magnified by darkness and a quarter-moon, the grey-brick roundness of Pentecost appeared immense. Its air of intense desolation was heightened, towards the north-west, by the ghost-village which still straggled towards its wall.

When men fretted out their sentences here, when they heated their brains and assured everybody they would be free next week, there grew up round it that huddle of cottages which lie near any country prison. Here lived the married officers, the non-convict staff, their wives and relatives and children: all the residue from that force which made the machine-shop hum, the food-tins bang, the endless line shuffle round and round the exercise yard. These houses, now, were as dead as Pentecost.

"Is everybody ready?" asked Stannard.

81

All five had gathered round the car-lights. Stannard had told them to wear old clothes: which Ruth interpreted as meaning black slacks and a red sweater, Stannard his ungainly plus-fours, the others sports-coats and flannels.

Ruth laughed softly. So did Dr. Laurier.

"You know," Ruth observed, "I thought this evening would never end. I almost choked over dinner."

"So did I," said Ricky, for some reason deeply impressed by this coincidence of thought. "I'm sorry Mother didn't come down after all."

"I assure you, Richard," declared the precise and conservative Dr. Laurier, "that Lady Fleet is in no danger. I have given her half a grain of morphia. We, on the other hand, have a stimulant."

All five were strung up, each of them not quite his or her normal self, which may account for much that happened afterwards. Each would have denied this. But if anybody had been watching them—and there *was* someone watching—that person would have seen it in a quick movement, a turn and gleam of an eye against the head-lights.

"I should have thought," said Ruth, "that you people who lived in this district must have been terrified. I mean, of escaped prisoners."

Stannard chuckled, his lips folded back from gleaming teeth.

"My dear, you are still confusing local prisons with convict prisons."

"I'm afraid I don't remember the difference."

"Come, now! If a man's sentence is anything from six months to two years, with time off for good behaviour, he won't endanger it by trying to escape. Some of them go mad, of course. But an attempted break is rare." Then Stannard's eyes narrowed. "Stop, though! There *is* an alarm-bell, aside from the ordinary main bell."

"What for?"

"You can see for yourself. Shall we go?"

From a bulging pocket he produced three flattish electric lanterns, of the sort carried on the belt by a policeman. Taking one himself, Stannard handed the second to Martin and the third to Ricky.

As they approached the high iron gates, the bright pale-white beams of the lamps flickered and roved. They touched the spikes atop the brick wall. They swept past the lettering. 'Fiat Justitia, MDCCCXCVI,' carved in stone over the doors. They raked the ground. Except for the ruts of heavy Army

82

lorries trundling paper-bales, no approach marred Pentecost's weedy gravel.

From his other side pocket—"Don't worry; I oiled the lock this afternoon!"Stannard brought out an immense old-fashioned key, rust-coloured but not rusty. To his annoyance he had to use two hands in turning it. Then the lock clicked with a heavy snap like a game-trap.

"Now!" he ordered, a little out of breath. "One of you at each door. Push!"

The big doors moved soundlessly (oiled hinges too?), and fairly easily. The breath of the prison, which at one time might not have been too pleasant, blew out at them. Now it was only a thick warmth overlaid by a mustiness of dried paper-bales. A little way ahead their lights caught a large arched barrier of vertical bars, with an opening in it like an ordinary door.

"Swing the gates shut," called Stannard. "We don't want intruders."

Martin and Ricky, their lamps hooked on their belts, complied. Inside they saw a heavy and complicated pattern of bolts, which they did not touch. The next moment they were shut up inside Pentecost.

Nerves sang a little more thinly, pulse-beats were a trifle faster.

"Just a minute." Ruth's quiet voice rose hollowly.

"It's all right, old girl!" Ricky assured her.

"But Stan told us at dinner," continued Ruth, "that they've stored this place full. If they've filled up the—the condemned cell and the execution shed, what are you going to do?"

"They haven't, my dear." Stannard's chuckle, echoing, sounded huge. "Either they were respectful or they hadn't the stomach. Our little self-contained flat is empty. Now follow me closely, and don't lose my light."

Martin Drake glanced at the luminous dial of his wrist-watch. Eighteen minutes to twelve.

Behind the barrier of vertical iron bars, they saw a mountain of brown-paper bales. Holding his lamp ahead, Stannard slipped sideways through the opening in the barrier, and edged to the left. Ruth, with an appealing glance at Martin, followed Stannard. Martin followed her. Dr. Laurier came next, with Ricky at the end.

Then they made a sharp turn to the right. They were in a narrow aisle—just broad enough for walking in a straight line—between the bales on one side and a grey-brick wall, with doors, on the other.

"You'll get used to the atmosphere," Stannard called from

83

ahead, where his light bobbed and splashed. His voice went up in reverberations, which seemed to roll back at them through dust-puffs from the bales. "They had a ventilating system. Quite a good one."

And Martin's imagination, heightened and tautened, began to bring this prison to life: with doors opening, bells ringing, the blank-faced men in the grey garb.

Just before the war he had visited Eastaville, a local prison like this one. He had been given only glimpses, which came back as much in sounds as in visual images. The wing they called B Hall: with its high tiers of cells facing each other across an open space, and a steel-woven net slung between to prevent suicides. Each oak cell-door painted yellow. Stung by bells, the unending shuffle, shuffle, shuffle, or march, march, march. A sense of suffocation; and the voice of a blue-uniformed prison officer: "Quiet, there!" A workshop: "Quiet, there!" A line of grey men, stiffly at attention near the door of the Governor's room, to get punishment or make complaint: "Quiet, there!"

"Turn to the right, here!" called Stannard.

Martin, peopling unseen corridors and galleries with old shades out of Eastaville, realized that they had all been shuffling as the aisle narrowed. Ruth coughed in the dust.

Their turn led them through an aisle of bales, then into another one between bales and wall, with another line of doors (*not* cell-doors) to the right.

"Why," Martin asked, "do cell-doors look so repulsive when they're painted yellow?"

"I beg your pardon?" demanded Dr. Laurier, adding to the burst of echoes which rolled to upper and outer air.

"Never mind!" said Martin.

Ruth, a gallant little figure in red sweater and black slacks, not quite so tall as Jenny, turned around and smiled at him.

"Here we are," announced Stannard.

Martin's heart jumped a little, then went on (it seemed to him) normally. With the image of Jenny in his mind, with what he had heard about Jenny over the 'phone, he told himself he was the calmest person there. This was going to be easy.

They emerged, one by one, into a completely cleared space. The beams of the three lamps converged. You could see that the corridor was ten feet wide. Ahead of them, cutting off the corridor, was a grey-brick wall; and into this was set an iron door, with a very small barred opening in it so that you could peer and talk through.

Stannard's breath was noisy in his nostrils. "Here are the

premises," he explained. "I have not even looked into the rooms. I have done nothing except oil the lock of this door."

He held up the key he had shown to Ruth and Martin that afternoon. He fitted it into the lock. And, with a squealing creak of hinges, the iron door swung inwards.

A sudden animation seized that whole group, and they began talking twenty to the dozen. Martin afterwards supposed he must have talked too.

The babble of their voices carried them through into a passage some eight feet wide and twenty feet long, ending in a dead-wall facing them. It was floored with very dirty asphalt. In the wall to the left, eternally the grey-brick, was a door which faced across to a corresponding door on the right.

Stannard, taking one of the lamps from Ricky, propped it up a little slantways against the floor and the dead-end wall so that it should shine straight down the passage.

"Would you like first—" he put his hand on the knob of the left-hand door—"to see the execution shed first?"

"No!" cried Ruth. "The other one. I mean, the beginning. I mean, after all, the condemned cell is the beginning."

Stannard turned to the other door.

"I have always understood," rattled Dr. Laurier loudly, "the condemned cell really is a room, with wall-paper and religious pictures."

"Oh, yes," said Stannard. (Damn the man, thought Martin; his voice rasps on you like a lecturer's). "Oak door," he went on. "Notice the little glass peep-hole high up. The condemned man had two warders—or wardresses, if it happened to be a woman—with him or her every instant of the time. That peep-hole was for the hangman."

"Hangman?" Ricky's voice went up.

"To judge weight and height for the proper drop."

Stannard had difficulty with the iron knob. Ricky wrenched open the scraping door. The first thing their lights picked up, inside, was a dilapidated rocking-chair.

And now the pull and swirl, of what Stannard had called atmosphere or vibrations, began to creep round Martin Drake. He could imagine someone sitting in that rocking-chair, someone who started up and cried, "Get out!" No, this wasn't going to be too easy. Martin subconsciously felt that, when he and Stannard drew lots, he would be the one to be locked up.

"Look there!" Stannard was saying. "Over in the corner. The rope."

"Rope?" Ruth almost screamed. "Not—?"

"No, of course not. Easy, my dear!"

85

"I'm all right. How dare you say I'm not all right?"

"Do you remember, this afternoon, when I told you about Hessler, the multilator of women's bodies? That he tried to escape from the condemned cell?"

"Yes. No! What about him?"

"The mercy and tact of our Prison Commission," cried Dr. Laurier, "are beyond praise. That picture of Our Saviour on the Cross is truly moving."

"Hessler, Ruth, managed to smuggle potassium cyanide into this room. He used it—"

"To k-kill himself?"

"No. On the guards. In cups of cocoa. When they staggered and tried to shout, he made a break. My *History of the Penal System* is very discreet. Undoubtedly they knew how he did it, but they won't say. In some fashion he got from here into the garden between this wing and the next. He had a rope thrown over a spike in the wall. They winged him with a revolver as he was climbing, and he fell back into a flower-bed. Hessler . . ."

"Listen, old boy," Ricky's voice hissed in Martin's ear. He seized his companion's wrist, and twisted it. "Over there! To the right!" A pause. "Well, damn me to perdition if . . ."

Ricky's exclamation drew round the slightly glazed eyes of the others.

"Afterwards," continued Stannard, "the prison governor insisted an alarm-bell be installed here. Idiot! Prize, thundering idiot! Look at that hanging rope over there! As if . . ."

But the others were not listening. They saw what seemed a crowning incongruity.

In the far corner, grimy but only a few touched with rust, lay a much smaller but better collection of rapiers and daggers than Martin had seen at Willaby's on Friday.

The rapiers were flung down in a heap, as they had lain for many years. The white lamp-beam played over cup-hilts, swept-hilts, ring-hilts, both the pointed and the double-edged. Ricky's eyes were fixed on a little ivory tag attached to one handle. Behind the rapiers stood a row of ancient dusty medicine-bottles, corked, and several empty bottles of whisky.

"Either I've got hallucinations," snapped Ricky, "or those swords belonged to my father."

"Your father?" exclaimed Ruth.

"Ages ago," Ricky tugged at his collar, "my father had a collection. Did you know that?" (Sir Henry Merrivale, had he been present, would have growled assent). "He got tired of 'em; Grandmother Brayle said he gave the stuff away; he put up those old guns you can see in the Green Room. But I could

86

swear, from that writing on the tags . . ."

He hurried over, catching his own reflection in a dust-furred mirror where so many of the despairing must have looked, and bent down.

"*You* remember, Dr. Laurier?" he added.

Dr. Laurier, for a moment hypnotized, uttered what for anybody else would have been a cry of delight. He darted over to the rapiers, pulling at one so that others rattled and tumbled down.

"Surely," he cried, "this is a . . ."

"It's damn funny," said Ricky. "How did this stuff get here? Why?"

Up went the influences or vibrations, up and up! Stannard inflated his thick chest and laughed.

"Are you a swordsman, Mr. Fleet?"

"No," said Ricky, standing up. "I never liked it. It seems— Dago, somehow. Like sticking a man with a knife. But," and sheer vanity bubbled out of him, "there was a time when I couldn't fly a plane, either. Fencing? I could learn it as easy as winking!"

"Indeed?" mocked Stannard, showing teeth against the red face. "When I saw you, you were such a *very* little pious boy."

Ricky whipped round, his grey eyes wide open in the dazzle of cross-light.

"I may have been no giant then," he said. "But I could put-the-weight twenty-seven feet three inches when I was eleven years old, and I've got a cup to prove it. How would you like to try a little strength-test now?"

"Thank you. But I have another kind of test in about ten minutes."

"Unquestionably," declared Dr. Laurier, "a Toledo blade. Note also the 'Christus Imperat' engraved on the blade near the hilt, and the beautifully wrought pattern on the cup-hilt itself. I must have more light. Excuse me."

And he almost ran out of the room into the passage.

Martin too, having handed his lamp to Ricky, had drawn out a rapier to his taste. Like Laurier's, it was no clumsy double-edge blade; like Laurier's it was thin and tapering, for play with the point. It had a large plain cup-hilt with broad quillons, so finely balanced in the hand that it seemed to bear its own weight.

"Excuse, *me*," Martin said—and also hurried out of the room.

It wasn't, he told himself, that he felt fear. But he felt shut up in there. The condemned cell, twenty feet square, with its

87

flowered peeling wallpaper, boiled with hatred and despair. He could have sworn (though he knew this for an illusion) that the rocking-chair swung a little.

But one touch of panic, real or only half-real, acts on human beings as on animals. Ruth, Stannard, and Ricky crowded after him.

At the far end of the passage, where the lamp stood slightly tilted on the floor, Dr. Laurier was bending over the thin Spanish blade to examine it. For some reason, his prim pince-nez and iron grey hair and hollowed cheeks looked grotesque above the sports costume, like a clergyman's head on a clown. He was trembling. He straightened up, with a flash of pince-nez, when he saw Martin with the other cup-hilt.

"Captain Drake!" he said eagerly. "Do *you* fence?"

"Yes. Most rapier-collectors do."

"Ah!" said Dr. Hugh Laurier.

He advanced slowly, silhouetted against the eye of the lantern, its white glow spreading round and behind him. Turning his body sideways, he bent his knees tentatively and swept out the still-sharp point in insinuating challenge. His wrist turned in that short semi-circular movement, engage and disengage, by which fencers feel, as though by antennae, for an opening.

Insinuating, insinuating, moving forward . . .

Martin, without any sense of incongruity in time or place, instantly crossed points.

All of them, now, were far from normal.

"This is good," Ricky threw at Martin. "Give him hell, old boy!"

"Take your pleasure, gentlemen!" said Stannard.

"Stop it!" cried Ruth.

Her voice was not loud, but it pierced and begged. She had dodged round to the door of the execution shed. If anyone had looked at her then (nobody did) that person would have seen Ruth was far more terrified of these sharpened points than of any forces in Pentecost Prison.

"Look here, Ruth, we're only playing!" said Martin. "Ricky!"

"Yes, old boy?"

"Put that lamp of yours at the other end, against the iron door. Propped up behind me just as the other one is behind him."

Tick-ting went the blades, circling and feeling round each other.

The two facing lights sprang up, silhouetting both fencers

and somewhat clouding each other's sight. *Tick-ting, tick-ting.*

Of course, Martin knew, this was only playing. Feint-lunges, as harmless as the hop of insects; much threatening and scrape of feet; cats darting with sheathed claws. Yet he could feel his own heated excitement, and feel through the thin blades the tensity of Dr. Laurier's arm.

"Only playing!" cried the latter, in a kind of ecstasy. *Tick-ting.* His eyes never moved from Martin's through the crossing-line of the points. "Only playing!" He made a feint of darting in.

"For God's sake stop," shrilled Ruth. "I can't bear swords! I can't stand it! I—" Then, in horror, she pressed one hand over her mouth.

The *tick-ting* ended abruptly. Dr. Laurier disengaged and lunged.

It was a full lunge, with stamp of foot on asphalt. Martin saw the glint on the blade; his wrist snapped two inches in parry; the point, scarcely rasping above a whisper, flicked past his right sleeve.

Hugh Laurier, slow and clumsy on return, stood wide open to a riposte that would have skewered him like a fowl. Movements are automatic, as in boxing; Martin checked his lunge in time, he felt the sweat start out on his body, and then stood staring at the Doctor, who had lowered his point.

"Captain Drake."

Dr. Laurier's husky voice, impeded as though by too-large a tongue, faltered. "I slipped!" he said with great earnestness. "I slipped!"

And he pointed to the gritty asphalt, where there was in fact a long gouge in grit from his right foot. The source of the accident was plain enough.

"But," said Dr. Laurier, fumbling at his pince-nez, "I should not have lunged even half so far. It is incredible. I can't think what made me do it. If any of my patients had seen me tonight—" He ran a hand over his long, hollowed face, exploring it in wonder. Then he added, in appeal, just five words.

"My life is very dull," he said.

Martin, however, had become somewhat light-headed with wrath.

"It's quite all right," he said. "But, if you want to play like that, I'll teach you how. Give me a hand, Ricky?"

"What's up?"

"There were a lot of old medicine-bottles in that room. The corks will do as buttons for these rapiers. Bring the light."

Ruth cried out in protest. Martin did not want to go into that condemned cell again, where to him the air was like a physical touch of evil. But in comparatively few minutes he might be in a worse place—across the passage—and locked into these rooms at that.

He fought it to the back of his mind, while he and Ricky stumbled again over the heap of swords and daggers. More of them clanged and rolled as the light moved. Martin put down his cup-hilt ready to hand.

"Big corks or little corks for the ends of the swords?" demanded Ricky. "There'd be more sport in little ones. If the point—" He paused, and Martin did not reply. They were both looking down at what had been revealed among the scattered swords.

It was an Italian dagger of the sixteenth century, of plain steel for blade, crosspiece, and handle, in a metal sheath of engraved design. It was not so large as we usually imagine such weapons. The blade, shaken almost out of a loose sheath, was so stained with blood that splashes smeared the crosspiece, and somebody evidently had tried to wipe off the lower part of the handle. It was fresh blood.

"Don't touch it!" said Ricky. "They tell you never to . . ."

"Got to touch it." Martin, far less bothered by this than by the evil old room, lifted it by the top of the dagger and the end of the sheath. He inspected it. "Antique," he said. "But—"

"But what?"

"The one cutting-edge has been ground to an edge like a razor. The point's just as sharp." He raised his voice. "Both the lawyer and the doctor had better come in here. Keep Ruth behind you; don't let her look."

There was a long silence, followed by a rush.

Stannard and Dr. Laurier carried the lamps. The former's black eyes were hard with suspicion. Dr. Laurier, dropping the Toledo blade with a clang on the other weapons, seemed miraculously transformed: any of his patients would have recognized him as Martin held out dagger and sheath half-together.

"We found it," Martin told the doctor, "in with the other things. Is that blood—recent?"

"Very." The pince-nez edged round the blade; the long, delicate fingers touched it. "I should say," he drew in his cheeks, "within the last half-hour. Of course, it may not be human blood."

"If you're anything of a pathologist?" Stannard suggested. Dr. Laurier nodded as though startled. "Then," Stannard

90

added, "you can discover whether it's human blood in a very few minutes."

"A very few minutes?"

"Yes, my dear sir. You and Ruth and Mr. Fleet are going home." -

Stannard took a deep breath. He thrust out an elbow and looked at his wrist-watch. Then he smiled.

"It is two minutes to twelve," he told them. "Time, I think, that Mr. Drake and I drew lots."

Chapter 10

A moment more, and they were all outside again in the passage between the doors: both closed now. The sheathed dagger, wrapped in a handkerchief so that he should not get blood on his clothes, had been thrust into the pocket of a dazed Dr. Laurier.

The tendency towards hysteria was mounting again.

"You quite understand the terms?" Stannard persisted.

"Quite." Martin tried to speak with a careless air, though his nerves were jerking like an alcoholic's. "Whoever wins the toss locks the other in, keeps the key, sits outside, and doesn't let him out until four o'clock—unless he yells for help."

"Exactly!" Stannard beamed. Then he looked at Ricky, and hesitated. "You recall the rope of the alarm-bell? In the condemned cell?"

"Yes. What about it?" snarled Ricky.

"It's very old. It probably doesn't work. But if you *should* hear the alarm-bell in the night, it will mean we are in serious trouble."

"What kind of trouble?"

Stannard nodded towards the door of the execution shed.

"Probably that Mr. Drake has gone mad in there," he replied.

"What makes you so infernally sure," demanded Martin, "that I'm going to lose the throw?"

"My luck," Stannard told him. "It never fails."

It was evident that he quite seriously believed this. Self-confidence radiated from him like a furnace; he kept patting his stomach, as though the luck rested there. Then, as he caught Ruth's eye, his tone changed.

"Not that it matters. In humanity, I should like to be the one who is shut up here. It would not, I think, trouble me much. My friend Drake has a disadvantage that will always beat him."

"Meaning what?"

"Your imagination, my dear fellow. You will see nothing, hear nothing; but you will feel. It is only when you *imagine* you see them crawling up from the gallows trap—men-eating tigers like Hessler and Bourke-Smith and pretty Mrs. Langton —that the brain will crack like a china jug." He turned round. "Have you got the folder of matches, Ruth?"

"I have them," said Ruth. "I wish I hadn't."

"Turn your back. Tear out one match, and tear off another much shorter. Give us the heads to choose. The short match is the loser."

Suddenly Dr. Laurier threw back his head and laughed, like a clergyman at a funeral. "This is most amusing!" he said. "This is really extraordinarily amusing."

Stannard bowed slightly.

"Have you got reading-matter, my dear fellow?" he asked Martin briskly, and produced from his conjuror's coat a pocket edition of the plays of Chekhov. "Come! Let's compare reading-matter!"

Martin took out a pocket edition of stories.

"What's this?" fussed Stannard. "*The Beach at Falésa. Markheim. Thrawn Janet. The Sire de—*" His bright black eyes grew incredulously chiding, then gently chiding. "Come, now! Stevenson!"

"If you," Martin said slowly, "are one of the clod-heads who don't appreciate Stevenson, then nobody can make you see his fineness of touch. But did you note the title of the first story? It's called *A Lodging for the Night*."

Stannard handed the book back. "Touché," he said.

Ruth swung round, holding up her hand with the match-heads above her clenched fist. The hand trembled slightly.

Only Martin and Stannard wore wrist-watches; these could be heard ticking in the pressure of silence. Martin moistened his lips. Stannard, comfortably smiling, nodded towards the matches.

"Won't you go first, my dear fellow? If not—"

"No, you don't!" said Martin.

They both lunged together for a different match. Ricky Fleet, his fists dug so deeply into the pockets of his coat that it seemed to stretch almost to his knees, watched with eyes round and fixed in a kind of incredulous hope. Both contestants, after a glance, opened a hand side by side; and Ruth expelled her breath.

Stannard had drawn the short match.

"Believe me," he said quietly and with evident sincerity, "it is best."

Then he became brisk.

"My dear Drake, here is the key to lock the iron door; together with your lamp and two spare batteries. Mr. Fleet," he indicated a lamp on the floor, "there is your light to guide your party to the main gate. It's a shade past midnight."

Martin felt Ricky clap him on the back at the result of the draw.

"That's all very well, Mr. Ghostmaster," said Ricky, leaning one elbow on the wall and making no pretense of liking Stannard, "but you led us in here. How do you expect us to get out?"

"Ah. Did you observe the floor as we came in?"

"Not particularly."

"In the aisle leading out you will find a length of heavy white string. I put it there this afternoon, a clue to the Cretan labyrinth. Follow the string; it will take you to the main gate."

In spite of everything, Martin thought, Stannard's all right. He's all right!

In a very short time he and Stannard were alone. The other three, obviously very nervous, watched while Martin stood outside the iron door, turned the key, and dropped it into his pocket. They saw the white splash of Stannard's lamp as he stood inside, close to the tiny square barred opening in the iron door.

"It's amusing," the barrister said, "that nobody's asked to see the execution shed. You and I can speak to each other through this opening. *If,*" he added very pointedly, "it is at all necessary."

The trembling echoes fell away to sharp-pointed quiet.

Ricky's bobbing light, Ruth's red and black slacks, Dr. Laurier's smile all faded amid rustles against bales. Martin switched off his own lamp. For a little time he watched Stannard, without speaking, through the little barred opening.

Holding the lamp ahead, Stannard opened the door of the execution shed. He raked the light inside. He started a little, though he must have guessed exactly how the room looked. It would look—

Stop that! Martin Drake shut up his own imagination.

93

Stannard, not quite so ruddy in the face, contemplated what lay inside. He turned back, entered the condemned cell, and after a moment emerged carrying an ugly-looking rocking-chair which Martin well remembered. Hoisting this awkwardly on one arm, Stannard returned to the execution shed, maneuvered in backwards, and closed the door. Utter darkness and silence descended on Pentecost Prison.

Martin hastily switched on his own lamp. The space between the iron door and the line of the piled paper was about ten feet clear. Brick walls and a brick floor. He set the lamp in a corner.

Got to sit down.

Standing on tiptoe, and with a heavy lift, he brought down one of the long paper bales. Pushing the lantern to one side with his foot, he thumped down the bale almost in the corner with its back to the wall at right-angles to the iron door. He glanced at his wrist-watch, thinking vaguely that Stannard's watch must be slow: his own registered a full fifteen minutes past twelve.

Only when he sat down and relaxed back against the wall, letting his arms and legs go as limp as a straw, did he realize.

God!

His head swam dizzily. His heart beat hard, though it was slowing down. There was sweat on his forehead, and his shirt stuck to his back. He hadn't quite realized the heat and oppressiveness in there. The others had been the same as himself, dust-grimed figures—except for Ruth, who in some inexplicable fashion preserved her freshness, the trim up-swept hair-do—but at the time he hadn't noticed it.

You couldn't call this place exactly soothing; yet it was soothing by contrast to that force which had put the black dog on his back in the condemned cell. Soothing! The lamp shed a thin beam at his feet across the floor. With Stevenson, and tobacco, he could easily pass less than four hours until dawn.

Smoking here? Yes; the paper bales were a good distance away. He lit a cigarette, drawing in smoke deeply and again relaxation; and out of the smoke swam Jenny, and Jenny's look, and Jenny's present address.

Well, Martin thought grimly, he had got that address.

Vividly he remembered how, at the telephone in the hall of Fleet House at well past seven that evening, he had got in touch with Dawson the butler at Brayle Manor. Dawson couldn't be overheard. The Old Dragon was upstairs at Fleet House with Aunt Cicely.

"I am sorry, sir," the voice told him. "I'm not at liberty to say where Lady Jennifer is."

"Yes, I appreciate that," Martin had answered. "But I'll pay you five hundred pounds if you do."

The telephone, so to speak, shook at its moorings.

If you want to bribe anybody, Martin thought, don't mess in small craftiness with ten-bob notes, or there'll only be haggling and you'll lose. Hit your man in the eye with a sum so staggering that he'll fall all over himself to get it.

"Go on!" jeered the telephone, in a startlingly different tone, but much lower-voiced. "How do I know you can pay that?"

"The banks are closed. But did you ever hear of Mr. Joseph Anthony? He's the biggest art-dealer in London."

"Yes, sir," the voice muttered respectfully. "We've had to—" the word "sell" seemed to tremble on his lips.

"His private 'phone-number is Grosvenor 0011. Confirm it with Information if you doubt me. I'm going to 'phone him now. You ring him in about fifteen minutes. Ask him then if he's ready, on my say-so, to send you his own personal cheque for that amount. The cheque will reach you tomorrow, and won't be stopped unless you've given me a fake address."

"The . . . the address is not on the 'phone, sir."

"Never mind. Get it!"

Then he had 'phoned Joe Anthony; and waited in agony, twisting his knuckles, for Dawson's return-call. Curious, too: once or twice he imagined he had heard somebody whispering in the background while he spoke to Dawson. Then the telephone pealed its double-ring.

"That's all right, sir," Dawson muttered. "The address is not exactly in London."

"I didn't suppose it was, or the old—she wouldn't have told me so."

"Care of Mr. and Mrs. Ives, Ranham Old Park, Ranham, Hertfordshire."

Serene satisfaction animated Martin when he wrote it down, and put it in his pocket. He was still sitting by the telephone in the hall when Lady Brayle herself came downstairs past the dying light from the tall arched window.

Martin, startled, did not get up. She did not look at him; was not conscious of him. On her face was an expression he failed to read. She marched on her flat heels, shoulders swinging a little, to the front door; and departed without a word to anybody.

Then there had been dinner in the high square room at the

95

back of Fleet House, candle-flames on polished wood making a shimmer against daylight through garden trees. H.M. and Masters had somewhat hastily departed after the interview on the roof, saying they were going to see the local police at Brayle. Ricky insisted on Martin's bringing his bag across from the inn. Then the long sitting in the back garden—Dr. Laurier arriving in his own car from just outside Brayle, Ricky rushing into the house to see how his mother was—until the position of the quarter-moon above rustling darkness told them it was time to . . .

Yes; he had got that address!

Sitting back relaxed, the cigarette-end glowing red against the darkness of Pentecost, Martin felt cool in temperature as well as mind; and he smiled. Tomorrow morning, very early, he would see what train-connections he could make for Ranham in Hertfordshire.

"With luck," he said aloud, "I might get there at breakfast-time."

The sound of his own voice startled him. By the Lord, he was jumpier than he'd thought! Not a whisper of noise had come from beyond the iron door. Stannard must be sitting in the rocking chair, perhaps wheezing a little as he read Chekhov, near the closed gallows-trap. Martin reached down for the Stevenson; and then flung his head round.

Something was moving and rustling among the paper bales.

Steady, now!

He dropped his cigarette on the floor and ground it out with his foot. Reaching down for the lamp, he directed it towards the aisle between bales and wall. Whoever it was, the person carried a light. Out into the open emerged Ruth Callice: her face anxious, her finger at her lip.

"What the devil are you . . . ?"

"Sh!" Ruth tiptoed over. "I know I'm breaking my promise. But I *had* to talk to you alone."

This was the Ruth he had known on Thursday night, and for so long: the dark-brown eyes softened and upturned, the lips half parted, that sense of "niceness" which so many persons found impossible to describe. Her sweater-and-slacks costume, Martin observed for the first time, became her very well. She looked at the iron door.

"Can Stan hear us?"

"I don't think so, unless you shout. The door of the—that place is thick oak, and he's got it closed. Where are the others?"

"They went home. I knew *I* was perfectly at home, if I had
96

a lamp and that thread guide-line." Ruth's smooth forehead slightly wrinkled; a smile curved up the corner of her lip. "Sit down," she invited, "and move over. Have you a cigarette?"

Martin put down the light in its old position with Ruth's lamp beside it, and lit cigarettes for both of them. With his eyes becoming accustomed to near-darkness, he could see that the paper-mountains had been built up on the side of windows. He was acutely conscious of something else: Ruth's physical nearness.

"I suppose," Ruh said softly, when the cigarette had several times pulsed and darkened, "you thought I behaved very badly today?"

He had forgotten all about it. "No, not in the least."

"Well, I did."

"Never mind your behaviour. Why didn't you ever tell me you knew Jenny? You knew I'd been searching for three years . . ."

"Pardon me," Ruth corrected. "I learned it just under a year ago. You got horribly drunk and told me all about it."

"Yes. That's true. I remember. Even so!—"

"Oh, I wish I could make you understand!" The cigarette glowed and darkened nervously. Ruth half turned. In near-darknss he could see the sincerity, the deep earnestness, in the gleam of her eyes. "I had to know whether it was right for both of you, and that wasn't easy. I had to decide what was best."

"You had to decide what was best for us?"

"Yes."

"Forgive me, Ruth. But can you, or I, or anybody else in this bloody Socialist world, say what's best for his neighbour?"

"I knew you wouldn't understand. You see, I'm very fond of Jenny, and I—am rather fond of you. Jenny's had a queer upbringing. Her father and mother, the Earl and Countess, never got on well. Her mother's dead. Her father lives abroad: in Sweden, I think."

"Yes. So Jenny told me."

"She's been brought up by this stately grandmother . . ."

"And you think the old she-dog can stop Jenny from loving me?"

"Oh, she'll love you." Ruth laughed. "She'll love you so desperately that in a year or two you'll be bored to death. Also, Jenny's terribly jealous. And she has almost no sense of humour."

Ruth dropped her cigarette on the floor and trod on it. Martin watched her.

"How many times have you been in love, Ruth? Did you

ever find a sense of humour much of a help?"

Ruth ignored this. She seemed about to add something else about Jenny or Jenny's family, but checked herself.

"And take you, for instance!" she went on, with soft and tender satire. "Do you remember what you said on Thursday night?"

Now the ability of a woman to remember some trivial remark, made possibly decades before, is a weapon which cannot be met.

"You said if you ever found Jenny again, and she was engaged, you'd use *any* trick, however underhand, to get her back again. And what, as it happened, did you actually do?

"Darling, your fair-play-and-no-advantages attitude was ridiculous. If Ricky Fleet hadn't been up to his ears with Susan Harwood, there'd have been trouble. You insisted on keeping your word about the vigil here, though I was a cat and tried to make Jenny even more jealous than she is.

"Look at your best, or rather your most popular, work! Look at your fencing! Look at Stevenson! You're an old-fashioned romanticist, that's what you are, only temperamental and a bit crazy."

Ruth said all this in a low voice, speaking more quickly as she went on. Martin dropped his own cigarette and crushed it out.

"What you say," he retorted, "may be true. If it is, it's no very deep damnation. Your friend Stannard . . ."

"Oh, Martin!"

"Why do you say, 'oh, Martin' like that?"

(Yet all the time he was becoming more heavily, acutely aware of Ruth's physical presence.)

"Poor Jack Stannard is only showing off, that's all. He despises younger men, and wants to show them up as ignorant louts. And he's rather tremendous, you know. And that grave bearing of his, shaking hands just as though I were made of fragile china, is so touching that sometimes I—" She paused. "Do you know why he arranged this whole expedition?"

Martin hesitated. "Well! I suppose because he thought you were, you know, more interested in me than you were."

"So you've guessed *that*," Ruth mocked softly.

(They were both breathing with a little more quickened beat.)

"I'd have known it, of course, if there hadn't been a kind of spell on my brain. In any case, since it happens to be wrong . . ."

"Who says it's wrong?" asked Ruth coolly, and turned round. "Suppose you kiss me."

Now here, it may be submitted, what is any man to do under such circumstances? Besides, human nature is human nature: to put the matter politely. Furthermore, ordinary social behaviour . . . Anyway, he did not treat her like fragile china.

Suddenly Ruth struggled and pushed herself away.

"This doesn't mean anything," she said. After waiting a while, she repeated in a calmer tone: "This doesn't mean anything."

The thought of Jenny, even in Martin's present state of mind, partly sobered him.

"I know!" He got his breath back.

"I wouldn't have an affair with you," said Ruth, "and I certainly wouldn't marry you, for anything on earth."

"I know that!—But, for the sake of academic clearness, why not?"

"Because you have your way of life; you're an idiot; and you wouldn't change it one little bit. I have my way of life; I'm practical; and *I* wouldn't change it one little bit. It would be horrible."

"Jenny—" he stopped. "There's Stannard, you know."

"Do you think you're joking?"

"No!"

"Because I might, just conceivably might, be able to care a good deal for him, if only," said Ruth with intensity, "if only he were more of an idiot!"

"For God's sake," exclaimed the other, taken aback by what seemed to him the deep seriousness and complete illogicality of this remark, "isn't that the deadly charge you've been levelling at me?"

"Oh, you don't understand." Ruth was almost crying "I shouldn't have come here. You shouldn't have let me talk to you. It's your fault."

She reached across, took up her own lamp, and stood up. She moved softly away from him, turning round only at the aisle. Her dark-brown eyes were soft again. Her lips made a movement of lightness.

"I shall get over this very shortly," she told him. "In the meantime, I warn you by your own code that I'm *rather* jealous of Jenny. Against that, I *am* trying to do the decent thing and what's right. What I really came here to tell you . . ."

"Yes?"

"I *can* tell you, because it hasn't directly to do with Jenny

99

herself. Years ago," said Ruth, "a child was found murdered and mutilated at a place called Priory Hill, not very far from here."

Then she was gone.

The old brick prison might have echoed with ghostly occupants shaking their cell-doors. Was Hessler, who also murdered and mutilated, listening with his ear to the little grille of the iron door? Across and beyond the paper bales Martin could see the tops of high windows, with vertical bars; but the lighter sky beyond made darkness here more dense.

Ruth . . . he must forget that subject, Martin told himself. Suppose Jenny had seen them? No harm in it, only natural; but hard to explain. Lord, suppose Ruth told Jenny? "I'm *rather* jealous of Jenny." Stop! Mentally he closed the lid of the incident with a bang.

Still not a whisper, not a chink of light, from beyond the iron door. Under the rules of the test, the man inside was permitted to get up and walk about. Could anything have happened to Stannard?

Martin would have shouted to Stannard, except for the practical certainty that it would bring the barrister to the iron door, sardonically to inquire whether his friend outside needed help.

Yes, Ruth—careful!—did right to respect Stannard. Aside from anything else, the Great Defender was as clever as Satan. Another memory stirred in Martin's head: a festal occasion at his club, viewed through a gauze of whisky, in which a certain eminent judge had spoken with great indiscretion. He spoke of Stannard, who had been briefed for the defence in the Cosens murder case.

"Gentlemen," His Lordship had declared, his speech being rendered here as free from alcoholic slur, "gentlemen, counsel for the defence produced an unexpected alibi. It was not only, gentlemen, that we couldn't prove the flaw in it; we couldn't even *see* the flaw in it. And that thus-and-so Cosens, as guilty as Judas, walked out a free man."

Well, there was no question of ali . . .

Great Scott, no wonder Stannard hadn't become restless! Martin, blinking hard at the luminous dial of his watch, saw that the time was only half-past twelve. It should have been two o'clock, at least. But he held the watch to his ear, and it was ticking.

Swung round once too often in the emotional bowl, exhausted, Martin sat down heavily on the paper-bale. His head felt very heavy. The light of the lamp began to grow yellow (somebody using it too long before?), and he hastily replaced the battery with a spare one.

With heavy movements he groped along the wall, found a nail there, shifted along the bale, and hung the lamp sideways so that its beam should shine past his shoulder. He groped down again for the Stevenson he had found in the library at Fleet House.

Begin with the first story, yes. Title-page, table of contents, foreword, so! Begin with the fine scene of the snowflakes sifting over mediaeval Paris. Begin . . .

The type blurred before his eyes. He had a hazy consciousness that the book was there, the light was there, and he was there; but not for long. His head and shoulders lolled back against the wall. Martin Drake, with the lines of tiredness drawn slantwise under his eyes, was asleep.

What woke him he did not know at the time, or for nearly twenty-four hours afterwards.

But it was a noise. It made him start up, nerves twitching; it made him jump to his feet, miry-eyed, and peer round until he realized where he was. His first impression, possibly created by a dream, was that the alarm-bell on the roof was ringing.

"If you hear the alarm-bell in the night," someone had said, "it will mean we are in serious trouble."

But a bell would have gone on ringing. Besides, a deeper memory suggested, this had been something like a crash: not very loud, yet loud enough to jolt thin sleep. Martin's head remained mazy. By concentration on his wrist-watch, he saw the hour was two o'clock. Then Stannard flashed through his mind. Yanking the lamp off the wall, he hurried to the iron door and played the beam inside.

"Stannard!" he yelled.

The oak door to the execution shed was still closed. So was the other one.

"Stannard! Are you all right?"

To his relief he heard the "Yes! Quite!" of the other's unmistakable tones, muffled by the oak door. But in the voice was a curious wild inflection which in his relief he did not stop to analyze.

He groped for the key in his pocket, but hesitated. He would not offer Stannard the insult of asking whether he wanted to be let out.

What vaguely puzzled Martin, as he returned to his seat, was the fact that he had been able to sleep in the place of bogles. But this wasn't the place of bogles. Wasn't there some legend about iron, cold iron, keeping them off?

101

It was within the rules, both stated and implied, to sleep if you could. You could drowse in the rocking-chair, or even on the ruddy gallows-trap. Martin hung the lamp on the wall again, his hand heavy.

When he leaned back against the wall, he felt no sense of crick in the neck or stiffness in the back. His senses were padded. Once more, from here, he bellowed out at Stannard; and very faintly Stannard's voice told him to mind his own damned business.

Right you are, Mr. Great Defender.

Sleep coiled insidiously, sleep soothed with shadow narcotics.

Though it might have been unusual under such circumstances, Martin afterwards remembered his dreams as being cozy and pleasant. He became somehow entangled with the love-scene between Blanche and Denis in *The Sire de Malétroit's Door;* and the old Sire de Malétroit, who was going to hang somebody in the morning, bore a baffling, dissolving resemblance to Lady Brayle. The old Sire de Malétroit . . .

Look out! *Thud!*

This time what woke him was toppling off the bale, his hands and arms in semi-consciousness saving him as he struck the floor. It was an ugly feeling, that sense of a helpless fall. But he was awake, chilly and sharply wide-awake, when he crawled up from the dirt-sting of the floor.

The corridor swam in a dim grey twilight which seemed as dingy as the prison. Outside the tall barred windows he could detect a white mist, wisps of it, past grime-speckled panes. Once more he consulted his watch. Two minues to four o'clock.

A great exultation sang in him, though he felt as if he had slept in a barrel. It was nearly all over. Give it dead to the time—exactly to the ant-busy travelling of the watch's secondhand—and then unlock the door.

The beam of the lamp still shone straight across, against murky daylight. Stevenson, unread, had sprawled open on the floor. If there could be degrees of silence, Pentecost Prison seemed more utterly silent now than at any time during the night. And Stannard?

Martin let the full two minutes tick round. Then, drawing the large key out of his pocket, he went over to the iron door.

"Stannard!" he shouted.

Chapter 11

Shading his eyes, Martin peered through the grille.

Grey traces, very faint, showed a vertical glimmer along the edge of the execution shed door, which stood about an inch open. Obviously, as in the case of the condemned cell, that room must have some kind of window.

"Stannard!" he called, with the same formula. "Are you all right?"

"I'm here. I'm—" The voice seemed to answer somewhat hollowly, and from a distance away, though the oak door stood a little open. Odd, perhaps. Who cared?

"The time's up," Martin shouted back, "and I'm unlocking this door."

He did so, after which he pushed the iron door partly open with a squeak and squeal of hinges. There was a ringing clatter as he threw the key inside on the floor.

"Thanks," he added, "for an entertaining evening. You're free, and I'm free too."

The thought of Stannard's company, on the way back, almost revolted him. In his exuberance he felt like talking to empty air instead, so that he could use rich words unheard. Putting Stevenson in his pocket, and picking up the lamp, he took long strides to get away from there.

Faintly, once, he thought he heard Stannard calling something after him. But the light found the white-string guideline with ease; amazing he hadn't noticed it before! Nevertheless, in his daylight mood, it was of a pattern with all the other incidents of last night.

Every action, every speech, had seemed quite natural at the time; even inevitable. Yet now, when the images unreeled before him—those evil forces (imagined?) in the condemned cell, a fencing-match in which he had nearly been murdered by the sedate Dr. Laurier, a blood-stained dagger, an alarm-bell with its rope in the cell, an amorous passage with Ruth Callice—it became a phantasmagoria which struck him with wonder. The little talk with Ruth seemed to him inconsequential, as though it had never happened; even amusing. He would tell Jenny about it.

In less than two minutes, at rustling quick-step through what was now only a dreary storage-building, he reached the main gate. All phantasmagoria, like that skeleton in the clock. Briefly he wondered what Sir Henry Merrivale might have been doing with the skeleton in the clock.

Through the arched frame of bars like a portcullis, he saw that the tall iron gates stood wide open. Beyond lay thick white mist, drifting and with rifts in it; the mist would presently vanish before heat and sun, but meantime it muffled the world in eeriness.

As he passed the opening in the portcullis, switching off the lamp and putting it in his pocket, Martin laughed aloud at this so-called "eeriness." He could have danced or hit the air a right-hander. Then, just outside the prison gates as a rift in the mist floated past, he saw Jenny herself. She was obviously waiting.

For a moment he stood still, with a notion that this might be part of the fantasy.

By coincidence, Jenny also wore slacks and a sweater: coloured brown, with a light coat thrown over her shoulders. As soon as he saw her, other considerations of feminine appeal were forgotten. Her yellow hair curled to her shoulders. She was smoking a cigarette, which she instantly threw away. They ran towards each other.

"How the devil did you get back here?"

"I was never away," Jenny confessed. "I thought I could take that train. But I couldn't face it. I told the taxi-driver to come back. Because—" She stopped. "So you'd have paid five hundred pounds just to learn where I'd gone?"

"If that butler has blabbed, the old lady will sack him."

"Dawson," said Jenny, "isn't a butler. I suppose he is, in a way, and Grandmother insists on calling him that. He's butler and handy-man too; we don't employ much of a staff of servants. Anyway, I caught him when he was going to take your money. I was afraid you could hear me whispering in the background."

Realization bumped him. "Come to think of it, I heard something."

"Of course I rang up Mr. Anthony after you did, and said it was all a joke and he wasn't to send any cheque. Dawson nearly wept. Then I made him ring you and give the address, or you might have come to the Manor. But—"

Here, raising her blue eyes, Jenny began such a bitter denunciation of her own character, such a writhing of self-

104

loathing, that it would have been considered strong even by her worst enemy.

"Martin, I knew you had to go through with that 'bet.' I wouldn't have you back out. That's what makes me so vile. There's one excuse," her eyes looked at him oddly, "that perhaps helps, and I've got to tell you soon. But Ruth had got me absolutely furious. Then, when I saw you running across the road after her . . ."

He ended her rush of speech in the appropriate way, which was an effective way. At the back of his mind it occurred to him that he wouldn't just yet tell Jenny about that small brush with Ruth last night. Presently, of course! But not just yet.

Presently Jenny spoke.

"So I had to sneak out this morning and meet you. Otherwise," she said happily, "you'd have been ripping away or chartering a special plane or heaven knows what. Where do you want to go now?"

"Anywhere you like. We might go and throw a bucket of water over your grandmother?"

"Martin! You mustn't . . ."

Jenny stopped. Suddenly she began to laugh, with such full infectiousness and delight that Martin joined in without knowing why. It warmed his heart to see this girl growing healthier and more exuberant at every minute, as though she had been let out of prison.

"If you think the idea is as funny as all that, Jenny, it would be still better to use a fire-hose."

"Wait!" cried Jenny, shaking all over and wiping the tears of joy from her eyes. "Do you mean to say you haven't heard about the perfectly awful thing that happened last night? In the public road between the Dragon's Rest and the Manor?"

"No."

"Well, Grandmother and Sir Henry Merrivale . . ."

"Godalive, don't tell me those two had *another* knock-down row?"

"Yes."

"*He* threw a bucket of water over her, I suppose?"

"No, no, it wasn't anything like that." Jenny, the wings of her yellow hair falling forward, pressed a hand over her mouth and began to shake again. He straightened up her shoulders. "Darling," she assured him, "I shall be a perfect model of prim correctness. I've been trained to that. You're at the Dragon, aren't you?"

"No; at Fleet House."

"If you don't mind wading in wet grass, there's a wonderful short-cut over the fields."

"We will roll and revel in the wet grass. Lead on."

About them the white mist so muffled sight that even the prison was hardly visible twenty feet away. Sometimes the mist would drift past Jenny, obscuring her until the smiling face emerged. Their footsteps crunched in weedy gravel; once, on the edge of the gravel approach, Jenny hesitated.

"Good heavens, what about Mr. Stannard? What about everything?"

"Stannard," he replied, "is A-1. He'll be out in a minute, so let's go ahead. *I* saw no ghosts. In fact," concluded Martin, telling one of the more remarkable lies of his life, "there was practically no excitement. Let's hear about this row."

The wet grass swished and soaked to their knees as they went down across an almost invisible field in the mist. The shape of a tree swam dimly past, to be blotted out as though by magic. They walked happily, arm and hand linked; but Jenny was now frowning.

"You see," she explained, "Grandmother's now got the skeleton."

"She's got . . . you mean the skeleton-clock?"

"Not the clock. Just the skeleton. Heaven alone knows why she wants it," Jenny bit her lip, "or why anybody wants it. It all started very seriously. Grandmother had gone to visit Aunt Cicely, and got back home about a quarter to eight."

"Yes. I remember."

"I was a bit uneasy when she got home. I shouldn't have been, and I won't be again. But I wondered what she'd say when she found I hadn't gone to visit Mr. and Mrs. Ives after all. She just looked at me in the oddest way—" Jenny hesitated—"as though it didn't matter. She said: 'Jennifer dear, I must think hard for five minutes.'

"Whenever she says that, I know it means she's thinking about legal proceedings. Grandmother's got a passion for law suits. She's always trying to prove something from old documents of 1662, or things like that. *I* imagined she was thinking about the fair (you'll hear about it) that opens on Monday.

"Anyway, she came back in fifteen minutes looking grim and sort of triumphant. She made me sit down in a chair. She said: 'Jennifer, mark my words! The unspeakable Merrivale —' "

(Martin could hear Lady Brayle saying it.)

" '—the unspeakable Merrivale,' Grandmother said, "in the

presence of no less than four witnesses, distinctly promised to give me the clock if I answered "a few" questions. These questions I did answer, as the witnesses can testify.' "

To Martin's memory returned a view of the library at Fleet House, with H.M. and Lady Brayle standing on either side of the desk like offenders in a magistrate's court. He saw Ruth, Stannard, Ricky and himself with their backs to the white marble mantelpiece.

"Jenny," he said, "that's true. He did say so!"

"Anyway, I'm afraid I couldn't follow the legal lecture she gave me. Something about possession of the clock including possession of its contents: as, *par example*, and to wit, when it is sold at Willaby's with a skeleton inside. Then she called for Dawson to get out the electric car. Do you know what an electric car is?"

Martin reflected.

"I dimly remember having seen, or at least heard of one. It looked like a two-seater carriage with a dashboard, but no horses; nothing in front except the dashboard and a glass windscreen. You steered with a handle instead of a steering-wheel. Yes! And it was used by stately ladies who didn't want to travel fast."

Jenny nodded.

"That's it exactly. Grandmother has one, and it still works. But it's never used except on *very* special occasions. I asked Grandmother what it meant, but she only smiled that peculiar smile and said I should understand in good time. What's more, she told Dawson she would drive herself, because she wanted me as a witness.

"It was broad daylight, not more than half-past eight. Along we went in the electric—'brougham,' Grandmother calls it— with Grandmother sitting bolt upright and never looking more grand, and *me* sitting bolt upright, eyes ahead, and feeling *awful*. We got as far as Fleet House, and then turned round in a graceful curve to the main bar of the Dragon's Rest."

Martin Drake was beginning to taste ecstasy.

"Is that the one she usually patronizes?"

"Martin!" said Jenny. Her eyes belied her seraphic countenance.

"I beg your pardon. Go on."

"Of course Grandmother wouldn't let me go in. She stationed me just outside the door. It was Saturday night, and they were pretty noisy. They're not supposed to sing, but the constable doesn't interfere much. A group in one corner were harmonizing on a pirate chantey with a refrain like, 'Skull and

107

bones, skull and bones; ho, the Jolly Roger.'

"When Grandmother walked in, every man of them looked up as though he'd seen the hangman. But Grandmother loves—" Jenny's voice poured with bitterness—"*how* Grandmother loves being the lady of the manor. She raised her hand and said, 'Please, my good men, be at ease.' Then she beckoned to poor Mr. Puckston.

"I couldn't hear much of what they were saying. Mr. Puckston seemed to be telling her the first bar-parlour was used as a private sitting-room by Sir Henry Merrivale, and H.M. was out, and the door was locked. Of course you can guess how Grandmother dealt with that. Mr. Puckston unlocked the door, Grandmother went in; and in a minute Mr. Puckston followed her with a pair of wire-cutters.

"Then the door opened again. Out marched Grandmother, with the skeleton slung over her shoulder. The head was hanging down her back, and she had the legs in her hand.

"One poor old man, who must have been eighty, spilled a pint beer-glass straight into Miss Partridge's lap. Grandmother never stopped or looked round. She marched straight out to the brougham, sat the skeleton up in the seat like a passenger, and told me to get in.

"That's where the fireworks really started. As I was getting in, I looked round. In the middle of the road, about thirty feet behind us—well, there was Sir Henry.

"His eyes were bulging out behind his spectacles, and his whole corporation was shivering like a mountain. I can't reproduce the tone, and, anyway, nobody could reproduce the volume, of what he said.

"He said: 'You stole my skeleton.' Then he turned round to the people in the door, who'd crowded out with their glasses in their hands, and said: 'Boys, that goddam hobgoblin stole my skeleton.' By this time we were off to a flying start.

"There wasn't any motor-car outside the Dragon at all. Only a lot of bicycles, and a farm-cart with Will Harnaby's horse. H.M. was so mad he really and literally couldn't see straight, and he fell all over the farm-cart when he tried to get up. But he did get there, and he did grab the reins and whip, and off we all went.

"Grandmother was bending tensely over the steering-lever, putting on every ounce of speed; and Sir Henry was standing up and whirling the whip round his head like a charioteer in *Ben-Hur*. Only, you see, that electric car couldn't possibly do twenty miles an hour. And Will Harnaby's horse couldn't do fifteen.

"That's where——" Jenny faltered a little—"Grandmother gave me the instructions. She said, with that smile of hers, I was to stick the skeleton's head out of the side-window so it faced H.M. And I was to move the lower jaw up and down as if the skeleton gibbered at him.

"Well, I did. I made the skeleton stick its head out and gibber about every twenty yards. And, every time the skeleton gibbered at him, his face got more purple, and his language was awful. Truly *awful*. I never heard anything, even in the Navy, that could . . ."

Jenny stopped. "Martin!" she said, in an attempt at reproachfulness which broke down completely.

He couldn't help it. He knew it wasn't really funny; it was funny only because you could visualize the expressions of the persons concerned. He had collapsed against a tree, beating his hands on the bark. Jenny collapsed as well.

"But, Martin!" she insisted presently. "You've got to see the serious side as well!"

"If you can see the serious side of that, my sweet, you'd appeal greatly to Sir Stafford Cripps. Besides, you haven't told me the ending."

"The ending *is* the serious side."

"Oh? Who won the race?"

"We did. By yards and yards and yards." Jenny reflected. "I'm perfectly certain Grandmother told Dawson to be ready. He was there at the lodge gates, where there's no lodge-keeper now. But the wall is fifteen feet high, and there are big iron-barred gates."

Prisons, it suddenly occurred to Martin: striking the amusement from his heart. Pentecost, Fleet House, Brayle Manor, all were prisons; though for the life of him he could not think how this applied to Fleet House, where the impression had come only from feeling.

He and Jenny were walking again through the mist. A white tide of mist-under-mist washed across the grass, then revealed it, ever moving. Its damp could be felt and breathed.

"Go on," he prompted. "What happened after your electric flyer got through the gates?"

"Dawson closed and locked them. Grandmother drove the car a fairly long way up the drive. After that she walked to the gates again. By that time she and H.M. too must have done a little thinking, because . . . well, because it was different. H.M. was sitting outside the gates on the seat of the farm-cart, with the whip across his knees and no expression on his face at all.

"Grandmother put her own face almost against the bars,

and (don't think I've forgotten a word!) she said: 'It may be conceded that you won the first round, Henry; but can there be any doubt about who won the second?' "

Martin whistled.

"Jenny," he declared, "something tells me there is going to be a third round. And that the third round will be a beauty."

"But that's just what mustn't happen!" Jenny, peering at him past the side of her yellow hair, was again the eager and the breathless. "Oh, I suppose it doesn't matter if it's something silly, like making skeletons gibber. Though even there I doubt whether your H.M. is as clever as Grandmother."

"You think that, eh?"

"Yes. I do."

"Wait," advised Martin.

"But the skeleton-in-the-clock," Jenny told him, her thin and arched eyebrows drawn together, "is a different thing. It's serious, and—it may be deadly. Do you realize, from what H.M. said at Willaby's and from every bit of gossip floating about, that H.M. thinks this skeleton is a vital piece of evidence?"

"But evidence of what?"

"I wish I knew. And he told us straight out what he thought about Sir George Fleet's . . . death."

"*You're* sure it was murder too. Aren't you, Jenny?"

She stopped short and turned round, her lips apart. "Martin! What makes you ask that?"

"Because every single time you've mentioned it, you hesitate before you say 'death.' Besides, for some reason yesterday you started to be passionately interested all of a sudden, and wanted to learn all about it. Why, Jenny?"

Instead of lessening as they walked, the mist was becoming thicker. Already, some distance back, a hedgerow had loomed unexpectedly in their faces; they groped for the stile. Now a fence emerged with almost equal materialization from the white twilight. They reached the fence, and Jenny put a hand on it.

"Martin. Did you ever wonder why I didn't offer to go with you on the ghost-hunting expedition?"

Martin felt uncomfortable. "Well! I thought you were . . ."

"Jealous? Yes, that was true. Afraid of ghosts? Also true, a little." Her lips and eyebrows apologized gently. "But I told you there was another reason. Martin, I want you to know *everything* about me. I do, I do! But I can't tell you now because if I'm wrong it's not merely being mistaken; it's—it's sordidly stupid."

"Jenny, I don't care. I'm not a detective."

She shook her hair violently, and settled the coat over her brown sweater as though more conscious of mist-clamminess.

"It all comes back to that utterly meaningless skeleton," she said. "And now Grandmother's got it locked up somewhere."

"For innocent reasons, of course." He tried hard to make this a plain statement, without any inflection of question.

"Naturally. You see, under everything, Grandmother is just a sentimentalist."

Martin found his reason rocking. *"Your grandmother,"* he said, defining the words with care, "you call a sentimentalist?"

"Oh, she isn't easy to live with. I hate her sometimes. But she *is* kind-hearted, and you'd see it if it weren't for the arrogance. Grandmother is shielding somebody." Jenny hesitated. "She says the skeleton is legally her property. She also says nobody, not even the police, can take it from her unless they can show *why* it's a vital piece of evidence. Is that right?"

"You'd better ask Stannard. But it sounds reasonable to me."

"Then that means," cried Jenny, her eyes shining under lowered lids, "the police don't know themselves. It means . . ."

Here Jenny, whose gaze had wandered along the line of the fence, uttered a cry and ran to Martin. Some little distance down beside the fence, a man was standing motionless.

A drifting mist-veil hid everything except his legs, as he stood sideways to the fence. Then the moving veil slowly swirled past and up. Martin saw clearly a large and somewhat burly figure, with its blue serge suit and its ruddy face dominated by a boiled blue eye, under a bowler hat.

"Chief Inspector Masters!" Martin said.

Masters lifted one foot experimentally, and set it down with a faint squelch. If he did not happen to be in a good temper, the Chief Inspector never showed this in his professional countenance.

"Morning, miss. Morning, sir," he greeted them, as offhandedly as though he were in a London office instead of a mist-wrapped Berkshire field at half-past four on Sunday morning. Bland as ever, poker-faced as ever in public, he walked towards them and looked hard at Martin.

"Still alive, I see," he added.

Chapter 12

We talk with scorn of prophetic instincts. Martin felt one then, as sharp as the twinge from a bad heart; but, like the mist-movings, it drifted away and was lost in an instant.

"Still alive?" he repeated, and laughed. "Is there any reason why I shouldn't be alive?"

"We-el!" smiled Masters, with a tolerant and amused wave of his hand. "As you described it to Sir Henry and me, this execution shed business was to be a swell affair. But *you* don't seem to be hanged by the neck or snuffed out by any ghost, do you?"

Martin, studying him, saw that Masters had the appearance of a man who has walked hard to keep just ahead of somebody. In addition to his reddish eyelids, there were certain familiar dust-stains on the blue serge which had not quite been erased by a handkerchief or the mist-damp.

"Chief Inspector," he said, "were you at that prison too?"

"We-el!" said Masters, as though he debated this himself. "That's a very interesting question, sir. I might have been, and then again I might not have been." He drew closer, confidentially. "The fact is, a minute ago I heard you two saying something about a skeleton and a clock."

"Please don't start to browbeat me," begged Jenny. "Go and see my grandmother."

"Browbeat? Now, miss!" Masters was reproachful. He grew more confidential, like a Balkan diplomat. "I'll just tell you something about that skeleton, if you like. It wasn't Sir George Fleet."

Jenny's eyes opened. "Who on earth ever said it was?"

"Still, miss, one or two people seem to have got the idea." His eye swung towards Martin. "What about you, sir?"

"It did occur to me, yes. But not very seriously."

"Oh, ah. And that's right. Yesterday evening at the police-station, we got a message from London. From a supply-firm that keeps records as far back as the Flood, it'ud seem. Dr. Pierre Laurier, the old one who's dead, bought the skeleton as an anatomical specimen in 1912.

"Also last night, before he went to join you on the (hurrum!)

112

ghost-hunt, Sir Henry and I talked with 'young' Dr. Hugh Laurier, who's forty-eight years old. Lives just outside the town-limits of Brayle."

"This was after the Ben-Hur chariot-race, I gather?" Martin asked.

Masters frowned at him slightly, and addressed Jenny.

"Dr. Hugh, miss, told us all about it. When it became (hurrum!)—well, what you might call not fashionable to have skeletons hanging about in doctors' offices, his father put it away in a cupboard. It wasn't till shortly before his death in 1936, when he was old and maybe a bit fanciful, that this Pierre Laurier . . . was he French, miss?"

"Yes. His name was formerly De Laurier. That means," Jenny spoke wearily, "he was a nobleman, and Grandmother simply— Never mind. And the Fleets! He was supposed to have a hopeless passion for Aunt Cicely."

Masters made a broad wave of the hand.

"Anyway, miss, the old doctor with the beard took this skeleton, and put it in a clock after he'd taken the works out, and stuck it up in his back parlour as a kind of . . . kind of . . ."

"Memento mori?" suggested Martin.

Masters considered this.

"Oh, ah. Just so. If that means what I think it does. Like the people who put up sun-dials with a motto, *'It is later than you think.'* "

'It is later than you think.' Yes, Martin had heard that before. When Masters leaned towards Jenny, his head suddenly emerged out of a mist-wreath like a fatherly Spanish Inquisitor.

"Now come, miss!" he urged persuasively. "That's the living truth. And there's no harm in anything; I'll take my oath to it. Why does her ladyship, your good grandmother, want to cause a lot of unnecessary fuss and bother? Just why does she want the thing anyway? Eh?"

"If it comes to that," said Martin, instantly putting a guard between Jenny and Masters, "why do you want it yourself?"

"Ah! I'm afraid that'd be Official Secrets, sir."

"But there was nothing secret about why Lady Brayle wanted it: as a present for Dr. Hugh Laurier. She was bidding for it at Willaby's, until H.M. topped her. Afterwards he gave it to her. That's all."

"Is it, now?" Masters asked affably. "Then why did she take the skeleton alone? And not the clock?"

Too late Martin saw the flaw in his argument. But Masters dismissed the matter.

"What I really wanted to say," he declared, this also being a lie, "was I've got lost in this ruddy mist. How can I get back to the Dragon?"

"This is a landmark," Jenny assured him, putting her hand on the fence. "Follow this, no matter how far it seems to go, and you'll come to the main road. Then turn right and follow the main road. You can't miss it."

"Well, now, miss, I'm much obliged!" Masters' fatherly heartiness was overpowering. "The fence, eh? Not a countryman myself." His look at Martin was almost a sardonic wink. "Good day to you!" He followed the line of the fence a few feet; then turned round.

"By the way, Mr. Drake. Have you got the time?"

"It's getting on towards five."

"Ah!" Masters shook his head regretfully. "Pity! Bit too early to wake up Dr. Laurier. I wanted to know whether that blood on the dagger is human blood."

"What blood?" cried Jenny.

But Masters, at the deliberate walk he had never lost since he was a policeman on a beat, had disappeared into the mist. Jenny's eyes asked Martin the same question.

"It's a joke," he growled. Like other things, he had forced the matter of that dagger out of his consciousness; shut the lid on it. "Just some horseplay at the prison. That fellow," he snarled, "was only trying to scare you when he didn't know a thing. Let's forget it."

They climbed the fence, navigated several ditches, and walked for some time in silence when his words seemed to ring with vibrations in Jenny's voice.

"You're quite right," she said. "Let's forget it! Today is—Sunday, isn't it? Let's forget it! Let's enjoy ourselves!"

"And tomorrow," said Martin, "you go to London with me. You must have *some* friends who aren't under the eye and grip of Grandma, and you can stay with them. We can get a special license soon, if you don't mind being married in a registry office. Will you do that?"

"Of course," Jenny said simply "Anywhere, any time. I *did* think it would be better to get Grandmother's approval, because she says she's beginning to like you; but—"

Martin stopped short.

"Listen, Jenny angel." He touched her moist cheek, and looked down at the eager blue eyes. "It's a good thing I'm reasonably honest. Anybody you like seems able to deceive you. I can no more imagine your 'good grandmother' giving us

114

her approval than I can imagine her canoodling with Sir Henry Merrivale."

He felt a compression in the chest; such an immensity of tenderness that he could not have expressed it.

"It'll be all right, you know," he said. "You needn't worry. I'm not exactly broke, and . . . damn it, come on! We're nearly home!"

For the white, square solidness of Fleet House loomed up ahead in a mist-rift, seen partly from the north side and partly from the back. They were nearly on the edge of a flowergarden, whose paths they managed with care, until they emerged across a clipped lawn at the back of the house. To Martin Drake, this morning, Fleet House had no forbidding quality at all.

"I suppose," Jenny said, in a voice which asked to have the supposition denied, "you'll want to sleep for hours and hours?"

"Sleep? Sleep!" He chortled from deep springs of happiness. "No, Jenny. What I want is a bath, a shave, and a change. But first I want quantities of very black, very strong tea."

"I'll make it for you."

Martin surveyed the back of the house. "But how do we get in?"

"Darling, nobody ever locks doors hereabouts. Anyone can walk in anywhere."

"But we'll wake the whole house up, won't we?"

"Wait; I've got it!" breathed Jenny. She pointed to a middle door hardly discernible through mist. "I'll go into the kitchen and make tea; Aunt Cicely won't mind. You go on up to the roof."

"The roof?"

"It will be above the mist, and clear air. We can do it without disturbing anybody, and we'll have the whole place to ourselves. I'll be up as soon as the kettle boils."

"That," declared Martin, "is one of the better ideas. But can't I help you?"

"Please let me do it myself," begged Jenny Her look was irresistible . . . "If you knew how much I want to . . . to show . . . Please let me do it myself, and bring it up to you!"

"Yours to command, Jenny." It pleased him immensely. "Can I get up to the roof from here?"

Jenny indicated a small door at the north-west corner.

"The stairs," she said, "are enclosed. It's a kind of thin box. Do be careful, because they're nearly as steep as a carpeted ladder."

"I know. I've gone up there from another floor." He looked at the kitchen, and then at Jenny. "Ten minutes?"

"Less, if I can make it."

With even more acute exhilaration, Martin sauntered through mist-wreaths towards the door. It was set up well above ground-height, on five concrete steps. The stairs, if he remembered correctly, were very narrow; they turned back the other way at each landing, which had a window and a door. Though half expecting to find the door bolted, he discovered it was open. He had shut himself into the cramped stair-well, whose dingy carpet showed holes and whose window-light filtered through mist, when another door at his right hand opened.

Framed in the doorway, against the dim-lit background of the dining-room, stood Dr. Hugh Laurier.

From his hard white collar to his polished shoes, from the precision of the dark necktie to the pressing of the dark blue suit, Dr. Laurier was so immaculately groomed that Martin felt like a tramp dragged out of an areaway. On Dr. Laurier there might never have been a speck of dust in his life.

"Capta—I beg your pardon: Mr. Drake."

His voice had the pleasant, engaging professional level.

"Ordinarily," Dr. Laurier uttered a short laugh, "it would be hard to explain my presence at this hour. It would, indeed. But I was like the boy with the serial story. After going home, I returned here. I *had* to know what happened."

"You'll have to ask Stannard," replied Martin, feeling at his unshaven chin. "He'll be along in a moment."

"Mr. Stannard didn't come back with you?"

"No."

"Isn't that rather odd?"

"Nothing odd about it. I didn't feel like having company, that's all."

Martin started to take a step up, but the doctor detained him.

"Mr. Drake. One other matter. I could not—" Dr. Laurier emphasized the words more than italics can convey—"speak of this in the presence of others. I want to say a word or two; then ask you not to remember it."

"Of course."

Dr. Laurier peered behind him. In the dining-room, the tall curtains of heavy red velvet were still drawn closely. The light of a single small bulb in a wall lamp touched his grey hair, his pince-nez. Martin remembered him silhouetted against a different radiance.

116

"Mr. Drake. My slip with the rapier was honestly an accident."

"But, man! I never thought it was anything else!"

The other smiled whimsically.

"So many times," he said, "I have thrown myself under my opponent's guard. Or dropped sideways, on one knee, to cut with the double-edged blade!"

If this referred to the rules of fencing, it was weird talk. Dr. Laurier saw Martin's expression.

"In imagination," he explained dryly. "Are you well read in the history of small-arms?"

"I'm afraid not."

"There was the 'Fifty-fifty,' where you threw yourself in to catch his unedged blade in your left hand and kill him with the right. If your left hand in the least slipped, you were a dead man. There was the Spanish 'Low-High' with double-edgers: you parried a cut low to the right; you dropped on one knee to cut across the back of the knees above the ankles; then rose and thrust him through the side. There was the 'Vanity': a very narrow mirror set into the blade along its length. Only a thread of it, unperceived till play began; but it blinded him with its flash.

"There was the *botte de Jésuite*, mentioned in *Esmond*. It really existed, and was a perfectly fair device of swordsmanship, unlike the others; they were outlawed.—But I bore you," Dr. Laurier added evenly.

"Not a bit. But some other time . . ."

"I speak," said the doctor, "of what interests me privately. It is the hobby of a lonely man. Do you understand?"

"I do."

"Nor am I a good swordsman as yet. Who can be, with so little opportunity to practice? My father fought two duels."

Martin, who had been about to get away as politely as possible, felt the tangle of ugly incidents catch him again like a net of hooks.

"By the way," he said. "Chief Inspector Masters wants to see you."

Dr. Laurier looked frankly puzzled.

"Chief . . . ah, yes! He and some other man came to my home last night before I joined you here. They asked some questions, completely mysterious to me, about a clock formerly owned by my father."

"That's not on his mind now. He wants to know," Martin cleared his throat, "whether what we found on that dagger was human blood."

Dr. Laurier remained silent for a brief time.

"I regret to say," he answered, "that it was human blood."

Martin climbed the treacherous stairs. Would the lid bang on memory this time? Not quite, perhaps; but enough. Oh, to the devil with it anyway! In a very short time, any minute now, Jenny would be here. And he emerged on the roof.

Jenny was right. The roof-top lay just a few feet above the mist. In every direction it swam and hovered, so that only a few tree-tops showed green like islands. Far over across the way, the front of the Dragon's Rest lay submerged well above its gable-windows, the three gables rising to steep peaks with plaster faces and window-curtains drawn close.

The sky was clear and warm; no sun, but the hint of a sun. Dead stillness here, and it seemed as lonely as Pentecost.

As Martin took a few experimental steps to see how they sounded on concrete in this mist-world, the thought of Pentecost made him glance round.

Pentecost Prison—the observation occurred to him quite gravely—had not moved. Though it was a very long distance away, he could see the mist lapping nearly to the top of its circular wall. He could pick out no details, and wished he could.

By the way, oughtn't Stannard to be showing up soon? As Dr. Laurier had asked, where *was* Stannard?

Martin made a complete circuit of the roof, studying the short chimneys and the plentitude of garden furniture. A flick of disquiet touched him when he thought of Stannard. But the man had distinctly said he was all right; he must have lost his way in the mist.

Hold on! What's wrong with this roof-top?

Nothing *wrong*, exactly. Yet . . .

Martin was now standing towards the front, but turning slowly round to study it eastwards. There stood the orange-and-chromium chairs, settees, and tables, vivid against brownish concrete and a pale sky. When he had come up to the roof yesterday evening to see H.M. and Masters, he had taken no particular account of the furniture. Yet it seemed to him now that it was now arranged—especially the folding beach-chairs—in a different pattern.

Nonsense! The furniture didn't get up, sportively, and rearrange itself overnight. Such furniture, which suggested cocktail glasses and a portable gramophone, could hold no suggestion of the sinister. Then why was he having this damnable feeling of being watched?

Watched from where?

This was only reaction from last night. That exhilarated mood couldn't have lasted anyway. A number of people were peacefully sleeping underneath him.

"But I've seen the other kind of murderer too," he could remember Stannard saying, at a time which now seemed weeks instead of days ago. "That's why I don't scoff at spiritual evil."

Very well. Yet, whatever constitutes spiritual evil, it is confined to the dark and the unseen way. It has no strength, it is even ludicrous, in the calm early hours of a Sunday morning, on a commonplace roof-top where the furniture suggests a place for a party.

Martin strolled towards the northern side—careful of that ledge, now!—near the front. Again he looked towards Pentecost Prison, wondering about Stannard. As he did so, two sentences went through his head.

"I regret to say that it is human blood."

And, recurring from another time, another he had remembered before:

"If you should hear the alarm-bell in the night, it will mean we are in serious trouble."

He would like to see that alarm-bell. It would show the exact position of the condemned cell, where its rope hung. But, at such a distance, this was impossible. Idly he had noticed beside him a square table with a glassy-looking orange top. It might do for the tea-tray when Jenny arrived. On the table, he now suddenly observed, lay a pair of field-glasses.

Martin laughed aloud. This was like making a wish and having it answered by a flick of the lamp. They were very old glasses of antiquated pattern: the leather scuffed and peeling, the leather strap worn thin. But they might, as a matter of curiosity, find the bell on top of the prison. He picked up the field-glasses.

"Jenny, where's that tea?" he called aloud.

Easy! Mustn't go bawling 'where's that tea' when people are trying to sleep on a lethargic morning with all the windows open. He had said it only because again he felt that someone, with steady and shining eyes, was watching him. Never mind! He turned back to the field-glasses.

It is later than you think.

What made him hesitate, and inspect the glasses more closely, was not the motto on the sundial. It was an idea. He was not well posted on the facts of the Fleet case; H.M. and Masters had said little or nothing. But he did know, from two persons' accounts, that Sir George Fleet had come up to the roof with a pair of field-glasses.

Martin's first idea, characteristically, was a recollection of that grisly ghost-story by M. R. James, in which such glasses contain a fluid brewed from dead men's bones. Then, with a hot-and-cold sensation, he wondered if he might have solved the Fleet mystery while still knowing only a part of the facts.

You could, they said, play strange tricks with optical illusions.

As for the technical side—curse the technical side: he had no knowledge—that could only be guesswork.

"But suppose," Martin said aloud to the mist-world about him, "there's something wrong with the lenses that make distances wrong. He walks towards the front of the roof. He thinks he's farther from that six-inch parapet than he really is. He comes nearly to the edge, starts to take another step, stumbles as though he'd been pushed . . ."

It could be tried. Martin, facing towards Pentecost Prison and well back from the edge, lifted the field-glasses to his eyes. The lenses were polished, in focus for about a hundred yards, and very clear. Yet such is the power of suggestion, in such fashion can it poison, that he could not keep the glasses at his eyes for more than a brief look. He rattled them down on the glassy-looking table.

This infuriated him. Were those glasses left here, so very obviously, either to entrap or hoax him? Nonsense; it was all nerves.

Very deliberately, to show himself it was so, he turned round. He sauntered to the front of the roof at the middle, and stood just inside the little ledge. Deliberately he looked out over a countryside submerged in mist: left, right, and across to the gables of the Dragon's Rest.

Then two things happened.

A distant sound—on its first tremor faint and creaky, but gathering volume, gathering voice—shook out with a creak-and-clang, creak-and-clang, metallic bell-notes banging across a hush of morning, clang-and-call, clang-and-call, so that Martin stood rigid with realization of what it was. The alarm-bell at Pentecost was ringing.

He did not turn round. He had not time to turn round.

A pair of human hands, just behind him, lunged out and gave him a violent shove in the middle of the back.

Martin had just that flash-hundredth of a second, with the bell-note in his ears, to understand he had been pitched forward—head foremost, but a little sideways—pitched forward over the ledge into a sea of mist. After that he felt no pain; he felt nothing at all.

Chapter 13

From the right came a faint, steady ticking, just outside the circle of a shaded light. The ticking grew stronger (it was a watch on a table) just as did reality. Consciousness looked out through almost-closed eyelids.

The first thoughts of Martin Drake were those which he had once or twice entertained during war-time. They were as follows:

Well, here I am again. What the hell's happened *now?* Pause for long reflection. Either this is damn serious or it's not serious at all, because I don't feel much. Ah, clever idea. I'm not flat on my back; I'm propped up somehow.

Still with his eyelids open only a slit, Martin sent tentative movements through his body. He felt stiff and shaken, but he wasn't bound up in anything. His right shoulder and a part of the chest pained, but his exploring left hand found no splint or bandage. He had a slight headache; yes, but only what felt like a smallish, narrow, oblong bandage.

Whereupon memory returned like an electric shock.

This wasn't war-time. He had been jabbed in the back by somebody's hands; he had taken a half-turning dive over the ledge into mist, with a bell-note in his ears and panic in his vitals. Sheer incredulity at the fact of being alive shook him fully alert; and he looked round wildly.

At his bedside, to the right, was a large face, squarish and wrinkled, with an acquiline nose and a steady grey eye.

"Captain Drake," said the Dowager Countess of Brayle.

Martin shut his eyes, and opened them again.

(And upon thy dazzling face, O madonna, I must first rest my eyes after being picked up off the flagstones and somehow pieced together. It couldn't be Jenny. It couldn't even be a good-looking nurse. It had to be You).

"Captain Drake," pursued Lady Brayle, "I will tell you very briefly what you wish to know. First: you are in the bedroom of the late Sir George Fleet. Second: the time is nearly ten o'clock on Sunday night. Third: Dr. Laurier has had to put five stitches across your forehead. Aside from this and some bad bruises, you have suffered no hurt."

121

Martin, propped up on both elbows, was staring at her incredulously.

"No—hurt," repeated Lady Brayle, with measured emphasis. "Dr. Laurier has kept you under opiates all day, in case there were effects of shock. *I* thought it unnecessary; and indeed," she glanced at him, "that appears to be the case."

Martin leaned back on his pillow, head aching, to consider this. Then he pushed himself up again.

"Let's get this straight," he begged. "I fell off a forty-odd-foot roof on to flagstones? And all I've got are some bruises and five stitches in my head? How did *that* happen?"

"You owe your life to Providence. Remember that, Captain Drake, in your prayers tonight."

"Yes, but how did Providence operate?"

Lady Brayle's lips tightened.

"Also," she said, and looked away, "to an accident. I believe your acquaintance, the unspeakable Merrivale, was somehow concerned in it."

"Old H.M.? What did he do?"

"You may or may not have observed," said Lady Brayle, "that outside this house, some distance above the front door, there is a very large awning coloured orange. This is usually kept folded up on an iron frame."

"Wow!"

"I beg your pardon?"

Only too well Martin remembered that orange-coloured awning; and, yesterday, H.M. standing in the middle of the gravel path, his fists on his hips and an expression of malevolence on his face, looking up at the awning above Martin's and Ruth Callice's heads.

"As for Henry," continued Lady Brayle, now with a handkerchief at her lips, "I sometimes think, you know, he must be feeble-minded. According to the maid Phyllis he actually gave money to the gardener—"

"I know! I was there when Phyllis said so!"

"Ah, but for what purpose? The gardener was to go out in the middle of the night—the middle of the night, if you please!—and lower the awning so as to shade the terrace!

"By such acts of stupidity," said Lady Brayle, her voice rising strongly, "does good come about in this world. When you fell, I am informed, the loose canvas of the awning broke your fall like a firemen's whatever-the-term-is. Then the awning ripped, and let you slide through. You have had a most extraordinary escape, Captain Drake."

"The Old Maestro!" Martin said softly.

"I'm afraid I don't understand," said Lady Brayle.

On the bedside table there were cigarettes and his lighter. Martin, in the act of stretching out a painful right arm for them, stopped and looked at her. His glance said, 'Whatever is going on in that twisty brain of his, he saved my life and you know it.' Lady Brayle's lofty stare replied: 'Kindly refrain from mentioning objectionable subjects.'

This duel of glances became, as it were, so silently audible that anger gathered round Lady Brayle's mouth. Martin's stare did not fall. Instead Lady Brayle rose up from her chair, shaking shoulders which appeared massive in heavy tweed, and paced up and down the room.

"It may be conceded," said Lady Brayle, "that Henry sometimes possesses the vulgar cunning to outwit criminals."

"Thank you."

"But he is despicable," said Lady Brayle, breathing hard.

"I hadn't observed it."

"Constantly he consorts with low company. Never once does it enter his head—" this was the real grievance—"that their station is in any way inferior to his. His childish vanity, which makes him seriously imagine he is a model of deportment like Lord Chesterfield, is infuriating. On his vile tempers and obscene language I need not dwell. Even now, I believe, he is downstairs explaining to poor Cicely how he was once a Cavalier poet."

"Lady Brayle," Martin interrupted, "where's Jenny?"

Lady Brayle flowed into this without even seeming to notice the change of subject.

"Jennifer," she corrected him, "has gone home. On my specific order. Her behaviour here today was unladylike and even disgusting. No less than twenty times, by my own counting, Dr. Laurier had to assure her you were not at death's door. The speech she addressed to you—well, I make no comment."

This bedroom, uncompromisingly masculine, was a large square room with striped wall-paper and heavy oak furniture, dimly lighted by the bedside lamp. Lady Brayle stopped short in her pacing and loomed over the bed.

"Captain Drake," she began formally.

There was something strange in her tone. Martin, in the act of lighting a cigarette, blew out the lighter-flame.

"Yes?"

Lady Brayle seemed to be pushing, pushing hard against some door inside herself, to struggle out. It was a difficult business.

"I sat here tonight," again she pushed at the door, "for one specific purpose. I wished to say—" She stopped. "From what I had heard of your behaviour from certain sources, I was beginning to believe you possessed the qualities (and also the imperfections, which are just as necessary) of a gentleman."

There was a pause.

At this point (perhaps) Martin might have ended the feud. But he didn't trust the old girl an inch, not one inch. And his face showed it.

"Thank you," he said gravely. "You sat here tonight to tell me that?"

"Yes, yes, of course!" retorted his companion, with rather too much haste, "What other reason could there have been?"

"I can't say."

"But I no longer," snapped Lady Brayle, "think my belief to have been a true one." Her voice became colourless. "It remains only for me to give you your orders. On the table beside you you will find a yellow pill. Take that, with water from the glass, and lie back. Tomorrow you will be perfectly fit."

Martin, putting down cigarette and lighter, instantly threw back the bed-clothes and slid his legs out of bed. He was wearing his own pyjamas, and his slippers were beside the bed.

"If you don't mind, Lady Brayle," he suggested pointedly, "I'd like to get dressed. —You've guessed, of course, that Jenny and I are to be married."

"That, Captain Drake, can await discussion later."

"Can I reach you tomorrow morning?"

"Fortunately or unfortunately," replied Lady Brayle, taking up a handbag from the chest of drawers, "no. I am driving tonight to visit some friends at Priory Hill, and I shall not return until the afternoon. Then there will be the fair."

"The fair?"

"Has Jennifer told you nothing of the fair?"

Martin drew his hand down over his face. "She did say something . . ."

"Among my records," Lady Brayle informed him triumphantly, "there is a document, dated 1662. By permission of the King, an annual fair may be held within the park of Brayle Manor. The town-council," she shook her shoulders, "have opposed this project. I have informed them that I will sue them for five thousand pounds if one of their representatives sets foot inside the park.

"Cromwell, by which I mean the vile Oliver, sought to suppress these fine old wholesome English customs. Doubtless there will be grinning-matches through horse-collars, and quarterstaff bouts; perhaps even a Maypole."

Lady Brayle, having reached the door, spoke as though she were addressing a public meeting. Then her face seemed to close up; to retreat.

"Now," she said, "you must excuse me. My friends at Priory Hill wish to hear the details of a—of a most unpleasant affair at Pentecost Prison this morning."

"The bell!" exclaimed Martin.

Until this moment, his own grace-of-God escape from death had swept away everything else.

"The alarm-bell," he said, "was ringing from Pentecost. The alarm-bell from the condemned cell. Stannard . . . What happened there?"

Lady Brayle regarded him coolly.

"You have had your orders," she informed him. "You must not excite yourself." And she went out and closed the door.

Martin stumbled over his slippers when he sprang forward. Then he stopped and put them on. Pain knifed across his forehead, the effect of opiates still lingered, and (to tell the truth) not many of his joints seemed to work well. But he had his wits with him.

Thank the Lord he had brought that suitcase across from the inn last night. Across the room stood a gigantic wardrobe, with a long mirror. As he reached out to open the door of the wardrobe, he saw his own face.

Wow! Though the bandage was small enough, he had not counted on the swelling and discolouration of the forehead, which made him resemble someone out of a horror-film. Never mind appearances; and somebody had given him a shave. Inside the wardrobe were clothes: clean, fresh clothes.

When Lady Brayle opened the door, it had disclosed a modern bathroom. Martin brushed his teeth, doused and doused his face and head in water, and felt better. Physically, that is. While he dressed, automatically putting on his wrist-watch, the full implications of this business spread through his mind.

Whatever had happened to Sir George Fleet, his own fall had been no accident. Some person, man or woman, had lunged with a solid pair of hands and sent him over the edge to crush his skull on flagstones. Someone hated him that much.

Why, for God's sake? And who?

It was nonsense. It couldn't be anybody he had met hereabouts. In imagination, their faces all smiled at him. And yet Stannard's 'spiritual evil,' his 'man-eating tiger' of fancy, might be close. What made Martin Drake shiver was not so much the attempted murder as the consciousness of all that hatred directed against himself.

H.M. had somehow foreseen this. He must get to H.M. And the old man, Lady Brayle had said, was downstairs now.

Trying to find the position of his own bedroom, Martin threw open the window-curtains on windows wide up in the breath of a perfect summer night deepening from dimness into dark. Sunday would be early closing for the Dragon; across the road he could see the last customers being turned out against a background of lighted door and small-paned lighted windows.

His bedroom was at the north-east corner front. Hence—

Martin went through the bathroom, obviously an addition making two rooms smaller. The room beyond was dark. Groping across it, he felt his knees begin to shake and the sensation that someone was following, just behind, to push him over an edge.

"Steady!" Martin said. But you can't argue with feelings like that.

Groping wildly, he bumped into a desk and after a moment found the chain of a desk-lamp. When the light sprang up, healing to nerves, he sat back heavily in the desk's swivel-chair.

And Martin waited to get his breath back.

He was in Sir George Fleet's study, no doubt of it. That was where Stannard had sat with his host before Fleet hurried up to the roof, just as Martin had heard Stannard speak of it.

Along the west wall were the gun-racks, behind folding glass doors. A ledge of silver cups, kept bright, ran round the other walls. Cricket-bats, once the whitest of white ash and now brown-grey from use and age, were inscribed in red with the dates when George Fleet had made a century. Between the windows, where the desk stood sideways, hung a picture of a man who must be Fleet himself. Aunt Cicely—old ghosts, old and deep loves;—must have put it there.

Stern kind of bloke, Martin thought. Thin military-looking face, ridged hair parted in the middle, cropped moustache. Then Martin glanced down at the desk-blotter, and in a few seconds began to grin.

It was only a grey-covered book, open and face down. But its title, which was *The Cavaliers, 1625-1649*, made it seem an odd book for this particular room. Martin turned it over and glanced at the flyleaf. He was greeted by the following formidable and menacing announcement of ownership, done in red crayon:

ME—H.M.

The old maestro himself seemed to scowl out of that flyleaf, warning with ferocity an attempted book-pincher to keep away. Martin's grin became a laugh, and he got up. It was infernal nonsense, letting these bugbears weaken his knees and letting him grow soft. Noting the position of the door, he switched off the lamp and walked slowly to the door.

The upper hall outside was luxuriously furnished and softly lighted. At the rear was the staircase, beside its tall arched window. He went downstairs without a tremor, walked to the front of the lower hall with its polished hardwood floor; and hesitated. But he did not hesitate long.

Green Room and library, which were on the right as you faced the front door from inside, showed no light. But a faint glow filtered out from the left-hand door at the front.

Also, Martin heard a familiar voice.

"Honest-Injun," the voice rumbled with a faint note of surprise, "you'd like to hear all about it?"

"I'd love to," said the attractive and still-young voice of Aunt Cicely.

"You want to know what Charles the First said about me?"

"I do, really,"

"Ahem!" said the other voice, beginning to take on a stern, stuffed air.

Martin peered round the edge of the door.

In a drawing-room rich with the luxury of twenty years ago, Aunt Cicely was sitting at one side of the tall mantelpiece just opposite. In her upraised face there was no trace of amusement; she was, Martin saw, deeply fascinated. At the other side of the mantelpiece, his back to it, Sir Henry Merrivale stood swelling with the same stuffed, heroic look.

The muffled lamps, dull red or white, struck gleams from a wine-coloured carpet. It was a setting for romance.

"This here," said H.M., whipping out a pocket-book and extracting a typewritten slip, "is a quotation from the *Dictionary of National Biography*, edition of 1889. It ain't there now, because a lot of people have got born since and they don't pay any attention to the arts. But here's just what it says.

" '*Merrivale, Sir Curtius, first baronet. (1583-1645?). Knighted by James I., created baronet Charles I. Poet, duellist, and lover of fair women.*' "

Here H.M. gave a short cough, and glanced sideways behind his spectacles.

" '*He is best known for his lyric poetry, later collected by Anthony à Wood. Many present-day critics, including Mr. Andrew Lang, consider his best work—notably the lyric*

127

called, "Come rest in this bower, my honey-haired bride,"—*to be the equal of Herrick.'* How's that, hey?"

"It's lovely!" said Aunt Cicely, her eyes far away. " 'Come rest in this bower, my honey-haired bride.' Could you recite it?"

H.M. touched his neck and made a long challenging noise.

"You got a throat-spray?" he inquired.

"Really, I . . ." Aunt Cicely looked round vaguely. "I'm afraid . . ."

"Never mind," H.M. consoled her. "We'll come back to that. Lord love a duck, I'll give it all the organ-stops I had when I played Richard the Third for Henry Irving. You just lemme go on with this."

"Of course, Sir Henry."

" *'Charles the First'*—are you gettin' this, hey?—*'Charles the first is said to have remarked of him: "No man of fairer manners was ever about us." His tragic marriage to Lucy Baimbridge, and the duel that followed, are well known. In the middle years of his life there is a long gap, which Anthony à Wood was evidently unable to trace.'*

"A gap in his life?" exclaimed Aunt Cicely. "What tragic fate was it?"

"Well," said H.M., "they stuck him in the coop."

"I . . . I beg your pardon?"

"Into the 'foul, heynouse' jail of Newgate they stuck him," roared H.M., beginning to fire up. "Three times they did. It was a put-up job, of course. The Cecils did it."

"You mean they persecuted him?"

"Oh, my wench!" said H.M., momentarily forgetting the heroic atmosphere and shaking his head dismally. "It was the scummiest piece of work in history, and I'm goin' to write a monograph to prove it.

"Looky here!" he went on with inspiration. "You just imagine him (or, as it might be, me) standing up at the Old Bailey to face his accusers the first time. You imagine him (or, as it might be, me) in a big lace collar, with his Cavalier hair down to his shoulders, lookin' up at the bench like this."

Here H.M., with his arms hooked out at his sides, squared off and directed a glare of martyrdom about half way up the opposite wall.

"The place," he added, suddenly turning round to explain in a normal voice, "was as full of Cecils as the Café Royal is of drunks on Saturday night. Got that?"

"Yes, I follow you! But . . ."

"But Curtius Merrivale (or, as it might be, me) folded his

128

arms, like this. And he looked up at the judge. And: 'Me lord,' he says, 'this is a frame-up.' 'Have no fear, Sir Curtius,' says the judge, who was an honest man; 'for well I know,' he says, 'that there is hokey-pokey goin' on in this court.'"

"Stop it!" cried Aunt Cicely.

"Hey?"

"You're joking. You're teasing me! I don't like it."

H.M. was completely taken aback with amazement.

"Honest to God!" he said in purple-faced earnest, and lifted his right hand to take the oath.

"But they didn't say it in those words, surely?"

"Well . . . now! I was only giving you the gist of it, sort of. The original's in a manuscript I got at home."

"But you make it sound so terribly *unromantic!*"

H.M. considered this. "H'm, yes. Maybe I did make it a bit on the dry and legal side, at that."

Aunt Cicely leaned her head sideways against a wing of the chair. The dim lamp-light, in that corner dark red, made her blonde good-looks seem those of thirty instead of over fifty. One frail-looking hand trailed down over the arm of the chair.

"I've always half-believed in reincarnation," Aunt Cicely murmured. "'His tragic marriage to Lucy Baimbridge, and the duel that followed,' she quoted softly, from H.M.'s slip of paper. "Was she beautiful?"

"Uh-huh. Absolute stunner. I got her portrait at Cranleigh Court."

"My own marriage," continued Aunt Cicely in the same faraway tone, "was very happy. The world didn't understand George. He was dominant; I love dominance. Of course, with George, there was always the terrible responsibility of . . ."

"Aunt Cicely, seeming to wake up, paused. Only now did you notice that she wore rather heavy make-up, because of the pallor underneath. A bright, arch animation swept round her an aura of charm; and she almost bounced in the chair, hands clasped, to pour eager questions at H.M.

"You were saying, ma'am?" asked H.M., in a sharply different tone of voice.

It was here that Aunt Cicely caught sight of Martin in the doorway. She sprang up in consternation and solicitude; and, as he advanced in what seemed to him a steady manner, she extended both hands with their flowing sleeves.

"Mr. Drake!" she exclaimed. "You shouldn't have got up!"

Martin touched the cool fingertips.

"There's nothing wrong with me, Lady Fleet," he told her. "It was very kind of you to take such trouble." Then he turned to H.M., the rush of gratitude showing in his face. "Sir," he said, "I don't know how I'm going to thank . . ."

H.M., to conceal an exploding embarrassment which he would have denied under torture, raved and bellowed and shouted at him (for getting up) to such an extent that nobody could understand what the great man was saying. But Martin cut it short.

"H.M., how did you know someone might try to—to—" he hesitated.

"To push you off the roof?" H.M. supplied.

"To . . . *what?*" cried Aunt Cicely in horror.

H.M., his expression wooden, replied only by extending his own hands and making a lunging motion.

"But it was an accident," pleaded Aunt Cicely, retreating. Her eyes and mouth begged them to reassure her. "Sophia said so. Dr. Laurier said so. I've always thought something might happen when the young people used that roof for parties, with drinks and everything. But they get older, you know, and you simply can't do anything with them."

Her voice ran on, telling them Sophia said it only went to show, but Martin was not listening.

"H.M.," he insisted, "how did you know?"

H.M. looked uncomfortable.

"Oh, my son! I didn't know! It was only one of about eight possibilities, where I had to block the approach-shot somehow. Though, mind you, I thought it was the most probable."

Where I had to block the approach-shot somehow . . .

"Very early this morning," said Martin, clearing his throat, "Jenny and I met Masters in a field near here. I asked him if he'd been at the prison during the night. Was he by any chance keeping an eye on *my*—welfare?"

"That's right, son. All night."

"Are you trying to tell me—" the words sounded wild, but Martin could not help using them—"that I've been a kind of focus for murder?"

"Uh-huh."

"But that's impossible!"

"Son," returned H.M., without any swelling of dignity, "I'm the old man. I've got to believe," scowling ferociously, he rapped his knuckles against his bald head, "what this cokernut tells me is true. Even when Masters thought I was loopy and you won't believe it even now. I couldn't tell *you*, because— well, never mind the because. You were in a sweet whistlin' ring of danger. And you still are." H.M.'s tone changed. "Did you see who shoved you off that roof?"

"No."

"Got any idea who it was?"

"No. What's more, I'll swear my side of the roof was empty!"

Then Martin flung this aside.

"Never mind the roof," he said. "What about the alarm-bell? I heard it ring as I went over. What happened?"

"Lord love a duck, didn't old Sophie tell you?"

"No! Either she was cantankerous, or she thought it wouldn't be a good thing to tell me. Is Stannard all right? I'll never forgive myself if anything happened to Stannard. Where's Stannard?"

"Stannard?" echoed H.M., in a huge puff of astonishment. "Oh, my son! Stannard's as right as right as rain. Though," H.M. added in a curious tone, "he did get a bit of a shock. Something like you, only in a different way."

"Then if he . . . what *did* happen?"

H.M. looked at the wine-coloured carpet; teetered bulkily back and forth on his heels; hesitated, as though he could not quite place what he meant to say in the scheme of things; and looked up again.

"Murder," he answered.

And, at the same moment, the front door knocker began to rap sharply.

Chapter 14

To the sleek room, in tone dull-red and white and dark gold, these dim lamps lent at once an intimacy and a kind of religious hush. In a far corner stood a grand piano, with Sir George Fleet's framed photograph on its dull-gleaming top.

The questions which rushed from Martin—"Who was murdered? Where in the prison? When?"—were shushed by a particularly meaning look from H.M. Martin sank down into a deep sofa, feeling the pain-throbs above his eyes. All of them heard the nonchalant maid, Phyllis, saunter through the hall to open the front door.

"It's the cops again, m'lady," rose the bored voice of Phyllis from outside.

The cops, on this occasion, were represented only by Chief

131

Inspector Masters. Masters, holding a brown cardboard file in his left hand as well as the brief-case in his right, coughed with discomfort at the door of the drawing-room. His bowler hat was held under his arm.

Aunt Cicely responded automatically. Though clearly still frightened and shocked, it was apparent she had resigned herself to the belief that somebody, somehow, would take care of this matter. In white, with flowing sleeves, vivid against a Burgundy carpet, she turned to the newcomer.

"Mr. Masters! It was *so* kind of you to come!"

"Well, ah—" said Masters, completely off balance by this reception of a police officer, "I'm not here on official business, as you might say. I just wanted to pick up Sir Henry."

"*Do* please make yourselves at home!" urged Aunt Cicely, with such sincerity that even Masters believed it. "I shall have to run along to bed now, but do make yourselves comfortable. Have you got the Ovaltine, Phyllis? That's a good girl! And I must have someone to talk to before I . . . Phyllis! Where is Lady Brayle?"

"Gone home, m'lady. Long ago."

Aunt Cicely fretted. "Then I wonder . . . Mr. Masters! Is Ricky over at the Dragon?"

"Not there now, Lady Fleet. It's been closed for half an hour."

"Then I suppose," Aunt Cicely said, "he must be with Susan Harwood." And she gave a bright, inquiring smile at Martin Drake.

(Careful, now! But you don't know anything about Susan except that Ricky wants to marry her and Ruth says he's deeply enamoured, so you're safe in admitting ignorance. Besides, the maddening questions . . .)

"Susan is a dear girl," said Aunt Cicely. "But, of course—!" She laughed deprecatingly. "I mean; her father being a farmer. Not serious; and what matter? No woman can resist Ricky. I've always told him so. And I must confess," her attractive laughter rang again, "I've always been rather proud of it. It seems to reflect credit on me, somehow. What was I thinking of? Oh, yes! Retiring. Of course. Will you say good-night for me to everyone?"

Radiating charm with her smile, giving a whisk of the loose sleeve, Aunt Cicely left them.

It was just as well, Martin thought, that a harmless if somewhat feather-headed siren had gone. The tension which invaded that room, when H.M. and Masters faced each other, set his nerves tingling again.

132

"Got the stuff?" demanded H.M.

"All of it," Masters growled. "I'm fair sick of interviews, and that's a fact." He dropped hat, brief-case, and cardboard file into a chair.

Murder.

Thanking Grandmother's Providence first of all, Martin's thoughts raced on, the person killed couldn't have been Jenny. Jenny had been here today, hovering over him, her behaviour being 'unladylike and disgusting.' Lady Brayle and Aunt Cicely were both very much alive. So was Dr. Laurier, whom he had met here in this house early in the morning.

(In front of him, like mumbled voices heard in a crowded room, he was conscious of H.M. and the Chief Inspector talking away. Masters was pointing at Martin, and asking questions about the fall off the roof. H.M. was growling that the victim seemed to have no evidence; and up went Master's blood-pressure again. But little of this penetrated to Martin.)

The person killed, he was thinking, couldn't have been Stannard either. Stannard was as right as rain. Now he knew it couldn't have been Ricky, because Ricky's mother had just asked whether her son was at the pub. That left only . . .

"Look here!" Martin exclaimed, and jumped up. "Was it Ruth Callice?"

Both the others—Masters with his face red instead of ruddy, H.M. taking out a cigar—swung round.

"Burn it all, son, don't start shoutin' like that," complained the latter, making fussed gestures. "Was she what?"

Martin felt a hollow of dread, with a pulse to it, inside his chest.

"Was she the victim? Did somebody kill Ruth?"

Yes, his voice had been loud. In the north wall of the room towards the west, a door opened. It opened to show a glimpse of a billiard-room, corresponding with the library on the other side of the house.

Ruth Callice came out of the billard-room, and John Stannard after her. They were noticed neither by H.M. nor by Masters. But Martin saw them, and slowly sat down again.

"Listen," said H.M., standing in front of Martin. "The victim hasn't got anything to do with you; and I'm trying to drive it through Masters's head that the victim hasn't got anything directly to do with the case either."

"Ho," said Masters, and snorted like a bull. "A murder slap-bang in our laps, and it hasn't got anything to do with the case."

"Regardin' motive," H.M. insisted over his shoulder, "no."

133

He turned back to Martin. "You put up at the pub, didn't you? Didn't you meet the Puckstons?"

"Puckstons? That's the—?"

"Yes. Father, mother, and daughter."

"I met Puckston, yes, and I think I saw his wife. I don't remember any daughter."

"Enid Puckston," said H.M. His expression was not pleasant. "Only a kid . . ."

"Oh, ah," muttered the Chief Inspector. "Only a kid. Like the one twenty-two years ago."

"She was the pride and joy," said H.M., slowly and heavily, "of those people's hearts. Goin' to a fancy school, she was. Not harming anybody."

"Last night at Pentecost," Masters interrupted, "she was stabbed through the heart and (hurrum!) pretty badly mutilated. What's more, for a fair-to middling certainty, she was killed with that dagger your crowd found in the condemned cell."

For some time nobody spoke.

To Martin, Enid Puckston was only a name, not even a person to be visualized. Yet the ugliness and brutality struck through. At this point, too, he became aware that Masters was speaking not for information, but for effect; that the corner of Masters's eye had caught Ruth and Stannard over there by the billiard-room. Martin shook his head to clear it.

"Stabbed and mutilated," he repeated. Then he looked up. "Was she—?"

Masters now spoke almost blandly.

"No, sir. She wasn't violated, if that's what you mean. Or any attempt like it. Might have been anybody's crime. Might have been—" here Martin could have sworn the Chief Inspector was about to say 'man or woman,' but checked himself—"might have been anybody who'd got what they call a strong sadistic nature. With their flummy talk nowadays," he added.

"Where was she found?"

"Ah! As to that, now!"

Straightening up, with an air of surprise and grave welcome, Masters turned round in the direction of Ruth and Stannard.

"Evening, miss! Evening, sir!" he intoned, as though he had just seen them. "Didn't notice you in the dark. I'd be glad to have a bit of a chat with both of you, if it's convenient."

"Yes, of course," answered Ruth, whose eyes were fixed on Martin. Abruptly, as though breaking loose, she ran across the room and took Martin's hands.

"So you're up and about!" Ruth added, scanning his face and forehead. She added, as though in reproach: "Martin, you look *horrible.*"

He grinned at her. "No worse than a hangover. Honestly!"

Stannard approached more slowly. H.M. had spoken of him as having had a shock, and you could well believe it. Some of his strong vitality—not too much, but some—seemed to have ebbed from him. The black eyes had no glitter; he smiled, though with visible effort. As he moved towards them he put one hand on the back of a dark-red wing chair as though his ankle hurt him.

What had he seen in that execution shed last night?

But, for that matter, Ruth herself looked far from well. She was as trim as ever, the small light-brown curls gleaming above the rounded face, her dress a close-clinging green. Yet she looked physically ill. And Martin began to understand the strain which had been growing on everybody all day.

The strain grew and grew. They seldom spoke of it. And yet

. . .

"Martin," Ruth began, and braced herself. "Some people are saying what happened to you was an accident. It wasn't, was it?"

"No. It wasn't."

Very much, now, he was conscious of H.M. and Masters in the background.

"What did happen?" asked Ruth. Then, without waiting for a reply, as though afraid of a reply she went on:

"All *I* know is that I was waked up about a quarter to five by that alarm-bell going. Then I heard a crash—"

"Great Scott, Ruth, did I fall as hard as that?"

"It was the tea-tray!" said Ruth, and snatched her fingertips away from him in a reproachful way as though he had somehow insulted her.

"What tea-tray?"

"Jenny," Ruth explained, "was carrying a loaded tea-tray through the dining-room to those little back stairs. She heard you—she heard that thud on the awning, and the awning ripping wide open, and something hitting the flagstones. And would you believe it?"

Here Ruth turned to Stannard, who, though he must have heard the story half a dozen times, only nodded.

"Would you believe it?" Ruth said to Martin. "Jenny says the front door was partway open, with mist in the hall. Jenny simply threw the whole tea-tray to one side and rushed out. She found you lying on the terrace in the mist, with blood

135

coming out of your forehead. Then Jenny began screaming. By that time I was there, and Ricky came flying downstairs in his pyjamas. Poor Cicely was tired out and slept through it. Fortunately Dr. Laurier was on the spot."

Stannard, smiling, had been examining the trim of his fingernails and polishing them on the sleeve of his dark-grey suit. He grew grave now. He approached Martin, limping a little, and formally extended his hand.

"My dear fellow," he said in his husky hearty voice, "real congratulations on a lucky escape."

Everybody I meet, Martin thought, seems to want to shake hands.

"It *was* you ringing that alarm-bell?"

Stannard's look was wry. "Yes. For my sins."

Well, then, here was one hand free from attempted murder and one face without hypocrisy. Martin already liked Stannard; he liked the man better now.

"But," Ruth prompted. "Up on the roof?" She made a tentative gesture.

Martin thought he had better get it over. He told them everything, from the time he and Jenny walked through the mist to the time somebody's hands lunged out. He could see Master's black notebook, the shorthand travelling steadily. H.M. had sat down near the tall white marble mantelpiece, with its dull-gold clock and its dull-gold candelabra against dark-red walls.

When the recital was finished, neither Ruth nor Stannard commented. They did not even speak. Too much repression! Dangerous! The person who did speak, after studying Martin, was Chief Inspector Masters.

"Field-glasses, eh?" ruminated Masters. "A pair of old field-glasses, on an orange-topped table near the north-west side of the roof!"

"That's right."

"Would it interest you to know, sir, that other witnesses who went up there later didn't see any field-glasses?"

"I can't help that. They were there earlier."

"I say, Masters." H.M. raised his head briefly. "Could they 'a' been the same glasses George Fleet used on the famous day?"

Masters simmered. "For the *last* time, Sir Henry—"

"Will I stop babblin' about field-glasses, you mean? Oh, Masters, I know there were no hokey-pokey spikes to stick him in the eye! But I gather the field-glasses weren't busted; they

136

fell just wide of the terrace and on the grass. And that's why the policeman picked 'em up and carried 'em inside."

"Yes!"

H.M., an unlighted cigar in his fingers, craned round in his chair to blink at Martin.

"Now tell me, son," he said. "Supposing (just supposing!) these were the same glasses! Were they a good pair? Good lenses? Easy focus? No blurrin' that would . . ." He paused. "Were they?"

"As I told you," Martin returned, "I didn't look through them very long. But they were in first-rate condition. I'll swear to that."

"That's good news," breathed H.M. "Oh, my eye! That helps a lot."

Masters was unable to yank down his bowler hat on his head, since he was not wearing it, but his gesture conveyed this.

"The field-glasses," he said, with strong self-control, "were in A-1 order. They had nothing wrong with them. And *therefore* (eh?) they're a great big smacking-sure help to us?"

"That's right, Masters."

"Er—just so." Masters addressed himself to his notebook and to Martin. "Anything more you can tell us, Mr. Drake?"

"I don't think so." This atmosphere had become dangerously explosive, and Martin tried to lighten it. "I woke up with Lady Brayle sitting beside me. I annoyed her, and she annoyed me, so I decided to dress and come downstairs. In here I found H.M. telling Aunt—telling Lady Fleet about his previous existence as a Cavalier poet and duellist." He grinned. "By the way, sir, you ought to talk to Dr. Laurier."

"What's that, son? Hey?"

"Dr. Laurier. He's an authority on old-time fencing. He can tell you all about the 'Fifty-fifty' and the 'Low-High' and the 'Vanity' and everything else. Incidentally, he says his father fought two duels in France."

Masters barked him back to attention. But Masters himself had a grievance, and was annoyed enough to air it.

"A fat lot of good," he growled, "this gentleman Laurier did us last night!"

Martin, knowing a question would shut him up, said nothing.

"All *he* kept talking about," Masters growled, "was his father, with the big grey beard, when the gentleman was old and a bit scatty, sitting in a rocking-chair in front of that

137

infernal skeleton-clock, rocking back and forth and muttering something in French that Sir Henry says means, 'Would a man of honour have done it?'

"Ah, but not done a murder," Masters added. "Because, according to the record, he was in this very room talking to the butler when Sir George Fleet pitched off the roof." Masters started, and woke up. "Hurrum! Sorry! Off the subject! Now, Mr. Drake! What I wanted to ask—"

But he never asked it.

Masters's gaze had strayed towards H.M.; and, after a pause, Masters's expression became that of one who sees a prayed-for portent in the sky.

H.M. had sat up straight. His mouth fell open, and the unlighted cigar dropped out and rolled on the carpet. His look was fixed straight ahead behind the big spectacles; his hands were on the arm of the chair, his elbows hooked as though to push himself up. His voice, astounded, started from deep in the cellar and was at the same level when it emerged.

"Wait a minute!" H.M. begged. "Lemme think! Stop babblin' and lemme think!"

Nobody spoke. Martin, Ruth, and Stannard exchanged inquiring glances; Masters remained very quiet indeed; and H.M. fiercely pressed his hands over his head.

"But that couldn't be," H.M. addressed the empty air. "It couldn't be, unless . . . yes, burn me there was!"

His hands dropped again to the arms of the chair. With some effort he propelled himself to his feet.

"I got to go and look at something," he explained, with an air of haste and absent-minded apology. "I've been an awful ass; but I got to go and look at something now. You stay here. You play bridge or something." And he lumbered across to the hall door, where he turned right towards the interior of the house.

"By George," breathed Masters, "the old bounder's got it!"

Martin stared after H.M. "Got what?"

"Never you mind that, sir," Masters said cheerfully. "We'll get back to business. Now, Mr. Stannard!"

"I beg your pardon?" Stannard was obviously surprised.

"I said a while ago," Masters told him smoothly, "that I'd like a word with you. If you don't mind, I'd like to take a statement from you as to what happened in the execution shed last night."

The other stood motionless, a vertical line between his black eyebrows.

"If memory serves, Inspector, I gave a statement to the police this morning."

"Yes, sir. But that was to Inspector Drake. County Constabulary."

"True. And what then?"

"The Chief Constable's Office—" Masters was suave—"have got in touch with our people in London. *I'm* in charge of the case, you see. Now, about that statement . . ."

Stannard pushed back his cuff and glanced at his wrist-watch.

"It's rather late, Inspector."

"I'm afraid I've got to insist, Mr. Stannard."

Dead silence.

The light of battle sprang across that room as clearly as the opposing lamps had shone behind the fencers at Pentecost Prison last night. And Martin knew why.

Too often had John Stannard wiped the floor with the police, including Chief Inspectors of the C.I.D., in a battle of question-and-answer at the Central Criminal Court. Masters knew this; Stannard knew he knew it. They looked at each other.

Last night, Martin reflected, Stannard could have wiped the floor with Masters in such an engagement. But Stannard was shaky now; there was some horror inside him; his eyes were dull; his movements, perhaps mental as well as physical, seemed slow. Then he glanced towards Ruth Callice.

To Martin's astonishment, Ruth was looking at Stannard with an expression of . . . well, not nearly as strong as hero-worship; but something deeply moved and as near to love as made no difference. What had been happening during the past twenty-four hours? Ruth veiled her look instantly, slipping back into H.M.'s chair.

And Stannard smiled.

"I'm at your service, Inspector," he said. And vitality seemed to flow and expand through him.

He sat down at the other end of the sofa from Martin, crossed his knees, and took from his pocket a cigar in a cellophane wrapper.

"I'll make the statement," he went on, "mainly because," he looked sideways, "I think my friend Drake deserves to hear it."

"The trouble was," Martin blurted, "I thought I might have left you there helpless or dying or—God knows what."

"No. You played the game strictly according to the rules. Unfortunately, however . . ."

Sharply Masters cut across the amenities.

"You might begin," he said, "from the time Mr. Drake locked you up behind the iron door at just past midnight. Well?"

"To tell the truth," Stannard admitted, "I was not as easy in my mind as I led others to think. I have—some imagination too. But there it was: it had to be done, and more than done. So I opened the door of the execution shed." Again he looked at Martin. "You never saw it. Nor did any of the others. I'd better describe it. It was—"

"I don't want to hear any of that, sir," snapped Masters.

"Oh?" Stannard slowly turned his head back. "You 'don't want to hear any of that?'"

"No. Not by a jugful!"

"Thus," Stannard said evenly, "denying a witness his right to give testimony in his own way. The other name is coercion. May God help you if I ever quoted your words in court."

Sting went the mental whip across Masters's face. Masters, dogged and conscientious, was inwardly raving. But he remained impassive, with sheathed claws.

"Hurrum! My mistake. Go on!"

"It was a good-sized room," pursued Stannard, taking the cellophane wrapper off the cigar, "though with not a very high ceiling, as in the condemned cell. Its walls were brick painted white, pretty dirty, with two small barred windows near the top of the opposite side.

"I picked this up, detail by detail, with my light. In the centre of the floor, which was stone, I saw the gallows-trap: two big oblong wooden panels, fitting closely together and set flush with the floor-level. They would drop together when you pulled a lever. An iron beam stretched across the ceiling just over this trap. In the left-hand corner—concealed from a condemned man as he entered by the opening door—was a rather large vertical lever which controlled the drop.

"My dear Drake, do you remember the *feel* of the condemned cell just over the way? Yes; I can see you do. Well, this was worse. I had expected that. As soon as I opened the door of that execution shed, the whole room seemed to jump at me. It did not like visitors."

Chief Inspector Masters interrupted harshly.

"Just a minute, sir!"

"Yes?"

Masters had to shake his own head to clear it of a spell. Like the mist on the countryside that morning, this dim-lighted drawing-room became invaded with the shapes and sounds of Pentecost Prison.

"I ask you!" persisted Masters. "What kind of talk is that?"

"It is true talk, Inspector. Write it down."

"As you like, sir."

"A dirty white brick room, a trap, an iron beam, a lever: no other furniture," continued Stannard. Instead of lighting the cigar, he put it down on the arm of the sofa. "But I had seen a rocking-chair across the passage in the condemned cell. I went over there, fetched in the chair, and, as a matter of honour, closed the door behind me.

"I put the rocking-chair in a corner, the far corner from the door, looking obliquely across the gallows-trap towards the lever. I hung my lamp over the back of the chair and tried to read *The Cherry Orchard*. This became impossible. The influences, previously poisonous, were now devilish.

"No, Inspector! Don't make faces. I saw no ghosts and I heard none. I am prepared to admit the influences *may* have been imaginary, though I don't believe it. Everything centered round that gallows-trap.

"There, of course, the condemned person had dropped on his long or short rope—according to weight—into a brick-lined pit underneath. It was natural that these currents of hatred, of malice, of despair, should come from there or seem to come from there.

"Then I did the worst possible thing.

"I put down my book. I did what I called in my own mind —" a sardonic grin tightened back Stannard's lips—"the act of a boxer riding with the punch. I lit a cigar. I rocked in the chair, and deliberately exposed myself to whatever was here. I tried to imagine what an execution would look like. In short, I did exactly what I said Drake would do.

"I knew I was somewhat rattled; but not how rattled until . . ."

"You remember that I was sitting in the corner of the execution shed. I had been imagining the hanging of Hessler, who had tried to escape from the condemned cell. I had been wondering about this: when the doctor and other officials went down into the pit to make sure the hanged man was dead, how did they get down? Ladders? But I saw no ladders. All of a sudden I woke up from these thoughts.

"My cigar, which for some reason I had been holding near the tip, had burnt down and was searing my fingers. And I was not sitting in any corner. I was sitting in my rocking-chair on the gallows-trap itself."

Stannard paused.

He moved his right hand towards the cigar on the arm of the chair, and suddenly drew back again. Ruth Callice, a little way back from the light which touched Stannard's cheek, sat back with her eyes closed. There were bluish hollows under Ruth's eyes.

"The explanation, of course," said Stannard, "is so simple as to be almost comic. I mention it as a matter of: say unconscious muscular reaction. You're familiar, I imagine, with old fashioned rocking-chairs? And how they moved when you swung? I had simply rocked myself there.

"This sobered me. I threw that chair back and stamped out the cigar. My burnt fingers seemed to pain out of all proportion. It was now getting on towards two o'clock in the morning. And I decided to carry out an idea that . . . well, it had been in my mind from the first. I would try out that idea, and get rid of its fears."

"Idea?" demanded Masters. "What idea?"

Stannard grimaced.

"I wanted to see what would happen," he replied, "if I threw the lever and the trap fell."

Chapter 15

Stannard essayed a smile.

"There was no reason," he said, "why I shouldn't have done this before. One cause of my reluctance," he brooded, "may have been shrinking from mere *noise*. Just as all of us shrink from making loud noises in an ordinary house at night.

"I had some idea, perhaps from fiction, that it would be a boom or a crash. Logical reasoning should have told me that such trap-doors, in use, would fall smoothly and without noise. Or, at a time like this, that the machinery might not work at all.

"In any case, I laid hold of the lever and pulled. It moved a little, but only a little. I pulled again, harder. A rasping noise followed, either from the lever's mechanism or from under the trap-door. Then I laid hold, blind-determined, and put out all my weight with both hands. And the trap fell.

"With luck there would have been no more than a heavy creak. But the right-hand trap-door, too heavy for its old hinges, ripped loose and fell into the pit with a crash which seemed to bring down the roof."

Martin Drake stared at the past.

The crash which had roused him out of sleep—loud, yet not very loud because it was muffled by a heavy oak door and the inside of the pit—the crash which had roused him, at two o'clock, was just that.

But Stannard was speaking again.

"If I had expected a noise," he said, "I never expected a noise like *that*. It dazed me. Immediately afterwards," he turned his head towards Martin for a brief look, "my friend Drake called out from the grille of the iron door: 'Stannard!' And then: 'Stannard! Are you all right?' I shouted back, 'Yes! Quite!' Though I fear my voice showed—never mind.

"While I was tugging at the lever, I had put down my lamp on the floor. Now, in not quite the best state of mind, I went over to the edge, and turned the beam of the lamp down into the pit. It was square in shape, a brick-lined shaft much bigger than the oblong trap."

Stannard paused.

"Well, Mr. Masters," he added, "Inspector Drake must have told you what I saw."

"What you saw?" exclaimed Martin.

"I saw a very young girl," said Stannard, "lying on her back. Her eyes showed whitish slits, and her mouth was open. Her bodily mutilations: well, those are for the morbid. But this I saw; and it seemed to me that all the evil forces in that room were settling down on her like flies."

With a murmured apology Stannard rose to his feet. Limping a little, he went slowly to a gilt table in the middle of the room. On the table-top, of eighteenth-century mottled marble, had been set out a decanter of whisky, a syphon, and glasses. He now faced Martin and Ruth; and Masters, twitching round his own chair, also faced Stannard.

"Enid Puckston," said Masters. "Now we're getting to it!"

Stannard's eyes were glittering darkly as of old. His hand trembled very slightly as he tipped whisky into a glass.

"Enid Puckston," Masters repeated. "Did you recognize the girl, sir?"

"No. Never saw her before."

"But you guessed she was murdered? And recently?"

Stannard, in the act of pressing the handle of the syphon, gave Masters a long and almost affectionate look.

143

"Yes, Inspector," he answered. "I guessed that." Soda hissed into the glass.

"You were one of a group of people (eh?) who found a blood-stained dagger—with fresh blood—over in the condemned cell?"

"I saw it shortly after it was found, if that's what you mean."

"Just so. Didn't you (hurrum!) associate that dagger with the murdered girl?"

"Not at that moment, I think. Afterwards, naturally."

Masters was snapping at him now; and Stannard, motionless with the glass in his hand, seemed to throw his replies through half-shut teeth.

"Mr. Stannard, do you know what a person is required by law to do when they find a murdered body? —Mind your answer."

"Inform the police, I believe. —Mind your grammar."

"Ah!" said Masters. "Now I understand Mr. Martin Drake was within easy calling-distance of you . . ."

"Come to think of it," Stannard frowned, "*he* called to *me*, for a second time, shortly after I saw the girl's body. His voice seemed to come from farther away, as though he'd moved back from the grille. But he called, 'Are you sure you're all right?' "

"Did you answer that?"

"Yes. I told him to mind his own damned business."

"So you could have called for help. And yet you didn't?"

Stannard's gaze wandered towards Ruth.

"Inspector," he said tenderly, and took a deep pull at the whisky and soda, "I wouldn't have 'called for help,' as you put it, for anything on earth."

"What did you do next?"

Stannard took another deep pull at the whisky and soda, emptying the glass.

"I put my lamp on the floor. I put my hands on the edge of the shaft, opposite the side on which the trap door had fallen. I let myself hang down inside, stretching my arms to full length. Then I let go, and landed on my feet in the blood beside the dead girl."

Masters was badly jarred. "You mean—you thought you might give help of some kind?"

"Never mind my motives. That's what I did."

"Oh, ah. And then?"

"The shaft, as I had noticed before," Stannard's husky voice had grown huskier, "was ten feet deep." His vitality seemed to be ebbing, despite the whisky. "I couldn't get out. I was shut in. And I had no lamp. Consequently, all I could do was sit down in a corner and wait for daylight."

"But *why* in lum's name did you do that? If you knew the shaft was ten feet deep?"

"Chief Inspector!" Martin said sharply. And, though Masters turned a sinister eye which threatened prison or worse, Martin ignored it. "If you'll let me ask Stannard just one question, in my own way, I'll guarantee to get you out of this trouble. Is that fair, or isn't it?"

Masters made a disgusted gesture in surrender. Stannard, who had been leaning his weight with both hands on the marble-topped table, looked up with some attempt at lightness and humour.

"Your question, my dear Drake?"

Martin looked him in the eye.

"You were beginning to have the horrors," Martin said. "But you wouldn't give in. You meant to show these young swine they were pretty small beer when it came to nerve. So you deliberately dropped down into that shaft, and left your light behind, to sit in the dark near a—an ugly sight, until you were let out at four in the morning. Is that true?"

There was a silence.

"You put it bluntly," said Stannard. "However, that's true."

Ruth had sat up, her hands clenched. Despite her self-control, the tears stung to her eyes.

"Stan, you idiot!" she raved. "You utter, absolute, and complete *idiot!*"

Stannard, though clearly as blind as a bat regarding women, appeared to sense a new quality here. But he did not believe it.

"Ruth, my dear," he began, and hesitated. He was again sedate and grave. "If any foolishness of mine ever gives you the slightest concern," he said, "it will have been worth it."

And, to conceal the horror growing in him, he blundered back to the sofa and sat down in his old place. Hastily he picked up the cigar and clipped its end with a cutter; Martin passed across a pocket-lighter.

"There's little more to tell," Stannard drew in smoke deeply, "though it was perhaps—no matter. I told you I couldn't get out. There was, of course, a door at the bottom of the shaft."

"A door?" said Martin.

"Yes. Logical deduction, as I sat in my corner, convinced me that there must be one. You know the facts: you should be able to see why the door was there, its purpose, and where it led. But the door," Stannard said thoughtfully, "was locked. I found it after groping round the walls in the dark. Locked!

That, Inspector, should give you a clue to the mystery of the girl's death. As for my plight when daylight came . . ."

"Martin," Ruth cried, "only opened the iron door, and threw the key inside!"

"One moment," Stannard intervened. "It was not Drake's fault. Tell me, my dear fellow: when you fell from the roof this morning, was your wrist-watch smashed?"

The villain of the piece shook his head.

"No. It was the first thing I heard when I woke up. Ticking on my bedside table. I'm wearing it now."

"Tell me the time, will you?"

"It's . . . ten minutes past eleven."

"No," contradicted Stannard. He smiled and coughed out of cigar-smoke. "I examined your watch today. It's something over ten minutes fast. *Now* do you see why I was so badly caught?"

Martin, reconstructing last night, saw himself hauling down a heavy paper-bale to sit on: that was just after the vigil began. He remembered looking at the luminous figures of his watch, and thinking Stannard's own watch must be fast because it was well past twelve. But—Stannard was right—his watch must have been fast.

"Stan, you mustn't keep thinking about it!" urged Ruth.

"But I was never more controlled!" said Stannard. "Would you believe, Inspector, that in my brick corner I alternately dozed and woke up, and dozed and woke up? In darkness the—the poor girl beside me seemed to my imagination worse than she had looked in light. The quiet, the damned quiet! And the influences of people who'd *dropped* there!

"Presently I waked from my doze. My lamp had gone out on the floor above me; but there was a dim kind of grey from the two little windows up above. I kept my eyes on my wrist-watch; it said thirteen minutes to four. Before going down there I had opened the door of the execution shed a little way—you remember?"

"Yes. I remember," Martin said grimly.

"So that Drake would be sure to hear. Thirteen minutes to go. Then . . .

"Then Drake's voice cried, 'Stannard! Stannard! Are you all right?' Bracing myself for those last extra minutes, I was completely off balance. I managed to croak out, 'I'm here. I'm—' Whereupon he said the time was up, and he was opening the iron door. I heard the door open, and the key clatter inside. Then he said something about entertaining evening, and he was free and so was I.

"I was paralyzed. I could not utter a word. Such is the nature of an unexpected voice. Then, since he seemed to be going away . . ."

"Damn it," protested Martin, whose guilty conscience troubled him, "how could I have known you were down there?"

"You couldn't have. It was my own—call it what you like. I did find my voice, and start to call after you. You heard that?"

"Faintly. When I was on my way out."

"So I knew myself in a trap for heaven knew how long. I was there with what remained of Enid Puckston, and the other things. The only possibility was to break down the door I spoke of, the door at the front of the shaft.

"Inspector, have you ever tried this? On many, many occasions in fiction I have read, 'Twice he hurled himself at the door, and on the third attempt the lock splintered.' Well, try it. If this had been a proper prison door, I shouldn't have had a chance. But it wasn't.

"It became an endless series of kicks with a heavy country boot. Once or twice I stumbled over—Enid Puckston. I think it took half an hour. The last frantic kick, which wrenched my ankle and made me think I was done, tore the lock out of the door.

"I had my pocket-lighter, which I had not used except for a cigar or two. In front of me was a short brick passage running straight. Can you guess what it was?"

Masters, who long ago had swung his chair round again, spoke in an expressionless voice.

"No need to guess, sir. I *know* what it was."

"Oh?"

"It was the way the prison doctor and governor and the rest came down to certify death after an execution. Also the way they carried the body up again, so the prisoners wouldn't get a look at it from windows."

"Ah! So I reasoned! The passage must lead to—"

"To the prison mortuary on the ground floor of Wing B," Masters said slowly. "Along a little passage, turn left to another passage, up a flight of steps into the mortuary. Mr. Drake was sitting all night with his back to one wall of the mortuary."

"*I* was?"

"Oh, ah. The door's a little way down from where you were sitting, in the wall between the aisle and the paper-bales. Listen, Mr. Stannard!"

Masters held up a pencil and studied its point.

"We know how you got up into the mortuary, pretty well done in," said Masters, "*and* with a bad ankle. You managed to get to the condemned cell, and rang the alarm-bell till the rope broke. The constable found you there afterwards. Now could you give me some *answers?*"

"What the devil do you think I've been doing?"

"Now, now! No call to get excited!"

Stannard's cigar had burnt down raggedly. He dropped it into an ashtray beside the sofa. With some fervency Martin wished that the Chief Inspector, who could at times be as yielding yet as smothering and stifling as a feather bed, would end a questioning which was having such bad effect on——Ruth, for one.

"You smashed the locked door to the underground passage. Oh, ah! You had a pocket-lighter? Oh, ah! Was there a key in this lock on the other side?"

"No."

"Though you'd been told no doors were locked at the prison except the main gates?"

"It *was* the only locked door." Stannard, his black eyebrows raised, leaned forward and again seemed to throw back the words through half-closed teeth. "The hinges of the front gates were oiled, though *I* didn't oil them. The lock and hinges of that door were oiled, though *I* didn't oil them. Are your wits beginning to wake up?"

"Maybe, sir! Maybe! Were there blood-spots in that underground passage?"

Ruth tried to, and only just succeeded in, stifling a gasp.

"Yes," Stannard said briefly. "I didn't tread in them."

"And blood-spots in the other passage? Where it turned left, I mean?"

"Yes."

"And blood-spots on the stairs up to the mortuary?"

"A few."

"What was Miss Puckston's body lying on, sir? On the floor, or on anything else, like?"

"She was lying," Stannard pressed his hands over his eyes, "on a fairly large travelling-robe or lap-robe, plaid in colour, with each corner rather twisted up. As though . . ."

"Ah! As though somebody'd twisted the ends together like a parcel, and carried her there?"

"I can't be expected to answer that."

"Just so. Still——!" Honey flowed in Masters's heavy voice. "Didn't you investigate any blood-spots in the mortuary?"

Stannard stared straight ahead.

"There was a door in the mortuary," he replied, "which led out into a big fan-shaped garden, with a prison wing on each side and a spiked wall at the end. It was on the side of the condemned cell. There was a white moving mist. The garden had gone to ruin, but it was overrun with flowers. Red, blue, yellow; I don't know their names.

"Yes, yes, I went out there! In a square patch of grass there was a scuffed space where the travelling-rug may have been placed. That was the way Hessler must have gone."

"Who's this 'Hessler' you keep mentioning?"

"A mutilating murderer."

"What about him?"

"He poisoned his guards in the condemned cell. Logic, Inspector! He ran to the execution shed, opened the trap that would receive him, and jumped down. He reached the mortuary by way of the passage and the stairs. They shot him in the shoulder as he was climbing the spiked wall, and he fell back into a flower-bed. All this I saw too: in the mist."

With some effort Stannard got up. All his vitality had gone; his jaw sagged. He caught a brief flash of it when he addressed Ruth and the others.

"My dear," he said formally, and took Ruth's hand again as though she were made of china, "Lady Fleet has asked us to stay on tomorrow. I can rearrange *my* engagements to suit it, if you can?"

"Yes! I can arrange it! Of course!"

"Thank you. And now, gentlemen," added Stannard, quite convinced they would believe every word he said, "this country air has a tendency to make me sleepy. Yes. It's past eleven, and I think I'll turn in. We have had—ah—a most interesting discussion. We must continue it soon. Yes. Good night."

And the shortish, stocky barrister, his dark hair gleaming, sauntered to the door while he firmly put down his bad ankle to keep from limping: facing the world with defiance, as though he carried a sword.

There was a long silence, even after they faintly heard his footsteps slacken and slow down on the stairs.

"I didn't think," Martin said slowly, "there were any knights-errant left in this world. But, by God and all honour to him!—there goes one of them!"

Ruth, who was standing and looking anxiously at the door, immediately showed her state of mind by attacking Martin.

" 'Knights-errant,' " she scoffed in her quiet voice. "Don't you see all he needs is somebody to look after him?"

"The Great Defender?"

149

"Oh, rats!" said Ruth. "All he needs is someone to—to let him be a *little* idiotic but keep him solid and distinguished, which you've got to admit he is. And take you, Martin!"

Again he recognized, as he had recognized last night, that long-lingering if tender note of satire: which, like an arrow on a string, must be drawn to full arc before it is fired. Mentally, he shied back.

"Hold on, now! This is no time for discussing my imperfections!"

"You loathe being taken care of. For instance: are you hungry? You know you haven't had a bite to eat since last night?"

For some reason Martin's gorge rose sickeningly at the very thought of eating.

"Woman," he said, "if there's one thing on this earth I *WILL NOT* stand, it's being pestered with admonitions to eat something. Especially when I'm working. Food!" He was about to say, 'to hell with food,' when the mocking imp at the back of his brain reminded him that he also was shaky, from a fall off a roof, and not quite rational.

"You see?" smiled Ruth, turning up her palm.

"See what?"

"You like the clinging-vine," said Ruth, "who undoubtedly would manage your house so inefficiently, Martin dear, that you'd get furious and run it yourself." Ruth hesitated, and tears came into her eyes. "I don't know what I'm doing here," she said, "I *must* see poor Stan gets safely upstairs."

And, her green dress flashing, she ran out of the room.

During these remarks, which he had not heard, Chief Inspector Humphrey Masters was for once off his official dignity. He leaned back in his chair, his boiled blue eye contemplating a corner of the ceiling. On his face was a trace of reluctant admiration.

"Now if I might ask you, Mr. Drake," he mused, after ruminating for a while, "what did you make of that little 'statement?'"

"With Stannard, you mean?"

"Clever!" said Masters, shaking his head. "Oh, ah! Just as wide as they make 'em; and I've met a few in my time. Did you notice he never once mentioned the alibi?"

"*What alibi?*"

"Come, now! You found that dagger at close on midnight. Even allow a mix-up with watches: 'tisn't much one way or the other. Dr. Laurier testified (and testifies) the blood was fresh within half an hour. Say half-past eleven or a bit later. The police surgeon says Enid Puckston might certainly have been killed round about half-past, though he's like all doctors about allowing much leeway."

"Half-past eleven! But that means—!"

"Now, was she killed with that dagger?" Masters mused.

"Inspector Drake tells me old Sir George Fleet gave away his rapier-collection about November of 1925. Sir George never did like steel; he preferred guns; and after there'd been a knife-murder at Priory Hill he gave the stuff away to Major Colwell, the Governor of Pentecost. But *was* the Puckston girl killed with that dagger?

"There's very strong evidence she was. You can't identify a knife-wound certain-sure like a bullet-wound. But unusual blade; unusual wounds corresponding; fits exactly. Blood-group type's same. Yes; there you are."

Whereupon Masters sat up straight.

"Sir, that girl *was* killed in the garden between the two prison-wings. There's evidence: I tell you straight. She was carried down under the gallows-trap in a travelling-robe. After (mind you) being brought to the garden alive. And that took time. Lots of time. What's the result?

"It's this. Every one of you five people who went to the prison, and were together even before then, has got an alibi as big as a house. Eh?"

"I hadn't thought about it. So that's the perfect alibi, is it?"

"We-el!" said Masters, regarding him with broad and fishy skepticism. "No. I don't say perfect. *I* could pick a flaw in it. But it'd go down with a jury like peaches and cream. You'd want strong evidence to upset it?"

"And you think you can upset it?"

"If you ask me whether I *want* to upset it," Masters said violently, "the answer is: yes. I smacking well do! If you ask me whether I *can* upset it, the answer is: probably. I'll know tomorrow. There's a little camera-trick, Mr. Drake, that might interest you."

Sir Henry Merrivale, at this point, lumbered very slowly into the room and passed them without appearing to see them. H.M.'s big face wore a mottled pallor, and there were beads of sweat on his forehead. It struck Martin Drake with a chill of dread. And Masters—who had sworn at the time of the Bronze Lamp case he would never again be worried by the old man's carryings-on—uttered a roaring oath and jumped up.

"Have you been on that roof?" Masters demanded.

H.M. did not reply.

He went over and stood with his back to the fireplace, his

151

feet wide apart. Fumbling for a handkerchief in his hip pocket, he mopped his forehead slowly and returned the handkerchief. His eyes were blank. After a long time he spoke.

"Masters," he said, "we're not finished yet. But if we play the cards right we'll finish soon. Masters, we've got the swine good and proper."

And the tone of his voice stung Martin Drake like a red-hot wire.

"We've got a beauty," said H.M., envisaging the murderer. "What sticks in my gorge," he tugged at his collar, "is that Puckston gal being killed just merely for the reason she *was* killed. Masters, we've got a real vicious 'un. And, oh, so innocent!"

"Sir Henry! Listen!"

"Hey?"

"I knew you'd twigged it," Masters said with satisfaction, "as soon as you shouted out to let you think, and then rushed off to the roof. But what have you *got?*"

"I know how Sir George Fleet was murdered."

Masters reached for his notebook.

"And don't you forget that," said H.M., pointing a finger malevolently, "because it's the keystone of the whole business. Everything falls down without it." And, Martin noted with disquiet, H.M.'s face was still pale.

"I won't forget," Masters assured him. "And—?"

"I can tell you the truth about that goddam skeleton in the clock."

"Ah! Just so! Anything else?"

Again there was so oppressive a quiet that they could hear, above H.M.'s head, the almost noiseless gold clock ticking between its two candelabra. The satiny dark-red walls, with their high cream-coloured curtains, seemed to have a stifling quality despite their open windows.

"Y'know," said H.M. thoughtfully, "I've been an awful dummy. Almost as bad a dummy as when I nearly slipped up in that Goblin Wood case. It was because I never connected the pink flash with wood."

"You never connected the pink flash with . . . *what?*"

"With wood," said H.M., reaching over to knock his knuckles on a table.

"Goddelmighty," whispered Masters. "Listen, sir! When Sir George fell off that roof, the only wooden-made things on it were the frames of the beach-chairs and the wicker settee! And all of 'em were fifty feet away from him!"

"I know that."

"Was somebody hiding behind them?"

"No."

Masters wiped his forehead. H.M. was persisting in mazy speculation.

"Y'see, Masters, you've got to find two units, sort of, like the wood here and the skeleton in the clock with old Dr. Pierre Laurier rocking back and forth in front of it. But, burn me, still they don't fit into a pattern until you connect 'em together with a real clue . . ."

Here H.M. roused himself out of his reverie.

"I say, Masters. Am I making myself clear?"

"Curiously enough," retorted Masters, with towering and stiff-jawed dignity, "you are not." Then slow suspicion dawned and grew clear in his expression. "Sir Henry, are you trying to do me in the eye again?"

"Oh, my son! No! I wouldn't do that!"

"Oh, no," said Masters in a hollow voice. "Oh, no. No. You never have, have you? Oh, no. In a pig's ear you haven't!"

H.M. looked at him steadily.

"I'm not doin' it this time son. Honest. It's too serious."

This almost if not quite reassured his companion, who again opened the notebook.

"And I got all the details," he insisted, "straightaway?"

"Every detail," H.M. reassured him, "goes on the table tonight. For our conference. We've been dealt some awful good cards, but a little conjuror's hokey-pokey won't do any harm when it's our turn to deal."

"Then what was all that flummery a minute ago? First you started gabbling about a beach-chair, and then about the skeleton and Dr. Laurier . . ."

"Wait a minute! I didn't . . ."

"And," Masters rode him down, "you said they were connected by a real clue."

"Oh, Masters! The whole place is flooded with clues."

"Maybe so. You talked about a 'real' clue, that bonged down out of the air, like, and hit you on the head. I can't see the wood for the trees. I don't see anything, except that the alibi is a fake. Where did you *get* this 'real' clue? Where did it come from?"

H.M. pondered.

"Well," he said, "from my reincarnation."

Chapter 16

"Stop," said Masters, extending his arm like a traffic-policeman. "Stop just there."

Despite Masters's effort to be calm, the hoarse and strangled note in his voice betrayed him. He must do more than count ten now. Snapping the rubber band round his notebook, he carefully put it in his pocket.

"Sir," he continued, as one who weighs his words but gets louder and louder, "I've been mixed up in these cases for more years than I'd like to count. *I* get the credit. Oh, ah! But I've got blood-pressure, and I've got a family to think of!"

"Sh-h! Quiet! Don't wake up the house!"

"I've been kicked in the pants," said Masters. "I've been hocussed and flummoxed. I've had poisonous snakes dropped at my feet. I've been told to face a mob of reporters, without a word to say for myself, when you'd promised a world-beater of a story. All right: that's fair enough; I don't complain. *But this is too much.* —Reincarnation!" breathed Masters, and clasped his hands in prayer to heaven.

"Sh-h, now! Sh-h! Sh-h-h!"

Masters subsided. A healing peace settled through the room.

"And now," bellowed H.M., in a voice which made the curtains quiver, "are you goin' to stop being a goop and listen to a word of explanation?"

Masters was silent.

"I've been reading a lot of literature," continued H.M. "I don't believe it as I oughter, because I don't remember as much as I oughter. *But* there was one thing I did read, and it slipped through without more than scratching the surface of the old man's mind, until somethin' was said that made me remember. And it tore the hocus-pocus wide open. *Now* do you see?"

Masters peered at him suspiciously.

"You're not off your chump? You *don't* remember how you wore a big hat and recited limericks to Charles the First?"

"Well. No. Not much. And, Masters, for the love of Esau stop drivellin'. This is a murder case. And I'm scared."

"You?"

"Me," returned H.M., with all the impressiveness this conveyed. "We've got to act fast, son. If we can keep this feller," he pointed to Martin, "if we can keep him alive for just one night . . ."

(Again that sense of hatred, gathering round and pressing against him! Martin, weak from lack of the food he told Ruth he hated, sat down and lit a cigarette whose smoke made his head swim.)

"If we can do that," said Masters, "he's out of danger?"

"Not necessarily. But a certain innocent-looker will be occupied with other things. We'll be the attackers and not standin' at defence. Now, son!" H.M. pointed. "When you first barged in here tonight, I asked you whether you'd got the stuff. You said you'd got all of it. Where is it?"

Masters indicated the chair where lay his bowler hat, the brief-case, and the brown cardboard folder.

"You don't want to go through all that tonight, do you?"

"I don't want to go through any of it, Masters. I only want to ask you a question."

"Well sir?"

H.M. scowled and adjusted his spectacles.

"You've got," he stated rather than questioned, "you've got from the local police files some testimony from *everybody,* and I mean everybody, who was here at Fleet House on the afternoon of November 4th, 1927?"

From the thick-filled brown folder Masters took out a typewritten slip with pencilled notes.

"I have," he said. "Also what happened to each of 'em afterwards. The word 'here' means within a radius of three or four miles."

"So! Read it out loud!"

"As follows," said Masters, clearing his throat. "Lady Fleet (here), Dowager Countess of Brayle (here), Earl and Countess of Brayle (one dead, one in Stockholm), young Fleet (here), Dr. Pierre Laurier (dead), Lady Fleet's companion (dead), governess (dead), butler (at Reading), parlourmaid (here), first and second housemaids (one here, one in Australia), gardener (dead). In addition to these persons's testimony, Stannard's too."

"Stannard!" interrupted Martin. "But he didn't give any statement then'"

Masters grinned.

"No, Mr. Drake. Still, I'm told that in Sir Henry's presence and yours he said he'd talked to a newspaper reporter at the

155

train. The area's not so large that a few 'phone-calls wouldn't cover it." Masters tapped the cardboard folder. "They sent a copy of the press-cutting by hand."

H.M. pressed his hands hard to his forehead.

"Here's the burnin' question," he snapped. "You or I got testimony, today or yesterday evening, from all the witnesses who weren't dead or out of reach. *Does it agree with what they said twenty years ago?*"

"Ah. Almost to a T." Masters's eye grew thoughtful. "Almost too close, don't you think?"

"No, son. Oh, my eye, no! *You're* not likely to forget the first h.e. bomb that fell close to you; now are you? Or the circumstances? No. And that's a great help."

"It's a great help to know there aren't any contradictions?"

"That's right."

Masters shut his eyes. "Anything else?"

"You don't mention Dr. Hugh Laurier as bein' there. Or wasn't he qualified for medicine yet?"

"He'd qualified a few years before; he was helping his father. But he was in London that day. He missed the train, and didn't get back till later."

"I see," observed H.M. in a colourless tone, and dropped his hands. "Finally, son, in that brief-case you got the Scotland Yard dossier, in a blue folder, with the statements of Simon Frew and Arthur Puckston. One with the binoculars, the other with the telescope." H.M. stretched out his hand and waggled the fingers. "Gimme that folder!"

And now they both saw, with growing alarm, the extent of H.M.'s disquiet.

"This folder? What for?"

"I'm goin' on a little errand," said H.M. "It'll be short, but it won't be sweet. I'm dreading it like the Old Nick." He put the folder under his arm."

"Ready when you are, then!"

"You're not goin', Masters."

Masters stared at him. "In case it's slipped your memory, Sir Henry, I'm the police-officer in charge of this case."

"You're still not goin'," H.M. said simply. "You'd only scare him. Don't argue, burn it! This is the first card we play; and I got to play it. Now that young feller," he nodded towards Martin, "is the one I want to go with me. If he'll do it. Hey?"

Martin staggered up from the sofa, crushing out his cigarette.

"I'll go with you to Land's End," he said, "if you don't mind my ringing up Jenny first. I've been intending to do it all night;

156

and every time somebody walloped out with something I had to hear."

H.M. spoke sharply.

"You can ring her up, son, but you won't get any answer."

"My God, she hasn't gone away with Grandmother?" Martin thought back. "The old lady said *she* was going away overnight. Did Jenny go?"

"No, no, no," H.M. told him in a fussed and malevolent way. "I made her promise, before the old hobgoblin sent her away from here, to take two nembutal pills as soon as she got home. Son, it wouldn't wake her if the whole town of Brayle fell down. All right: you be stubborn and cloth-headed. Try it!"

Martin did try it. He sat at the telephone-table in the dark rear of the hall, listening to ghostly little ringing-tones which had no reply. Surely Dawson or somebody must be about? Never mind. It was late. He put down the 'phone.

Suddenly Martin realized he was in the dark. A gulf of mist, in his imagination, opened in front of him; somebody's hands lunged out; the solid floor melted away for a plunge outward

⋅ ⋅ ⋅

None of that! Martin went back towards the lighted drawing-room, timing his steps slowly. Himself: a focus of hatred. And again, everlastingly, why? The atmosphere of the drawing-room intensified this thought, since Masters and H.M. had evidently been talking rapidly. It seemed to Martin that the Chief Inspector, in utter incredulity, had just opened his mouth to protest. Afterwards they did not speak.

They turned off the lights in the drawing-room. They went out of the house softly, Martin slipping the latch of the front door. In a fine night, the quarter moon dimmed by a sweep of stars, they crossed the road.

At the Dragon's Rest, whose front showed no light, what might be called the hotel-entrance was in its south side, the narrower end of the building. As Martin made for the hotel-entrance door, Masters preceding him and H.M. following him, he glanced southwards because Brayle Manor was somewhere there.

It seemed to him that in the distance the sky had a faintly whitish glow, conveying a sense of movement. No sounds; or were there? The glimmer wasn't fire. He could tell that. But

⋅ ⋅ ⋅

"Oi!" whispered H.M., and shoved him inside.

A narrowish passage ran the length of the inn from south to north. Beyond the left-hand wall lay the three bars. In the right-hand wall was a cubicle for signing the visitors' book,

157

then a door to the dining-room where Martin remembered having had lunch on Saturday, then more doors to the end. The walls, white-painted, had at one side a design of brass warming-pans framing a sixteenth-century crossbow; and the light of a shaded lamp shone on ancient scrubbed floorboards.

"See you later," whispered Masters, and tiptoed up the narrow staircase towards the bedrooms.

H.M., taking Martin by the arm, impelled him down the passage to the far door at the right end. H.M. knocked gently.

"Come in," said a voice which Martin guessed must be Mrs. Puckston's.

Mr. and Mrs. Puckston, whose child had been murdered and hacked last night, were in there. If H.M. had not gripped his arm, Martin would have turned and bolted.

H.M. opened the door.

It was an old-fashioned kitchen-sitting-room, its brick walls painted white. In what had once been the immense embrasure of the fireplace, there now stood a big coal cooking-stove with many lids, and a kettle simmering on one of them. In the middle of the room, with a frayed yellow-and-white cloth and an electric light hanging over it, was a table set for an untouched supper.

Arthur Puckston, back to the door, sat on the other side of the table and faced the stove. His freckled bald head, with its little fringe of grey-reddish hair, and his thin drooping muscular shoulders, were motionless. Mrs. Puckston, dark-haired and stoutening, sat in a corner chair and sewed.

Then Puckston looked round.

The tears were running down his face despite his spasmodic blinkings. His eyes remained gentle. He saw who was in the doorway. First startled, then deeply ashamed, he whipped his head away and began swabbing desperately at his eyes with his coat-sleeves. But grief had beaten him. His arms dropped. He did not care.

"Mr. Puckston," said H.M., in so gentle a tone that Martin could not have thought it possible, "I know we're intruding. Will you believe I only came because I know I can help you?"

Mrs. Puckston, tearless but dull-glazed of eye, looked up.

"Won't you sit down, please?" she asked quietly. "We understand. Arthur suspicioned—at least, he hoped—you'd come."

The two visitors sat down on their side of the table, their eyes fixed on the cloth.

"Norma," Puckston said in a slow, dull monotone, "I've got to explain."

"That's not necessary, Arthur."

"I've got to explain."

With great care Puckston slowly hitched his chair round. He too looked down. His right hand, blue-veined, automatically brushed and brushed and brushed at the table-cloth.

"What I've got to explain, sir, is that we only opened the 'ouse tonight because I'd promised the Choral Society they could have the two parlours for their practice after chapel. Because it was hymns, you see. We thought that was only right and proper. Because it was hymns. And Mr. Bradley, from the Chapel, he said so too.

"Of course, we didn't go out there. But Norma and me, we reckoned it would be right and proper if we sat out in the passage, there, and listened to the hymns through the wall. And we did. And I was feeling fine, I was feeling just as fine as I could be, until it came to that part of the hymn about while the nearer waters roll, while the tempest still is high.

"And I don't know," he went on, shaking his head while he brushed and brushed at the table, "I can't just rightly say, what made me make such a fool of myself. Breaking down like that, and coming in 'ere so they wouldn't know about it. I didn't know I was so soft. I reckon it was just that part of the hymn, that's all."

Both of his visitors, one of whom could not bear this, made an instinctive movement to get up.

"No!" said Puckston, and stretched out his hand. "Don't go, if I've not offended you. Sit down. I was hoping you'd come."

They sat down.

"Don't think about it, Arthur!" said Mrs. Puckston. But there was a heavier glaze in her eyes as she sewed.

"I won't," said her husband. He concentrated hard for a moment, before slowly moving his head sideways. "Norma, haven't you got a cup of tea for the gentlemen?"

The sewing slid from his wife's lap. "Arthur, I never thought of that. I've never been so bad-mannered in all my born days."

"*But please don't . . .*"

"Easy, son," muttered H.M., and gripped Martin's wrist as the latter started to speak. H.M. looked at Puckston, who had ceased to care whether they saw the tears on his face. "You said, Mr. Puckston, you hoped I'd come here. Was it about anything in particular?"

The other started to speak, but fell to brushing the cloth instead.

"Mr. Puckston," said H.M., "this person who—hurt your little girl."

As Mrs. Puckston moved the kettle from the stove-lid, the white-brick kitchen was as still as death. Mrs. Puckston, an iron hook in her hand to remove the stove-lid and see to the fire, did not seem to breathe.

Puckston swallowed. "Yes, sir?"

"Do you want me to nab that person, and see that there's punishment?"

The lid rattled back. From the stove leaped up a yellow lick of flame, curling high; momentarily it painted the kitchen with yellow brightness; and, had he been facing it, you might have fancied a reflection in Puckston's eyes.

Then the lean man's shoulders sagged.

"What's the good?" he asked dully. "Like old Sir George. Years ago. You can't beat 'em."

"I know this country," said H.M. "It's asinine, sure. It's full of fatheads. But there's been justice here for nearly a thousand years."

"Old Sir George . . ."

"Could *he* take your land from you, when he tried to?"

"No, by God 'e couldn't!"

Rattle went the stove-lid, back into place.

"Arthur," said his wife, herself near to breaking down, "I don't think I'll make tea. I think there's some bottles of the '24 port that the gentlemen would like better. I think I know how to find them."

Then she was out of the room. Her husband, struggling to pull his wits together, pressed his hands flat on the table. His mildness, his weary look, showed he could scarcely do it.

"Can—you help me?" Puckston asked.

"If you help me."

"How? I'll try. Yes; I'll do it."

"Son, I warn you: the first bit is goin' to hurt. It'll keep you thinking about your daughter."

"Go ahead."

From his inside breast pocket H.M. took out three postcards. One, postmarked July 5th, read, *Re Sir George Fleet: examine the skeleton in the clock.* The second, July 6th: *Re Sir George Fleet: what was the pink flash on the roof?* The third, July 7th: *Re Sir George Fleet: evidence of murder is still there.* Clearing a space on the supper-table, pushing away cutlery and a bottle of Worcestershire sauce, he put down the exhibits.

"Son," he said quietly, "you sent these postcards."

The other's mouth quivered like a hurt child's.

"To be more exact," added H.M., "you dictated the
160

substance and Enid put it down in correct grammar and spelling, with schoolgirl flourishes."

" 'Ow did you know that?" asked Puckston.

"Never mind. It's not important. What I . . ."

" 'Ow did you know that?" repeated Puckston, with the insistence of the drunken or the damned. The tears had started again.

"Oh, son! From your antiques here I thought you *might* subscribe to Willaby's catalogue. I asked Lady Br——I asked somebody in this district if you did, and she said yes. She also said she got her last catalogue on July 5th, which is the postmark on that first anonymous card.

"Y'see, that was the catalogue that listed the skeleton in the clock. Somebody got it on July 5th, and fired off an anonymous postcard to stir up the police about the Fleet case. There weren't likely to be two such curiosities as that clock floatin' about."

"I'm not saying I didn't do it." Puckston had the palms of his hands pressed over his face. He rocked back and forth. "But why did it have to be *me* who sent the postcards?"

H.M. expelled a slow, deep breath of relief. They could hear the throb of the fire inside the stove, and Mrs. Puckston moving somewhere in the cellar.

"Well . . . now. That's what we're coming to. And it'll be easier. Because it's about Sir George Fleet's death."

H.M. snapped his fingers down at one side, without looking away from Puckston. Martin rightly interpreted this as an order to pick up the blue Scotland Yard folder, which H.M. had dropped.

Puckston was not composed now, but he was more composed. Any mention of Fleet could rouse him. His light-blue eyes, bloodshot and reddish at the lids, tried to focus on H.M. out of a long, wretched face.

"Do you remember," continued H.M., turning over the typewritten pages of the folder, "what happened the day Fleet died?"

"Do I remember when I first walked out with Norma?"

"You didn't like Fleet. Hey?"

"I wonder," said Puckston, shutting his eyes, "if that man ever thought how much I looked down on him. 'Im, with 'is money made out of the fourteen-eighteen war! Me, whose forbears 'ave owned this inn a matter of two hundred year! But you can't make the nobs see that. They don't notice!"

"Let's come to the day, shall we?"

161

"Glad to."

"You, accordin' to your testimony, were sitting on the top of the north gable with a telescope. You were watching the hunt. You heard the shout Fleet gave. Now lemme read you a part of your statement verbatim."

H.M. found the passage and ran his finger down it.

I looked round. I saw something pitch over the little ledge, but it was so quick I did not see what it was. I looked—

H.M. paused abruptly. There was a space of silence, while Martin found the sweat stand out on his forehead.

"Y'see," H.M. said very gently, "that second sentence just can't possibly be true."

"Why not?"

"I'll tell you. If there's one thing of general agreement, it's that Fleet gave a shout and immediately fell. If you doubt that, see the testimony of Simon Frew, who had the binoculars on the middle gable and is admittedly an honest witness.

"But what about you? You were on the north gable, watching the hunt: either the hounds streakin' to the north, or the field galloping round Black Hanger to the east. You heard a yell: that's all. You couldn't have known where it came from, except somewhere behind you. You couldn't have known what it meant. By the time you could swing that telescope round, Fleet must have been dead on the flagstones.

"Yet you claim, see, that out of all the space of sky and land comin' round into view through your telescope, you managed to pick out the exact spot where Fleet was standing *just as he fell*. Son, it won't do. It's plain ridiculous."

Again there was a silence.

In Puckston's expression there was no fear, no wrath, no shrinking; only a curious twitch of the mouth which Martin could not identify.

"What did I do, then?" Puckston asked.

"I'm goin' to suggest," pursued H.M., turning back a page and tapping it, "that the same thing which happened to Simon Frew also happened to you."

Puckston shut his eyes.

"*You* saw the field gallop round the side of Black Hanger. Through the telescope they all seemed to be waving and smiling at *you*. You wondered who it could be for: just like Frew. You turned round and raked your telescope along till

162

you saw your enemy, George Fleet, a few seconds before he fell. Is that true?"

"Yes," said Puckston without opening his eyes.

"But you were looking at him sideways—a good distance sideways—instead of face on. That's how you came to see . . ."

"See what?"

"The pink flash. Just like open and shut, wasn't it?"

Were they coming at last, Martin wondered, to the explanation of that tantalizing obscurity which (Masters seemed to think) was connected with a wooden beach-chair? He, Martin Drake, had been pushed by a pair of hands. Or could he swear he had? The soft, gentle growl of H.M.'s voice went on.

"To clinch it," said H.M., "here's a final bit of your story. You tell in this record (Oh, lord love a duck!) about how Dr. Laurier ran out on the terrace, and the constable came up. Now you're speakin', son."

And they saw, through Puckston's eyes, the scene played against the white facade.

Dr. Laurier said something, and Bert picked up Sir George's binoculars and walked into the house. Dr. Laurier said something else, and Lady Brayle came out with some kind of cloth. I said aloud, 'The bastard is dead.'

Puckston stared at a salt-cellar on the frayed white-and-yellow cloth.

"I never made no bones about what I thought of him. Maybe I oughtn't to have said that, with the hymns tonight and all. But that's how I felt. And still do."

H.M. held up a hand for silence.

Dr. Laurier put the cloth over his head. Lady Fleet came out and started to faint, but they talked to her a while and she went in. The governess and the boy came round the house then, but Dr. Laurier yelled so loud you could hear to go back. Dr. Laurier made as if he was examining all over Sir George. I did not see anybody at the windows. Bert came out and seemed to argue with Dr. Laurier about who carried Sir George. Bert took his head in the cloth and Dr. Laurier took his legs. They carried him in the house. Lady Fleet came out again once and looked up. That was all I saw before I slid down.

Puckston smote the table.

"And there's not a word of a lie in that," he insisted. "Simon could—"

"Sure, son. I know. It agrees with what Simon Frew said, and the other fellers who were farther down on the roof. But, considering what I've read, can you tell me more about the pink flash now?"

Puckston looked vacant.

"I was sure what it was." Again his hand mechanically brushed the table-cloth. "Anyway, I was pretty sure. But . . ."

"But you were glad Fleet was dead. And anyway you didn't want trouble, because you were scared of the nobs."

"Nice lot, aren't they? Lady Brayle . . ."

"Sure, Sophie's one of the bad examples. That's because she's so goddam cloth-headed. She ought to be either ousted or made popular. But when you sent that anonymous card with the fancy words 'pink flash' . . ."

Any reference to those cards, no matter with how gentle probing, seemed to send Puckston frantic.

"Enid didn't know nothing about it," he pleaded. "It was only a lark, don't you see? She loved larks. That's how they got her up to Pentecost, because it was a lark. Because all the gossip was round they were looking for ghosts. Because . . ."

Puckston got up. He stumbled across to a kitchen dresser with an oil-cloth top, fumbled in a drawer, and brought out a table-cloth to dab at his eyes. Then he turned round.

"It was Enid," he said, "who thought of saying 'pink flash.' I—I hemm'd and hawed." Puckston's freckled bald head stood out against the white-brick wall. His thin shoulders, square like a scarecrow's in the old blue-and-white shirt, were humped up.

"I hemm'd and hawed, not wanting to say much. And Enid, she said, 'Well, Daddy, what did it look like?' And I told her. And she thought for a minute and said, 'I know, Daddy! We'll call it a pink flash.' And she put it down."

"Ah!" said H.M. *"Now* we got it!"

"Got what?"

Statement and question were flung across that warm kitchen. Martin knew that a scale-pan hung in the balance, that a gambler prepared to play.

"You've been torturin' yourself," said H.M., "because you thought *you* were responsible for that kid's death. You thought some swine believed she knew too much, and killed her."

Puckston put the table-cloth in front of his face.

"I don't hold many things sacred," said H.M., "but I swear you on what I do hold sacred that you're wrong. Wrong! That

164

wasn't the reason! It wasn't even a reason you or I could understand."

The table-cloth fell to the floor. " 'Ere! Are you trying to . . . ?"

"No. I can prove it, son. And if I do prove it," said H.M., with such a radiance of conviction that the other did not move, "will you help me with something else?"

Ten seconds ticked past. Puckston walked across to the table and extended his hand. H.M. gripped it. After this he slid back in his chair with a Gargantuan thump, and breathed noisily. Slowly his head turned round.

"*You*," he glared at Martin with incredible malevolence. "What are you doin' here, son?"

"But you asked me to—"

"You go out in that passage," H.M. ordered sternly, "and you wait there till I talk to you. You've served the purpose. Now the garden's lovely. Sling your hook."

Martin felt no surprise now when he remembered having heard that Chief Inspectors sometimes came within an ace of murdering Sir Henry Merrivale. He knew why. Deeply he could sympathize. In fact, as his eye caught a bowl of Jell-o on the sideboard, he wondered how its contents would look if they were tastefully pressed down on H.M.'s skull.

But he went out into the passage and closed the door.

"You've served the purpose." What purpose? Why had he been brought to see the Puckstons? He was beginning to suspect H.M. of a purpose in everything, but what purpose in this?

The long passage, with its single dim lamp, lay shadowy and deeply cool. At the other end of it lounged Masters himself, with the hotel-entrance door wide open to the fragrant night. Masters's face was a mask of inquiry as Martin joined him.

"Don't ask me what happened," the latter begged. "He's verified what he wants to verify. Do you understand?"

"Do I!" Masters growled with fervour.

Yet the Chief Inspector, or what could be seen of him in dimness, appeared serene, breathing the fragrant air, almost humming a tune and smiling. Martin pointed southwards.

"By the way, what's that whitish glow away over there? In the direction of Brayle Manor?"

"Can't say, I'm sure."

"Probably doesn't mean anything. Still," Martin was uneasy, "it did strike me he hurried me in here when I tried to look at it. Er—you've heard about his feud with the Dowager Countess of Brayle?"

"Have I!" snorted Masters.

"He won the first round by a thrust with a guisarme. She definitely took the second by making a skeleton gibber at him and insulting him behind locked gates. I've wondered before this if he might——well . . ."

"You know, Mr. Drake," said Masters, shaking his head and folding his arms portentously, "I've tried to stop it; but I can't. It's a sin and a shame how that old bounder carries on!"

"At his age, you mean?"

"Oh, ah! Just so! It'd be a great pity if he (hurrum!) made it worse."

"It would, Chief Inspector! It would! What worries me is that it always upsets Jenny, and I won't have Jenny upset!"

"Of course," Masters observed musingly, after a long pause, "the lady *is* a bit of a handful."

"Are *you* telling *me?*"

"Do you know what she said to me," continued Masters, with his eye on a bright star outside, "when I tried my ruddy best to get that skeleton back?" Here he mimicked heavily. " 'My good man, you are perfectly well aware you cannot remove the article in question until you can show just cause why you need it. Should you set foot inside the park without a warrant, I shall instruct my gardener to use his gun.' ——Urr!" said Masters suddenly, making a noise like a dog.

"And do you know," Martin demanded, "what she said to me? Listen!"

Whereupon they both stopped and looked at each other, conscious of a meeting of minds.

"Let's face it, sir," Masters said benevolently, and lowered his defences. "There *may* be trouble."

And the richest and ripest trouble of all, as regards proceedings between Sir Henry Merrivale and the Dowager Countess of Brayle, had its first stir at eleven o'clock on the following morning.

Chapter 17

It was nearly eleven before Martin finished his breakfast on Monday morning.

When he turned in the night before, he had been too tired to bother with the sleeping-pill Dr. Laurier had left for him. He woke to a morning of soft breeze and gentle sun, so stimulated and refreshed that he felt ravenous for food. Certain instructions, which H.M. had made him promise to carry out overnight, now seemed nonsensical.

Martin sang in his bath. A harassed but punctilious Dr. Laurier, who arrived while he was shaving, changed the bandage on his forehead and told him that with luck the stitches would be out in no time.

Somebody had tried to kill him? But he had only to think of Jenny, and other matters for the moment seemed of no consequence. When he went downstairs, he met nobody in the cool house. In the dining-room he was served breakfast by a maid other than Phyllis; and, since Fleet House was supplied with great quantities of food from an unspecified source, he ate with appetite.

But it was the telephone he wanted. Emerging through a series of passages which brought him out opposite the staircase at the back of the main hall, Martin at last heard sounds of life. Voices—apparently those of Aunt Cicely, Ricky, and H.M. himself—drifted down from the direction of the drawing room.

Then the 'phone rang; and it was Jenny.

The first part of their conversation need not be recorded here. Doubtless Sir Henry Merrivale would have described it as mush, adding that Jenny and Martin seemed to have achieved the seemingly impossible feat of getting into an intimate embrace over a telephone. But there seemed to be a faintly odd note in Jenny's voice.

"You haven't forgotten," he asked, "that this is the day you and I are going to London?"

"We—we can't. Not yet, anyway. Tonight we might."

A sense of impending disaster crept into him. "Why not?"

"Martin," breathed Jenny, "*why* does your H.M. insist on persecuting my poor grandmother?"

(I knew it! By all cussedness and the ten finger-bones of Satan, I knew it!)

"But what's he doing to her now, Jenny? He's here! In the drawing-room!"

Martin, do you know where I am?" asked Jenny.

"What's that?"

"I'm under the main staircase, with a thick oak door closed so I can speak to you. Hold on a second, and I'll push the door open. Listen!"

Martin jumped. The sound which poured out at him, even

167

over a telephone, made him yank the receiver away from his ear before putting it back to his ear again.

It sounded rather like Blackpool on August Bank Holiday. But the crowd-noises were over-ridden by music, in which Martin (too imaginatively, perhaps) thought he could detect one brass band, a panotrope with a bad needle, and the steam organ of a merry-go-round. High rose the strains of *Waltzing Matilda,* closely contested by *Cherry-Ripe* and *The Daring Young Man on the Flying Trapeze.*

The strains were blotted away as Jenny closed the door.

"Did Grandmother," she asked, "tell you anything about a fair?"

"Well," Martin searched his memory, "she did say something about it, yes. *I* thought she meant some sort of rustic fair with a Maypole."

"So did she," Jenny answered in a weary voice. "But it's the biggest travelling fair in the British Isles. They took half the night to set it up. You see, they—they sent Grandmother some sort of paper, six months ago. She said solicitors cost too much money, when she knew all the law anyway. And she signed it."

For a moment hope began to stir in Martin. After all, six months ago! It had been Grandmother's own fault. H.M. couldn't have had anything to do with this! He said as much.

"Yes," said Jenny. "But have you met a Mr. Solomon MacDougall?"

"Not to my knowledge."

"He's the owner or the man who manages it or something. Anyway, H.M. met him when he was looking over the ground yesterday . . ."

"Oh, my God!"

"And H.M. pointed out something in the contract they didn't know themselves. They intended to use Rupert's Five-Acre, which would have been bad enough. But H.M. said wouldn't it be a wonderful attraction if they had lines of booths and stalls and freak-shows up the main drive to the front door? And that's not the worst, either. Have you ever ridden in a Ghost-Train?"

Martin had. But he wanted to let Jenny pour her heart out.

"It's a big place like a house, dark inside. You ride in a little railway through terrific screams and howls and screeches. Do you know where H.M. persuaded them to put the Ghost-Train?"

"No, my sweet."

"Under Grandmother's bedroom windows," said Jenny.

168

"Er—yes. What I mean is: I see "

"On the roof of the Ghost-Train house," said Jenny, "there's a papier-maché skull on a pole. It's painted green. It turns round and round. And, every time it turns round, it looks in the bedroom window and chatters *two* sets of teeth."

"Jenny," said Martin, "wait just one minute. Hold the line and wait. The culprit's here. I'll . . ."

With a shaking hand he put down the 'phone beside its cradle. To say that he did not know whether to laugh or swear is to understate a real conflict of mind: it boiled inside him, tearing him both ways. Grandmother Brayle was not due home until this afternoon. To watch her behaviour then would be worth much. On the other hand, H.M.'s craftiness seemed always to separate him from Jenny; and he was resolved to get Jenny away today.

At this point of both murderousness and mirth, he became conscious of the great man's voice from the direction of the drawing-room. It was now raised to a serious and oratorical pitch, holding his listeners.

H.M. said: "What we got to remember, y'see, is the noble *dignity* of Curtius Merrivale. I wish I could paint you the picture of Charles the First sittin' in that noble Banqueting Hall, designed by Inigo Jones, with all his family gathered round just as you see it in the portraits. (Mind, I don't say these are the exact words; it's the idea.) And Charles the First would say, 'Sir Curtius, will you not favour us with some amusing conceit?'

"And Curtius Merrivale would get up, sweepin' off his plumed hat like this, and he'd say:

" 'There was a young girl from Bel Air,
  Who used to—' "

"H.M.!" thundered Martin, with full power of lungs. It was enough to bring even H.M. to an abrupt stop. And Martin, torn between two feelings, could only sputter mentally.

"Did you," he shouted down the hall, "put a damn great Ghost-Train under Lady Brayle's bedroom?"

This question, whatever else may be said about it, was at least arresting. It roused attention and curiosity. After short silence, there was movement.

Ricky Fleet, in white flannels and white shirt, with tears of emotion in his eyes after what had been a long narration by H.M., raced and skidded along the hardwood floor. He was followed by Aunt Cicely, now seriously angry with H.M. for his romantic anecdotes. Last of all, with a lofty air, marched H.M. himself.

"Didn't you," Martin demanded, "put the biggest travelling fair in England slap on the main drive of Brayle Manor?"

"Well . . . now," said the culprit in question.

"But what's this," asked Ricky insistently, "about a train running through Grandmother's bedroom?"

At the same moment, in a hall touched by sunshine through the open door to the terrace, Ruth Callice and Stannard appeared at that door, followed by Chief Inspector Masters. Martin, like the skeleton, almost gibbered as he explained while the others gathered round.

"Jenny?" He turned back to the 'phone.

"Yes, dear?"

"How long has this uproar been going on? Why didn't you ring me?"

"But I only discovered it myself," Jenny protested, "about twenty minutes ago. Before I left you last night, you see, H.M. gave me two nembutal sleeping-pills; he got them from Dr. Laurier; and he made me promise to take them as soon as I got home. And I was so worried about you——"

Martin kept the receiver a little way back from his ear. Jenny's small, soft voice was distinctly audible to everyone who had gathered round.

"So," repeated Martin, "H.M. gave you some sleeping-pills, so you wouldn't know. Yes, I remember he said he did."

Sir Henry Merrivale, wearing an incredible air of righteousness, had folded his arms and stood like a statue in a park.

"Dawson and some of the others," pursued Jenny, "tried to wake me in the night, but they couldn't. While we had the lights and the noise, I mean. The first I knew was when I heard someone yelling, 'Get your fresh cockles and winkles.'"

"Did they—er—ring up your grandmother at wherever she's staying?"

"Priory Hill? No. They were afraid to."

"When is your grandmother due to come back?"

"At one o'clock, for lunch. I think she's bringing that clergyman back, the one who's so terribly dead-set against horseracing."

"Holy cats, they haven't got a race-track there, have they?"

"No, no, no! Of course not. And I'm not crying, Martin; I'm only laughing and I can't stop. If you could see this place! Can you please come here soon?"

"I can be there," Martin told her, "immediately. Wait for me!"

"And so can I be there," Ricky declared in ecstasy. "I'll run you over, old boy. I'd heard about this fair, but I never thought it was going to be anything like this."

Martin looked at H.M.

"Y'know," said the latter, taking a reflective survey of the faces round him and then leaning one elbow against the wall, "I think I must be the most reviled, misunderstood poor doer-of-good in this whole floatin' earth! I try to do Sophie some good, I honest-Injun do! And . . ."

"How are you going to do her good by sticking winkle-stalls and coconut-shies all over the lawn?"

"Never you mind," H.M. told him darkly. "They don't understand the old man, that's all. They see the result, when it's all over. Then they say, 'How curious! The silly old dummy did it by accident.'"

His peroration—in which he inquired, rhetorically, whether he was indignant when a skeleton stuck its head out of an electric car to blow raspberries at him; and replied by saying he was the most forgiving soul on earth—his peroration was cut short by the husky chuckle of Stannard.

Stannard looked in fine form this morning, hearty and clear of eye, with hardly a trace of limp.

"Ruth," he said, "something tells me this would be a sight worth seeing. Would you care to go?"

"I'd love to!"

"I'm going too," announced Aunt Cicely, tripping up several steps and running down to look at them, in unconscious pose against the tall window. "Only not until this afternoon, when I'm properly dressed."

Ruth looked worried.

"Cicely, do you think you ought? You heard what Dr. Laurier said only this morning. Shock, or excitement . . ."

"Ruth, I'm not an invalid!" laughed Aunt Cicely. "*I'm* the only person who keeps on talking about my heart. Besides," she nodded at them decidedly, "there's an unanswerable reason. Ricky wants me to "

"Ricky, don't you think you're being a bit inconsiderate?"

"Look here!" said Ricky. "The reason is—"

He hesitated, looked at them, saw in a wall looking-glass that he wore no coat or tie, and took the stairs three at a bound. "Tell you later!" he said.

"You for a sun-hat, my dear," Stannard touched Ruth's

arm, "and I for a suitable cloth cap. I have an instinct that this will be a memorable day."

"Oh, ah," Chief Inspector Masters muttered under his breath, "it will be for somebody."

Masters said this when he and H.M. and Martin stood in an otherwise empty hall. And Martin felt again an unexpected coldness round the heart when he saw him look at him: Masters with the unmirthful smile of one who knows all the facts, H.M. with his fists on his hips.

"So!" the latter growled softly. "You think I'm not attending to business, hey?"

"You don't mean this travelling-fair business is a part of another scheme to . . ."

"It's the same scheme, son."

"To catch the mur—?"

"Quiet, sir!" muttered Masters; and his tone was deadly serious. It was as though the blare of fair-music dwindled in Martin's ears; then grew louder with an implication of what it was to conceal.

"But, H.M.," he protested, "Jenny tells me you saw this man What's-his-name, who manages the fair, yesterday morning or afternoon. If I've got the facts right, you didn't tumble to the whole solution until late yesterday night. Then how could the fair have—?"

"Son," said H.M., "when I talked to that fine feller Solomon MacDougall I was having—hem!—maybe evil thoughts as well as holy thoughts. About skulls that chattered: you see what I mean? But I also saw last night how the cards were bein' dealt straight into our hands. See what I mean?"

"No."

"Anyhow, it's so. If you hear Masters or me say, 'Pip,' you jump to it and ask no questions. Got that?"

"Right."

Their looks were still in Martin's mind ten minutes later when the old car, with Ruth and Stannard in the rear seat, Martin in front with Ricky, moved along the main road southwards under a canopy of mellow sunlight. It moved so slowly that Dr. Laurier's car passed them, the doctor giving a pince-nez flicker of greeting and touching the brim of his hat. At sight of the other car, Ricky blurted out what he had to say.

"I want to explain," he said, "why I seemed to be such a hound towards Mother."

From their previous conversation, it had been clear that Ricky no longer felt any distrust of Stannard. Sheer admiration of Stannard's conduct in the execution shed would have done that. Stannard's friendliness was apparent too, though he treated Ricky as an indulgent uncle would treat a nephew of sixteen.

"My dear boy!" The husky chuckle remonstrated. "You can't be called a hound for inviting your mother to a fair."

"No, that's just it!" Ricky appealed to Stannard as much as to Martin. "But—it's about Susan Harwood."

Stannard whistled. "You don't mean they're going to meet?"

"They've met already, in a way. At charity do's. But this is different. Martin, you'll stand by? You're in the same boat."

"I'll do anything I can, of course."

Ruth, tapping her fingers on her handbag, said nothing.

"Susan knows about it," Ricky explained, with one eye on the road and one eye on his companions, "but Mother doesn't. At one o'clock I'll be strolling with Mother. The place will be near, but not too near, a lemonade-stall or an ice-cream stall or something like that."

"Ricky," Ruth cried, "what *are* you planning?"

"*Will* you be quiet, old girl, and listen to me?"

"Honestly, Ricky . . ."

"I'll introduce 'em," Ricky ignored the protest, "and then I'll out with it. I'll say this is the girl I'm going to marry, and wouldn't they like to get acquainted? Mother can't make a scene in public. Then I'll say, 'Just get you an ice; excuse me a moment.' "

"Ricky," cried Ruth, "you coward!"

Former Wing-Commander Richard Fleet, D.S.O. with bar, did not in this instance deny it.

"I've told Laurier," he confided; "but he's an ass. They'll stroll away, Susan and Mother, and I'll follow. If you see me beckon, crowd in. If you see me motion to keep away, keep away. Anyway, I can't lose 'em when I follow."

"We're with you," said Martin. "But why not simply elope with the girl? That's what I'm going to do, this afternoon or tonight."

"You're . . . *what?*" exclaimed Ruth.

"Never mind. We were talking about Ricky."

"I can't do it," said Ricky, referring to elopement. He was desperately in earnest, so much so that his eyes brimmed as they had brimmed a while ago, though perhaps for different reasons, when H.M. was telling stories. He scarcely noticed the road; the car had gathered speed; yet his instinctive timing never put them in danger. "This is the only way. Mother'll understand it."

173

"All good luck, my boy!" smiled Stannard. "But, my dear Drake. You were saying—?"

"Martin doesn't mean it," observed Ruth.

(Oh, don't I?)

For now, beyond tall trees at a bend in the road, there rose above a crowd murmur the predominating brass-band strains of *Waltzing Matilda.* In contrast to the stuff which passes for music nowadays, this noble tune must set a stuffed mummy to whistling and tapping its foot. Martin Drake began whistling too. He was going away with Jenny.

Round the curve they swept into the straight. The fifteen-foot-high brick wall of Brayle Manor, which they had seen stretching westwards, now ran past the road on the right. All the noises of the fair were sweeping out at them now.

On the left-hand side of the road, an immense enclosed field had as the sign over its road gate, PARKING, is 6d. Though petrol was supposed to be scarce, you would not have learned this by the glow of sun winking on the backs of so many cars. On the other side of the road seethed mild pandemonium.

The broad iron-grilled gates stood wide open. The head of a perspiring ticket-seller stretched out over the half-door of the gate-keeper's lodge. From the opposite side, hoarsely, rose the chant of a man with vari-coloured balloons and white hats bearing such mottoes as *Kiss Me Quick.*

As Martin crossed the road from the parking-lot with Ricky, Stannard, and Ruth, a police-car containing Masters and H.M. drew up not far from the gates. Then Martin noticed, stuck on each side of the wall at the gates, a huge poster showing an equally huge photograph of the Dowager Countess, wearing a tiara and a smile. Underneath, signed and in red letters, ran what was clearly a quotation from a letter.

"If the civic authorities of Brayle attempt to prevent this fair, or so much as set foot inside the park, I shall sue them for five thousand pounds."

Several newcomers were reading it with stunned admiration.

"Now listen, sir!" Martin heard the Chief Inspector's voice hiss. "You're going to behave yourself?"

An empurpled visage appeared above the shoulder of Ruth Callice.

"What d'ye mean, behave myself?" the face demanded.

This was the last Martin could catch, since they were pressing through the swirl of the crowd. To his surprise he saw Dr. Laurier up ahead. After procuring their tickets, feeling the gravel of the broad drive crunch under their feet, they seemed to be in clearer space while voices and music rolled over them.

174

"*Kick the football! Kick the football, burst a balloon, and win a fine prize!*"

"'*Ow's yer strength, gen'lemen? 'Ow's yer strength? 'Ere we—*"

The churning, tinkling melody of the merry-go-round, blowing hard with steam-pressure, swept across the voices like mist. Another (alleged) melody, made even more ghoulish by a loud-speaker and a deep voice singing, intruded.

"*With 'er 'ead TOOKED oon-der-neath 'er arm,*
    She wa-a-a-lks the bluidy TOW-ER—"

"*This, ladies and gentlemen, is the Mirror Maze.*" A loudspeaker again, with a semi-cultured voice. "*Biggest and finest attraction of MacDougall's Mammoth. The Mirror Maze. If you are unable—*"

"Stan!" cried Ruth. "Where are you?"

"Here, my dear! Take my hand!"

Laughter and giggles broke above them like rockets. Everybody seemed to be eating potato-crisps and then throwing the empty bags in your face. Then they emerged into a comparatively wide open space: where, Martin gathered, two lines of attractions crossed.

"*If you are unable to get out of the Mirror Maze,*" the loudspeaker gave a rasping chuckle, like a loud parody of Stannard, "*directions will be given by—*"

"Sir Henry! Wait! Come back here!"

Martin, getting his breath to plunge towards the house and Jenny, turned round. But nothing appeared to be seriously wrong.

Just to the right was a booth set out as a miniature racetrack with its counter a little higher than waist level. Metal horses, each about five inches long and with its jockey's colours brilliantly painted, stood at the starting-gate of an oval course. Grandstand, spectators, greensward, all were realistically done. Along the front of the counter ran a line of squares, each inscribed with the name of a horse and its colours. Projecting underneath each space was a crank-handle by which you made the horses run.

"It's all right, son!" H.M. assured Masters testily. "Burn it, I'm just havin' a look."

Behind the counter sat a dispirited-looking man, chewing a broomstraw, who had started to get up. Now he sank back again hopelessly.

H.M. inspected the track. He sniffed. He ran his eye

critically over the horses, like one inspecting a parade at Epsom. Then something seemed to take hold of him as though with hands, and he swung round.

"I'll give you five to one the field," he burst out. "And eight to one," he glanced behind him, "Blue Boy." His eyes gleamed. "I'll teli you what I'll do: I'll give you *ten* to one on Blue Boy!"

Ricky sprang forward.

"Here's ten bob on Blue Boy," said Ricky, slapping the money down on the corresponding counter-space. "And, just for luck, I'll have another ten bob on Squaw's Feather."

"For myself," said Stannard, instantly whipping out his note-case, "I fancy Bright-Eyes. With the dark brown colour; eh, Ruth? One pound on Bright-Eyes!"

"Uh-huh. One pound on Bright-Eyes," repeated H.M., who had scrabbled out with a notebook and the stub of a pencil, and was hastily recording. Then he lifted his voice to the whole fair-ground.

"I'll give you five to one the field," he bellowed. "Anybody want to make a little bet?"

"Goddelmighty!" whispered Chief Inspector Masters.

Now there are many words which will instantly rivet or turn the attention of an English crowd. You may say them over to yourself. But perhaps none is quite so potent as the word 'bet.' Materializing and mingling, the crowd pressed in ten-deep towards the counter, with cries and queries.

The man behind the counter, who had swallowed his broomstraw as he leaped up, now appeared to be racked by the convulsions of cyanide poisoning. He was writhing forward across the race-track, his hands outstretched.

"Oi! Gov'nor! The gent with the bald 'ead! For gossake! Oi!"

"What d'ye mean, oi?"

"It's against the LOR."

"What d'ye mean, it's against the law?"

"It's gambling," whispered and blurted the other, his eyes now rolling horribly *in articulo mortis*. "*I* wouldn't mind, see, but it's against the LOR. You'll 'ave the coppers on us!"

"Oh, my son! Don't you know no coppers can get in here today?"

"Whassat-forgossake?"

"This here Lady Brayle—" H.M. was in good voice; it carried far—"thinks people's liberties are bein' interfered with. Couldn't you have guessed that from what she wrote on the posters out there?"

A hum of approval, growing to a roar, spread out over the crowd. Dust and gravel flew. At his last extremity the dying man's eye seemed to catch some flicker beyond, a signal from an arm in a grey-and-black checked sleeve, which said, 'Yes.' The pangs of agony dropped from him.

Whang went the cymbals from an invisible brass-band; and, by one of those inspired coincidences which really do happen, the band crashed into *Camptown Races*. Martin, his head down and pulling Ruth after him, was fighting his way through a pressing crowd with silver in its hands. His damaged forehead took some dizzying knocks, but he got through.

Ruth Callice, her straw sun-hat squashed down, removed the hat and regarded him helplessly.

"Martin," she said, "is H.M. married?"

"Yes."

"Have you ever met his wife?"

"No."

Ruth shut her eyes, puffed out her cheeks, and seemed lost in questions of fancy in her own mind.

"This stout gen'leman will give you five to one the field; ten to one Blue Boy! Don't crowd, now! Keep back so's the 'andles can be turned. Lady Brayle wants you all to 'ave a fling!"

"Ruth," Martin said, "I've got to hurry. Excuse me if I go ahead."

He had still fifty or sixty yards of the drive to cover. But the stalls and booths were fewer; he could almost run. A yellow balloon, lost from someone's hand, sailed past on a rising breeze. He could see that the oak trees, set back twenty feet from the drive, allowed room for the stalls inside. But the bigger exhibits, like the Mirror Maze, the merry-go-round, and something which called itself Mermaids' Paradise, raised their garish colours well back on the lawn behind the trees.

Well, the bandage was still on. And he reached the terrace.

Except to glance along the front, Martin hardly looked at Brayle Manor. Between two square grey-black towers, one at each end and of great age, had been built a Tudor or Jacobean frontage, with latticed windows, which seemed almost of yesterday by comparison.

Martin banged the heavy knocker on the front door. There was no reply. He banged and banged until the noise, in his head, grew louder than the band and the loud-speakers and the merry-go-round. He thought he heard some sound from an oriel window, projecting out over the front door, and he stepped back. But a voice spoke from behind the front door.

"Is that Mr. Martin Drake?"

"Yes!"

With a rattle of bolts and the click of a key, the heavy door

177

opened under its low-pointed stone arch. Inside stood an elderly man in butler's canonicals, very shabby and clearly Dawson, with whom he had held that conversation about the five hundred pound...

He was in a dim, polished Tudor hall, low of ceiling and so much in twilight because all windows had been closed, all curtains drawn, against the noise.

"Martin!" said Jenny's voice.

A broad, low staircase, with carved balustrades, ascended along the left-hand wall. A heavy hinged panel at the side of the stairs stood more than part way open, and Jenny's face peered out at him.

"Martin," she said without preamble, "Grandmother's on the telephone."

Chapter 18

Martin strode over, hearing Dawson shut and lock the door behind him. Jenny was now regarding his forehead with far more consternation and concern than seemed possible if he had suffered serious injury.

"Just a minute, Jenny," he said. "What have you told her?"

"She only just started to speak. She said, 'Jennifer, I—' and that was where Dawson opened the door."

Taking the 'phone from Jenny's hands as she moved out from under the stair-opening, Martin sat down on a low little chair and cleared his throat.

"Lady Brayle? Martin Drake here."

To tell the truth, Martin was beginning to feel sorry for the old girl. True, she had brought the whole mess on herself by inviting MacDougall's Mammoth into her grounds. But H.M. was the evil genius. And, in the third round, H.M. had landed such a knockout punch that his adversary was still unconscious after the count. Or was H.M., actually, the evil genius? Martin was beginning to have other ideas. Still, the fact remained . . .

"Indeed," said Lady Brayle. "I was not aware, Captain Drake, that I wished to hold any conversation with you."

Calm and even of voice, conscious of no interest but her

own and not apparently caring who knew it, the lady with the cold grey eye spoke indifferently.

"So?" muttered Martin.

"However! I have heard certain rumours, which I do not believe, concerning the Manor. You will not trouble to comment on the facts. This would not interest me. You will merely be good enough to confirm or deny these rumours."

Martin held the telephone away from him and studied it. His temper, like a red line on a graph-paper, zig-zagged violently and then slowly soared high.

"Where are you now, Lady Brayle?"

"Really, that is not the slightest concern—"

"It may be. Where are you now?"

"I am at the Priory Hill vicarage, about two miles north of Brayle. I am in Mr. Barnham's study."

"Is that the clergyman who's so dead-set against horse-racing?"

Distantly, but still audible, the band-music swayed and jigged:

> "Oh, I put my money on a bob-tailed nag,
>   Doo-dah, doo-dah—"

"Has it occurred to you, Captain Drake, that I am waiting for an answer?"

"Madam," Martin said gently, "I can't answer your question as it deserves to be answered, because I don't know. I have a theory, but it may not be right. Sir Henry Merrivale," he hoped he could keep his promise, "will ring you in half an hour and explain everything."

"You will regret this, Captain Drake. When I return home, I shall carry a riding-crop. It will be most unpleasant for the first half dozen people I meet inside my gates."

Martin put down the 'phone and ducked out from under the stairs. Jenny, her wide-spaced blue eyes filled not only with concern, clutched his arms.

"You didn't say anything to insult her?"

"I don't think so, and I don't care."

"Darling," Jenny asked quietly, "have you any idea how lordly *you* can look and sound, when you get annoyed with somebody?"

"*Me?*"

This, to him, seemed so nonsensical that he put it down to some fancy of Jenny's romantic brain. He glanced round the dim, heavily stuffy hall, where the lean and sallow-haired

Dawson in his shabby butler's-clothes seemed a kind of symbol.

"No," Jenny answered his thought mockingly with a smile on her entirely irresistible mouth, "we didn't make the house look like a place of mourning because of the noise. It's a sort of gesture: when Grandmother comes back. Upstairs at the window we've been having a kind of signally-game with Mr. MacDougall. I don't know what it means, but he says it's frightfully important. Come along!"

Again the front-door knocker rapped, but far too heavily for it to have been Ruth Callice. Martin had his own guess.

"Chief Inspector Masters?" he shouted; and, at an affirmative reply, he nodded to Dawson.

Masters, having already pushed out a dent in his bowler hat and dusted off his blue serge suit, crossed the threshold with brief-case and cardboard folder under one arm; and he had the air of a tethered bull.

"Sorry to intrude, miss," he said, being not quite sure of Jenny's title and knowing she didn't like it anyway, "but this is business."

Jenny had gone rather white. "Yes," she acknowledged, and pressed Martin's arm. "After all, someone tried to kill Mr. Drake."

"And did kill that Puckston girl," said Martin.

"I wanted to ask—" Jenny began. "Will you come upstairs, please?"

She led them to an octagonal room, of white walls framed in dark oak, above the front door. Here was the big oriel window with its three leaded panes—two slantwise, the other facing straight out—which looked down the gravel drive with its crowd, its gaudy exhibits, the oak-trees, and the green lawns.

Geraniums in flower-pots, as a homely touch, stood just inside the ledges of the diamond-paned windows. The dark oak window-seat ran round all sides of the octagonal room as well; like the chairs, it had flattish flowered cushions. With one window-light partly open, the babble now sounded at its loudest.

"Mr. Masters," Jenny began.

Jenny, in white, her knees crossed, sat at one side of the window. Her elbow was propped on one knee, her chin in her hand.

"I think," she smiled, "I like H.M. far better than Martin likes Grandmother. But doesn't he ask the oddest questions sometimes?"

"Does he, miss?" inquired Masters, who was at his blandest

180

card-sharper's air as he put down hat, brief-case, and folder.

"He talked to me for ages yesterday at Fleet House. First all about certain things," her eyes moved towards Martin, who was sitting beside her, "when he hadn't been present. Then, if you please, something that seemed to be about Grandmother's influence over me!"

"Is that so, now, miss?" inquired Masters, as though hearing a mildly surprising revelation.

"And that's absurd, of course!" Jenny had some intense purpose behind this; her eyes were lustrous. "You see, my parents were estranged. They sent me away to school from the time I was ten and onwards. Grandmother was always hovering about, it's true. But most of the vacations were abroad with my parents. Then came the war and the Wrens. It's only since the war that Grandmother's had much 'influence.' I was wondering if H.M.—"

"Yes, miss?"

Martin who had got up and was staring out of the window, interposed.

"Where the devil *is* H.M., by the way?"

Masters's own temper flared as he sat down in a chair opposite Jenny. Everything grated now, everything jarred like a bad slate-pencil on a bad slate.

"Whatever he's doing," the Chief Inspector snapped, "he's not attending to business."

"There's a Derby-Day crowd round that race-track," said Martin, "all waving shillings. Is he still being bookie?"

"When I last saw the gentleman," Masters replied with dignity, "he was starting some kind of darts-contest." Masters looked at Jenny, not without sarcasm. "I suppose, miss, your grandmother doesn't keep a cellar full of beer?"

"Good heavens, no! She used to drink wine, but . . ."

"N-no," intoned Masters, "I didn't think she would keep a beer-cellar. And especially I didn't think she'd keep it in barrels with her photograph pasted on, and 'Here's how from Lady Brayle.' As to what the old bounder's *doing* . . ."

"I can tell you what he's doing," said Martin. "He told Arthur Puckston last night he'd been thinking for several days Grandmother ought to be ousted or made popular. He's trying to make her popular. And do you know what'll happen?"

Masters didn't care, and said so.

"She told me she'd come back with a riding-crop. And she will. Isn't that so, Jenny?"

"Darling," pleaded Jenny, "she tried to make friends with you. I told you she was beginning to like you, but you wouldn't

181

believe me. I didn't see her last night, because she went straight on to Priory Hill. Surely she tried to make friends with you?"

"Possibly. Anyhow, it didn't work. Now she'll come back with a riding-crop. She'll lay it, right and left, across anybody she sees. Then there'll be a riot and real trouble."

"I don't doubt it at all," Masters agreed, almost with satisfaction.

Then he whacked his hand down on the arm of the chair.

"Mr. Drake," Masters said, "this is a murder case. We had everything planned and even timed to a minute to catch the murderer. But Sir Henry's gone off his rocker, just as he did once at Coney Island, and what chance have we got now?"

"To catch—?" Jenny's face had gone even whiter. "But it couldn't possibly be . . . anybody we know?"

Belatedly, Masters remembered official caution and his usual manner.

"Is that so, miss? Why not?"

"Well!" Jenny laughed, not convincingly. "*I* didn't do it. Grandmother certanly didn't. For the rest, there's the alibi!"

"Oh, ah, miss? What do you know about an alibi?"

"Only what Ruth Callice told me yesterday." Jenny shivered violently; even her mouth seemed distorted; Martin quickly put his arm round her shoulder. "About a blood-stained dagger somebody used to kill poor Enid Puckston, at half-past eleven or thereabouts."

"Anything else, miss?"

"Ruth said Mr. Stannard—he's a tremendous barrister—had suddenly snapped his fingers and said to her, 'You know, I was so tired and groggy I completely forgot to tell Inspector Drake about that alibi. No, wait,' he said, 'let them find it out themselves.' But he told Ruth."

"You can forget the alibi too, miss," Masters remarked quietly. "It's shot to blazes."

From outside the window the churning tinkle of the merry-go-round, silent for a time, began to rise loudly with *We're All Together Now.* In the octaganal room, with its white walls and its red geraniums inside the window, the tune seemed to swirl round as in a bowl, above the babble of voices.

"So you did upset the alibi!" Martin muttered. "How?"

Masters looked complacent.

"We-el! No harm in telling that. You people who were in the condemned cell when you found the dagger, you were doing a lot of talking . . ."

"Chief Inspector, how do you know so much about that conversation?"

Masters eyed him grimly.

"Aren't you forgetting, Mr. Drake, that *I* spent the night in that prison? Oh, ah! Keeping an eye on *you* to make sure nobody nailed you?"

"You could hear everything we said all the time?"

"I'm an old-fashioned copper," Masters said dryly. "I've had trickier jobs when I was a sergeant."

"But where were you during the 'test'? I mean, when I'd locked Stannard behind the iron door, and the others had gone?"

Masters snorted.

"Making myself comfortable," he said, "on top of that mountain of paper. Lummy! We'd get sixteen hours at a stretch in the old days when I was a sergeant. On Saturday night I was facing the iron door. I could see you, Mr. Drake, by your own light, sitting on the paper-bales. I couldn't see down into the aisle, between the bales and the wall with the doors; but I could get there at one jump if I had to."

Here Masters smiled a peculiar smile.

"D'you think I'm a liar, sir? You look a bit funny. For instance! At shortly past twelve, you had a visitor."

The visitor had been Ruth Callice, of course.

Martin, his arm round Jenny's shoulder and the caress of her hair under his cheek, felt such a cold rush of guilty conscience that he was within a quarter-syllable of speaking out and denying it. At the same moment Jenny raised her head round and up, looked at Martin casually, and returned to her former position without comment. After a quick heat of emotional temperature, Jenny's shoulder seemed to become as cool and lifeless as though it did not exist at all; as though it rested there out of mere politeness. If there could have been a mental conversation between them, Jenny would have begun.

(Please don't think I'm annoyed. I knew it would happen *some* time that night).

(What are you talking about?)

(The same thing you're thinking about. How far did it go?)

But Masters, or so the Chief Inspector believed, had no intention of giving away a fellow-male.

"A visitor," he repeated judicially. "Well, no harm in that I could see it in two seconds. Later the—hurrum!—the bloke went back the same way. Then nothing happened until a quarter to one. But at a quarter to one I heard someone else rustle in that aisle."

Both Martin and Jenny were jarred out of their mental conversation. Both sat up. The sound of *We're All Together*

Now, mixed with crowd-babble, seemed to swirl higher.

"Somebody else?"

"Somebody, anyhow. It was just a bit of a faint rustle you could hardly hear, 'Strewth!" said Masters. "If I'd been younger in the force, I might have got the wind up myself.

"You wouldn't have heard it in any case, Mr. Drake. You were sound asleep. I got ready. I thought it was creeping towards you. Anyway, it wasn't. My eyes were enough used to the dark so I could make out the outlines of the doors in the wall. Just so! You remember, I told you last night there was a little camera trick that might interest you?"

"Yes! What about it?"

"Ordinary camera," Masters said, "borrowed from the local police. Infra-red film, infra-red bulb, from the chemist at Brayle. Useful to have along with you. Take photographs in the dark; not a glimmer to show you're taking 'em. *If* you know where to aim a camera.

"I could see that the end door opposite the bale-mountain— Mr. Drake was sleeping against the same wall about ten feet from the door—started to open. Soft as soft! And wider. No sense for me to yell lum's name if nothing was after Mr. Drake. I snapped a picture at the door before it closed.

"We-el," resumed Masters, tapping the brief-case on the table beside him, "I got the print from the chemist this morning. Not a good picture, no. But a picture of Enid Puckston."

"Of . . . what did you say?"

"Of Enid Puckston," repeated Masters, and tapped the brief-case again. "Creeping in backwards. Facing the camera. On tip-toe," Master's face darkened, "and with a 'What larks!' delighted look. Like a kid playing a prank. Somebody's hand was on her arm, drawing her in."

Masters drew a deep breath.

"*And this*," Martin demanded, "*was at a quarter to one in the morning?*"

"That's right. And—come now! Blimy-O'Reilly! Can't you see the trick of it?"

"I can see that the dagger we found among that heap of rapiers . . ."

"Oh, ah! Exactly. It'd been planted there, with fresh blood on it, to make what you think what you did think later.. That somebody'd killed the girl about half-past eleven. But the girl was still alive. Not even in the prison!

"You're the arms expert, Mr. Drake. And that Italian dagger you found, now! I told you knife-wounds can't be identified

184

certain-sure like bullet-wounds. Would you say that dagger was (hurrum!) unique?"

"Lord, no. There are plenty of them. I've got one something like it in my own collection."

Masters bent forward, his fingers spread. Every word he spoke seemed to pounce.

"Then: a quarter to one. Everything dark and quiet. Somebody from outside leads Enid Puckston along the aisle. Creeping, hardly a rustle. Soft as soft. Like a cat! Door opens (no noise; notice that), door closes. They're in the old mortuary.

"Somebody takes her across the mortuary, out into the garden under the windows of the condemned cell. Somebody kills her there with another dagger. Enid's carried the travelling-robe; it's in the photograph. Somebody carries her body, soft as soft, down the underground stair from the mortuary, along the passage, through a door, into the shaft under the gallows-trap . . ."

Masters, reverting to his normal tone, sat up straight.

"How was I supposed to know," he demanded, "there'd been a murder in the prison that night? I was uneasy, like: oh, ah! But my job was to follow Mr. Drake. And I did, when he left at what he thought was four o'clock. I followed you both," he looked at Jenny, "down over that field."

Now here was a characteristic of Jenny: that, though she had been furious a few minutes before over a little matter concerning Ruth, it seemed swept out of her mind at anything concerning Martin.

"You said," she exclaimed to Masters, "the murde—this person—you said this person was 'somebody from outside.' "

Masters pulled himself together, remembering official caution.

"Did I say that, miss?" he inquired, eyeing the brief-case. "Then I must have meant it, mustn't I?"

"So in that case . . ."

"As for the trick with fresh blood on the dagger that wasn't used, that's easy. Lummy! The whole alibi-trick was only a conjuring principle. Sir Henry could tell you that. People *won't* believe what's as clear as daylight. People *won't* believe how small a space a body can occupy; and, when a dozen girls walk out of a little cabinet, there's no hocus-pocus: the girls were honestly there. They *won't* believe the time a thing happened, from a coin-change to a couple of bodies, was back-to-foremost. Sir Henry could tell you that. But will he? Oh, no! He was supposed to be here fifteen minutes ago . . ."

185

Martin Drake, stung by memory, fumbled at his wrist-watch.

"Fifteen minutes!" he echoed. "It's more than half an hour!"

"What do you mean, more than half an hour?"

"I promised Lady Brayle——"

"Martin, you did!" Jenny began to move apprehensively.

"——that H.M. would ring her in half an hour. If she doesn't hear from him, she'll be here and start a riot!"

"Agreed," said Masters.

"Then you never will catch your murderer," said Martin, whose brain burned to know the look of somebody's face. "And *I've* got a score to settle too."

"You have," agreed Masters, looking at him in a curious way.

"Isn't there any way to find H.M.?"

"Find him?" said Masters. "That's easy enough. By the signalling system. But get him here? Ho! He's off his chump, I tell you!"

"What's this signalling business?"

Jenny hurried to a writing desk, and took up a sheet of paper with a list typed on it. Hastening to the middle page of the window, she raised her right arm and waved.

From some forty yards down the drive, there appeared the conspicuous sleeve of a grey-and-black checked suit. (Martin had seen that sleeve before, near the race-track booth.) A hand waved. Then, startlingly, the hand held high a square card bearing the large number 7.

Jenny's finger, on the typewritten sheet, found the number 7 and indicated to Martin, opposite the words *Mirror Maze*.

"That's Mr. MacDougall," she said rapidly. "For some reason he thinks H.M. is wonderful. He thinks H.M. was born to the show business. Martin! Wait! Just a moment!"

Martin scarcely heard Jenny's last words as he ran.

Outside the front door, a still-rising breeze swept his face. The sky was overcast, though it did not look like rain. Empty bags of potato-crisps danced past, and a small girl's hat.

"This, ladies and gentlemen," Martin could remember a voice through a loud-speaker, though he did not hear it amid the blatter now, "is the Mirror Maze. Biggest and finest attraction of MacDougall's Mammoth. The Mirror Maze. If you are unable——"

It was half-past twelve. Though a fair number of people still cluttered round the attractions, most of the crowd had retired farther back to eat out of picnic boxes. They sat on the greensward, encamped like an army, with white napkin-cloths and glinting thermos-flasks. As for music, only the band whooshed and boomed softly with Scottish airs. But in the drive, where Martin ran like hell, it was different.

"Get a fish, now! A wood-en fish, with a re-al hook, out of re-al running water. Each third fish contains a number a number, which—"

"See how easy it is? Just throw the wooden ring, like this, over the peg!"

"Come-on-Redjacket! Bill, turn that crank faster! Come-on-Redjacket for 'alf a crown!

This was the place.

Near the race-track, where the crowd bounced him round its edges like a roulette-ball, a wide space had been left between both lines of booths and stalls to form a sort of cross-avenue.

Beyond the open space on his right, set some hundred feet back, was the Mirror Maze. It stood alone; nothing anywhere near it except the Whip and the Dodgem.

"'Ave your try at the coconut-shy!" a voice was intoning, that of a little man who hopped from foot to foot under the spell of his own rhyming. *"'Ave your try at the coconut-shy!"* An arm snapped forward; the wooden ball clacked against the coconut; the coconut toppled and fell. *"That's the stuff, sir. One—cigarette! 'Ave your try at the coconut-shy!"*

It jigged through Martin's head, like the little man jigging back and forth, as he turned off the drive and ran towards the Mirror Maze. The loud-speaker had been right in calling the Mirror Maze its biggest attraction.

The structure was very large, circular in shape (odd, wasn't that, for a mirror maze?), and 'practical' in the sense that it had been built of very light wood painted dull silver. The words MIRROR MAZE stared at Martin in red letters.

But there was nobody at the ticket-seller's place. Nobody to speak into the microphone of the loud-speaker. No visitors. Nobody at all. Over the door hung a curtain of black felt, a good deal heavier and thicker than the under-felt for carpets.

The sky was growing darker, over a buzz and paper-crackle from an army at sandwich-eating. Some female singer, whose voice reminded Martin of Lady Brayle, had joined the brass-band and urged it to softness. Martin heard one line above the heavy lion-purr of the band:

"Ma-a-a-x-wel-l-l-ton's braes are bo-o-n-n-ie—"

187

Then he ducked past the mattressy black felt, became entangled in another black curtain, and twisted himself free from that.

"H.M.!" he shouted.

Inside the circular structure was another structure: almost as large, but square and painted black. It had only one door, opening into a broad corridor, dimly lighted and lined with polished looking-glass.

To Martin, as he crossed the threshold of the Mirror Maze, it seemed he was walking into a gigantic box-camera.

"Oi! H.M.! Where are you?" he called. But the shout seemed lifeless, flat, stifled, as he strode along the corridor.

(I know it's an optical trick, but this corridor looks as long as something at Versailles. It isn't actually broad, either; I can touch each side by stretching out my hands. Also, I can see the joinings down the mirrors. Of course the corridor's not long! Two turnings here.)

Martin took one turning. He walked a dozen feet farther, and took another.

"H.M., don't try to play the fool! This is only a little place; you can't help hearing me. They know you're here!"

Exasperated, Martin paused. He looked round with curiosity, and then with some feeling other than exasperation.

He was the only living soul in this maze. Yet he was not alone. Everywhere he was pursued, surrounded, and furtively glanced at round corners, by images of himself.

The dim yellow light, from some concealed source along the tops of the mirrors, turned the place into a shiny, shadowy labyrinth, all straight lines and right-angles, short passages and long, with one looking-glass occupant.

Martin Drake, turning to one side, confronted himself: he looked, with the discoloured forehead, exactly like a pirate. He turned to the other, with the same result. He walked forward again, his footsteps clumping, to what seemed to be the junction of four passages. As he circled round, a whole band of pirates multiplied and circled with him.

(All right. If H.M. is up to some crafty game, let it be taken as done. I'm going to get out of here.)

That would be easy, of course. He had only to remember where he came in, which must be comparatively close. But the fact was that he couldn't remember where he came in.

Well, what of it?

All that would be required of him, as Stannard had said, was a little logical reasoning. A sense of direction, too. Here— observe, now!—was the junction of what appeared to be four corridors. One of them looked like a dead-end. Martin edged in, reaching out his fingers to touch his own reflected fingers, and met the glass. Good! He'd established that.

Now the other corridor, opposite, must be fully twenty feet long. It had a mirror there facing him; but a long corridor must have a turn at the side which (now he remembered!) was the direction he had come.

Martin, heated with elation, took five strides forward. And . . .

God!

Out of nowhere, leaping, a full-length mirror rushed at him and banged him full body and face.

Only the sudden vision of his own eyes—appearing hideously magnified by their closeness—made an instinctive recoil and lessened the shock as he smacked full-tilt into his own reflection. What angered him was the real shock to the nerves it had given him in a childish place meant for amusement.

"Now let's consider this!" Martin said, unaware he was speaking aloud.

"Looking-glasses can't suddenly move across in front of you. Any more than a lot of beach-chairs can rush at you and push you off a roof."

That was a grisly thought. What brought such an idea into his head?

"Therefore," he argued, and still aloud to all his ghost-selves, "there's an explanation. This mirror I ran into: it's the end of the passage I was trying to reach.

"Got it! A mirror at the end of the passage gives a double length of reflection. You judge it by the floor. If it looks twenty feet away, it's actually only ten. I went tearing forward, like Grandmother Brayle, and as a result—!" He stopped.

That was a sound, not from his imagination, clearly if very faintly heard, which registered with him. It was, 'Brayle,' or 'Lady Brayle.'

Despite its layers of looking-glasses and its double roof, the Mammoth Mirror Maze was not exactly soundproof. Nobody could mistake the slowly gathering roar from a little distance away, to Martin's heighted senses carrying a note of anger; the shouts; the heavy drumming of crowd-feet across open grass.

The old girl had returned.

She must have returned, he reflected, almost as soon as he himself had dived into this place. She had started raising hell at the main gates, and must have got some way up the drive with her riding-crop before . . .

Well, he'd *got* to get out of this place. Martin tried again.

What drives a man frantic, even under the most ordinary circumstances, is that he cannot make speed even when he refrains from making haste. The more he says it to himself—slowly, slowly, no haste or you'll fumble—the more matters become snarled. The clock-hand crawls; the chance is lost.

"If you are unable to get out of the Mirror Maze," Martin's memory brought back the words from the loud-speaker, *"directions will be given by—"*

Given by whom? Given how? He had heard no more.

Martin, trying to keep from a run and holding out his hands against obstacles, hurried always into a dead-end. His watch kept ticking steadily, tiny digs of urgency. If only he hadn't come in here alone . . .

But he was not alone in the maze.

He discovered this as he whipped round the angle of a corridor, and stopped dead.

This corridor (his eye, used to it now, could judge accurately) was twenty feet long. Ahead of him, back to Martin, walked a man in a brown coat and blue trousers.

A grey soft hat was pulled down on the back of the man's head, concealing even the neck. In the dim light, in the secret silvery cavern, no details could be seen. And, though the man wore heavy boots and walked heavily, he made not a sound. All this went through Martin's head while the man took three steps.

"Hoy! There! Wait a minute!"

Martin ran forward. The air itself took form against him. His outstretched hands thumped into an invisible barrier which jarred him to the shoulder-bones and stopped him in his tracks.

It was a polished sheet of thick plate-glass: invisible, stretching across the whole corridor and cutting it in two. No wonder the man's steps had made no sound!

Martin, his hands against the glass, stood there for a moment and tried to think straight. This wasn't a predicament: it was merely damned ludicrous. He was not in the Cretan labyrinth, or even in Pentecost Prison. He was in a trumpery two-by-four pavilion at a country fair, and yet as excited as though . . .

Whereupon, although the corridor was empty except for Martin, a voice spoke. The voice had a note of slyness; it was not loud; it even whispered. The voice said:

"You had better leave, Mr. Drake. If you can."

Chapter 19

About a quarter of an hour before that voice spoke to Martin, there was at Brayle Manor a scene far more wrenched with emotion, far deeper in the springs of human life.

Sophia, Dowager Countess of Brayle, almost staggered as she moved up the broad oak staircase in the dim house. Her fashionable hat was disarranged on the grey-white hair. The fashionable dress, also a little disarranged, did not now conceal her stoutness. From the limp fingers of one hand dangled a riding-crop. Nevertheless, most noticeable of all was the look of utter stupefaction in her eyes.

Lady Brayle stumbled a little on the top step. She went over to the octagonal room, whose oriel window faced the drive, and opened the door.

In the window-seat, his back to the leaded panes, Sir Henry Merrivale sat smoking a cigar. Chief Inspector Masters stood beside him. Jenny, at the other side of the window, looked at the floor.

Lady Brayle groped for and found a chair. She sat down heavily. She drew her breath heavily through her heavy body. For a few seconds she stared at the carpet, and then looked up.

"They cheered me," she said.

Her tone was one of incredulity, though perhaps she had not meant it as such. It was that of one half-waking from hypnosis.

"They cheered me!" she repeated.

Nobody else spoke.

Lady Brayle seemed vaguely to notice the riding-crop in her hand. As though nobody else in the room knew what happened, she went on.

"I—that is, Mr. Barnham was kind enough to send me over in a car. An open car. With a driver. I gripped *this* in my hand. From some distance away one of the wr-wretches saw the car coming, and ran to tell his fellow—other people. As we swung in at the gates I stood up and gripped *this*. For I could hear them roaring. But . . .

"They were lined up on each side of the drive and beyond. Heaven knows how many of them. Some waved balloons, and some waved Union Jacks. They were shouting and cheering for me. Then, I believe, some wr-wretched band struck up. They began to sing."

It was unnecessary to tell her listeners, even if they did not know. For at that moment, beyond the oriel window, the band struck up with the same tune and the voices joined again.

> *"For she's a jolly good fel-low,*
> *For she's a jolly good fel-low,*
> *For she's . . ."*

Out it rolled, one repetition after another, over the ancient oak-trees of Brayle Manor. Lady Brayle put her hands over her face.

"Sophie," growled H.M., taking the cigar out of his mouth, "you come to this window and wave your hand at 'em. Don't say anything, or I'll wring your neck. Just wave."

"Henry, you fiend!" said Lady Brayle.

"Uh-huh. But you do what I tell you."

Lady Brayle got up, shaking and adjusting her shoulders, and moved over to the window. Beyond the sky showed dull, almost lead-coloured, with the red geraniums in their flower-pots against it. Lady Brayle lifted her arm in the manner of one unaccustomed to do so.

When she returned to her chair, after the tumult subsided, she was still half-dazed.

"As—as the car went up the drive," she said, "I confess I was stunned. I . . . I could only make some response, as a matter of courtesy, by waving *this.*

"At the terrace there were calls for 'speech.' This, naturally, was a duty I could fulfil admirably. I was about to do so, when my attention was attracted by a revolting noise from that window there. I looked up, and saw projecting from the window a quite horrible face, which I discerned to be Henry's. He was holding a flower-pot.

"He informed me (pray forgive me for repeating such words) that, if I were to speak one word of what I had intended to speak, he would drop the goddam flower-pot on what he described as my onion.

"The fiend told me to do only what he called my routine, which I have always considered somewhat graceful. It consists in calling for three cheers, and taking two steps backwards while raising my hand. I . . . I confess that the volume of the cheering: I never heard it before."

Lady Brayle thought for a while. Then her mood changed.

"This is pure sentimentality," she said abruptly, and

192

whacked down the riding-crop on the table, where she left it. "How very amusing! The cheers of a vulgar mob!"

"Sure," agreed H.M. "We know you're above all that." He contemplated the glowing tip of the cigar, he frowned down at his big shoes, and looked up again. "But don't you find it just a bit comfortin', Sophie, now that you and I are old?"

There was a pause. Then Lady Brayle heaved herself to her feet.

She went over to the little writing-desk, with her back to them. While the others pretended not to notice, she removed a hat disarranged from (mere) feelings, straightened her dress, repaired her face while peering into the mirror of a compact, and shut up her handbag with a decisive snap.

When she returned to the chair, and sat down with dignity and grimness, she was herself again.

"And now, Henry," she suggested briskly, "shall we have this matter out between us to a finish?"

"Grandmother!" cried Jenny.

But again two strong personalities, with a sort of silent blare, faced each other.

"Sophie," H.M. said mildly, "don't tangle with me again. I'm just warning you."

"'Tangle with' is an expression I have heard before. It is a vulgarism, probably transatlantic. But I will make you pay for your childishness, believe me."

"Uh-huh?" said H.M.

"First of all, I will admit that an error of judgment on my part admitted this revolting display," she nodded towards the booths and stalls outside, "under the impression that it was a simple rustic fair, and . . ."

"Oh, Sophie," groaned H.M., taking the cigar out of his mouth. "You knew smacking well what kind of show it was, or you wouldn't have had correspondence and signed a contract on MacDougall's Mammoth letter-paper. You wanted money; who's blamin' you? But you're spinnin' this little piece of hooha, for your friends, about how you've been taken in."

Jenny, really shocked, uttered an exclamation and sat up straight. Her grandmother regarded her with mild surprise.

"You find this strange, Jennifer?"

"*I* don't care," Jenny told her with a sort of loathing, "whether you go out in the street with a tin cup and a dancing bear. But why must you be hypocritical about it?"

"One has one's responsibilities, Jennifer. I fear you would not understand that."

"For years," cried Jenny, "you've been saying you would do

this, and you would do that, but you wouldn't stoop to tell lies."

"And I never do," replied Lady Brayle, quite sincerely believing every word she said, "except when I consider it just. As, for instance, telling your friend Captain Drake you had gone to London instead of Ranham Old Park."

Then she whipped round to H.M., coolly.

"But a fair in Rupert's Five-Acre is one thing. A detestable display on the approach to Brayle is quite another. When I heard of it, Henry, I was *quite* prepared to use this riding-crop on the vulgar."

"Sure, Sophie. I know that. What's more," said H.M., with a shadow of huge and ghoulish pleasure on his face, "you're goin' to get another beautiful surprise when you look out your bedroom window."

"And *you*," pounced Lady Brayle, "were responsible. I shall sue—"

"By the way, Sophie, what are they payin' you? The show's here for a week; you bargained for that. What are they payin' you by the day?"

"I believe," answered Lady Brayle, lifting one shoulder with an air of indifference, "it is the beggarly sum of ten pounds."

"Well . . . no. As a matter of fact, you're gettin' sixty."

"Sixty pounds a day?"

"That's right. And fifty per cent of the car-park profits. I had to do some swift work on that first part; but here it is." He fumbled inside his breast pocket and took out a cheque. "This is MacDougall's first of the week's rent. D'ye want it, or shall I turn it back to him?"

"This," Lady Brayle conceded with grace and dignity, "somewhat alters the complexion of matters." She allowed a space of silence. "I accept."

"Here you are, then."

"I am not mercenary," said Lady Brayle, taking the cheque carelessly, scrutinizing it with great care, and then hastily putting it in her handbag. "I do not think," again she brought out the cheque for examination before shutting it up, "I do not think that my worst enemy could call me mercenary. But one has one's rights."

"Definitely, Sophie. Nobody's denying it."

Whereupon Lady Brayle gave him a peculiar smile.

"Another point, Henry. Those photographs of me outside the gates, which by the way are not bad," she adjusted her shoulders, "were no doubt the work of Mr. MacDougall. But this strange popularity of mine, which I had never noticed

194

before: I can guess it might be some of *your* work. Was it, Henry?"

"Uh-huh."

"And why, pray, do you take such trouble on my part?"

H.M. looked embarrassed. "Well, Sophie, there were a lot of reasons."

"As, for instance?"

"You used to be an A-1 sport. You'd still be a human being if you'd only for the love of Esau stop thinking what's vulgar and what ain't. Most of all, I realized—only last night, it was!—why you stole the skeleton out of that clock."

Chief Inspector Masters started to speak, but checked himself.

Against the dark sky outside, the walls of this little octagonal room appeared starkly white. One of the leaded window lights, propped open, rattled at its catch in the rising wind. Masters, heretofore, had been paying small attention to the conversation; he was looking out of the window, on edge, waiting for a signal. Now, as H.M. mentioned the skeleton and the clock, it was as though someone had flung down a coiling snake.

"Ah!" said Lady Brayle, and grew rigid. "I thought we should come to some bargaining-point about your precious skeleton. Well, you won't get it."

"I'm sorry about that, Sophie. Then I got to take it."

"The law, my dear man . . ."

"Didn't you hear what I said?" H.M.'s big voice rose sharply in the little room. "I said I knew why you stole the skeleton. That means I know why it's such vital evidence. And I can take it."

Lady Brayle, with both hands on the arms of the chair, pushed herself up.

"If you think I'm bluffing," H.M. added, "I'll give you a little tip. Masters here has applied to the Home Office for an exhumation-order."

"And what, precisely, does that mean?"

"It means they're goin' to dig up the body of George Fleet."

"Henry, are you entirely mad? The skeleton I have here is not that of Sir George Fleet!"

"I know it, Sophie," said H.M. "It's not Sir George Fleet's," he added, "except for a little bit."

"A little bit . . ."

"Which you can't see," snapped H.M., "until you take it out of the clock."

Lady's Brayle's whole manner and tone altered again.

195

"For God's sake," she pleaded, "and for the sake of old friendship, let the dead rest! You don't know how horrible it is! You don't . . ."

"MacDougall's signalling," Masters reported, stolidly but with quicker breathing. "It's the left arm for X? Oh, ah!" He lifted his left arm and waved it. A pause. "Card's up. It's number 7." From the window-seat Masters picked up a typewritten sheet of paper. "It's the Mirror Maze, all right. Nobody made any mistake. X is the Mirror Maze."

"So!" grunted H.M., throwing his cigar out of the window. "And pretty near on time, too. Looky here: where's young Drake? *He* ought to be with us."

"How should I know where he is?" demanded Masters "I told you he went charging out of here, looking for you, not two minutes before you got here! I don't know where. The young lady just pointed to some number on the list, and out he went."

"But it was there!" exclaimed Jenny. "The Mirror Maze!"

"Oh, lord love a duck." H.M.'s mouth fell open. "This is bad, Masters. This is bad."

"Eh? What's up?"

"You know what might happen," said H.M. cryptically, "if our dewy-eyed innocent meets the wrong man in that ruddy maze. Masters, come on!"

They paid no attention to protests or entreaties. In a very short time, under the dark sky and with the crowd milling towards shelter against possible rain, they saw the maze ahead. H.M., at a curious pigeon-toed run which made children stare, was able to keep up with Masters.

The circular structure, dull silver with its red letters, loomed up. Out from a fringe of the crowd hastened a lean youngish man, in a grey-and-black checked suit and with a beret on his brilliantined black hair. To a man in overalls he handed a bundle of big numbered placards. The young man had a shrewd, shiny, razorish kind of face, now one focus of eager interest in the eyes.

" 'Owzit, cock?" he asked H.M. affectionately. "Did I do it right?"

H.M. began to rave.

"But you *was* in there," protested Mr. MacDougall, "even if you only looked round. And I wasn't to signal when you come out, was I?" he broke off. "Oi! Charley.' "

A well-dressed young man, in the ticket seller's cage, rose up over the top of the booth.

"I was to drive them out," Charley answered in dubiously refined tones, "at twelve-thirty. I was to come back at a quarter

196

to one. If anybody wanted tickets, I was to tell 'em the maze was full and would they come back later. Except the *right* one. I was to give the right one a ticket, or tickets—"

"Your friend's inside," said Mr. MacDougall. "In we go!"

Though they writhed through the thick felt curtain in a cursing wedge, nevertheless H.M., Masters, and their companion stood still and said nothing on the other side. They were all listening.

The great black box, like a camera with a faintly illuminated door of looking-glasses, stood silent inside its circular wooden shell. Softly the eager MacDougall led the way into the maze. Its soft-gleaming corridors led them on at first one angle, then another.

"Looky here, son," muttered H.M. "We can talk now, can't we?"

"We can talk," said Mr. MacDougall, "until I give you the sign we're near you-know-where. Meantime, we're buried." He looked round at all his reflections. "I don't envy your friend, cock. No fooling: this maze is a bastard. No fooling: it's the best there is. No fooling: ninety per cent of 'em don't get out 'less they take directions from the loud-speaker inside.'"

"Which loud speaker?" demanded Masters.

The other, hunching up padded shoulders, regarded Masters with exaggerated expression of pity and hopelessness. Evidently he did not like coppers.

"This maze is a square within a circle. See?"

"Well? What about it?"

Mr. MacDougall pointed to the ceiling.

"There's a loud-speaker in every corridor. Only you can't see it (see?) 'less you look close. There's a microphone out in the circle, where it's open space. Bill Fraser keeps talking to the people in 'ere. Bill can't see 'em. 'E can't 'ear 'em. But Bill talks to 'em as if he could, things that'd apply to anybody. And they jump and laugh nervous and Christ how they enjoy it! 'Careful, lady; that's a dead-end.' 'Mind, the gentleman with the bowler hat: you're taking a wrong turn.'"

Still there was no sound in the maze except MacDougall's voice.

"About every ten minutes Bill will say, 'If you can't get out, follow the black arrow.' Them black arrows are painted high up on the glass, see? You can't find 'em 'less you're told about 'em. That leads to . . ."

"*You know me, don't you?*" whispered a thin, faintly husky voice from empty space.

Mr. MacDougall, despite his knowledge, jumped as though

stung. He adjusted his beret over the shrewd, shiny face.

"That's not Bill Fraser," he said to H.M. "That's your murder-party starting now. Come on!"

They gave only one glance towards the fretted circle in the ceiling which showed the source of the voice. Following MacDougall, they hastened and stumbled forward among their own images. They took another right-angled turn—and came face to face with Martin Drake.

Chief Inspector Masters, who expected to meet his own reflection, was even more startled to see somebody else. Martin had just put down on the floor a piece of white paper torn in a thin strip from an envelope. A wave of relief went over his face, and something else as well.

"It's the pipes at Lucknow," Martin said, and flung down the shredded envelope.

"This your friend?" hoarsely inquired Mr. MacDougall. "Good!" He eyed the strip on the floor. "Beg-pardon-I'm-sure; but what the 'ell are you doing?"

Martin looked at him. "For some minutes, now," he said, "I've been putting these down to block up what I KNOW are dead-ends."

"Never mind that," snapped a glowering H.M. "Son, I've been worried. Have you met anybody?"

"Not met," said Martin. "I *saw* somebody with a damned brown coat and blue trousers, walking away from me. Then I ran into a sheet of plate glass. Then a voice; I found afterwards it was a loudspeaker; advised me to get to blazes out of here. That was when I started putting down papers. I wonder if Houdini ever tried this blasted place?"

Mr. MacDougall, immensely pleased, did a little tap-dance; and then nervousness smote him.

"Now look!" he urged. "I'm leading the way. Three more turnings, and we're there. When I give the sign," he made gestures like a temple-dancer, to illustrate, "don't start to speak or mess about. For gossakes don't! We'll be too near 'em!"

"Near them?" repeated Martin. "Near whom?"

"Go on!" urged the insistent voice from the ceiling, as though it were eerily feeling its way along the mirror walls. *"Come a little closer! It's not so dark you can't make me out!"*

"Son," H.M. said to Martin, "do you know who's speakin' now?"

"No!"

"It's Arthur Puckston. Puckston was the feller in the brown coat."

"You don't mean Puckston is the . . . ?"

"Puckston's talking to somebody. That somebody killed George Fleet, killed and mutilated Enid Puckston, and almost murdered you: all the same somebody. We're ready, Mac-Dougall."

Though it took them three turnings and one fairly long corridor, it was only a matter of seconds until MacDougall gave the signal. Then Martin tried to straighten out his thoughts.

They all now stood facing down a short passage, not more than six or eight feet deep, with no other passage turning out of it. They stared at a dead-end of looking-glass.

"*I don't say much,*" sounded Puckston's voice from the ceiling. "*I was never one to say much, was I? Would I make trouble?*"

Only a bumbling murmur answered with something like "What do you want, then?" Whoever somebody was, Puckston was crowding the voice away from the microphone. Whoever somebody was . . .

Then Martin realized the presence of something impossible.

Straight ahead, reflected in that glimmering dead-end, he saw H.M.'s bulk and impassive eyes, Masters in down-pulled hat and with pencil moving on a notebook, himself like a pirate, MacDougall in beret peering round the angle of the passage. Crowding images of them sprang up wherever you looked. But . . .

"*I know you killed Enid.*" Puckston's breathing was now audible. "*I wanted you to hear that, like. That I know you killed 'er.*"

"You can't prove that." (Whose voice?)

MacDougall had told them almost with tears that they must not utter a whisper, not make a shoe-scrape, or the slightest sound would betray them. But on the floor lay a piece of paper which Martin had dropped there.

He had explored that passage. It was made of solid looking-glasses. If the microphone were outside this mirror maze in the circular shell, you could clump about or talk without being heard.

Then where were Puckston and his companion? Standing there invisibly, by some optical trick?

"*I tell you again, I don't want to prove it. If I did, I'd a' gone to the police.*"

"With what evidence?" (Come closer! Come closer!)

"*I dunno. I didn't think.*" Puckston's breathing grew shorter

199

and heavier. *"You killed my little girl. That's all I know."*

No reply at all, now. Masters was silently raving.

"You killed my little girl. Why did you do it?"

"I had to. It was a kind of—expression."

"What's that?"

"I said a kind of expression. Don't sob. You—"

"But you did kill 'er?"

"Yes! What's so bad about it?"

Clearly, not loudly, but with smooth and articulated viciousness, somebody's voice moved straight on microphone. Martin Drake realized, with horror, whose voice it was.

"We mustn't worry over these things. They happen," said somebody's voice. *"You seem sensible. I'll take care of you."*

"No, by God!" said Puckston. And every effect was shattered; his voice, with the sound known as blasting, pierced the ear but smothered clearness. *"No, by God! I'll take care of you!"* And through that bubbling blatter there came a faint noise as of a hammer thudded down on meat.

"Stop it!" shouted Masters. "Stop it! The confession is—"

It was too late. And the maze gave up its last secret.

Before Martin's eyes what seemed a solid mirror at the end of the short passage rippled like water, soundlessly, distorting the staring reflections. Then it curled and disappeared. Somebody, back to the watchers, staggered into the passage: reeling out of nowhere, piercing a dead-end, straight into the watchers' faces.

Arthur Puckston, forcing back that reeling figure, no longer stooped. His narrow bald head, his staring blue eyes, loomed like an image of mania. He was hitting for the face with a countryman's blows: unskilled, straight, murderous. Then all the group collided, and flew apart.

Martin, flung backwards, tripped and caught himself as he went down. Master's yellow pencil rolled underneath him as he got up, among reeling reflections less like a mirror maze than like a kaleidoscope. Puckston, still shouting, had driven his adversary into a short passage at right-angles to the other.

But it was all over.

One last blow Puckston landed before Masters locked both his arms from behind. Puckston's adversary, flung back against a mirror at the end of the passage, struck it with too great weight. With a crunching noise, opening in slow cracks, great shards slid down and splintered on the floor as the figure slid down and lay motionless.

"Y'know," said H.M. in a calm and meditative tone, "it's interestin' to nab this feller in a house of mirrors. He may be

200

the most vicious, he's certainly the most conceited murderer, I've ever met."

And all of them, panting, looked down amid smashed glass-shreds at the unconscious figure and bloodstained face of Richard Fleet.

Chapter 20

The policeman, pacing his beat through Moreston Square, South Kensington, glanced up to see the lighted windows on the top floor of number 16. It was the Thursday night—or, to be exact, the Friday morning—exactly a fortnight after he had seen lights burning so late in Miss Callice's flat.

From St. Jude's tower the chimes rang and rippled with the hour of three. The policeman smiled and sauntered on.

If he had looked into the comfortable living-room on the top floor, he would have seen in its easiest chair a large, stout, barrel-shaped gentleman in a white linen suit, with a cigar in one hand and a strong whisky-and-soda in the other.

Ruth was there, and Stannard, and Jenny, and Martin, and, as it happened, Lady Brayle. The light of the silver-shaded wall-lamps touched unquiet faces. It had taken a long time, and a very fair amount of whisky, to work themselves toward hearing what H.M. had begun to say.

H.M. drew deeply at the cigar, scowled, and put down the glass on the table beside him.

"Y'see," he said, "the boy-murderer is not at all uncommon. I don't have to tell you that. Usually he's psychopathic, as Ricky Fleet is. But, as a rule, he's nabbed straightway and shoved into confinement where he can't do any more harm.

"What's interesting here is to watch the boy-murderer who's grown up into a man-murderer. Still protected and cosseted by his mother! Still not believin' a soul now alive has suspected him! To watch his reaction to grown-up life; watch him squirm, watch him wriggle, watch him blurt out things, watch him smile and smile, until he's told his last lie. All that, y'know, you saw unroll in front of your eyes.

"Now if we're goin' into the grisly details," continued H.M., "there are some things we got to understand about Ricky Fleet.

"He really is a charmin' and likeable bloke. His good-nature

201

is absolutely genuine. His generosity and free-handedness are genuine. His bravery, where he could be crazy-reckless but cool-headed at the same time, was genuine too. If you think those qualities can't belong to a murderer just balanced between sanity and insanity, think of Ronald True. Or Patrick Mahon. Or—my eye, how recent this is!—Neville Heath."

H.M. grunted.

At the end of the sofa opposite sat Jenny, her eyes fixed intently on him, and Martin with his arm round Jenny. Ruth sat at the other end of the sofa, with Stannard perched on its arm. He was an effulgent Stannard, beaming.

"To start at the beginning," continued H.M., eyeing a pile of papers on the table beside his glass, "Masters sent me a heap of testimony about the death of George Fleet. Together with three apparently scatty postcards about 'examine the skeleton in the clock' and 'what was the pink flash' and 'the evidence is still there.'

"I'd decided, before we went to Berkshire, that Fleet's death was murder. I argued the salient points with Masters at the Dragon's Rest on Saturday. You people haven't seen these typed sheets, maybe . . ."

Martin intervened.

"I've heard some of it," he said. "I heard you prove to Puckston, out of his own testimony, that he couldn't have swung that telescope round when he said he did. Did that make you suspect it was murder?"

"Oh, my son!" groaned H.M.

"It didn't?"

"Not so's you could notice it. All it showed was that Puckston had been lying, and there might be a lot of hokey-pokey in his statement. But *what* hokey-pokey? No, son. The glarin' give-away is in the testimony of an honest witness, Simon Frew with the binoculars, supported by others. Frew was lookin' straight at Fleet from the middle gable. I'll read what he said, just as Masters read it to me."

H.M. fished among the papers at his side, drew out a blue-bound folder, and grubbed through it until he found what he wanted.

Sir George was there. I could see all round him. He had his glasses to his eyes in one hand, and was waving with the other. Then it looked like somebody gave him a hard shove in the back. He stood there for a second. He shouted. He fell head-first.

H.M. threw the folder back among the papers.

"If somebody gives you a hard shove in the back," he said, pointing his cigar at his listeners, "you don't 'stand there for a second.' You go straight over. As Martin Drake can tell you.

"Nobody pushed Fleet, or the pusher would have been seen. Nobody threw a weight at him. Aside from no weight being found, and no place to throw without bein' seen, it would have made Fleet lurch or stagger even if he didn't pitch straight over. He still wouldn't 'stand there for a second.'

"When I read that first, I felt a frizzlin' kind of feeling,"—H.M. indicated his corporation,—"here. Like devils at work. Fleet was in pain, intense pain. Or weakness. Or both. That look 'like a hard shove in the back' was muscular jerk and reaction which would give the same gestures.

"If you'll think about that for a bit, you'll get the key and the lock together. *I* didn't get that give-away straight off—being goop-witted, which the same I often am not—but I got it later."

Jenny, under Martin's arm, turned her head up to look at him uneasily, inquiringly, while a shiver went through her. He could think only of unshaped devilries against a lurid-glowing red sky.

"But, H.M.," Martin protested, "that's one of the things we do want to understand. *How was Fleet killed?*"

"You be quiet," H.M. ordered austerely. "I've got somethin' else to tell you."

Before resuming, he also mentioned the fact that he was the old man.

"Honest," he said, "what bothered me most in that bundle of Masters's testimony was the boy. I mean the tow-headed twelve-year old boy, Richard Fleet. The Scotland Yard bloke didn't take a statement from him; only the local police did. But he got into the other statements, and he worried me.

"Whatever else George Fleet was, he was dead-keen on sport and dead-keen on the Army. Take his own career! As Masters said, he'd been sent to boarding-school when he was a tiny 'un—ten or even less—then to Harrow, and then to Sandhurst. He couldn't finish Sandhurst, because he had to take up his dad's business. Oh, my eye! Don't you see a man like Fleet would be dreamin' of a career for his son just like the interrupted one of his own? Dreamin'? He'd have had it planned in detail from the first cradle-squawk.

"But this son, at twelve, was still at home with a governess. Why?

"Was the boy delicate and rabbity? No: he was a pocket

203

athlete. Thick-witted? That wouldn't have mattered at a school; but, anyway, he was very intelligent. Did the fond mother step in and say she couldn't have her darling away? No: George Fleet ruled that roost and his word was law.

"Then why?

"Let's take the boy's governess, this Miss Upton. H'm. There were bits about *her* in the testimony that bothered me. But let's jump ahead and use what you all knew or heard for yourselves.

"Miss Upton was the rummiest kind of governess I ever heard of. She was sort of immense, with a build like Sandow the Strong Man; and she knew how to put on a real wrestlin'-grip. She was with the family for four years. Correct?"

It was Jenny who answered, Jenny with shining eyes but with the weighted and harassed air of one who has guessed too much.

"Correct," Jenny almost whispered. "I reminded Ricky himself, when he spoke about her."

"And on that roof of gaiety and delight," said H.M., "your Ricky told me—in his careless and laughin' way—she was with him till he was fourteen. Now it's fourteen instead of twelve. And at this time, he added, they *pensioned her off*. A pension after four years' service? I tried to keep from doin' more than blink. Either that was a lie, or else Miss Upton couldn't stand it and Cicely Fleet had to buy her silence.

"I wonder if you've begun to catch the unnatural atmosphere of Fleet House twenty years ago? The nervous, stampin' father, who wallops his son (as the son told me) like blazes. The pretty, well-meanin' mother, who loves everybody and hopes George will get a baronetcy; and there mustn't be any scandal. Lemme give you one reminder: at Priory Hill, in November of 1925, a child was murdered and mutilated. Immediately afterwards George Fleet suddenly tore down his collection of rapiers and daggers from the wall, and gave 'em away. At that time young Fleet was in his eleventh year—Why didn't they dare send him to school? You answer."

A cold shock of horror spread through his listeners and lay inside them like lead, although two of them at least had been expecting it.

"I'm afraid, y'know," H.M. shook his head, "that in a way I did Masters in the eye. I warned him about it at the pub on Saturday afternoon. That little bit about Fleet gettin' rid of his weapons was in the original dossier I read in London. It bothered me worst of all. I rang up a friend of mine at the *Evening News,* and asked him if anything unpleasant had happened in this district about November, 1925. Cor! I got a answer.

"Masters learned this later, and told you. I knew beforehand. That was why I told young Drake, at Willaby's on Friday, to keep an eye out for real trouble. Because . . . well, now! You'll see.

"H.M.!" Ruth Callice intervened softly "I've been a friend of poor Cicely for years. I knew she was hiding some kind of secret; but I never guessed it was an awful thing like this. And yet when I first visited there—the impression wore off later—I thought of that house as something like a prison."

(So, thought Martin, you did get the feeling too! Like mine, it wore off).

"And now," said H.M., with a sort of malevolent patience, "I want you to see everything happen from Saturday to Monday. You!" He pointed his cigar, long gone out, at Martin. "You went harin' down to Berkshire on Saturday.

"You sent a message to Ricky Fleet, who was at Brayle Manor, that an enemy was waitin' for him at the Dragon. Your gal and Sophie were there when he got the message. I've heard this from a very particular source.

"Didn't it strike you as a bit odd that he should come over there so quickly? The proper reply to you should have been, 'I'm waiting at your service here at Brayle Manor; came and see me.' Above all the sweet fireworks of heaven, didn't it seem odd that your gal, should have come flyin' over there on a bicycle, as frightened as blazes, to anticipate him?"

Martin looked at Jenny, who had turned her head away.

"It did seem funny, yes. But Jenny said she had to know what happened between us."

"Sure. And that was true, as far as it went. Now: presto-chango: watch! In the doorway of the second bar-parlour at his most charmin', stands Richard Fleet grown up. At his prime. Intoxicated by his war-success; but modest, not showin' it. Assured by this dotin' mother there's not a woman alive who can resist him. Quite believing it. With conceit runnin' in his veins like blood. Down he sits, takes out his pipe, and asks what's up.

"And you give it to him between the eyes that you love your Jenny, she loves you, and you mean to get married."

H.M. drew a deep breath.

"Son," he went on, "do you remember how Ricky Fleet sat there for a few seconds, with his leg over the chair-arm: not movin', just lookin', without any expression in his eyes: creepy as creepy?"

"Lord knows I do!" Martin answered. "I started to shout out something about being sorry, and I could hear what seemed like the skeleton-clock ticking in the other room . . ."

"If he'd had a weapon then," H.M. observed very quietly, "you'd have been a dead man."

"You mean . . . about Jenny and Ricky and their engagement . . . he really *did*—?"

"Oh, son! He'd fallen head over heels for her. He just couldn't believe, in his vanity, that *any* woman could prefer another feller to himself. Burn it all, when you were at Willaby's the day before, why didn't you take the word of the one person who did know? I mean the gal herself?"

Jenny, her face flushed, still looked away from Martin; but she gripped his hand as she spoke.

"I told you Ricky was in love with me," she said. "That sort of thing—well, you always know. I'm afraid, at Willaby's, I showed I was frightened. I kept telling you about his good qualities and—and looking at you and wondering if you'd see anything wrong. Once, if you remember, I started to talk about Ricky's father's death; but it stuck in my throat."

"Yes. Yes, it did."

"When you mentioned Sir Henry Merrivale, I didn't know what on earth might happen. I'd always heard of Sir Henry as a real sleuth: a strong, silent, unemotional man . . ."

"Hem!" said H.M., endeavouring to look modest. "Thank-'ee, my wench."

"Jenny, listen!" Martin insisted. "Ricky Fleet: you didn't know he was a . . . ?"

Jenny regarded him with horror. "Oh, God, *no!* It was only a feeling of something horribly wrong; of how he might turn on you. I couldn't talk about it. He was our friend. I liked him; but I couldn't endure his touch. As I told you afterwards—if I happened to be wrong, it would only be sordidly stupid."

"We will now," said H.M., "return to Richard Fleet, in the bar-parlour, when he'd just got that staggerer between the eyes. How he did pull himself together! How he *forced* the blood in his face, and that look of relief and 'Thank God.' His charm poured all over the place." H.M. looked at Martin. "But from that moment, in his eyes, you were a dead duck."

(Much, so very much, became comprehensible to Martin now.)

"What did he say?" pursued H.M. "Oh, he was all bounces and smiles! He never in the world could have married the gal, and he was awful relieved. He'd grown up with her! Cor! He gave the impression they'd lived in each other's pockets for about twenty years; and he'd as soon have thought of marrying a sister.

"But what was the truth?

"The gal there," H.M. pointed at Jenny, "told me on Sunday. She'd been at school from the time she was ten. Her holidays were spent with one or the other of her parents abroad. Then came the War and the Wrens. In other words, he couldn't possibly have seen much of the gal for about thirteen years. And what happens then, hey? She comes back at the end of the war.

"And he sees her. He goes straight overboard. Presently, as they say, a marriage is arranged.

"But Ricky Fleet (in the bar-parlour with Drake) is all dewy-eyed innocence. He's mad-keen on a gal named Susan Harwood. She was his newest, ripest conquest. (Of course, son, you heard his philosophy of marriage; you knew he saw himself as a boundin' faun, all Pan-pipes and breathin's in the grove). Oh, he was goin' to marry Susan!—Then in walked our Jenny."

H.M. shook his head. Again Martin saw the dingy bar-parlour.

"She's just been having a blazing row with Ruth Callice here, across the road.—Don't interrupt me, dammit, either of you! Before she came in, Ricky Fleet made a dramatic business of 'what was he goin' to say to Jenny?' Son, do you remember what he did?"

Martin nodded.

"I thought he was acting a little. He looked at himself in a wall-mirror, to see if his posture was right. He was preening a good deal."

"Uh-huh. And Ricky Fleet's passion for looking at himself in mirrors, at exactly the time when nobody except a vanity-swollen feller would, is going to figure in this business again.

"Anyway, in came Jenny. Very soon she asked you would you please, please take her driving that night and not go to the prison. That wasn't merely because she was jealous of Ruth, or

. . .

"Will you two gals for the love of Esau shut up? Both of you? And lemme get on with this? All right: now put a sock in it!

"Ahem. Well. If Ricky Fleet did happen to hate Drake, something pretty unpleasant might happen to Drake at the prison. You gather the wench had naturally been listenin' to most of the talk between you and Fleet, even though the windows were closed? All wenches do.

207

"But most of all she thought she could get these nasty crazy suspicions out of her mind—at least, she might—if she brought up the death of George Fleet and made Ricky Fleet tell about it. Then she could be sure her suspicions were all moonshine.

"He had begun tellin' about it, when they were interrupted first by Dr. Laurier and then by Ruth Callice. There was a rumpus; I came in at the end of it. But just think of Ricky Fleet as he talks about his old man's death!

"I'll take my oath, here and now, he'd practically forgotten about it. It was swept into the dustbin, lost and gone, like a dim sort of prank we remember that *might* have raised trouble in boyhood. His brain's most rational, admittedly; and it's tipped over the edge with hatred for Martin Drake, who's under his charm and thinks he's the best feller in the world."

Martin's feelings, in retrospect, had more of an inward shudder than can be rendered here.

"The coppers are investigatin' that old, dim prank of twenty years ago? Well! What does Ricky Fleet care? They can't do anything. For I'll tell you this much:

"Only three other people, who protected him, ever knew he killed his father and how he killed his father. The first was his mother. The second was old Dr. Pierre Laurier, with the beard, who (we know) cherished a romantic passion for Cicely Fleet. The third was Miss Upton, who told lies by the bucket to save him when the tow-headed boy came babblin' to her with fear.

"Now, twenty years later, Dr. Laurier was dead. So was Miss Upton—see Masters's list of witnesses—and couldn't retract any lie for the boy's alibi. And one more fetchin' point: Ricky Fleet never knew anything about that skeleton in the clock, what it was or what it meant.

"But, shortly after he'd hared away from that explosive argument at the Dragon, and hurried back home, he did begin to get shocks.

"Watch his behaviour now!

"There was something wrong with his mother. Something seriously wrong. Ricky Fleet was worried. He knew it couldn't have been caused by any casual reference made to a twenty-year-old death by Stannard . . ."

"Thank you," Stannard intervened gravely. As he sat on the sofa-arm, bent a little forward, Stannard's black little glittering eyes were absorbed in the story.

"What upset his mother? When young Fleet hurried home, and followed her partway up the stairs (Drake and Ruth Callice saw that scene), all she'd say was that there was something he'd got to learn soon; and that she'd just put in a telephone-call for her now-closest friend, Sophie Brayle. But *we* can guess what was wrong with Cicely Fleet.

"It was the sight of that ruddy .great skeleton-clock being carried into the door of the pub just opposite. I'd sent it on ahead of Masters and me, by the carriage-people. Masters and I stopped at a couple of pubs in Brayle and didn't get there till late afternoon. Aunt Cicely must 'a' thought the secret was on the point of coming out.

"But what about Me?

"I was dragged into Fleet House, along with Sophie there, by Ricky himself. I was shanghai'd, I was, and shoved into the library with the rest of you people. And Ricky Fleet had just before that got another shock.

"He'd recognized, or half-recognized, Stannard as being the man standing at the upstairs study window. It jumped at him out of the past: Stannard was the bloke who looked down, when he came round the edge of the terrace that day, and he saw his father lyin' with a smashed head under the tapestry-cloth.

"But let's take the events in their order! In that library, first off I had a bit of a dog-fight with Sophie. At least she gave confirmation to my notion (remember?) that Arthur Puckston might 'a' written the anonymous postcards about the pink flash and the skeleton-clock.

"Whereupon in tripped Aunt Cicely, at her artificial archest and most charmin', to carry away Sophie for a private talk. And there occurred something that was embarrassin' to the point of the horrible."

During all this Lady Brayle might not have been in the room, might not have existed. She sat over by one open window, staring blankly ahead of her, an untasted glass of sherry on the window-sill. She did not seem arrogant or even friendly: only like one who had been lost, and still gropes.

"Do you remember that incident, Sophie?" H.M. called softly.

"Yes." The stiff lips writhed as the grey-white head slowly turned. "I remember."

"What was said?"

"I made some mention of a blade, a sword, which I wished I could have brought back from Willaby's as a present. There—there was real horror in Cicely's eyes. She blurted out, 'But you must never . . .' Then Cicely stopped and turned it off with some reference to Dr. Laurier. What she meant, I imagine, was, 'You must never bring a sharp blade into this house?'"

209

"That's right," agreed H.M. "And then (hey) she took you upstairs and told you the whole truth?"

They spoke to each other across the length of a room, Lady Brayle with her head turned sideways, trying to control the writhing of her mouth; but they spoke without incongruity.

"Poor Cicely," Lady Brayle went on, "could hardly speak for sobbing. About the skeleton in the clock. About that half-mad, or altogether mad, boy who—" She stopped. "I do not suppose, Henry, you now have much respect for my word of honour?"

"That's where you're wrong, Sophie."

"Never, until that moment," the lips writhed vehemently, "had I the least suspicion, let alone knowledge, of the situation. To think I would allow Jennifer, after that, to be married to . . ." She floundered. "My late husband, who commanded the Grenadier Guards, once said that a person who allowed . . ."

"Yes. Sure. But Aunt Cicely would have allowed the marriage, hey?"

"Oh, Henry!" The other made an impatient gesture. Again she struggled to free herself from reticence. "You're hardly a person to understand mothers, especially, people like Cicely. That is—"

"Her son was 'cured' of this. It had been only childish aberration. Nothing like it at Cambridge or later. The 'poor boy' had been misunderstood. Cicely wished to believe it so; and it was so. She could not even bear to have him *know* about the skeleton. She ought to tell him; but why remind the boy? The skeleton must be removed. I am Cicely's friend. I could not let her down."

Lady Brayle turned her head away, and looked out of the window. And now Martin remembered her look, on that Saturday evening, when she left Cicely Fleet and walked downstairs past Martin at the telephone table.

"I knew I was right," cried Jenny. "She *was* shielding somebody!"

"God help me," Martin said uncontrollably, "I thought that business of stealing the skeleton was funny."

"Not to me," said Lady Brayle without turning round.

"Looky here," howled H.M., bringing his fist down on the arm of the chair. "Who's tellin' this story? I'd got you people in the library early that Saturday evenin', after Sophie and Aunt Cicely had gone. Ricky Fleet then 'denounced' Stannard as the one who'd been lookin' at him from the study window. Before that he said one thing that gave me a shiver. Can you spot what it was?"

210

Stannard lifted his shoulders in negation.

"Somebody asked him what he'd seen up there at the window. And it was, *'The face of somebody I'd never met. The face of a total stranger. Looking down like God.'*

"Looking down like God.

"Cor! There's your boy-murderer's conscience, leaping out of him and speaking through the mouth of a grown man. That's what he remembered best! That's what he thought all those years ago! And," H.M. looked at Stannard, "he rounded on you pretty savagely."

"I noticed," Stannard pursed his lips, "he was nervous and truculent while you were questioning me. He would have been a difficult witness to handle. And all, you say, because of this repressed—?"

"Ho-ho!" rumbled H.M. "Not so's you could notice it. It was because you said at least one thing that could help to denounce him."

"I did?" Stannard asked in surprise.

"You were in the study when you heard Fleet shout and fall on the flagstones? Right! You then went to the window and stood there looking down? Right!

"But you further said you stood there *five minutes* before the governess and the boy came round the edge of the house to the terrace. In Ricky Fleet's story of it, which he gave me almost immediately afterwards when we climbed up to the roof, he said he and Miss Upton were *just startin' from the back to the front of the house when they heard the shout.* What sort of frozen-snail-with-lumbago takes five minutes to walk from back to front?

"His memory might be bad? Sure! Your memory too? Of course! But there was a certain way of checking it. Across the way, at the pub, there were six witnesses on the roof though only two on the gables. All agreed in their first testimony."

H.M. picked up the blue folder, and stabbed at it with his dead cigar.

"After Fleet's body struck the terrace, Dr. Pierre Laurier ran out of the house. The local policeman walked up the path to the terrace, picked up the field-glasses from the grass, and went in: presumably to 'phone the police-station. Dr. Laurier called to Lady (the Dowager Lady) Brayle, who brought a cloth out of the house. Dr. Laurier put the cloth over Fleet's head and shoulders. Cicely Fleet then came out and started to faint, but they talked to her 'a while,'—I'm quoting, so note the 'a while,'—and she went in.

"Then, and only then, did the governess and the boy come

211

round the side of the house. Lord love a duck! For the precedin' events, you could easily allow five minutes.

"But did the boy and the governess say the things, twenty years ago when it was fresh in mind, as Ricky Fleet said to me as well as to Jenny and Martin Drake? Including, for instance, that fancy touch about hearin' Dr. Laurier say, 'Get the tablecloth out of the hall?' So I asked Masters to check over their statements made to the local police.

"And they had said the same things. Therefore they were both tellin' a pack of lies. Q.E.D."

Again H.M. threw back the blue folder among the other papers.

"But there was another great big lie," he went on, screwing up his face hideously, "that the old man had to see through before the solution was so blazin' obvious. That lie has caused half the mystery in this case. It had to do with how Fleet was murdered.

"When I went up to have a look at that roof-top for the first time, I was stumped and flummoxed. I couldn't think of anything but colour. I talked more about colour than an interior decorator. Because I'd got my mind fixed on that pink flash.

"So I went to the front of the roof. And then this here venerable scalp did start to stir a bit with wheels workin' inside. I hadn't quite visualized the surroundings. Arthur Puckston had been over on that north gable, in a position to look at Fleet sideways—well sideways.

"It went like this: Puckston probably wrote the anonymous postcards; only a postcard mentioned the pink flash; Puckston had told lies in his statement to the police; Puckston looked sideways . . .

"The pink flash must have been that lurid-glowin' sky on something white or whitish. It must have *moved*, pretty sharply, or there wouldn't have been any flash. It couldn't have been up in the air, or Frew would have seen it. But—stop a bit!—Puckston could see what Frew couldn't see: he could see behind Fleet and a part of the roof-floor. Down on the floor . . .

"Now think! That look of intense pain or weakness, or both, which strikes the victim all of a sudden and holds him there for a second . . ."

"A sword!" interposed Stannard.

"No!" said H.M. sharply. "That's the one thing it couldn't have been, in spite of the tinge of steel in all this case. Because why?

"Because a sword or sharp blade would have meant blood. Because that's the one thing that couldn't be concealed. Remember, Fleet's body was lying smack in front of a number of witnesses. Lemme quote again; and I've been over it so much I can quote from memory."

H.M. closed his eyes.

Bert (the policeman) came out and seemed to argue with Dr. Laurier about who carried Sir George. Bert took his head in the cloth and Dr. Laurier took his legs. They carried

. . .

H.M. sat up.

"Even if old Dr. Pierre Laurier had been up to hanky-panky, he couldn't have concealed any blood below the shoulders.

"Then: bang! On Sunday night this feller——" H.M. pointed to Martin—"came weaving his way downstairs after a fall off that roof, and he tells me I ought to see 'young' Dr. Laurier if I wanted information about swordsmanship in remembering (hem!) my reincarnation. He mentioned a cut called the 'Low-high.'

"Now upstairs I'd got a book called *The Cavaliers,* which I'd been readin'. As I distinctly told Masters at the pub on Saturday, it was a blook on swordsmanship. The 'Low-high' was a cut by which the trickster dropped down and cut viciously across the backs of both his opponent's legs just above the ankle. And the only way anybody could have attacked George Fleet would have been round his feet or ankles under that six-inch parapet.

"A sword wasn't used. But at the same moment I remembered what else was hangin' on the wall of the study upstairs. *You,*" he glared at Martin, "must have seen for yourself. And I remembered Dr. Laurier in the rocking-chair."

H.M. drew a deep breath.

"Y'see, this wasn't intended to be an impossible crime. Only one big whitewashed lie made it so. A twelve-year-old young 'un had been beaten too much by a father he hated. He was goin' to stalk his father just like a red Indian. Only he was goin' to kill him.

"He knew (he said so) his father was goin' up to that roof to watch the hunt when it came near. George Fleet always did. How did the twelve-year-old get up there? By a door, leadin' to the back garden, and a staircase going straight up there. Could he stalk the old devil, in all the excitement of the hunt, without his father seein' him?

213

"Easy! And why? Because of field-glasses.

"Y'know, Masters kept goin' on at me and raving when I insisted there was only one thing I wanted to know: were they good field-glasses, nothing wrong or wonky about them?

"That would have been my question no matter how Fleet had been killed. Lord love a duck! Suppose you or I look through a pair of field-glasses, and the vision don't seem to come into focus when we fiddle with the wheel?

"Well, we get mad; we get a vague sort of idea there's something wrong with the scenery and turn 'em somewhere else. We look round. We take the glasses away from our eyes and examine 'em all ways. But, if they're good, we don't notice what's goin' on around us.

"Fleet didn't. That twelve-year-old maniac—with a certain boy's weapon you'll guess—crawled belly-flat like a red Indian under the ledge of the north wall, and then under the ledge of the east wall towards where his father was standing. Remember: not a soul looked round until shortly before Fleet fell. Once the boy was under that front ledge on the east side, nobody could see him: not even Puckston. I think Masters may have told a couple of you that people won't believe how small a space can hide a full-grown adult, let alone a small boy.

"I'd dismissed that possibility at first, because I kept thinkin' of somebody startin' a tussle with the legs or ankles of a powerful man like Fleet. And Masters never dreamed of a kid. But also remember: Ricky Fleet, as he'd told Stannard in the condemned cell at Pentecost, wasn't what you might call ordinary in another way. He could put-the-weight a distance of twenty-seven feet three inches when he was eleven. A lot of grown men couldn't do that.

"On he goes, just as crazy-excited as we've seen him on other occasions, with the music of the hunt to encourage him. The hounds were after the fox; he was after the wolf. He's carrying something out of the realm of sport, but a nasty heavy weapon if you remember it's . . ."

"A cricket-bat!" Jenny whispered. "He told us they'd given him a new cricket-bat that week!"

"And when it's new," said H.M., "it's the whitest of white ash. Don't see it as an ordinary cricket-bat: see the heavy broadness taperin' on each side to the very-narrow-rounded edge that's like the edge of a wooden blade.

"One hand, lyin' flat with his left arm under him, was all Ricky Fleet needed. It was the narrow blade of the bat. Out and back it went: flash! open and shut! It smashed across the back of Fleet's legs just above the ankle, the most painful of all

214

places. It fractured the bone in both legs without drawin' a drop of blood. Fleet jerked in horrible pain; he couldn't stand straight, and—

"That's all. After the first thirty seconds or so, no witness (see testimony!) was studyin' that roof. They all looked down at the terrace, while the boy crawled back by way of the north ledge. But I'm bettin' *he* never thought anybody could see him at any time, except maybe God.

"*You,*" H.M. said to Martin. "Burn it, you must have seen the row of cricket bats in Fleet's study! On Sunday night I remembered 'em; I remembered the 'Low-high' cut; I wanted to look it up in my book. And I remembered something else too: Dr. Laurier, old Dr. Laurier, rocking back and forth before the skeleton-clock mutterin', 'Would a man of honour have done it?'

"Done what? We know that after Fleet fell Dr. Laurier (quote) 'made as if he was examining all over Sir George.' *He* ordered the constable to take the head, in spite of an argument, and *he* took the legs. He was the old family friend, the one who cherished Aunt Cicely, and he knew all about the boy's psychopathic traits. He saw in a second this wasn't accident. Finally, remember, he was the police-surgeon.

"The awful creepin' danger was that the coppers, especially Scotland Yard, would tumble to the fracture at the *back* of both legs, when Fleet fell in a way where that couldn't have happened. Then the gaff would be blown.

"At the post-mortem there wasn't much danger—everybody's concentrated on the stomach-contents, as usual—of too-close investigation. Laurier had sworn (which was the lie I told you about) there hadn't been other injuries to the body. But Aunt Cicely intervened, weepin' and pleadin'. And at her insistence old Laurier . . . amputated just above both ankles before burial.

"It was a fat-headed thing to do; but our Cicely pleaded they couldn't *prove* anything against her boy, which was true, if that was done. Also (here I'm on ground I don't know) there had to be hanky-panky with the undertaker.

"I won't go into grisly details," growled H.M., "about how Laurier removed flesh and sinew from what was left. It was only long afterwards, when age wore on him and he got a bit senile, that he built the skeleton-clock for his parlour, *where everybody could see but nobody knew,* as his penance. Anybody here examined that clock?"

"Yes. I have," said Martin out of a thick throat.

"Did you look inside? Look close?"

215

"There was some kind af platform round the ankles and feet, apparently to keep the skeleton upright . . ."

"Dr. Laurier took his old anatomical-specimen skeleton," said H.M., "He removed what had to be removed, and he attached—what had to be attached. It was a skillful job of fittin'. But any medical man could have seen at a glance that the ankle-bones and feet of a big man don't belong to the skeleton of a small man. *Unless* there's a wooden platform built up round 'em which gives you only a glimpse of the feet and curves round the ankles. You can't probe the truth about that skeleton until you take it out of the clock. And I hadn't time before Sophie stole it.

"So y'see, as regards that nasty business of murder on the roof, there was only a twelve-year crawlin' back unseen, and out to his governess now screamin' what he'd done and how he'd got to be protected. That's why they took five minutes to get round. Nobody'd notice if Ricky Fleet was scared. Nobody'd notice him anyway. But it must 'a' made him nearly faint when he thought he saw God lookin' down from his father's study window.

"*You*," and H.M. pointed to Stannard, "said something else to the grown-up Ricky Fleet that shook his nerve too. You called him a '*grubby* little boy.' It was twistin' and wrigglin' in his mind just later when I asked him about his father and Ricky Fleet blurted out: 'He never minded how filthy dirty you got.' He was thinkin' about how almighty dirty he got when he crawled along that concrete roof to kill his father."

There was a long silence. H.M. picked up his whisky-and-soda, and drained the glass with a volcanic gurgle. Then he set it down.

"There's not much more to tell except what you know already," he went on. "That expedition to the prison on Saturday night . . ."

"Where," Ruth said, "Ricky later killed Enid Puckston. H.M., *why?*"

"Listen, my wench. Young Fleet said himself it was an 'expression.' An outlet. Did you ever see a golfer smash a golf-club against a tree? Or a woman throw a whole breakfast-tray in somebody's face? Well, that's normal; he wasn't.

"Burn it, Ricky Fleet had been hurt. His girl preferred somebody else to *him*. His vanity was scratched raw. There was young Drake, the cause of it all. He wouldn't dare face Drake without a weapon, any more than he'd have dared face his father. (That was still lurkin'; got it?) But he had to *hurt*, had to inflict *pain* on a helpless person, before he killed Drake.

"No, it's not pretty. I warned you long ago it wasn't.

"He prepared it all beforehand. Do you recall, when you were all sitting in that dark back garden just before you started for the prison, how he kept rushin' back to the house—apparently to see how his mother was?"

"Yes," said Martin. "Very well."

"The last time, just before you left, he made his preparations. On this occasion he was goin' to give you a good grown-up sophisticated alibi. He had the dagger and its sheath. He cut his own arm, got plenty of blood for the dagger; and the sheath would hold it without staining him, except for smears on the handle, if he wrapped it in a handkerchief and put it in his pocket. Just as you later did when you shoved it in Dr. Laurier's pocket.

"You went to the prison. Who deliberately called your attention to that pile of rapiers and daggers in the condemned cell? *He* did. You didn't find the dagger, as he'd hoped when he shoved it in there under cover of so much darkness. But back he went with Drake after the fencin' match—"

"By the way," demanded Martin, "was 'young' Dr. Laurier concerned in this?"

"Not in the least, son. He's only a bit of a snob, that's all. His most valued patient is Sophie there, and when he had tea with her on Saturday she must have dropped a hint that 'Captain' Drake was endangerin' Jenny's marriage. Hence the faintly sinister hints in the bar-parlour when he first met you."

"But to get back to—?"

"Sure, if you'll stop interrupting. Ricky Fleet, when you and he went back to get corks, smackin' well made sure you'd find the dagger. He helped tumble over some swords and put his light straight on it. As to how the weapons got there, it's clear he'd been using the prison for some time . . ."

"Using it? He told me," said Martin, "he'd often wanted to explore the place, but he couldn't get in."

"Oh, my son!" H.M. said dismally. "Anybody could get in there. You don't have to be a locksmith to understand that. You just have to go and take a dekko at the main gates. The bigger the lock, the simpler it is. And the easier it is to get a wax impression, if anybody wants to.

"Son, there were too many doors with oiled hinges inside that place, as our friend Stannard pointed out. Even if Stannard himself had been up to some kind of funny business—"

Here the barrister chuckled.

"—why in the name of Esau should he have oiled the hinges

of those high front gates? Admittedly all your party were goin' there. No; it was somebody who wanted no betrayin' gate-creaks when he slipped in.

"Ricky Fleet had been usin' the prison for his amorous adventures, Pan-pipes and nature-worship, which weren't of a sadistic kind. Masters has discovered he got back the rapier-dagger collection from the ghost-village . . .

"Ghost-village? You saw it. Built beyond the prison. The Governor's house was there. George Fleet gave that collection to Major Colwell, and Major Colwell left it behind when everybody decamped. So Ricky Fleet had a second dagger, very like the first, when he led Enid Puckston toward the prison to kill her."

Martin cleared his throat. "H.M. Was she one of Ricky's —?"

H.M.'s expression was heavy and bitter.

"No, son. That's the real irony of this case. She liked and admired him an awful lot, as I could tell when I heard her mention him at the pub. That's all it amounted to. But— haven't you wondered why Puckston sent those anonymous postcards in the first place?"

"You mean she wasn't one of Ricky's conquests, but—?"

"Her father thought she might be," replied H.M.

He was silent for a moment, glowering.

"Mind you, Puckston didn't *know* the boy Richard Fleet had done that murder years ago. He'd seen what he knew was the light on a cricket-bat. He guessed nobody but a kid could have crawled under that ledge unseen. He had no proof and anyway he didn't want trouble. But if Enid had fallen for this bloke years later—! So he sent the postcards, with her help but without her knowin'; and then he thinks she's been killed, by the same boy grown up, because she knows too much! Do you wonder at Puckston's state of mind on Sunday night?"

"No," Martin answered. "No. I don't wonder."

"Anyway, Ricky Fleet took that gal to the prison, to see a 'ghost-hunt', at goin' on for one in the morning. He butchered her with all the hate in him. He left the body under the gallows-trap, as a rare sight for somebody if the trap was opened. Masters has told you that story, including the reversed alibi. Finally, Fleet slipped out again without a whisper to catch Masters's ear.

"I don't think, though, he slept very well the rest of the night. And then you two," H.M.'s finger indicated Martin and Jenny, "had to go yellin' under the windows at going on for five in the morning, and give him his heaven-gilded opportunity to shove Drake off the roof."

"But why didn't you warn me?"

H.M. drew himself together. He stuck out towards Martin a face of such utter loathing, such indescribable contempt, that the other felt his scalp stir with hostility.

"Look here, you something-something'd thus-and-so," he said. "There's a feller here in London," he mentioned a famous painter, "you think is a friend of yours. I, bein' the old man, happen to know he hates your guts."

"That," Martin said quietly, but with buzzing ears, "is a very bloody lie."

"Darling!" cried Jenny.

"You think so, hey?" inquired H.M., with a contempt which was one vast sneer. "He was in Spain with another feller he hated, and he shot that feller in the back without givin' him a chance. What do you say to *that*, you credulous so-and-so this-and-that?"

"I say," returned Martin, sticking out his own neck, "that I will prove you a thus-and-so this-and-that liar. I will take him to any lonely place you name, with a loaded revolver in my pocket. I will hand him the revolver, and—" Even with badly buzzing head, Martin stopped short.

"Y'see what I mean?" inquired H.M., with a sort of malignant apology.

"I deny that! I . . ."

"Your feelings, son, ring up as plain as l.s.d. on a cash register. Even when," H.M. glanced towards Lady Brayle, "it was half the world to you that they shouldn't. Ricky Fleet would have had to shut you up even quicker than he tried to do.

"And didn't he try! It was a matter of seconds for him to nip up, get the field-glasses out of his father's study where his mother kept 'em, rearrange the chairs on the roof, and . . .

"Are you askin' why? Listen. What's the impulse of anybody who finds a pair of field-glasses on a roof? It's to try 'em, ain't it? People in general (we all did it ourselves on Saturday evening) walk straight to the centre-front of a square roof. You'd have done it on Sunday, with your attention distracted, if you hadn't got suspicious of the glasses. Your bravado took you there instead. The chairs were arranged like a series of rocks for hiding places, while somebody in bare feet crept up behind you.

"To wind it up, on Sunday night I tumbled to the trick of the murder on the roof. And that opened every other door: the skeleton in the clock too. *Puckston,* nobody else but Puckston, was our salvation if we could get him to help.

"He'd written the postcards, probably with the help of his daughter. It seemed to me the poor devil would be over at the Dragon, writhin' in agony with the fear Enid might 'a' been killed because of that. Mind you, I didn't know then he suspected something between Enid and Ricky. And at that time I didn't know old Dr. Laurier, with one too many brandies in his bar, had once given him a hint about what the skeleton-clock meant.

"But—*if* I could show him he wasn't in any way responsible for his girl's death—it seemed to me he'd help us yank a confession out of Ricky. I even took Drake along, as one nearly killed by a maniac. But Puckston didn't even notice Drake's horror-film forehead; and he wasn't necessary.

"The crowds at MacDougall's show were just what we needed. Puckston 'phoned Ricky early in the morning. Ricky arranged to meet him—just as he was willing to meet Drake, with somethin' goading his mind—in the darkish outer-shell of the Mirror Maze.

"But young Richard had plans laid too. He'd arranged a quite genuine meeting between his mother and Susan Harwood, timed for one o'clock. You see why? That was his time to meet Puckston. So he told everybody about it, even Dr. Laurier, with this addition, '*If you see me motion to keep away, keep away.*'

"Neat idea. He could then go where he liked, to meet Puckston, and he could keep any of his friends from followin' him if he waved. All the same, even when we were discussing who was goin' to the fair, he couldn't keep away from his own reflection in the hall mirror. *Just as, on Saturday night and of all places and times, he'd taken a look at himself in the mirror of the condemned cell.*"

"And about his emotional state Monday morning. Did you notice, there in the hall, he had tears in his eyes?"

"But, H.M.!" protested Ruth. "If what Cicely told me was true, he was laughing. You'd been telling some perfectly outrageous anecdotes about your ancestor. Including one about reciting limericks to Charles the First."

"Well . . . now!" said H.M., with a cough and a deprecating wave of his hand. "I didn't really think, y'know, the lofty muse of Curtius Merrivale would ever descend to limericks, even if they'd been invented. It was Masters put the idea in my head by sayin' so the night before."

"Then what—?"

"I was always careful to be very comfortin' and cloth-headed in front of Ricky Fleet. He didn't think he'd got to worry about the old man." Then H.M.'s voice changed sharply. "He wasn't amused then, my wench. He'd been listenin' with all his ears to Drake's end of a do-you-love-me telephone conversation, with that gal there, which didn't amuse him at all.

"When four of you went out there in the car, I heard later, he nearly lost control of himself. He was rigid, nearly ready to burst, hardly keepin' back the tears. That was after Drake had said *he* meant to elope with Jenny if he had to.

"I didn't know this at the time; but cor! I was worried. When I gathered that crowd round the race-track booth, and yelled and bellowed the odds, it was only partly to make Sophie popular. I wanted the jostle of a big crowd so I could make sure Ricky Fleet wasn't carryin' a weapon. He wasn't. But when I heard Drake was in the maze . . .

"You know the rest. Puckston and the dewy-eyed innocent were near a microphone (it was darkish, so the feller didn't see it) outside what looked like a solid mirror. It was only the silver paint usually used over plate glass, for what's known to gamblers as a two-way mirror, but in this case on cardboard and curtain.

"Puckston . . . so! I should 'a' realized, the night before, he was powder packed into a cartridge. He exploded. Ricky Fleet was a first-rate athlete and as strong-built as you'd find; but against that man he hadn't the chance of a celluloid cat in hell. He collapsed in the pieces of smashed looking-glass. And that's all."

There was long silence, extending almost to discomfort. All of them, except Lady Brayle at the window, looked everywhere except at each other. Finally Ruth, smoothing her skirt over her knees and looking steadily down at it, managed to speak.

"There is one thing." Her face was flushed. "Jenny, dear!"

"Yes, dear?" answered Jenny, without looking at her.

"I was in the prison that night. You know what I mean. I made a suggestion to Martin."

"Ruth darling," said Jenny sincerely, "I don't mind. At least—"

"I don't mean *that* kind of suggestion!"

Martin felt like dropping through the floor. Jenny was so surprised she almost looked round.

"About Ricky's—unbalanced state of mind," said Ruth tensely. "I apologize. It was horrible of me. I honestly thought there might be something—well, odd about your side of the family."

Lady Brayle, outraged, turned round majestically. Jenny, with an exclamation of pleasure, put her hand across towards Ruth.

"And that's the only reason you went there?" Jenny did not stop for an answer, which was just as well. "Ruth, everybody thinks that very same thing when your parents are estranged, and everything seems mixed up, and you have a grandmother as reserved and reticent as mine!"

"Ruth," Stannard said softly.

All through H.M.'s recital his strong personality had been repressed, buckled in, to the steady gleam of attention in his eyes. Now, sitting on the arm of the sofa, his husky chuckle seemed to dominate the room. He put his hand under Ruth's chin and tilted it up so that he could look at her eyes.

"What has been," he smiled, "is no longer. What is," he smiled again, "shall continue."

"Always," said Ruth. Her look left no doubt of that.

"By God," Stannard said suddenly, looking up radiantly and lifting his fist, "I can conquer the world!"

He checked himself. His hand dropped, and he looked whimsically at H.M.

"Sir Henry," he said, "it seems an extraordinary thing that only a fortnight ago, in this room, I said I mustn't keep late hours. What is it now? Close on four." He glanced towards Martin and Jenny. "Exactly when, my dear fellow, are you getting married?"

"Tomorrow," Martin answered, "at Westminster registry office. We take the afternoon plane for Paris."

"My new car," chuckled Stannard, "is downstairs. Just as it was a fortnight ago. There's no petrol for long distances. But suppose the four of us drive out to Virginia Water and see the sun come up?"

There was almost a scramble to get up. Much attention from Jenny and Ruth was bestowed on H.M., who endured this with a stuffed and stoical look, like a world-weary Curtius Merrivale. Then it was broken.

"Captain Drake," said Lady Brayle, getting up from her chair beside the window and adjusting her shoulders.

Dead silence.

Martin instantly left the group and went over towards the window so that he could look her in the eye.

"Yes, Lady Brayle?"

"With regard to your proposed marriage with my grand-daughter."

"Yes."

They looked at each other for a full minute, which can be a very long space if you time it. The reason was that Lady Brayle could not speak. She was shaken; emotion tore her; but the lips would not move. Her large, rather flabby hands were folded in front of her. Her shoulders were back. Her eyes wandered in search of determination. Then came firm resolve, and clearly she spoke.

"The Gloucesters, I am informed, are a very honourable regiment."

There was a short silence.

"Very," agreed Martin. He reflected for a moment. "But in my opinion the Brigade of Guards, particularly the Grenadier Guards, must always rank highest of all."

Then, startlingly, tears came into the woman's eyes.

"Thank you, Captain Drake."

"Not at all, Lady Brayle."

They did not even shake hands. They understood.

And so, as the clock of St. Jude's rang out the hour of four, and white dawn showed faintly behind Kensington, the policeman was on his way back through Moreston Square. The car which had been standing at the kerb was gone. But the windows of Miss Callice's flat were still lighted.

A rumbling voice floated down clearly from those open windows.

"So they framed him, Sophie," the voice said. "And the only reason they framed him was because he killed one of 'em in a duel outside the War Office. But they indicted that fine character on a charge of promotin' fake companies to get Aztec gold out of Mexico, and three times they chucked him into the can. I tell you, Sophie, it was a cryin' scandal against the law!"

The policeman looked up at those windows thoughtfully. But, after all, duels outside the War Office are comparatively rare. And it was Miss Ruth Callice's flat. The policeman smiled and sauntered on.

The End.